Turning Trixie

A Novel by
ROBB GRINDSTAFF

TURNING TRIXIE
Copyright © 2022 by Robb Grindstaff

All rights reserved. No part of this book may be used or reproduced in any manner whatsoever, without written permission, except in the case of brief quotations embedded in articles and reviews. For more information, please contact publisher at Publisher@EvolvedPub.com.

FIRST EDITION SOFTCOVER
ISBN: 1622532457
ISBN-13: 978-1-62253-245-2

Editor: Jessica West
Cover Artist: Kabir Shah
Interior Designer: Lane Diamond

www.EvolvedPub.com
Evolved Publishing LLC
Butler, Wisconsin, USA

Turning Trixie is a work of fiction. All names, characters, places, and incidents are the product of the author's imagination, or are used fictitiously. Any resemblance to actual events or persons, living or dead, is entirely coincidental.

Printed in Book Antiqua font.

BOOKS BY ROBB GRINDSTAFF

Carry Me Away
Hannah's Voice
Slade
Turning Trixie

June Bug Gothic: Tales from the South [Short Story Collection]

DEDICATION

For all the incredible mothers in my life:
Linda, Lauren, Shelly, Terri, Jen, Judy, Dawn, Brandi, Amy C, Kathy, Amy F,
Nancy, Janice, Mary Jane, Teresa, Rachael, Rain, Kay, *and of course,* Mom.

CHAPTER 1

Tyler dropped his bike in the dirt and ran to the house. He knew how to ride, but when he really wanted to get somewhere in a hurry, running was faster. And this was a good time for a hurry.

After all, it wasn't every day a white Corvette crunched down the gravel country road and turned into their dirt driveway, a brown cloud spiraling into the pine trees lining both sides.

Ty's legs flipped one in front of the other in a blur. His bare feet slapped the ground and left a miniature version of the car's dust trail behind him. A lot of men pulled into their driveway, but none ever showed up in a ride this fine before. Ty imagined an older man in a white suit with a white cowboy hat. Maybe a TV star or a country singer.

The car door flung open. There behind the steering wheel sat his momma. The yellow-blond hair she'd left with a few hours earlier, now dyed platinum, was piled into a tall, wavy mound lacquered with enough hairspray to make it look as breakable as their Christmas vase.

"So, how do you like it?"

Tyler stared at the Corvette. "It sure is big."

Trixie glanced in the rearview mirror and pushed a wedge of hair back into place. "It's not too big, is it?" She swung her legs out to show off new red boots, white jeans tucked in. "I always told you the Lord would provide."

Tyler touched a finger to the metallic pearl door panel. "The Lord gave us this?"

"The Lord gave me the winning numbers for Powerball. Now go get some shoes on 'cause we're going to town. Golden Corral's got all-you-can-eat buffet."

With his best Converses on but still untied, Tyler jumped in the driver's side and climbed across the woodgrain console between the white leather bucket seats. He popped open the glove box, which contained only some paperwork and the little Ruger .22 pistol that Tyler only got to touch when Momma or Uncle Leon took him out shooting.

"Stay out of there."

Tyler slammed the glove box and struggled with the seatbelt.

Trixie leaned over to see herself in the sideview mirror while she tamped her hair down with both hands. "You sure this ain't too big? I don't want to be calling attention to ourselves just 'cause we're millionaires now. Let's say a little prayer and thank the good Lord for his bounty. Yes sir, my little man, our lives is about to change. Your momma's gonna be on TV tonight."

***

A crew member had shown Trixie to her seat behind the news desk where the anchors sat, right between the man and the woman who read the local evening news reports each evening: usually a fire, a train wreck, maybe a tornado spotted, a drug bust, and one feel-good story, like a kid who saved a kitten from drowning or a little old lady who'd fought off a burglar with her cast-iron skillet.

"Ladies and gentlemen," the man with salt-and-pepper hair said, "we have in the studio with us here a young lady who has just had a stroke of good fortune many of us dream of, but her dreams are now coming true."

It was odd seeing him in person. Her daddy watched him on the evening news as far back as her memory could go. He had a large college ring on one hand and a wedding band on the other that glimmered in the spotlights.

"That's right, Gregg," the woman on Trixie's other flank said. Her dark auburn hair rolled across the padded shoulders of a bright red dress. She was new, at least since the last time Trixie had watched the news. Maybe a year or more ago. "There were eight winners in last night's Powerball lottery, a total payout of more than $200 million. One of those lucky eight lives right here in east Texas, in the town of Pineywoods."

Trixie tried not to stare at the stage lights, but they burned into her retinas and left bright circles and blind spots in her vision. Her eyes watered. She hoped it didn't look like she was crying, or worse, ruin her makeup. The guy backstage who'd done her makeup did a better job in five minutes than Trixie could do in half an hour, and she hoped it would last at least through the evening.

"Let me introduce Victoria Burnet," the man said. "Victoria—may I call you Victoria?"

"Just Trixie please." Her head felt like it was on a swivel, switching back and forth between the man and the woman, both of whom wore more makeup than Trixie.

"Trixie," the woman said, "being the only winner from east Texas, you must feel like you just struck oil. What was your first thought when you realized you had the magic set of numbers?"

Trixie tried shifting in her chair rather than twisting her neck back and forth every time a question came from a different direction. She resisted the urge to wipe her eyes, blinked a few times to try to clear her vision, and looked at the woman. She'd already forgotten the woman's name.

"I figured it was a mistake. Thought I'd looked at the numbers wrong. So, I double checked them. Ten or twelve or a hunnerd times. But it was true."

"Yes, Vixie, it's definitely true," the woman said.

"It's Trixie, ma'am."

"Oh, pardon me. Trixie, of course. And you can call me Liberty. 'Ma'am' makes me feel so old. You may be one of the youngest Powerball winners we've ever seen. How old are you, if you don't mind my asking?"

"I just turnt twenty-three a couple months back."

"Married?"

"No, ma'am."

"Twenty-three," Gregg chimed in. "And you never have to work again. Where do you work, and do you plan on giving your employer your notice tomorrow, or just call in rich?"

Liberty chuckled.

"Well," Trixie said, "I don't really work for no one but myself."

"A businesswoman," Liberty said. "What kind of business?"

"I, um, well, I run a small farm. Family farm. It was my daddy's place, but he died when I was thirteen, and when I turned eighteen, Momma moved into town with her boyfriend Leon and gave the home place to me. Been tryin' to make a go of it but not quite there yet."

Gregg's turn. Trixie felt like she was being grilled by two detectives or something as she shifted back and forth between them.

"You going to keep farming," he asked, "or take some time off, travel the world, maybe hire someone to run the farm for you?"

Trixie paused. "Hadn't really thought about it much. I hired a fella a few months back to help with the farm, but I ain't sure there's anywhere I need to go. My boy starts school next month anyways."

"You have a son old enough for school?" Liberty looked like she was trying to hide her surprise.

"Yes, ma'am. Tyler's almost eight and will be startin' third grade."

Liberty couldn't keep the surprise off her face that time but moved in quickly with another question. "What's the first thing you're going to do with all this money?"

"I already did it. The only thing I wanted to splurge on. My old pickup was about to throw a rod, and I'd always wanted a Corvette. The car dealer's a client of mine so he let me drive it off the lot with a note that I'd pay once the money's in the bank."

"Client?" Gregg and Liberty both asked in unison.

"What kind of client?" Liberty asked.

Trixie froze. She couldn't believe that word had rolled out of her mouth. "Yeah, um, ya know, he, um, buys some vegetables and an occasional side of beef from my place." She was pretty proud of that recovery, and the news anchors' faces looked satisfied with that answer. And it wasn't a lie. He had picked up some produce a few times and a side of beef once. Even though he visited her farmhouse once a month, it wasn't for tomatoes and cucumbers.

"Well, we're about out of time, Miss Burnet—Trixie," Gregg stepped in to bring the segment to a close. "Congratulations on your winning ticket in Powerball."

"An amazing stroke of luck that will change your life," Liberty said.

"Weren't luck," Trixie said. "It was a gift from the Lord."

Liberty turned in her chair away from Trixie to face the camera. "Next up, Terry will give us the rundown on just how hot it's going to be for the next two weeks, and it sounds like we're in for a continued scorching. But first, a quick commercial break. We'll be right back with weather and then sports."

A quick countdown then the spotlights turned off. Gregg leaned over with an outstretched arm to shake Trixie's hand and leaned over close.

"I'd love for you to take me for a spin in that new 'Vette some evening," he whispered.

CHAPTER 2

Trixie sat at her vanity in her nightgown and pulled the pins out of her hair until her up-do was undone. She repeatedly brushed through it to bring the hair back down to the top of her head. It still poofed up on top a bit until she ran her fingers through it to mess it up. She couldn't shampoo her hair for twenty-four hours so the color would set, but she considered washing it anyway, maybe take off a little of the shine.

Before she could make up her mind, a faint tap-tap-tap rapped on her bedroom door.

"C'mon in, sweetie," she called to Ty, who poked his head in.

"That a-hole is here, Momma."

"Did Uncle Leon teach you that word? I don't wanna hear it again from your mouth until you're eighteen and live on your own in a different house where I don't have to hear it. And tell Ellis I've gone to bed and he needs to..." Trixie stopped midsentence, stood, and grabbed her light summer robe. "Never mind. You go watch some TV. I'll get rid of this a-hole myself. Once and for good."

Ty grinned at his momma saying a-hole.

"Don't look at me like that, little man. I'm over eighteen, so I can say it. You can't. Got that? Just like you can't drive yet, you can't shoot the gun by yourself, and you can't drink beer. And don't you ever smoke cigarettes. You want your teeth to look like your uncle's? Now get to the den. No, go watch TV in your room."

"You need me to go get Mr. Garza?"

"I've handled Ellis since before you was born. I think I can deal with him myself just fine. Now go."

Trixie shooed Ty down the hall while she slipped on the cotton, knee-length robe. She tied the strings in front and hooked the little bow at the neck as she padded barefoot down the hardwood stairs to the kitchen.

Ellis sat sideways at the kitchen table, his long legs stretched out, snakeskin boots crossed at the ankles. An unlit cigarette dangled from his lips as he sparked his Zippo.

Trixie snatched the cigarette from Ellis's mouth before the tip met the flame.

"No smoking in my house. And why are you here anyway?"

"I just wanted to drop by and see you, that's all." Ellis rubbed his lip. "Dang, girl, I think you pulled out a chunk when you did that. Look." He stuck out his lower lip like a child pouting. "Am I bleeding?"

Trixie stood over Ellis and crossed her arms. "You ain't bleeding near as bad as you will be if you don't get out of here. You know better than to come around anymore."

"Just wanted to see my girl, that's all. What's wrong with that?"

"First of all, I ain't your girl. Second, you ain't welcome here, you know that. You need me to call the cops? That restraining order is still on, ya know."

"I thought we might be able to make some kind of arrangement if we could sit down face to face and discuss it like adults."

"You wanna make an arrangement, you know where the courthouse is. You go see the clerk there, and they'll make all the arrangements you need."

Ellis raised one leg and rested his boot heel on the edge of the kitchen table.

Trixie swatted it off. "Keep your shitkickers off the table. This is where we eat. And get your ass out of my house. We have to breathe this air, and you're contaminating it."

"Look, I don't want no trouble. I heard you was on the news last night, thought I'd stop by and congratulate you."

Trixie walked over to the counter, where she straightened the dishtowel and put some odds and ends away in drawers and the cupboard.

"Since you come into some money, I figured you might have hung up your spurs. Or stilettos. Whatever it is whores hang up when they retire."

"Not that it's any of your concern, but yes, I've retired."

"Well, then, that's a good thing, girlie. Since you're not charging for it anymore, maybe we could get together, ya know, for old times' sake." Ellis pulled a toothpick out of his shirt pocket and slipped it into his mouth, where he rolled it back and forth with his tongue. "We could do it in my truck, just like in high school. You remember that, don't you? Of course you do. How could you forget? A girl never forgets her first time, right?"

"Neither of us was in high school," Trixie said, still at the kitchen counter with her back to Ellis. "You were a nineteen-year-old dropout. I was still in middle school. You remember that part?"

"Ah, yeah, but you were mature for your age. If you'd prefer to break in the hood of that 'Vette now—"

Trixie spun and pointed a chef's knife at Ellis.

"My boy is upstairs, and I don't want him to see you, hear you, or smell you. Now get out and don't you ever come back here."

Ellis stood and stretched his arms high over his head in a mock yawn, then picked his Stetson off the table and slipped it on. "All right, all right." He stepped through the kitchen door that led to the mudroom, where the screen door opened to the backyard. Ellis's pickup sat next to Trixie's new car at the end of the dirt and gravel driveway where it widened into a dirt and weeds lawn. He turned around in the mudroom and took a step back toward the kitchen. "Our boy sure is gettin' big, ain't he?"

Ellis jolted to a halt. He didn't look down, but Trixie made her point. The knife pushed against his sternum just firmly enough he wouldn't need to see it.

She stared into his eyes, which got considerably rounder. "You take another step forward, so will I. *My* boy ain't none of your bid'ness, remember?"

"I was just thinkin' maybe it was time we called a truce."

"We made a deal, Ellis Shackelford, and you're gonna live up to your end of the bargain." Trixie leaned forward against the knife handle a bit.

Ellis took a step back, tipped his hat, and walked out. Headlights flashed up the drive and spotlighted him as he opened the door to his truck.

Another pickup pulled in and veered to the side to allow room for Ellis to back out. Another tall cowboy in another Stetson stepped out of the second truck. The silhouette of his hat against the headlights turned toward Trixie.

"Everything a'ight here, ma'am?"

"Everything's just fine, Clay. Ellis was just leavin'." Trixie slipped the knife behind her back. "Why don't you come in? I'll fix you a cup of coffee." She backed into the mudroom to keep the seven-inch blade out of sight.

"You okay, Momma?"

Tyler stood in the middle of the kitchen in his baseball PJs, looking for all the world like a miniature Texas Ranger.

"Fine, I'm fine. Everything's fine." Trixie casually tossed the knife onto the counter like she'd just found it out in the mudroom. "What are you doin' up? I told you to go to bed."

"You told me to go watch TV in my room. But I heard you talkin' to that a-ho... uh, jerk, and I came down to see if you was okay."

"Ain't nothin' for you to worry about." Trixie pushed in the kitchen chair and straightened up anything else out of place. Tires crunched across the gravel as Ellis backed up and turned around. She waited for the angry spray of gravel against her new car, but he left nice and slow.

Ty still stood in the middle of the kitchen.

"Did you call Mr. Garza?" Trixie asked.

Ty looked down at his bare feet. "Yes, ma'am."

Trixie kneeled in front of the boy and put her hands on his shoulders.

"I said not to, and I mean for you to mind me. But it is nice to have a man around the house watchin' out for me."

"Yeah," Ty said. "With Mr. Garza living in the trailer, he's close enough to call if there's trouble."

Trixie pulled Ty in for a momma-bear hug.

"I wasn't talking about Mr. Garza."

***

"He's down and out. Finally." Trixie pulled out a chair and sat at the table across from Clay. She absentmindedly tugged at the bow-clasp on the collar of her robe to make sure it stayed hooked.

"He's a good boy." Clay sipped his coffee from a ceramic mug that read "O'Bumpkin's Pub" under a logo of the Texas and Irish flags crossed.

"I'm sorry he bothered you."

"No trouble at all, ma'am."

"And stop calling me ma'am. Makes me feel old. And feels extra weird since I ain't any older 'n you. But I'm glad you're here. Something I wanted to talk to you about."

Trixie surveyed the kitchen while she collected her thoughts. The cabinets needed paint, and one had a missing front. The vinyl floor tile, once white but now a dingy yellow, curled around the baseboards. The silverware drawer had come off the track again and lay at an odd angle.

"I'm thinking about selling this place. Can't get much for the house, but sixty-three acres has got to be worth something. Don't owe nothing but some back taxes my daddy never paid, and I can take care of that now."

Clay took off his hat and set it on the table, upside down on the crown so as not to flatten out the carefully steamed and curved brim.

"With your good fortune, I was afraid you might do that. But I can't say I blame you."

"I'm thinking I should get a nice place in town, somewhere more fittin' to raise a boy."

"What's more fittin' than raisin' a boy on a farm?" Clay leaned forward and propped his elbows on the Formica table. "Teach him chores, the value of hard work, taking care of some animals. When he's a little older, there won't be the distractions of town life, teenage boys runnin' around bored with nothin' to do but get in trouble, do drugs, that sort of thing. A farm's a good place to raise a boy."

Trixie crossed her legs and pulled the hem of her robe over her knees even though they were under the table. "Just seems like he'd be happier in town where he could have him some friends, not way out here where he has to spend an hour a day on a school bus. Maybe get him into Little League or Pop Warner so he could be around some positive male role models, ya know. A boy needs that sort of thing."

"Maybe. What does he think about moving to town?"

"I haven't mentioned it yet. I wanted to talk to you first about your situation. You interested in buying the place? I'd make you a good price."

"I can't come up with that kind of cash. I wouldn't even have a down payment to get a loan."

"If I sell, what would you do? I don't want to leave you out in the cold."

"Guess I'd try to find somewhere else to lease some land." Clay took a swig and set down his empty mug.

Trixie grabbed it and headed for the coffee pot on the counter. She refilled his cup and set it in front of him. "One more?"

"Since you put it that way."

"I could try to find a buyer who'd keep leasing the land to you."

"I'm not sure anyone is going to buy a farm and then lease the land and that old trailer to me. Least not for three hundred a month. I'd buy it from you if I could. It's exactly the kind of place I want to own someday. The land is perfect. House may not need much. Shore up the beams a bit, and some cosmetics."

"Maybe we could work something out."

"I won't be makin' any profit from the cattle until next year—at the earliest."

Clay and Trixie sat and sipped coffee. Trixie talked about one of those new colonial-style houses on a full acre with a manicured lawn at the edge of town. Still plenty of room for Ty to play, maybe get a dog, and only five minutes from school.

"I need to find us a church too," Trixie said.

"A boy needs to be in Sunday School, true enough. Didn't do me no harm."

Trixie playfully tapped her fist on Clay's bicep, which felt like a shirt sleeve full of rocks. "Question is if it did you any good."

"So far I've been able to keep eight out of Ten Commandments," he said.

"Which two do you struggle with?"

"Ain't no struggle. I just figure 80 percent is still a B average."

"Better 'n I did in school." Trixie refilled their mugs once more and turned off the empty pot.

Clay explained his plans for the hay he'd planted on the back side while the cattle grazed west of the creek during the growing months. Come fall, he'd bale the hay and put it up in the old barn, the one he'd reinforced so it wasn't quite the hazard it had been after sitting unused for the ten years since Trixie's daddy died. Next summer, he'd move the cattle to the east quarter, grow hay in the old pasture, and clear another ten acres so he could add a few more head of Herefords.

"But I guess if you're gonna sell, I better recalculate some plans." Clay stared out the kitchen window into the night. "I just love the dark out here. Don't you?" He swallowed the last of his coffee and slipped on his Stetson.

"Not particularly," Trixie said. "Can't see what's hidin'."

CHAPTER 3

The man cleared his throat — twice — and shuffled some papers on his desk before he glanced up to acknowledge Trixie's presence. He jotted a note on a folder and shoved some papers inside, then carefully placed it into a drawer. He looked up again but didn't make eye contact.

Trixie shifted in the chair and tried to tug her dress between the bare skin of her thighs and the vinyl seat. She'd chosen the blue and white flower print because it would be both cool and socially acceptable in public. The little black dress was a bit much for meeting an accountant in the middle of the day. The gray knit sweater dress was strictly for winter. The others, she'd decided after trying them all on, were too short, or showed too much cleavage, or too sheer for a sunny day. She'd go shopping for some more appropriate things after she got all the finances squared away.

"So, what can I do for you today, Mrs., uh," he glanced down at the handwritten note on his appointment calendar, "Mrs. Burnet?"

"It's Ms. Burnet, actually."

His bald head glistened with a thin sheen of perspiration from the east Texas summer swelter. The window unit air conditioner made more noise than cool. The vents pointed away from the desk, probably to keep from blowing papers around.

"What can I do for you, *Mizz* Burnet?"

"Well, I got this here letter." Trixie dug in her purse for the envelope. "It's from the Texas Lottery Commission, and it's all official. Certified and notarized and all that. I'm going to need some good financial advice on how to handle all this properly. Ya see, I want to make sure I don't just blow it all or have people swindle me out of it." She pulled the letter from the envelope and unfolded it.

On the desk in front of her perched a polished block of oak with a brass plate tacked to the front, MASON BROOKS CPA CFP engraved into the metal, the edges dull and brown with tarnish. Trixie moved the nameplate to the side so she'd have a larger space to lay the letter flat and smooth out the creases before handing it over. She moved the nameplate back, positioning it directly over the shiny, dust-free rectangle where it had sat apparently unmoved for years.

Mason held the letter in one hand but didn't look at it. He glanced around his desk and moved some papers. He opened a desk drawer and peeked inside, pulled out a stapler and a tape dispenser and a pad of sticky notes. When he didn't find what he was looking for, he put them all back in the drawer. He reached to the top of his head and discovered his reading glasses right where he'd left them.

"Let's see what we've got here."

He skimmed and skipped across the lines through the congratulatory greetings and the legal mumbo-jumbo until he lingered on one paragraph near the bottom of the first page. He pulled the second page around and read on, then back to page one.

"Well, I guess congratulations are in order, Ms. Burnet." He glanced at the letter again. "May I call you Victoria?" A broad smile exposed unnaturally bright dentures that matched the closely cropped white sidewalls of hair on a slick tire of a head.

"Trixie. No one calls me Victoria 'cept my momma when she's mad."

Mason adjusted his readers down his nose a bit and held the letter a few inches farther out.

"Well, Trixie, this is, uh, quite a sum of money you've come into. I'm glad to see you've got the good sense to seek professional financial guidance. So many young people in your situation would go for the lavish lifestyle and be sorely disappointed when their funds run out in a few years."

"Yes sir, I've read about that sort of thing. But I've got a little boy to think about, and my momma. I'd like to buy Momma a house and a home for me and Tyler—he's my boy. He'll be eight next month. I did go ahead and buy me a car. My pickup was so old I figured it weren't worth payin' to have it fixed, but beyond that, I'm just not real sure I have a whole lotta needin' or wantin', just wanna quit my job and be a stay-at-home momma and..."

Trixie stopped talking and looked down at her hands clasped together in her lap. She'd started babbling again. She had to stop that. Learn when to say just enough then shut up, that's what her momma always told her. Way back in middle school, or even earlier, her mother would tell her, "You just don't know how to stop the words that roll outta yer face."

"Have you given any thought to whether you want to take the annuity or the lump sum payout? Do you know what those terms mean?"

Trixie didn't look up from her hands. "Maybe you can explain it for me to make sure."

Mason pulled a calculator from the side drawer and started clicking numbers, glancing back and forth from the letter to the keys.

"The total payout for this lottery is $212 million, but you're one of eight winners, so..." Mason clicked a few more keys and jotted a figure down on a yellow legal pad. "Yes, that's just what the letter says, twenty-six and a half million is your share. Now you can take that in an annuity where you'll receive a payment once a year for twenty years in the amount of..." Mason's eyes skimmed the letter again. "Yes, here it is. That works out to $1,132,500 per year for twenty years, before taxes. After taxes, you should net about $600,000 a year."

"I ain't complainin'," Trixie said, "but that sure sounds like a lot less than millions, don't it?"

"It's still a lot of money, but you'd need to invest a goodly portion of it, because those annual payments will end when you're, well, if you don't mind my asking, how old are you?"

"Twenty-three." She could practically see the accountant's brain calculating the numbers to figure out how old Trixie was when Ty was born. Momma always told her she was an early bloomer.

"When you're forty-three, those payments will end. I recommend setting aside at least half each year, probably more, and investing it. That way you'll be able to make it last the rest of your life. If you decided to live on a mere hundred grand a year, well, that would be a dandy income for a young lady in these parts, and you'd have half a million dollars to save and invest each year."

Trixie squirmed to get a little more comfortable in the hard office chair, and the vinyl nearly peeled off some skin from the back of her thighs.

"What's that other option you mentioned, the lumpy thing?"

"A lump sum payout. Instead of paying it out over twenty years in an annuity, you get the net present value in a single payment now."

"You mean I could get the whole shebang right now?"

"Not exactly." Mason pushed his glasses back to the top of his sweat-beaded head. "Net present value. That means, how much money it would be worth right now. That comes to..." Mason fumbled with his glasses and scanned the letter, then clicked a few more keys. "About ten million dollars. And of course, there'll be taxes on that. So you might get about five or six million."

"So I can get $600,000 a year for twenty years, which is..." Trixie paused to do the math in her head but couldn't concentrate with all those zeros bouncing around in the heat.

"Twelve million dollars," Mason answered for her.

"Or I can get five million right now." Trixie pulled a tissue from her purse and squeezed it between her palms to soak up the sweat then dabbed it to her upper lip. "Well, twelve sounds better than five."

"Yes and no. Technically, they're about the same, depending on interest rates, inflation, and estimated return on investments."

Trixie chewed on her tongue and stared at the white stripes on Mason's head, reflections of the fluorescent light tubes.

Mason cleared his throat once more to break the silence.

"Let's look at it this way," he said. "If you took the lump sum, took the five million dollars right now, and let's say you bought that new car and a new house—"

"And a new house for Momma."

"And a new house for your mother. Then you take the rest and invest it. You put some in the stock market, some in bonds, and you put some into instruments—"

"I don't really play no instruments. Momma made me take piano lessons when I was a kid, but I weren't no good at it."

Mason suppressed a chuckle, but barely. "Not those kind of instruments. Cash instruments, like money markets and certificates of deposits and such." He went on to explain, in more detail than Trixie wanted or needed, about how she could take the big chunk of money now and invest it, live off some of the earnings and reinvest the rest so her investments would grow every year. "If you live another sixty years, you might earn twelve million dollars or more, plus your original five million."

"Well then, that's what I wanna do."

"Now, see, there are risks involved in that too. The economy could go bad and you might lose some money some years. If you take the annuity from the state, then there's no risk to you. You're going to get six hundred thousand a year for twenty years, and then it's going to end. You'd need to invest most of it every year."

Trixie managed to get the accountant to look her right in the eyes. "Mr. Brooks, what would you do if you won this much money?"

"Me? Oh, I don't play the lottery. I don't believe in it."

"But if you did. If you came into this much money, what would you do?"

"What I'd do might not be what you should do. Every case is different. Every individual is in unique circumstances. You have to look at your age, your family, what your financial goals are—"

"Mr. Brooks," she cut him off, "are you a certified financial adviser?"

"Yes, ma'am."

"Then I need you to do some advisin'."

Mason took a moment to wipe the sweat from his forehead on his handkerchief while he appeared to think about it.

"I've never met you before, Miss Trixie, and I didn't want to let on, but I do know who you are and I know, uh... well, I know what you do for a living—"

"Did," Trixie interrupted. "I was in the personal services bid'ness, but I'm retired now."

"Personal services," Mason repeated. "Sort of like me then." Mason chuckled a bit at his own joke.

"I'd say my services were a bit more personal."

That brought a full-on hearty laugh from the accountant, his dentures flashing in the sun that blazed through the window. "There aren't too many things more personal than someone's money and finances, but I think you probably have me there. Given how the folks in this town think, have you considered taking this money and finding yourself a new town to raise your boy? Somewhere people don't know you."

"I can't do that. My momma's here and she'll never leave. Besides, this ol' town is all I ever knowed."

"In that case, I'd advise you to take the lump sum payout. I can put together an investment portfolio that is safe and conservative but brings you in more than enough income to live a very nice life, take care of your family, and leave a healthy inheritance for your son and even your grandchildren some day."

"I'd like that. I'd like that a lot."

"My standard fee is 1 percent a year, and I'll work hard to make sure your investments earn a lot more than 1 percent."

"That what you charge everyone?"

"For portfolio management, yes."

"Do you have any other clients worth ten million?"

"No, can't say I do."

"Then I'll pay you a half a percent. But I'm gonna make up the difference in other ways."

"Now, I'm not sure that's something I can..."

Mason trailed off while Trixie ignored him and pulled another piece of paper from her purse, a single sheet of white, lined paper with the edges frayed from where she'd torn it from a spiral notebook. Some of the margins were pinched off in little scallops when she had subconsciously rolled a few spitballs as she'd written her notes. She handed the ragged page to Mason.

"What's this?" Mason fumbled with his glasses and scanned the handwritten scrawl of columns and ticker symbols and numbers.

"This here's the investment strategy I researched on the internets last night, and it's what I'd like you to maintain on my behalf. There's a list of the mutual funds and how much I want invested in each one. It's balanced so's I get maximum growth and income while preservin' my capitals. I figured about half in some of them high-cap stock funds with a modest international risk, a quarter in bond mutuals, mostly tax-free munies, and the rest in some of them cash instruments you mentioned, ya know, for liquidity. And I want to give some money to good causes too, help out them less fortunate now that God has blessed me. I'll want you to set up a charitable foundation, and there'll be an annual salary for you as director to help run that for me. But we'll deal with that later. Oh, and I want a 529 fund set up for Tyler. I figure if we put in five thou every year, by the time he graduates high school, there'll be enough so's he could pay for any college in the country he's smart enough to get hisself into. And he's pretty quick, that boy."

Mason shook his head and chuckled. His smile pushed the wrinkles on his forehead up higher. He stood and reached over the desk to shake Trixie's hand.

"If that boy's half as quick as his momma, you'll need to save enough to pay for Harvard."

CHAPTER 4

Trixie pulled as close to her momma's mobile home as she could, which wasn't that close since she couldn't see over the hood or judge the distance from her right front fender to the aluminum siding. She backed up twice to get a better view and try to get a little closer.

"You're gonna hit it, Mom," Tyler whined. "Just stop already."

"You shush."

Tyler shushed and glared at his mother.

"And don't you look at me with that tone of voice." But Trixie listened to her boy and stopped the car. "You'll need to get out on my side."

"Why'd you park so close then?"

"So other cars can get by. And who put the sass in your mouth tonight, little man? You better behave yourself at Gram's."

Trixie used a tissue to wipe a bug splat off the metallic pearl hood while Tyler crawled out, then she carefully locked the car and made sure she'd left room on the asphalt lane for other cars to get in and out of the trailer park.

The screen door banged open and a tall man stepped out to the wooden porch he'd added to the trailer a couple years back. "Lordy, Lordy, ain't that a ride fit for a princess?"

"Hey, Uncle Leon," Trixie said.

"Hey, Uncle Leon," Tyler echoed.

"Is that your new wheels, Mister Ty?" Leon rubbed a hand across his mahogany forehead and wiped the sweat on his gray steel-wool hair.

Ty grinned so wide his ears moved back an inch on his nearly clean-shaven head. Trixie'd taken him for a back-to-school haircut after the visit with the accountant. "Your gram and Leon aren't gonna want to see you lookin' like a ragamuffin," she'd said when Tyler protested. He'd settled into a pout by the time the barber had the apron on him.

Leon held the unpainted two-by-four stair rail and put one leg down, shifted his body slightly, then put his other leg down.

"Stay there, Leon. We're comin' up." Trixie had never gotten a straight answer on how old Leon was. It was a floating number. Somewhere between fifty and seventy. Coming down the stairs, he looked even older than that.

"I wanna see this masterpiece of American manufacturin'. Just gimme a sec." Leon turned sideways and grabbed the rail with both hands to take the second step, one leg at a time, then the third step to the ground. A grimace twisted his face for a split second.

"Your knee flarin' up?"

"Ain't nuthin'. Just a little achiness. Nuthin' my prescription won't take care of."

"So the doc's prescribing Scotch nowadays? Medicaid cover that for you?"

Leon rubbed his hand over Ty's nearly smooth scalp and whistled long and low as he admired the Corvette. "Ain't never touched Scotch. Gin. Beefeaters. Gotta be Beefeaters. I've resorted to gin-snobbery." He rubbed Ty's head again.

"Let's go in," Trixie said. "I hope you got the A/C runnin'."

"Your momma's in there cookin' something. Whyn't you go see if you can keep her from burnin' it this time?" Leon sat on the homemade wooden bench next to the porch. "Me and the boy'll be in shortly."

Trixie drew a deep breath and paused with her hand on the screen door handle before she threw it open.

"Hey, Momma. Somethin' I can do to help?"

"What in the name of our Lord Jesus did you do to your hair?"

"It's just an up-do. And a little color tint."

"Just a little," Sabine repeated with a grin. She turned back to the pot on the stove. "Looks like you got it chrome-plated. What's wrong with your natural color? Do you even remember what it is?"

"Mousy brown, same as yours."

"Hell, I don't even remember my own color. Turned gray the day you turned thirteen."

Trixie ignored her momma's dig. A lot happened when Trixie was thirteen that might have turned Sabine's hair gray. For starters, Daddy died. There were financial troubles since he didn't have any life insurance. Sure, she'd started running around with Ellis and her straight A's in school disappeared in a flash. But premature gray ran in the family. It made Sabine look much older than her forties.

"You should color it," Trixie told her. "I'll take you to the salon tomorrow."

"Oh right, missy. You know how much that costs?" Sabine stopped stirring and looked at Trixie's hair again. "Yeah, I guess you do now, don't you?"

"Don't start, Momma. Whatcha need me to do?"

"It's 'bout ready. Set the table and tell those men to get their behinds in here and warsh up."

***

Everyone sat back with a collective sigh, bellies full of chicken-and-sausage gumbo. Sabine stood to clear the dishes, but Trixie grabbed her arm and pulled her back to her seat.

"I need to call a family conference. I just met with an accountant, and we're setting up some investments and such. Figuring how much I got to spend on some things."

"Like that car out there," Leon said with a smile.

"Like that hair up there," Sabine said with a nod toward Trixie's up-do.

"Momma, stop it already. I want to do something for y'all now that I can."

"I could use some hair like that," Leon said, and Ty laughed so hard the last bite of French bread shot out of his mouth and onto the table.

"Stop it, all of y'all. Momma, I want to buy you a house. A nice house, with a small yard and a place you can grow some vegetables, maybe raise a few chickens like we did when I was little."

"What do I want with a fancy house? Whyn't you buy me a car?"

"'Cause you don't have a license, Momma."

"So? I still remember how to drive."

"Until that DUI is off your record, you can't drive. You'll go to prison."

"Don't go to prison, Gram."

"I ain't goin' to prison. I just need to be able to drive to the store or carry Leon to the doctor. Or maybe get my hair done or somethin'." Sabine couldn't contain her laughter, then Leon and Tyler joined in.

"I'm tryin' to be serious here. I wanna buy you a house. Get you out of this trailer park."

"Why would I want to move?" Sabine waved an arm around at her humble abode and the surrounding neighbors. "All my friends are here."

"'Cause this place is fallin' apart. Leon can barely get up and down the steps to the door. And it's dangerous. I can't even let Ty stay overnight here what with that trailer down the way cookin' up meth and who knows what."

"She's got her a point," Leon said to Sabine.

"Shut up and go smoke your cigarette."

"You stay right here, Leon. This is for the both of you."

"You're assumin' I'm gonna keep him."

"You're assumin' I'll be stayin'," Leon said.

"Where the hell else would you go?" Sabine snickered and playfully kicked Leon's good leg under the table. "Useless piece of crap, you are. If we move into some nice house with a yard, who's gonna do the mowin'? Me, that's who. Ever' time the grass gets tall, your leg'll start actin' up, so I'll have to do it. Then when it's done mowed, you'll have a miraculous recovery and walk a mile down to Sallie Mae's for your gin."

Leon grabbed Tyler's cheek between a thumb and forefinger. "That right there, young man, is why I advise you not to get married when you're growed."

"I ain't never gettin' married, Uncle Leon."

"And when you gonna stop callin' me Uncle? I been with your gram goin' on five years. I think it's time you called me Gramps or Grandpa or GeePaw or something sweet like that, don't you?"

Trixie interrupted before Tyler could answer. "He can call you Grandpa when you marry my mother and make an honest woman of her."

Leon snorted. "That'll take more 'n a marriage license."

Sabine kicked under the table again. Leon doubled over with a grunt and grabbed his knee, whimpering.

"Oh my God, oh my God, I'm so sorry." Sabine was up and kneeling at Leon's side in a flash, her kitchen chair tipped over with a clatter on the linoleum floor. "Did I get your bad leg? How bad is it? I'm so sorry, baby." Sabine rubbed his knee, then she stretched up and kissed Leon's forehead, her eyes shiny with restrained tears.

Leon peeked up from under the kiss, his wry grin exposing yellow teeth with three missing in front.

"It's not so bad," Leon said. "I think it'll be okay as soon as I can stretch it a bit. I'm goin' out for a smoke." Trixie caught the wink he gave Tyler.

"I hope your leg's not gonna have to be ampamitated, GeePaw," Ty said with a return wink.

Leon groaned as he stood and limped with slight exaggeration on his way out. Ty asked to be excused and, when Trixie nodded, scooted outside to sit with the old man where they'd carve pointy ends on sticks with their matching pocketknives, and Leon would point out the mourning dove and the titmouse flitting in and out of the few loblolly pines scattered around the trailer park. If they were lucky, sometimes a red-shouldered hawk or a turkey vulture would glide overhead, and Ty would run inside to report to Momma and Gram what they'd spotted.

Sabine scrubbed the gumbo pot while Trixie stacked the bowls and spoons in the dish rack to drip dry. Sabine handed the pot to Trixie, who wiped the water around in an attempt to dry it with the tissue-thin dishtowel.

"You're right about one thing," Sabine said after a long silence. "This place here is sure goin' to hell in a handbasket."

Trixie offered to buy her momma one of the just-built homes in the new subdivision on the north side of town.

"I can't let you do that. I know you've got money now, but that's too much. That just ain't right."

Trixie slid the pot into its spot in the cabinet as she suggested the new park off Highway 69 just south of town with half-acre lots. "How about a nice doublewide? They got a playground and community pool for when Ty spends the night."

Sabine didn't say anything while she finished washing the lid to the gumbo pot and set it in the dish rack, balanced precariously over the tops of Corelle Ware bowls and plastic drinking glasses. Then she headed for her recliner, the green one with the gold flecks in the fabric. The black vinyl recliner was Leon's. A scarred coffee table sat in front of the two chairs, a mismatched end table between them with a small brass lamp and a stack of white plastic coasters that read, "Sallie Mae's for Home Cooking Away From Home."

"We'll make sure it comes with a dishwasher," Trixie added.

"I never have trusted those things to get stuff clean." Sabine cracked open her second Diet Coke of the evening and took a swallow, followed by a barely suppressed belch. "And we'd need a ramp to the front door so that ol' bastard out there don't fall and hurt hisself again."

Ty banged through the screen door out of breath, eyes wide.

"Momma, Gram, come quick. The purple Martians are coming to roost."

"Martins," Sabine corrected him. "Purple martins. Not Martians."

Sabine rose from her chair with another belch and followed her grandson out to the porch where they could see the martin house Leon and Ty had built the week before. A flock of dozens circled and swooped, some diving full-speed into the little holes in the front and sides of the wooden box mounted on a fourteen-foot pole.

"Well, boy," Leon said as Trixie dried her hands and stepped onto the porch to join them, "looks like these little fellers like their new home."

"Can you take that thing down?" Sabine asked.

Leon shot her a quizzical look. "Down? The birds are just startin' to move in. Why would you want me to get rid of it? They eat the skeeters."

"Not get rid of it. Just move it. You think them purple 'Martians' will follow us over to a new place?"

Trixie slipped an arm around her momma's waist and gave a little squeeze. She headed back in to finish putting the dishes away, but mostly to hide a couple of tears on the verge of escape. She'd never been able to do something like this for her momma, or anyone else, for that matter.

It felt damn good.

CHAPTER 5

"Nobody wears ties."

"You do when you visit the Lord's house." Trixie straightened the slightly too long clip-on for the fourth time. Ty tugged at his collar, throwing the tie askew once more. Trixie ignored it this time. She would straighten it again just before they walked in so he'd look like her little man, at least for a minute.

"Why are we goin' to church anyhow? Someone die or somethin'?"

"Where'd you get that smart mouth? We're going to thank the Lord for all our blessings. And because we need to. We should go. We're going to go every Sunday now, so just get used to the idea. Now go get in the car."

Ty groaned and stomped down the stairs as loud as he could, which was much louder than usual in his new shoes, the ones with the black genuine leather uppers and rubber soles.

Despite her best intentions to arrive on time, Trixie wheeled into the crowded parking lot at Pineywoods First Church of the Risen Lord at 11:05 a.m. to find only two spaces open—one handicapped spot and one other. Two SUVs on either side had parked too close to the white lines for Trixie to maneuver into the opening, so she pulled through the lot and parked at a meter down about a block. She fumbled in her purse for two quarters before she saw the sign announcing free parking after six and on weekends.

She made Ty hold her hand on the way up the marble stairs to the twin oak doors, each with a small stained-glass window.

Ty slipped his hand from her grasp. "Gross, Mom. Your hand's all sweaty." He wiped his momma's perspiration on his black trousers with the razor-sharp crease and pulled at his collar to loosen the irritating piece of cloth once more.

Trixie grabbed the door's brass handle and hesitated. She considered pushing the large button for disabled access that would automatically open the doors but changed her mind. She looked at her boy, his tie still clipped to one side of his collar, but no longer neatly vertical to cover the buttons on his crisp white shirt. She'd stayed up late to iron it with spray starch so he'd look smart.

"You gonna open the door, or can we go home now?"

Trixie kneeled in front of Ty and fixed his tie once more.

"Look at me, little man. We need to put our best foot forward and make a good first impression. We can make some friends here. You and me both."

"I don't like nobody here."

"That's no kind of Christian attitude." Trixie stood and stared at the door handle but didn't make a move to grab it. She smoothed her black skirt with a sweaty palm and checked to make sure the top button of her white blouse was still fastened.

Ty pushed the disabled-access button, and both doors swung inward. The chorus of "Onward, Christian Soldiers" surrounded them like the doors were connected to a volume knob. They stepped into the foyer, another set of oak double doors in front of them. A gray-haired man in an equally gray suit and tie greeted them with a broad smile and offered a church bulletin to Trixie.

"Welcome to Pineywoods First Church, young lady. And you too, young man." He reached into his jacket pocket and pulled out a three-by-five card. "Once you get settled in, we'd be obliged if you'd fill this card out and drop it in the offering plate so we have a record of your visit." He reached into a different pocket and came out with two red ribbons, ones like a prize calf might get at the county fair, only instead of the FFA logo, the ribbon tails were embossed with vertical white letters: VISITOR. He bent over and pinned one on Ty's shirt pocket. The ribbon was almost as long as his tie. The usher reached to pin one on Trixie's new blouse, but she intercepted it.

"Here, I'll take that. It's silk."

He reluctantly let it go like he'd failed in his sacred mission to brand all newcomers and strays.

"Come with me, please." He pivoted and glanced over his shoulder to make sure the late arrivals followed. When he opened the next set of doors, the volume grew louder as six hundred voices poured forth with *"marching as to war."*

A robed choir of at least fifty stood at the front, on risers behind the pulpit, looking like giant purple drapes. The usher led Trixie and Ty halfway down the center aisle.

"... with the cross of Jesus going on before."

A deathly silence filled the sanctuary as the pipe organ's last note lingered and faded. The usher indicated with a flourish of his hand a pew on the right with enough space to squeeze in two more worshippers.

Before Trixie and Ty caught up to him, the congregation sat in unison. The only people standing in the whole congregation were Trixie, Ty, and the usher. The man and woman seated by the aisle stood to allow Trixie and Ty to pass by them on the way to the opening on the other side of their three kids, who pulled their feet back only after their mother prompted them with a wave.

Pew blockers, Trixie thought. *Some things never change.*

Trixie and Ty settled into their seats. The three kids to Trixie's left swung their legs up and out again, kicking the pew in front of them. Two boys and one girl, and it didn't look like three years separated the oldest from youngest. To the right, a multi-generational family filled out the rest of the pew. A husband and wife sat with their two boys, one about Ty's age, the other a surly teen. Trixie dreaded the thought of Ty's surly teen years, considering the attitude her not-quite eight-year-old already possessed. And considering the grief and gray hair she'd given her own momma when she turned thirteen.

On the other side of the surly teen sat the grandmother and a very old woman, probably the great-grandmother, with an oxygen tank next to her and clear tubes disappearing up both nostrils.

Trixie glanced around for other boys about Ty's age, and she spotted some here and there. He'd be able to make some friends here.

She put her arm around her boy and pulled him up against her, resting her hand on his shoulder a moment. She unclipped the tie and discreetly slipped it into her purse. None of the other boys wore ties.

During the prayer, with all heads bowed and eyes closed, Trixie took the opportunity to scan the congregation. Were she and Ty dressed appropriately? Were there any people her age? Did any other single moms attend, or were they all happily married couples with 2.1 kids and perfect teeth?

Across the aisle, one row in front of Trixie, the police chief sat next to a beautiful brunette a good twenty years his junior, along with four staircase boys, all younger than Ty. *Pretty fertile for an old guy. Glad I always made him wear a condom.* Trixie calculated how old Chief Hale would be by the time his kids graduated high school — about seventy or so, she guessed — and wondered why he would leave a beautiful young wife at home to come visit her farmhouse once a month. She'd learned years ago not to question these things too deeply. Besides, he had been her insurance. In addition to paying cash, Travis Hale ensured she operated her home business without legal interference. He never talked much, just stopped in to say hello and make sure no one, especially Ellis, had been giving her trouble. Might sit for a cup of coffee until she made sure Ty was sound asleep upstairs, then she'd lead him to the spare bedroom on the main floor, and the chief would be in and out in five minutes or less. He'd never hang around after that, just tip his hat on his way out the door and say, "Thank you, ma'am. Give me a call if there's any trouble."

The prayer ended, followed by announcements of various meetings like the Men's Bible Study on Monday night, monthly business meeting this Wednesday evening, and the Ladies' Society Circle on Thursday morning. The Teens for Christ would meet in the Youth Center on Friday after the season-opening football game, and would feature hot dogs, hamburgers and Christian rock and rap music. The oxygenated great-grandmother muttered and shook her head. And don't forget to visit the gift shop in the lobby selling Christian T-shirts, jerseys, and ball caps, with all profits going to feed the starving children in South Sudan.

After another hymn, the Rev. Parker Webb stepped up to the pulpit. Trixie knew his face from the newspaper ads in the *Daily Progress* that invited all those seeking God's grace to come to the Pineywoods First Church of the Risen Lord on Sunday morning to be filled with the Spirit, and from the TV commercials on the local station in which Rev. Webb walked among skinny African children covered with flies and sitting in the dirt. He bent down and hugged one, then turned to the camera to talk about the great work the Lord was doing through Pineywoods' special ministries.

Trixie could now provide a better life for Ty and for her mother, but she'd have plenty enough to do something bigger, something on a grander scale, to help those who had nothing at all. That commercial had sealed her decision on Pineywoods Church and Rev. Webb's special ministries.

He looked a bit different than Trixie expected. Clearly the same man, but his hair was now slicked back and dyed shoe-polish black. His hairline had receded a couple inches from the photo in the paper, and he'd put on a good fifty pounds since he'd filmed that video in Africa. Was it ten years ago? Twenty?

"I'd like to welcome all of God's children to the Pineywoods First Church of the Risen Lord on this beautiful Sabbath day."

The crowd murmured in response, "Good morning, Pastor," and a few sedate "Amens" echoed from scattered points around the sanctuary.

Not quite as rapturous a crowd as the Pentecostal church Trixie grew up in until she was thirteen. Not a month after her daddy's funeral, she met Ellis, a tall cowboy with dangerous-looking tattoos, a driver's license, and his "trusty white steed," which was an old rust bucket of a pickup truck. That was the year she fell from grace and didn't feel much like putting on a flower-print dress with a lace collar and sitting in Sunday School class knowing she'd thrown away her eternal soul in Ellis's truck.

"We want to give a special welcome to all our visitors this morning. If this is your first time in our midst, would you please stand so we can greet you properly?"

Trixie hesitated until the great-grandmother at the end of the pew nodded at her. No need trying to stay anonymous—everyone knew she was fresh meat. She stood, hoping her skirt hadn't wrinkled too much. She tapped Ty on the shoulder, but he slouched farther back, out of reach, burying himself into the seat. Trixie leaned backward just enough to grab his ear and tug him to his feet.

Around the congregation, a dozen or so more rose to their feet—some bounding up, proud for the attention, others standing slowly, unsure, red-faced. Hundreds of faces turned this way and that to spot the newcomers and give them a nod and a smile.

Ty slipped her grasp and sat back down.

Trixie wanted to sit down too, to escape all the people looking at her, studying her, taking her measure. A familiar pit of guilt rose in her gut like bile, the shame that first showed up at the Antioch Pentecostal Holiness Church the morning after she'd stained her purity with Ellis.

With the visitors still standing, Rev. Webb began to pray, thanking the Lord for leading new souls to join in the service today, for bringing an increase to the flock.

Three rows in front of Trixie, Lamar Reeves nodded at her without smiling then turned and bowed his head.

Trixie closed her eyes for the rest of the prayer.

Lamar could be trusted. He owned the First National Bank and was always honest with financial dealings. He'd helped Trixie out with the tax lien against the farm, and he'd always tipped well above her standard fee for his nonstandard requests.

Trixie shook away the image of Lamar, a respectable man, in a cloth diaper, suckling at her breast, an inappropriate memory to have in church while the pastor prayed. But she couldn't shake away her grin.

Yes, Lamar could be trusted. People could be trustworthy if they needed her discretion in return.

Trixie missed the "Amen" until Ty tugged on her skirt to let her know she was the only one still standing.

***

Ty fell asleep within the first thirty seconds of Rev. Webb's sermon.

Trixie tried to follow along, concentrating, listening for words of grace and forgiveness, for repentance and a new life. She kept pulling her drifting mind back to the pastor, but his lilting, singsong cadence lulled her until his words were background music she couldn't quite hear over the nonstop chatter in her head. A house for Momma. A new home for her and Ty. Was the Corvette a mistake? Maybe a more practical car, a minivan perhaps, would have been a better choice. What would she do with the farm? With Clay? She couldn't sell it out from under him, throw him back into the streets, or rather, back to sleeping in his truck parked on the side of a logging road, which was where he'd been before she'd hired him to fix up some stuff around the farm. He'd just stopped by and knocked on her door one day, asked if she would consider letting him live in the abandoned trailer at the edge of the woods by the back pasture. In return, he'd fix anything that needed fixing.

Rev. Webb turned to matters of God pouring out his blessing on his children, and his children showing their gratitude by giving back to the Lord through their tithes and offerings. And today wouldn't be just the normal tithes and offerings, but a special call to expand God's Kingdom on Earth, an opportunity to dig a little deeper and really show God how blessed you are. "Don't be selfish with God's blessings. To those whom much has been given, much shall be required."

She would talk to Mason about that Monday. Maybe the Pineywoods special ministries should be a priority for her foundation once the money came in from the lottery commission. The thought of spreading God's love and feeding starving babies eased the discomfort in her gut.

Trixie dropped a ten-dollar bill in the offering plate, along with the visitor's card, but she had to nudge Ty on the shoulder to wake him up, and again in the ribs to get him to part with the dollar she'd given him to tithe.

During the benediction prayer by another of the associate pastors, Rev. Webb strode down the aisle to take up his position at the door to greet members and visitors on their way out.

Trixie stood patiently in the exit line, while Ty shuffled his feet, yawned, and leaned against her, his shirt half untucked and one shoe untied. Trixie couldn't do anything about it now. That boy wouldn't stay put together if she'd coated him in Elmer's glue.

"Wonderful sermon, Parker," the man in front of Trixie said as he shook Rev. Webb's hand.

"Inspirational, as always," the man's wife said.

"Mr. Mayor, Mrs. Mayor, always so good to see you both."

The mayor gave a hearty chuckle. "When're you gonna stop calling me that?"

"When you're not mayor anymore. Or when we're out fishing."

"When you two are out fishing," Mrs. Mayor said, "you can call each other anything you want. In public, you're Mayor Callahan, and you should address our pastor properly as well. Forgive him, Reverend, but sometimes I don't think he can be civilized."

Trixie stared at the back of Mrs. Mayor's head, shifting from one foot to the other just enough to make sure Jasper Callahan didn't catch sight of her. He wouldn't acknowledge her, of course, but no need in letting Mrs. Mayor catch a spark of recognition. The shame flared again, but Trixie tamped it down. If the mayor and the police chief and the banker — all married men in positions of authority in the community — weren't ashamed to spend time with a hooker Saturday night and go to church Sunday morning, why should she feel guilty? Perhaps the reason they attended every Sunday was to repent and gain forgiveness for their sins of the week, and that's why she was here too. No shame in being a repentant sinner. No shame at all for turning from a life of iniquity.

Trixie had left that life behind the moment the TV announcer read the sixth ball that popped out of the lottery machine at 9:59 p.m. a week ago Wednesday. She'd canceled all her appointments without explanation.

Maybe without Trixie running her personal services business, without the temptation she provided, these men would also turn from their sins, maybe stay home with their beautiful wives and children. As long as some other poor girl didn't decide to fill a market need.

"Good morning to you, son."

Trixie nudged Ty so he'd know the pastor was talking to him, and she rested her hand on the back of his neck. Ty took a moment to grab the outstretched hand, and he gave it a good, manly up and down pump, which gave Trixie one of those tiny, proud momma moments.

"How are you doing, son?"

"I'm just wakin' up. That old guy talked so long I fell asleep."

Trixie pinched the back of Ty's neck, and a different kind of shame burned onto her face. She stuck out her hand to shake with the pastor and said, "I apologize for—"

"No need for that. If I had to listen to me, I'd probably put myself to sleep." Rev. Webb held onto Ty's hand and grabbed Trixie's with his left. "A growing boy needs his rest. Isn't that right, young man? And he's got a beautiful big sister to bring him to the right place for that."

"She ain't my sister. That's my momma."

"Well, you have a beautiful young mother." He turned his attention to Trixie, letting go of Ty's hand and holding Trixie's in both of his large, smooth hands with perfectly manicured nails. "It's so good of you to join us in worship this morning. I do hope you'll come again, maybe give it prayerful consideration if this is the church the Lord is leading you to join. Seats may be getting a little hard to find, but we always have room for more of God's children. We'll find room for one more if your husband wants to join you next week."

Trixie squirmed a bit under his intense stare, his friendly, smiling face with two bright blue eyes that burned right through her. "I'm not married, Reverend. It's just the two of us."

"The two of us against the world," Ty added. "That's what Momma always says."

"You two are always welcome here with our church family. Then all of us can face this sinful world together in God's strength."

"Thank you." Trixie tried to slip her hand from Rev. Webb's grasp and walk away so the people in line behind her could take their turns greeting the pastor, but he held on and pulled her back.

"Have we met? You look familiar."

"I know you from your TV commercials, but I don't believe we've ever met. I've never been to church here before."

"You prolly saw my momma on TV too. We won the—"

Trixie pushed her little man along and nodded to the pastor, who was immediately swallowed up by the four-generation family. Once outside the church doors, Trixie led Ty by the ear toward the car. "Didn't I tell you not to go around talking 'bout that? Don't be callin' attention to it."

"Ain't you goin' on the TV callin' 'tention?"

"Just get in the car."

"Can we come back here next Sunday?"

"I didn't think you liked it. Put you to sleep, you rude little man."

"I didn't like it, but I want one of those Christian ball caps."

"Only if you stay awake and listen to the preacher."

"Never mind then."

CHAPTER 6

With his backpack slung over his shoulder, Ty stepped off the bus and headed down the gravel road for the five-minute walk to his dirt driveway. He picked a broad leaf off a kudzu vine and used it to blow his nose. Mr. Garza had shown him how to spot poison ivy and poison oak, which wouldn't do at all as a tissue. He tossed the snot-smeared leaf to the ground and picked up a rock, a good round one about the size of a ping-pong ball. He chucked it as hard as he could toward the abandoned barn in the field, aiming for the open window at the top. It missed by a couple of feet but gave a satisfying thunk against the rotten wood.

He turned up the incline of the driveway, which ran beside the house, then curved around behind. His bike leaned against the tree, next to the tire swing Uncle Leon had put up. Neither the bike nor the swing held much appeal at the moment, but neither did the math homework or the teacher's note in his backpack. He hoped to drop off his backpack in the kitchen, grab a bottle of water and head out to the woods for a bit, but Mr. Garza's pickup sat in the driveway next to the Corvette, so he wouldn't be able to get in and get out without adults delaying him.

Sure enough, Momma and Mr. Garza sat at the kitchen table, drinking coffee, a bunch of papers spread out in front of them. If they were busy enough with adult stuff, maybe they wouldn't mind him so much and he could slip out undetected.

"How was your day?" Mr. Garza asked.

"Crappy."

"Don't say 'crappy,' little man. That's a bad word. You got any homework?"

Maybe he wouldn't be so lucky. Nothing else had gone right today, so why should this? "Nope."

"You got anything you need to tell me about? Anything you're supposed to give me?"

The next lie started to slide out as easily as the first, but he hesitated a moment too long. Something in his momma's tone alerted him. She already knew. The teacher must have called.

"Oh, yeah, almost forgetted."

"Forgot. Not forgetted. Let's have it."

Ty set his backpack on the empty chair next to Mr. Garza, unzipped it and pulled out a wad of crumpled papers. On top of the pile was his math paper.

"I thought you said you didn't have any homework."

"Oh yeah, I got this one thing. I forget—forgot."

"You're awful good at forgettin' things you don't want to do. Like makin' your bed this mornin' before school."

Ty shuffled through the papers—old papers that had been graded and returned, an announcement about the PTA meeting he'd never given to his momma, completed homework he'd never turned in because he'd forgotten. At the bottom of the pile was a wrinkled, smudged envelope addressed to Victoria Burnet. He handed it over and scraped the rest of the papers back into his pack, then turned to head to his room.

"Stop right there. You ain't goin' nowhere 'til I read this."

Ty groaned and slouched into the empty chair.

"And how do you have so much crap in there when school's only been going for a week?"

Trixie smoothed the envelope on her lap. As she opened it with a butter knife, Mr. Garza lumbered out of his chair and headed for the coffee pot, rubbing Ty's head on the way by.

"Says here you've been a disruptive influence, and Mizz Lipscomb wants a teacher-parent conference with me tomorrow after school. Says you're not paying attention in class and not following directions, and she wants to meet so's we can 'coordinate our efforts to positively affect your behavior and motivation.'"

Ty withered under his momma's gaze when she finished reading the note. Normally, he'd stare right back at her, but with Mr. Garza taking his seat again, the will to defy his momma evaporated.

"So what's goin' on inside that head of yours? Why ain't you listening to the teacher and paying attention in class? You're smarter'n that. I'm raisin' you better'n that, ain't I?"

"I dunno."

"I still got that leather strap there on the wall if you need some positive motivation. My momma used it on me, and it worked just fine."

Ty stared at the cracked, brown razor strop that hung on a hook by the door. Momma had told him about it and what it was good for, but she'd never used it on him. He figured she never would, but no need in putting her to the test.

Mr. Garza slurped his coffee and set his cup down. He rubbed Ty's head again and asked, "Is there something going on at school that's bothering you?"

"No. I just don't like school."

"I loved school," Trixie said. "In fact, I'm thinkin' I might go back. I've always wanted to put my GED to good use, so I'm lookin' at the community college or maybe some online classes."

"Fine. You go to school, and I'll stay home all day and do nothin'."

"Little man, you better watch that trap of yours. I'm here all day cleanin' up after you, doin' your laundry, cookin' you a good meal, makin' your lunch, and then you go and mouth me like that. You're gonna go to school and behave, and you're gonna finish school and go to college after that, 'cause you're gonna have the opportunities never afforded to me. You might think you don't like it now, but you'll thank me the rest of your life."

Ty hadn't meant to talk like that with Mr. Garza sitting right there. It just came out. Momma raising her voice at him didn't usually bother him none, but he wished Mr. Garza hadn't heard.

"You just gonna sit there and sulk, or you gonna tell me what's goin' on? We can sit here all night if you want. I got nothing else to do, remember."

Ty didn't mean to say anything else, but the words formed a knot in his throat, battling to get out against the tears he was trying to hold back.

"Carson called you a bad word and I punched him then he and Franklin and Walker said I gotta give them each a dollar every day or they're gonna beat me up on the bus every time I don't but you can't say nothing to the teacher or they're gonna whoop my tail for tellin' on 'em."

The words had won out, spilling out so fast he couldn't stop them. When they ended, tears followed, punctuated with a heaving sob he tried so hard to swallow in front of Mr. Garza.

***

Trixie was out of her chair in a flash, wrapping her arms around her little man. Ty buried his face in her neck, his tears and runny nose damp against her skin. She stifled her own sob. She had to be strong. No going all blubbery.

She held tight until Ty's sobs subsided and he pulled away.

"You're not gonna tell Mizz Lipscomb, are you?"

"She needs to know what's goin' on, and she might be able to help. But I'll think on it to see if we can figure out the best approach. No need in just makin' things harder on you, right?"

Clay rubbed Ty's head again then got up and went to the fridge. He came back with a can of grape soda, popped the top and set it in front of Ty, who took a big guzzle.

"I got to ask you something," Trixie said as she pulled her chair next to Ty and sat down. "Clay, would you mind steppin' outside a minute?"

"Not at all, ma'am. Didn't mean to interfere in a family matter here."

"You're not interferin' at all. I just need to ask my boy something private."

Clay slipped on his Stetson, rinsed his coffee cup at the sink, and went out through the mudroom.

Ty took another gulp of soda.

"I know I always tell you not to say bad words, but this time I'm gonna make an exception. It's not you sayin' a bad word, it's you tellin' me what someone else said. I need you to tell me what that boy said about me."

Trixie braced herself. What had some cruel kid said about her to her son? Would she have to explain what 'whore' meant? How would she deny it? Or worse, how could she admit it to her boy?

"Carson called you a bitch."

Trixie blew a sigh of relief. She'd never been so grateful for being called that.

"Why on earth would he say that? I don't even know that boy."

"When he said I had to bring three dollars to school every day for them not to whoop my ass—um, butt, I told him I ain't got no three dollars every day. So he said I should just get it from you 'cause you're a rich bitch now."

"Well, ain't no denying the rich part, is there now? And I'm gonna call up that boy's momma, and she's gonna find out firsthand how true the second part is."

"Don't you dare call her, Momma. You promised."

Trixie grabbed a napkin and handed it to Ty. "Blow. Better yet, just go wash up."

Ty polished off his grape soda and let loose with a belch louder than an east Texas thunderstorm. He started laughing.

"That ain't funny. That's downright nasty."

Ty belched again while laughing, and Trixie chuckled despite her irritation.

"What do you say?"

Ty belched out, "Excu-u-use me."

"Ain't no excuse for that." But she couldn't stop laughing.

Clay stuck his head through the screen door and grinned at Ty. "Everything okay in here? Sounded like something exploded. Smells like grape."

Ty darted up the stairs to go wash up, still trying to force out another burp.

***

Trixie looked for Room 17, wandering the hallways like an oversized salmon swimming upstream against a chattering, squealing current of kids headed to the buses.

The air in the hall was thick with humidity from sweaty children, and hotter than the direct sun outside. Cool breezes rushed from each open classroom door along with the kids. The old three-story elementary school building, the same one Trixie had attended, hadn't changed much, but at least they'd added window air-conditioning units to the classrooms. Back in Trixie's day, kids just sweated and sweltered and tried to get gulps of air from the occasional breeze through open windows. At least once a week, a red wasp would fly in, and the classroom would explode in pandemonium while the teacher ran around with a flyswatter and told the kids not to be afraid, that bees can smell fear and are attracted to it. "If you don't bother it, and you're not afraid of it, it won't bother you."

The idea of a stinging insect that could smell her fear frightened Trixie even more. She'd sit perfectly still at her desk, frozen on the edge of panic.

In those days, Trixie longed for October, when the heat would finally break, the windows could be closed, and the bees went into hiding for winter.

Now, the windows stayed closed and the air conditioners thrummed in every room. She'd imagined that would keep her boy safe, but she'd been wrong. There were other insects that could bite and sting, poisonous little bugs named Carson and Franklin and Walker. Maybe she should have brought a flyswatter.

She hesitated a moment at Room 17, Ms. Lipscomb's third-grade classroom, according to the poster beside the door. She took a deep breath and consciously lifted her chin a bit higher.

"Hello, Mizz Lipscomb. I'm Tyler's mother." She strode across the room with her hand extended for a shake, a bit early on her timing.

The teacher stood up behind her desk and waited until Trixie got closer before she reached out to take her hand. "It's nice to meet you, Miss Burnet."

Ms. Lipscomb didn't look any older than Trixie. With her dark brown hair permed in ringlets with golden highlights, giant hoop earrings, black jeans, a white blouse, and a tiny rose tattoo on the side of her neck, she didn't even look much like a teacher. At least not any of the teachers Trixie'd had.

If she'd known teachers were this informal these days, she'd have worn jeans instead of the rose-colored dress and matching heels she'd planned to wear to church next Sunday.

Ty sat in a desk on the front row, looking as uncomfortable as he had in church.

"Please, sit down."

Trixie glanced around for another adult-size chair, but there wasn't one. She pulled a chair out from the desk next to Ty and sat down. When the teacher sat down behind her desk, Trixie was back in third grade, called to the principal's office for a scolding.

"Tyler, why don't you get your book bag and go to the library to work on your math problems and spelling words while I visit with your mother?"

"Yes'm." Ty grabbed some papers from his desk, crammed them into his backpack and headed for the door.

"Come back here, little man. Don't I get a hug?"

"Mom, geez." Ty rolled his eyes and left.

Trixie shrugged it off with a smile at the teacher. Ty couldn't know how much that hurt her feelings.

"Thank you for coming down, Miss Burnet."

"You can call me Trixie."

"I prefer to keep the parent-teacher conferences more formal. Let me get straight to the matter at hand."

Trixie scooted her bottom around in the chair, trying to find a more comfortable position, but none was to be found.

"Tyler is a smart boy. He masters every subject and is usually the first to grasp a new concept. And that may be part of the problem here."

"How is bein' smart a problem?"

"I believe he's bored. While I'm working with the other children, going over and over the same material, Tyler has had it down since the first time through, and he's ready to move on to the next subject."

"Then maybe you should let him."

"It's not that easy."

"Why not? Just hand him a book and send him to the liberry. Tell him to come back and see you when he's done. That's what I do with him at home. He goes off to his room or sits at the kitchen table and reads while I'm cookin' supper. He comes and asks me if he's got a question, and if I don't know it, we look it up together on the internets."

"That's wonderful that you do that, but I have twenty-six children to teach, not just one. They all need to be brought along to the same level in order to pass their state tests. I can't teach advanced information to some kids and help others who are having trouble catching on, all the time trying to maintain order because your son won't stay in his seat or keep quiet."

Trixie shifted again in her seat, then stood and pretended to look at the drawings Scotch-taped to the walls. "So the problem with his misbehavin' in class is because he's too smart, he's bored with what you're teachin' him, and you don't have time to occupy his mind. Do I have that right?"

"Look, I didn't want this to turn into a confrontation. Let's start over. We need to be a team, a united partnership, to help Tyler learn—not just schoolwork, but proper socialization skills. He seems to have trouble making friends, and maybe he's trying too hard. He goes from sullen and not participating in class at all some days to being disruptive to the other students."

"He's seven, almost eight years old. And he's a boy. He'd prob'ly rather be out playin' in the woods or ridin' his bike."

"How do you handle him at home? You said he sits and reads. Doesn't he get bored sitting still? He does here."

Trixie thought about that a moment. It'd never been an issue. When it was time to read, he read. She walked to the teacher's desk.

"I don't rightly know. He comes home from school, and I let him play outside 'til time for supper. He hikes the trails in the woods behind our house and rides his bike on the cow path across the pasture. After supper, and after one hour of TV, I give him a book to read."

"What does he read at home?"

"Over the summer, he finished all the Jack London and Mark Twain books, a coupla *Harry Potter* books, and started on them *Hunger Games*." Trixie leaned over the desk, hovering over the teacher, and lowered her voice. "And I caught him once reading one of my books—ya know, one of them bodice-rippin' romances—but I told him he weren't quite old enough to read that. You know what he said? He said, 'Sure I am. It's easier than Huck Finn.'"

Ms. Lipscomb hunched over her desk and jotted notes. "I knew he was a fast reader, but if he read all that over the summer, he's more advanced than I thought."

"Whadda you got him readin' here?"

"Some short books written for third graders. It takes most of the kids twenty to thirty minutes to read one. He sets his down in two minutes, and when I tell him to pick it up and keep reading, he says he already has. I thought he meant he'd already read it at home. So I tell him to read it again to get it fresh in his mind for the quiz."

"Maybe he's just too advanced for third grade," Trixie said, standing a little straighter than before, unable to keep the pride out of her tone.

Ms. Lipscomb stood and walked around the front of the desk, where she half-leaned, half-sat against it. "Maybe. But I don't think he's socially ready to move up a grade."

"Maybe if he was with older kids and doing schoolwork that challenged him a bit more, he'd start behavin' better."

"I think it's more than that," the teacher said. "Is there a father at home, or a father-figure in his life?"

"No, never been no daddy in his life. He ain't never knowed any different, so he ain't missin' nothing there." Trixie thought for a moment. "But he's got his uncle. Leon does a lot of man-stuff with Ty that I ain't no good at. Takes him fishin', makes things out of wood, that sort of thing."

"Is there something going on at home that might be bothering him?"

Trixie picked up her purse to leave. "I don't think it's what's goin' on at home that's botherin' him. Maybe you should look a little closer at what's goin' on here in school before you start pointin' accusin' fingers at his home life."

Ms. Lipscomb flinched. "I'm not making any accusations. I'm just trying to figure out what might be bothering him."

"I'm just sayin'. If you got a boy name of Carson in this class, you better keep an eye on him and how he's treatin' Ty. My boy ain't gonna tattle on him, and I promised I wouldn't either. But I bet if you open your eyes, you'll catch the little bully in the act. Or maybe you just got too many kids to handle. Can't see bullying goin' on, can't see when a kid is bored 'cause he's too advanced for what you're teachin' him."

"You're right. There's no doubt our class sizes are too big. We need teachers' aides to help out, but they've been cut from the budget." Ms.

Lipscomb clasped Trixie's arm in a friendly, almost conspiratorial way. "You know, this is something where you could be a great help."

"You want me to be a teacher's aide?"

"Oh, no, I don't mean you. Our Parent-Teacher Association is trying to raise money to hire teachers' aides. I don't mean to be presumptuous here, but, well, everyone knows you were the big winner, and this is something that could use your support. It's not just for your son, but it would help all of the teachers and all our students." The teacher walked behind her desk, pulled a piece of paper out of a drawer, and handed it to Trixie. "This is the flyer that explains the program and the donation form."

Trixie glanced over the form and pushed it into her purse. "Yes, ma'am, we've been real blessed recently, and I plan on helpin' out some worthy causes. I'll have my accountant look this over."

"Oh, that would be wonderful."

"When does the PTA meet?"

"It, uh, we meet every third Thursday in the auditorium. Seven p.m. But I'm sure you must be very busy, so it's okay if you can't make it."

"Oh, I can make it all right. I've found some extra time on my hands of late."

Ms. Lipscomb extended her hand first this time and held on, placing her other hand on top of Trixie's in the politician's handshake. "I'm so glad you came down and had this conversation. I'll keep an eye out for anyone mistreating Tyler. I'm so glad I've finally met you, Trixie."

Trixie peeled away and headed toward the door. "It's Ms. Burnet. I prefer to keep fundraisin' requests on a more formal level." She left, then pivoted and stuck her head back in. "Which way is the liberry these days? I need to collect my little man."

***

Clay pulled the bicycle out of his pickup bed and set it up on the kickstand. He flipped open the lid of the toolbox and pulled out a screwdriver and socket set.

"I'll go put on some coffee," Trixie said. "Thanks again for doing this. No way I could have wrangled that thing into the 'Vette."

"No problem." Clay kneeled beside the bike and tightened nuts and bolts, lowered the seat, and checked the chain and hand brakes to make sure everything was adjusted.

Trixie couldn't wait to see Ty's face when he spotted the new bike, full of chrome and polish, with knobby tires perfect for riding the trails through pasture and woods. He'd be home in about an hour, time to whip up some chocolate chip cookies for a special Friday-after-school birthday snack.

Clay came in about the time the coffee pot beeped. He and Trixie sat at the kitchen table and waited.

"What do you think?"

"I think he's gonna like it just fine," Clay said.

"I mean about the farm."

"I think it's a generous offer. Maybe too generous. I'm not sure I can accept it."

"Nothing generous about it. I'm just rentin' it out to you after me and Ty move into town."

"Rent usually means I pay you."

"It's an investment for me. I still own the farm, you live here and run it for me. When you're profitable, I get a share."

"Might take a couple years to make any profit. And what if I never make a profit?"

"That's the investment risk I take. Besides, I got faith in ya. Then, when you're profitable, we can discuss you buyin' it from me."

"At fair market value. Not interested in a charity price."

The scent of warm, melting cookie dough wafted through the kitchen, and Trixie checked the oven. "Another five minutes. Perfect timing."

Trixie sat down again and opened the folder with all the real estate paperwork Mason had pulled together for her. She flipped through a few pages until she found the one she was looking for.

"This here shows the fair market value as of right now. If you go and turn it into a fully working, profitable farm, the value would go up, but that'd be due to your work. When the time comes, I'll sell it to you at today's value, not what it's worth after you drive the price up. Fair enough?"

"Fair enough."

"And it'll be owner-financed at no interest. No need in trying to get a mortgage from the bank and paying interest on top of that."

"That's not fair to you."

"Sure it is. The place is paid for and not doing me any good at all. Your payments will be extra income, which I don't rightly even need that. And if for whatever reason you can't make the payments sometimes, I'll work with you better'n the bank would."

"What if the farm fails? What if I can't make it profitable?"

"I don't reckon that'll happen, but if it does, worst-case scenario, the land comes back to me rather than the bank."

The screen door squealed open and slammed shut. Ty walked in, looking at Momma and Clay then scanning the kitchen.

"Who's here?"

"Just me and Mr. Garza. Who else do you think would be here?"

Ty sniffed the air and looked confused. "Some kid's bike is out there, and you're makin' cookies. Smells like company."

Trixie tried hard to keep a straight, serious face. "No one else here but us, and no one else comin'. So whose bike do you think that is?"

"What're you grinnin' at, Momma?"

"You're just growin' up so fast. Besides, an eight-year-old needs a bigger bike."

The screen door banged open as Ty ran outside, Trixie and Clay at his heels.

***

Clay held the bike up while Ty squirmed around on the seat to get comfortable, his foot barely reaching the lowest pedal.

"This handle is the back brake. Pushing down on the pedal won't stop you with this machine. Here, give it a squeeze."

Ty's outstretched fingertips couldn't quite get a grip.

"I can adjust that a little more so you can reach it." Clay helped Ty off the bike, grabbed a wrench and fiddled with the brake lever. He then lowered the seat even more, all the way down. "Here, try this again."

Ty climbed back on. His tiptoes rested on the pedal, his fingertips peeking over the edge of the brake lever.

"Remember, just use this lever to stop, not the pedals."

"What's this lever for?"

"That's the front brake. Don't use that. Let's just learn how to use the back brake first."

"Okay."

Clay pushed the kickstand up. "Lean it over this way to push off and when you stop."

"Be careful, little man."

Ty pushed off and wobbled to a start, but within ten feet, he had it vertical and running a straight line. He made a slow loop around the 'Vette and Clay's pickup and brought it to a perfect stop right in front of Clay, who had crouched, ready to catch him.

"How do you like it?" Trixie asked.

Ty didn't have to answer. The smile split his face like a fire log kissed by an ax. "Can I take it down the path?"

"Whyn't you ride it around up here a bit longer, make sure you're comfortable with it?"

"Aw, Mom."

"Just five more minutes. Then you'll be ready to hit the trails."

"Your mom's right."

"Okay." Ty pushed off again for another circle, then a third, around the vehicles.

Trixie waved and led Clay inside for more coffee. Then she stuck her head back out and yelled, "C'mon in when you're ready for some cookies."

Ty ignored her, concentrating much too hard on steering and pedaling and hand-braking to pay any attention to cookies.

***

"Awrighty then, I s'pose we got us a deal." Trixie signed the back page of the twenty-page real estate contract and pushed it over to Clay for his countersignature. A lease-option land contract with owner financing. Closing date would be tentative on when Trixie found a new home for her and Ty. Clay would move out of the trailer and into the house, do upkeep and maintenance it sorely needed, and run the farm. No rent until profitable, then half of the profit to Trixie until that rent reached a maximum of $500 a month. Then a thirty-year mortgage at 1 percent interest. Clay insisted on some interest; Trixie refused more than 1 percent.

Clay ate another cookie, wiped his fingers and lips on a napkin, and signed just above Trixie's signature.

"I can't thank you enough, ma'am. This has been my dream, and if it wasn't for you doing this, I doubt it ever would've happened."

"I told you before, stop calling me ma'am. And I'm sure you woulda found your farm eventually, but this one just seems to have your name on it. The land here likes you."

Tyler burst through the screen door.

"You ready for some cookies?"

"I don't want no damn cookies and I don't want that damn bike neither."

"Ain't no call for that kind of language. Now sit down here and tell me what happened."

Ty held up one bloody elbow. More blood oozed from a scrape underneath the shredded knee of his blue jeans.

"C'mere, let's wash that up. Then we'll see if we need to wash your mouth out too."

Clay lifted Ty onto the kitchen counter while Trixie got a washcloth, some antiseptic spray, and bandages. She cleaned up the injuries, and Ty never even whimpered with the spray.

"What happened, little man?"

"I couldn't pull the brake lever hard enough, and the pedal just went backward, so I just tumped it over so I wouldn't hit your car 'cause you'd have been mad. That bike is too big. Your car is too big."

Clay helped Ty hop off the counter. "Let's go try it again. I'll come with you."

"I don't want to. I can't ride it."

"I'll give you a hand. You just have to get used to it."

"I'll fall again."

"That happens. You fall off a horse, you just have to get back on it and show it who's boss. C'mon." Clay ruffled Ty's hair, just starting to grow back from the buzz-cut, and headed out the door.

"Go on. You heard him."

Ty groaned and stalked out behind Clay. "Maybe I oughta wear a helmet or sumthin'."

"I never wore a helmet when I was a kid, and it never done me no harm. Wait a sec." Trixie went to the coat closet in the living room and came back with Ty's winter stocking cap.

"What good is that gonna do?"

"It'll keep you from getting blood on my new car."

Ty groaned again and stomped out without the cap.

***

Trixie sat in the car, bouncing the heel of her hand on the steering wheel. She wanted to honk the horn but didn't want to call attention from the neighbors in the mobile home park.

The screen door popped open, and Sabine came down the stairs.

"You're gonna make us late."

"Just calm down. I had to go back and get my purse."

"Going to get your purse doesn't take ten minutes." Trixie dropped it into gear and pulled into the driveway across from Sabine's trailer to turn around. "We've got a Realtor waitin' for us." Trixie pulled onto the highway and headed through town to the south side, toward the nice manufactured-home park with half-acre lots and dishwashers.

"Pull over at that gas station on the left. I need a pack of cigarettes for Leon."

"For cryin' out loud, Momma. That'll wait until our way back."

Sabine huffed and went silent.

Trixie whipped across the road into the gas station. "Make it fast."

"I will, I will. Jeez, that house ain't goin' nowheres."

"Wait." Trixie shifted into reverse and backed out of the parking space.

"What is wrong with you, child? I said I'd be fast."

"Ellis is here. Let's go. We'll get Leon's smokes later."

Ellis stood at the pump, filling his pickup, glaring at Trixie and Sabine as they pulled back onto the highway. The same trusty white steed he'd had for the ten years since they'd first met, and it was old back then.

***

Trixie stepped off the school bus but wasn't ready to go home. She stood at the intersection of the asphalt county road and the gravel lane that led to her house. The only sound was the fading exhaust pipe of the bus as it headed down to the next stop, along with the ever-present crickets and the last of the cicadas. The ditches beside the road were overgrown with weeds waist high. Daddy hadn't gotten around to mowing them.

She stared at the redwing blackbirds perched on the electric lines above her head like notes on sheet music. She always wondered how they didn't get electrocuted. Turkey vultures circled overhead, waiting for something to die or that raccoon at the curve to get ripe.

Trixie's was always the next to last stop on the way home, the second stop in the morning. Only the three Banderas kids a quarter mile down the road had a longer bus ride each day.

The house would be empty. Momma went back to work today at the plastics plant, and Trixie returned to school for the first time in a week.

"Life goes on," Momma had said more than once. "We gotta get back into our old routines. We'll figure it out as we go."

How could there be old routines with daddy gone?

She didn't want to be in the house by herself. Too quiet. She hadn't been there alone since the funeral. Momma had been there, and usually other people coming and going, all the folks from Antioch Church bringing casseroles and potato or macaroni salads and desserts. Then dark would come, leaving only Momma and Trixie in the quiet. Momma would turn on the TV just for the background noise, but to Trixie, it seemed to echo in an empty space, like all the furniture was gone.

But all the furniture was still there. Daddy's recliner sat in the corner facing the TV, but neither of them dared sit in it.

It had started with a sore shoulder from lifting bales of hay over his head onto the trailer, and then into the loft, and then down out of the loft back into the feed troughs. Sabine had told him to see a doctor, but he knew it was just tendonitis flaring up, and once all the hay was put up, he could rest it a bit to heal up.

It didn't heal up. The ache spread down to his elbow and up to his neck. Couldn't raise his arm above shoulder height. Elbow swelled up overnight like a baseball under the skin. Ice packs didn't help none.

He wouldn't call the doc until Sabine spotted a golf ball sticking out the back of his neck. That was the first time he'd admitted his hips had been hurting more than usual too. Sitting on the tractor too many hours a day, he said. He wasn't getting any younger and had been wondering how long he could keep farming if he was getting arthritis like his daddy and granddaddy before him. But it was hitting him much earlier. They'd both managed to keep working into their sixties. He hadn't even turned forty yet.

While the doc was checking him over for arthritis, he asked Daddy about that open wound on his arm.

"Spider bite," Daddy said. "Must have been a brown recluse because no matter what I put on it, it never improves."

"How long you had that?" the doc asked.

"About a year. No, nearly two years. It was a year ago last fall. You got any ointment I could put on it?"

The doc sent him to Houston for more tests. And scans. And lying strapped down inside a giant tube.

Ointment wouldn't help stage four melanoma that had spread to his bones. Too many years in the sun for man with freckles and ginger hair who refused to see a doctor for a spider bite and a bit of tendonitis.

Momma told Trixie not to cry when she broke the news that Daddy had cancer. They had to be strong for him. Be positive. He'd get some treatments and they could make it go away. Maybe a surgery or two. But if they got all blubbery and sad, that wouldn't help. Doc had said a positive attitude was as important as radiation if he was going to beat this thing.

When Daddy died not three months later, Momma said not to cry because Daddy was in a better place, in heaven with Jesus, no more pain, and they shouldn't be sad.

Momma lost it at the funeral though. The tears poured out of her like the dam broke on Lake Livingston. Trixie held it in. Fought it back. Had to be strong for Momma now.

Momma cried for days almost nonstop. Trixie wanted to cry. Felt like she should. But she'd held it in long enough to go numb. A couple of times, she lay in bed at night after Momma was asleep on the couch and tried to cry. Nothing happened.

But ain't no way she'd walk into that house alone. She'd just hang around outside until she spotted Momma's car coming back from work. Two hours.

That's when a rusty old white pickup with a bed full of tools slowed as it drove past her, then stopped and reversed. A good-lookin' boy slid across to the passenger side and leaned out the window. He was grimy like he worked in a shop somewhere, with a bit of a scraggly attempt at whiskers. A half-smile, half-smirk held a half-smoked cigarette in the corner of his mouth. The homegrown tattoo of a dragon on the side of his neck looked like it had been drawn with a ballpoint pen by a six-year-old.

"What're you doin' out here by the road, girlie? You lost? Bored? Lookin' for a ride somewhere?"

CHAPTER 7

Plenty of spaces in the church parking lot awaited Trixie for the Wednesday evening business meeting. Maybe a couple dozen cars in the lot. Less than fifty people gathered near the front of the huge sanctuary that had been filled to overflowing on Sunday morning.

Trixie found a seat not too close to the front, but not so far back as to look unfriendly. A trifold brochure promoting the building project was stuffed into the back of the pew in front of her, next to the hymnal.

Trixie had overdressed in her new navy pinstripe skirt with matching jacket over a basic white blouse. The few women in attendance wore slacks; none of the men wore ties. Some were in shirt sleeves and khakis, sports coats folded over the back of the pews. A moment after Trixie settled into a seat behind the others, Chief Hale arrived in uniform, straight from work. He sat behind her, slightly to her right where she could just see him in her peripheral vision. She glanced over her shoulder at him, and he nodded politely like he would to any young woman he didn't know.

Mayor Callahan came in next, but when he spotted Trixie, he looked away and sat on the opposite side. He came in alone, no Mrs. Mayor to keep him civilized in public.

Rev. Webb, in a suit and tie, emerged from the side entrance and took his position behind the podium at the front, at floor level, not up at the pulpit high above the altar. He opened with a brief prayer for divine guidance on stewardship of the church's resources then called the meeting to order.

Lamar Reeves, the banker, read the monthly treasurer's report, and a unanimous voice vote approved it.

"Jasper," the pastor addressed the mayor, "you're next on the agenda."

"Thank you, Parker." Jasper made his way to the podium and the pastor took a seat on the front row.

The mayor unfolded a sheaf of papers and slipped on his readers, cleared his throat, and glanced up.

"Ladies and gentlemen, as you know from last month's meeting, we were very close to our goal. However, there have been some unfortunate changes in our circumstances, beyond anyone's control, which has resulted in a situation this evening that will require us to discuss some options for how to move forward with the expansion of our ministries."

Jasper paused and flipped through the papers until he found the right page.

"To date, we have raised funds and committed pledges that had us within $50,000 of our goal, the 10 percent down payment needed to secure commercial funding for the balance of the project.

"However, the recent changes in banking laws—I'm sure you've all heard about them in the news—have thrown a monkey wrench into the plans. Lamar, some of this regulatory stuff gets a little over my head. Would you mind explaining to the folks what we're facing?"

The banker returned to the podium and talked about lending regulations and capital investment requirements and down payments and other complex financial issues that Trixie had trouble following. But she understood the bottom line: the fundraising target had been moved by Congress. They didn't need to raise just another $50,000; they had to generate $300,000 more in donations and pledges in order to qualify for the loan.

Lamar took his seat on the front pew next to the pastor, and Jasper picked up where he'd left off.

"Our choices are simple. One, we double the target fundraising goal and go out to more people who haven't yet made a commitment. It's taken us two years to get this far, and our most faithful members have already pledged as much as we can ask of them. To raise another quarter million could take two more years or longer, considering we've already picked the low-hanging fruit, so to speak. Our second option would be to scale back the project to what we can fund with our existing resources. Maybe we make the overall project smaller, or we could build it in phases. Build the basics now, and once that's done and we're drawing even more people, we could raise funds for a second phase, and then a third."

Rev. Webb took over the meeting once more.

"We've already paid for the land," the pastor said. "Even with these changes, we're still almost halfway to raising the down payment. It will require more sacrifice from many of us, and those who have already pledged will need to be asked to give more so that we can make God's vision for the First Church of the Risen Lord a reality."

Trixie flipped through the flyer that detailed, with artist renderings, a cathedral on the edge of town with a spire that could be seen from the freeway, a sanctuary large enough to hold a growing congregation, classroom space for expanding the elementary school into a full-fledged K through twelve Christian academy, a gymnasium, and recreational facilities for the youth.

"In short," Rev. Webb continued, "God has directed us to build a house that brings glory to Him. We need to reach a little deeper into our pockets that are overflowing with God's blessings and give a little bit more back to Him who gave it to us, not be selfish with the material things of this world."

Behind Trixie, Chief Hale raised his hand. He rose to his feet when the pastor called on him.

"I believe you've got a grand vision, Pastor, but I think Jasper is right. We've about tapped everyone out who has money to donate. Maybe we should consider the phased-in approach."

"This is not my vision, Chief," the pastor said. "This is God's vision—a job He has tasked this church with accomplishing. And if we have faith in Him, He will bring us the resources. You say everyone in this church who is going to give has already given as much as they can. But maybe there's someone out there right now who hasn't yet committed, someone on whom God has laid a burden, a burning in the bosom to contribute to the Lord's work in a big way. And God will lead that person to us. If we lose faith in the Lord's ability to provide, He will lose faith in our ability to faithfully execute His commands. I'm tellin' ya, God has the answer, and these new obstacles are just a test of our faithfulness. I have faith. Have faith with me. God has the answer already. He just hasn't shared it with us yet. Not until He sees we deserve it."

As a few amens scattered around the room, all nodding in agreement, Rev. Webb met Trixie's eyes for a moment before he bowed his head and prayed silently.

On her way out, she picked up a fundraising packet for the planned Pineywoods Cathedral and Christian Academy like Mason had asked.

***

Trixie had started making sure the O'Bumpkin's mug was always clean for Clay when he stopped by. Seemed natural it would be his favorite cup, even though he wasn't the least bit Irish. But it was a big mug, ceramic with a crackled glaze and an oversized handle that fit his oversized hands.

"I've been to church twice now, even went to their bid'ness meeting, but I don't feel like I'm really meeting anyone."

Clay blew across the top of the coffee and took a sip. "Ain't no sense in going to a church where you're not feeling welcome."

"Oh, everyone's real nice to me there. I just need to find a way to get more involved, that's all. And maybe I can transfer Ty to the Christian school. Smaller classes, more attention from teachers. That's what he needs."

"You asked Ty about that yet?"

"Not yet. I don't want to move him to a new school until after I figure out how much I can help out with the building. I reckon I can afford the tuition, but maybe if I give a large enough gift, they'll let him go there all the way through high school for free. And I want to help feed those poor kids in Africa too. But Mason made me promise not to commit to nothin' until after he reviews all their numbers."

"Mason's a smart man."

Trixie's coffee had gone cold, so she walked across the kitchen and popped it in the microwave for thirty seconds. The fan blew silence until the timer beeped. Trixie held up the coffee pot. "You need a warmer?"

Clay stared into the bottom of his empty cup like studying a puzzle. "No, I think I'd better get. Got an earlier morning than usual tomorrow."

"What are you working on?"

"Me and a couple guys are fixin' up a roof for some old woman. She lives on Social Security, can't get around much, but she's still living in her own home. If she can't get her roof to pass inspection, the county will declare it unlivable, and she'll have to move into a nursing home."

"Well, that's a nice thing y'all are doing."

"Not as big a deal as feeding starving kids in Africa, but we do what we can."

CHAPTER 8

Trixie waved to Tyler as the bus pulled away, like she did every morning, even though he didn't want her to walk him to the end of the road and stand with him and kiss him goodbye on the cheek and wave like a doting mother in front of all the other kids. Then she walked back to the farmhouse in the hazy morning heat to shower and get ready for the Ladies' Society Circle meeting. She chose the designer blue jeans and the scoop-neck pink t-shirt. Nothing but women attending for coffee and pastries at nine a.m., so it wouldn't be as dressy as Sunday morning worship. More like Wednesday evening business meeting, maybe even more casual than that.

The Circle met at a different member's home each week. If she was going to join, she'd need to get that new house where she could host the meeting, rather than out in the boonies at the old farmhouse that was falling down around her ears. Thank goodness Clay had come around fixing some things.

Trixie followed her GPS to the address in the old-money part of town even though she knew exactly where it was. She'd driven through here before to admire the turn-of-the-century Victorian houses, but never in her twenty-three years had she ever had reason to stop at any of them. Today, she was invited into the big corner house at Third and Oak, the one with the turret-style corner room and the wraparound porch, the grounds that looked more like a city park than a yard. She'd always wondered who lived there.

She pulled the Corvette into the circle driveway in front and parked behind a Mercedes and an Escalade. Pulled forward a bit more so as not to park under any of the trees where birds would crap on the metallic pearl paint. Trixie turned off the engine but just sat behind the steering wheel and eyed the other half dozen or so vehicles.

"It's fine. I'll be fine. These women are no better'n me. I was asked to come. They want me here. I belong here now." She wasn't going to be the poor farm girl with a GED who lived down a dirt road, her mother in a run-down trailer park and her daddy long dead. She'd been around the big-money men and the men who ran the town and owned businesses, but she'd never been introduced to any of their wives, for obvious reasons. They lived a different life, in a different world where Trixie wasn't invited. Overnight, with the dropping of a numbered ping-pong ball, she'd become probably the richest woman in town.

Now maybe they'd accept her. In fact, they called her up with an invitation.

When sweat popped out on her forehead, Trixie climbed out of the car and headed to the front door, repeating the affirmation in her head: *I belong here. I belong here.*

"Welcome to my home, Trixie. I'm Marion Schleicher. I'm so glad you could join us as my guest today." Marion held Trixie's elbow and guided her through the foyer, across gleaming hardwood floors, past the wide staircase and the white plaster walls, the fireplace nearly big enough to park a car in it, and into a surprisingly cozy sitting room.

It looked like the waiting room for guests who hadn't yet been invited into the main part of the house.

"I'm the mother hen here." Marion squeezed Trixie's elbow comfortingly. "Let me introduce you to the rest of the chicks."

Five women in a wide range of ages and choices of attire sat on overstuffed antique settees and garishly embroidered, highly worn armchairs that looked like some old French king might have owned them at one time. Trixie figured Marion surely had the money to have them reupholstered.

"Everyone," Marion announced, "please join me in welcoming Victoria Burnet as our special guest and prospective new member."

"Y'all can call me Trixie, please."

Trixie remembered the mayor's wife from church and guessed her to be about midsixties. Mrs. Mayor sniffed and wouldn't make eye contact.

Trixie had never been good with remembering names, so she concentrated hard as Marion pointed around the room from one woman to the next with introductions. Trixie made sure to repeat each name, hoping that would help the name stick.

First up was Bee Callahan, the mayor's wife, who still wouldn't look Trixie in the eyes. Plump but not fat, hair and makeup looked like she'd had it professionally done that morning, wearing a turquoise dress and matching heels. If Trixie had been asked to describe what a Ladies' Circle member would look like, Trixie could have drawn the spitting image of Bee purely from imagination.

"Bee, it's nice to meet you." Trixie picked up on the little flinch in Bee's face, like she wasn't accustomed to a first-name basis with people she just met who were younger and not of her social status.

I might be scared of bees, but this Bee looks allergic to me.

Bee finally made eye contact for a brief moment, though she couldn't hold it and looked to her right, prompting Marion to move on the next introduction.

Reagan Hale, who Trixie also remembered from church, the young, beautiful wife of the just past middle-aged police chief. Reagan sat next to Bee on the settee, and Bee didn't look at all comfortable sharing a piece of furniture with the blue-collar crowd. Reagan wore blue jeans with the knees intentionally ripped, the kind you'd pay extra for, not the kind Tyler would come home from school in that were brand new that morning.

"Reagan, like that old president." Trixie tried to find something to relate to each name to help her remember. She'd studied Ronald Reagan in her GED classes. Her teacher didn't like him one bit, and as soon as she said it, she hoped Reagan Hale didn't take offense. "I saw you at church. You have such handsome boys. I just have the one boy. I don't know how you keep up with all of them."

Reagan smiled, and her neck turned a deep crimson, creating two distinct skin tones with her makeup hiding the blush on her face. "Why, thank you. They take after their daddy. Can't keep track of 'em all the time."

Truer words have never been spoken, Trixie thought.

Cass Reeves, wife of Lamar the banker, was next. *Bank, cash, Cass,* Trixie repeated in her head to remember, then regretted it, hoping she wouldn't slip and call her Cash by mistake. Cass seemed pleasant and polite but a bit aloof, not real interested in Trixie or anyone else there.

Angelina Webb, the pastor's wife. Not the image Trixie would have drawn of a pastor's wife. *Pastor's wife, angel, Angelina.* Angelina—not Angie, as Marion cautioned with a chuckle when introducing her—was a stunning beauty, raven-black hair cropped short, wearing large, dangly earrings, a low-cut blouse, and a skirt that was almost too short and tight for her to sit ladylike in the awkward armchair. Heels that would rival anything Trixie kept in her spare bedroom closet for customers who liked her to wear that sort of thing. Trixie still wasn't sure how anyone could actually walk gracefully in them. Fortunately, Trixie had never needed to walk more than a few steps.

"And this," Marion continued, "is Shelby Wheeler. Shelby is our newest member, and our youngest. She's got to be about the same age as you. We've lost a number of our longtime members in the past couple of years. We've been recruiting some fresh blood, so the Circle will remain unbroken and just doesn't die out in a few years as the Lord calls us each home."

Bee sniffed and looked to the side again, like she didn't approve of this transfusion.

The first 'Shelby' Trixie thought of as a memory aid was the Julia Roberts's character from *Steel Magnolias*, her momma's favorite movie. Momma would watch that movie every few months and bawl her eyes out every single time when Julia Roberts died.

Then there was her daddy's old car, a 1970 Mustang Shelby that was his pride and joy, even though it had sat in one of the barns, undriven and undrivable, for years. He'd rolled it into a ditch after too many beers. He couldn't file it with insurance as it wasn't registered or covered, and he couldn't afford to fix it. He towed it into the barn with the tractor until he could get the money needed for the parts to do the work himself.

He'd never had that much money in his whole life, and never would. Trixie had sold it to a scrap dealer for the parts, most of which had rusted years before, when Momma moved into town with Leon and left Trixie the farm on her eighteenth birthday.

Both of those Shelbys had met tragic fates. Trixie just knew if this young Shelby met some horrible death in the near future, it would be because of this ill-fated mnemonic device.

"Trixie? Trixie Burnet? Do you remember me from school? We were in middle school together. I thought you'd moved away or something. Oh, it's so nice to see you again."

Trixie could feel the puzzled look that had to be plastered all over her face. She hated it when someone remembered her, but she couldn't remember them. That was impolite, but she searched her memory of eighth grade and all she could come up with was her English teacher, Mrs. Fortunata or something like that, and Ellis. Ellis wasn't in eighth grade, but that's when she'd met him. Trixie didn't really have any friends—all the girls from middle school just morphed into a single entity of a mass of hormones and eyeliner, like a hallway full of extras in a teen movie.

"You look familiar," Trixie lied. "But it's been so long, I can't quite put a finger on it. What classes were we in together?" *Like that's gonna help me.*

"I was a cheerleader and in band and drama club."

Trixie didn't even recall that middle school had a band or drama club. She'd never attended any of the sporting events where she might have seen a cheerleader.

Bee cleared her throat to draw everyone's attention. "Can we table this trip down memory lane until after our meeting? I have a chamber of commerce brunch with the mayor in an hour."

"Oh, sure," Shelby said. "Trixie, you want to meet for lunch at Roy's Diner afterward?"

With ten eyes staring at her, only Bee looking somewhere else, Trixie was on the spot, like on those TV shows when the boyfriend pops the question at a family reunion, where saying no to the proposal is going to cause untold discomfort to everyone in attendance.

"I'd love to." *Why'n the hell did I say that?*

Trixie took the seat Marion offered her, an ornately carved dining room chair brought in as extra seating, a hard wooden seat with no cushion. She hoped this wouldn't be a long meeting.

"Bee, we don't have much to discuss on our agenda today," Marion said, bringing the meeting back to order.

Trixie was glad there wasn't much on the agenda because she wasn't sure how long her butt could sit still on that wooden slab.

"So, let's give Trixie a moment to tell us all a little bit about herself, then we'll dive right into the treasurer's report first, so if you need to leave early, you'll be able to."

Telling a little about herself hadn't been on Trixie's agenda. She looked around the room and fidgeted in her chair a moment. *I recently retired from being a call girl. Three of your husbands were regulars.*

But that wouldn't get her voted into the Circle. Just one "no" vote would blackball her from joining.

"Well, my name is Trixie. But y'all know that already. I've lived here all my life, out Highway 69 a piece, and back off down some county roads. Not like you'd just ever accidentally drive by my place. Anyways, I have a boy, Tyler. He just turned eight. That's about all there is to know about me, I guess."

"Are you married?" Bee asked. "Do you own a business or work?"

Trixie wasn't expecting a cross-examination either.

"No ma'am, not married, just me and my little man against the world. As far as work, I inherited my daddy's farm a few years ago, and I've hired a foreman to help me make a go of it in the cattle bid'ness. People always gonna eat beef."

That wasn't really a lie. She'd leave out the part of what she did for a living before winning Powerball. She'd leave out the lottery part too, but she suspected they already knew. She'd been on TV and written up in the *Daily Progress*. She further suspected that might be the reason she got invited here to start with.

She'd anticipated a much larger group of ladies. Four older women, two younger ones, and now maybe Trixie joining the Circle. Maybe there were more members who just couldn't attend today, some with day jobs or kids at home that needed tending.

And how many members died in the past two years that caused them to be out hunting for new members? The two newest, Reagan and Shelby, didn't seem to fit with the older women. Reagan looked like she was trying too hard to fit into a sorority that was slightly above her station. Shelby hungrily nibbled on some coffee cake and looked pleased as punch to be anywhere.

Marion, the president of the club and the oldest of the group, called the meeting to order and handed out a printed agenda. She jumped ahead two lines to call on Bee for the treasurer's report first, as promised.

Bee read a written report full of projects and numbers rather than handing out a copy to everyone so they could read it themselves, which Trixie figured would have been easier to follow and a lot less boring. The Circle had held a bake sale last month that raised $217, with net profit after expense of $109, which was duly deposited in the club's general fund account at First National Bank. This would go toward rebuilding the general fund before any more donations or scholarships could be provided.

Cass interrupted Bee's monotone recital. "What expenses did we have? We all donated baked goods and our time. The church doesn't charge us to use the hall."

"That damned newspaper charges us now to publish a notice about our events," Bee said.

Marion huffed. "Fred never would have done that. We ran that paper for forty-seven years and never had to resort to charging civic organizations to announce charitable events. I'm glad he's with Jesus now. This would kill him to see what that corporation is doing to his paper."

"I don't know why you sold it to some giant out-of-state company like that," Bee said. "Oh, the money, I guess."

"They had a good reputation." Marion defended their decision. "Wasn't anyone local who wanted to buy it or had the money to. But last year, they sold to some chain from up north. These people are all about squeezing blood from a turnip. Laid off half the staff and raised all their rates. They charge for obituaries now too, for crying out loud. That paper served this community well and provided a comfortable life for Fred and me. When his Alzheimer's started flaring up, we knew it was time to find someone else to take it over. But never in all my born days did I expect to live long enough to see what they've done to it."

"When I die," Bee said, "just send out a letter to everyone in town. Envelopes and stamps probably cheaper than giving that rag another dime."

Reagan added, with a bit too much excitement, "I could post your obituary on our social media accounts. It would be free."

"Why didn't we just use social media to promote the bake sale?" Shelby asked after licking cake crumbs from her fingers.

Bee sniffed. "None of the old ladies who come to a bake sale read that computer thing."

"Oh, you'd be surprised," Reagan said. "They all use it to keep up with their grandkids. And we can push the notice to people in our town, in the right demographic and psychographic segments, for as little as five dollars."

"Does anyone know what she just said?" Bee added with another sniff. Trixie couldn't figure out if it was a snobbish habit or seasonal allergies. "Moving on, we had eighteen dollars in bank fees due to our average balance dropping too low, but Cass here was able to sweet talk that husband of hers into waiving those fees."

"He can't waive the fees," Cass corrected her. "He paid them. Out of pocket. It was a donation. I still need you to get me that receipt for our taxes."

After the group had voted to approve the treasurer's report, Cass read the minutes of last week's meeting, which was about three lines of nothing important.

Marion took over the meeting again. "We only have two items for new business to discuss. First is the Annual Cast-Off Clothing Sale to raise funds for our scholarship. That's scheduled for October 28, so we've got a little more time, but we need to keep moving forward so it's not all a big rush at the last minute like last year. Based on where our finances are at the moment, we need to bring in about two thousand dollars in order to fund that scholarship. Last year, we netted fifteen hundred, so we need to up our game. I think we need to let Reagan do her social media thing to see if she can generate more donations of old clothes and get more people to come shopping at the event. We'll be setting up in the church recreation hall as usual. Angelina is in charge of that."

"It's all reserved," Angelina said. "Even got some men lined up to arrange the tables and booths for us."

"Reagan, what kind of budget do you need for social media?" Marion asked. "Maybe we skip the newspaper notices if that's outside our budget."

"I bet I can get the word out for fifty dollars. I'll post pictures I saved from last year's sale, and information about the scholarship. We're up to about two hundred followers on our page. I'm trying to get us up to five hundred before the sale." Reagan was clearly excited about being turned loose to do her thing, practically bouncing in her chair.

"It better work," Bee said, "or this whole thing will crash and burn. I'm going to call that editor down at the *Progress* to give her a piece of my mind, let her know how much our group has done for this community. Not to mention how much advertising our husbands' businesses spend with them. Maybe that will get her attention."

"Now, Bee," Marion said. "You go easy on her. She's new, and she probably has nothing to do with their corporate policies. It's some suits up in Wisconsin making those decisions."

Trixie sat quietly and watched the back-and-forth like a tennis match, but in her mind, she was doing an inventory of her professional clothes that she wouldn't be using anymore, from dresses to lingerie to shoes. There were short skirts, long skirts with revealing slits up to midthigh or even higher, skin-tight, shimmery dresses that didn't quite cover her entire butt. High heels, higher heels, even higher platform shoes, and spike stilettos that could put an eye out. There were nylons with garter belts, and negligees too numerous to count. She wasn't sure about some of the more risqué items. The Ladies' Society Circle might not appreciate selling see-through bras and crotchless panties at their Annual Cast-Off Clothing Sale to raise money to award a deserving young Christian lady from the local high school with a scholarship to the local Methodist junior college.

"Only one more item on our list," Marion said. "But Trixie, we have to ask you to go ahead and leave. We will be discussing and voting on your membership application. It's been such a pleasure to have you here. The next time you visit, I'll give you a tour of this old house. I'll give you a call later to let you know the status."

All eyes bore down on Trixie again, and her palms immediately broke into a sweat at the attention. She felt the urge to make a campaign speech to sway any members on the fence about accepting her as a member, but she thought better of it and stood with a quick, "Thank you for having me," with Marion at her side to escort her to the door.

"Don't forget about lunch at Roy's," Shelby reminded her. "Let's meet at 11:45 to beat the lunch rush."

"I'm looking forward to it," Trixie lied.

She climbed into her car, which had probably reached a hundred degrees inside at ten a.m. because she'd parked in the direct sun instead of the shade in the bird target range.

She set the A/C on full blast and checked the time. She had an hour and a half to kill before lunch. She could hit Walmart to pick out some better clothes for her new role in the community.

***

Trixie picked out a booth, about fifteen minutes early, and ordered an iced tea to wait for Shelby. She hadn't heard from Marion yet about the vote. Did Bee blackball her? It wouldn't surprise her, but she would be disappointed. She'd still donate her old wardrobe to the clothing sale. Maybe even the crotchless panties out of spite.

The door chimed as Shelby entered, talking on her cell phone. She waved at Trixie and slid into the booth, still talking.

After whispering "I love you" more than once, a little giggle, and smooching into the phone, Shelby finally ended the call.

"I'm so sorry. That was my fiancé, Austin. He's so hard to get off the phone. And he's at work, but he just keeps yammerin' on."

"I didn't know you were engaged. Where's he work at?"

"Down at the bank, of course."

Trixie didn't understand why that would be an 'of course' question. "So, when's the big day?"

"We haven't set a date yet. Still working out details. Probably next summer."

"I never understood long engagements," Trixie said. "Not that I have any experience with it, mind you, and I'm not tryin' to get in your bid'ness, but it seems to me like once you agree to get married, you know you're with your one and only, just go ahead and get married. What's the point of being engaged for a year or two or three?"

"Well, we haven't told his parents yet. They know we're dating. We'd been high school sweethearts back as freshmen and sophomores but went our separate ways for a few years after that. Guess we both needed to grow up. Then we reconnected. We've been dating for six months now. We just have to wait for the right time to spring the news on them. Give me a little more time to win over his mother. She's a tough cookie, as you know."

"Why would I know?"

Shelby looked at Trixie, confused. "Mrs. Reeves, from the Circle. Cass. Sometimes I just call her Ass—not when she's around, of course—'cause she can sure act like one."

The connection dawned on Trixie, and it wasn't pleasant.

"Your fiancé is Austin Reeves, son of the bank owner?"

"Yeah. Well, I called Mr. Reeves the bank owner once and he corrected me. He's the president of the bank and he's one of several owners, he told me. But between him, his father, Cass, and Austin, they have controlling interest, so I'm not sure how being owner or being president is that different. Plan is for Mr. Reeves to become chairman of the board when his daddy retires in a few years and then make Austin president."

"Sure sounds like you landed a big fish."

Shelby's face went blank for a moment, with a flash that looked offended. "That's not why—"

"Oh, no, I didn't mean it like that, not like you were just marrying him for the money. That just came out sounding all wrong. I do that a lot. I start talking and my words don't always come out the way I intend for them to. I just meant... I just meant it's good that he's financially secure and knows what career path he is on. I'm sure he must be a wonderful guy." Trixie squeezed her napkin to soak up the sweat.

"Oh, okay, I understand completely. That's kind of like me too. That's partly why Cass doesn't like me much, I think. I've stuck my foot in my mouth around her more than once."

"You didn't call her Ass to her face, did you?"

Shelby busted into a cackle that turned heads in the diner their way. "No, not yet anyway. But I sure have thought about it."

"I don't think she thought much of me either," Trixie said, something else in common with Shelby besides middle school and the Ladies' Society Circle. "By the way, I haven't heard from Marion yet. Can you tell me how the vote went? Did I get in? I don't mean to press you for confidential information if you're not supposed to tell me. I can wait for Marion to call me."

"Really? She hasn't called you yet? I'm surprised she didn't call you before you got out of the driveway. You're in, of course. The whole thing didn't take a minute."

Trixie breathed a sigh of relief. "Bee didn't blackball me?"

"Bee? Hell, no. Pardon my French. Bee made the motion to accept you. Then it was all in favor say aye, and everybody said aye, then we adjourned. Why would you think Bee was going to blackball you?"

"She'd hardly even look at me, wouldn't talk to me, acted like she couldn't stand being in the same room with me. I wasn't too sure about Cass either."

"Bee treats everyone like that, but everyone just ignores her."

Even her husband, apparently.

Shelby continued, "And Cass, well, it's not that she doesn't like anyone. More like she doesn't trust anyone. I think it's something to do with her background. Austin told me she grew up dirt poor, raised by her aunt on a farm. She met Lamar after high school and suddenly went from rags to riches, marrying into the richest family in the county. His mother never did accept her. And Austin says she's paranoid that something awful is going to happen and she'll be poor again. That's made her real protective, thinks everyone is after her money. Thinks every girl is after Austin for the money."

"That's kind of sad, really." Trixie wondered if this was something she'd have to think about when Ty started dating.

"It is. Austin says she always told him he had to marry someone who had as much or more money that they do, that that was the only way to know they weren't after his money."

"You have more money than the Reeves?"

Shelby's cackle again split the air just as the waitress walked up to take their order, nearly jumping out of her sensible shoes.

After they ordered, Shelby wanted to talk about middle school. Trixie never could place the name or face, even when Shelby pulled out her phone and showed some eighth-grade photos she'd posted to Facebook.

"I'm really sorry, but I just don't remember much about middle school. Were we friends?"

"No, not really. I just knew who everyone was, even if I didn't hang out with them. I was always naturally good with names and faces."

"Not a skill I ever much developed. I was a bit shy—okay, more than a bit. I never could even look people in the face back then. I looked at my shoes mostly. So, I never remembered what people looked like."

"Don't be offended," Shelby said, "but the main thing I remember about you is that you developed a little earlier than the rest of us, and we were all jealous of your figure."

Shelby talked about transferring to the Christian school for her freshman and sophomore years, where she met her high school sweetheart, now secret fiancé. Then her daddy got laid off at the plant, and she had to go back to public school for her last two years of high school, when she and Austin drifted apart.

That explained some things for Trixie. In her sophomore year, she'd gotten pregnant with Tyler and dropped out, so she wouldn't have seen Shelby again, if she'd ever seen anything more than her shoes anyway.

***

Momma had told her, "If you're old enough to be allowin' that stupid boy to get you pregnant, you're old enough to earn a living and raise a kid. It's my time to be a grandma, not be raisin' your kid for you."

Trixie wanted to argue that she didn't allow herself to get pregnant, but she held her tongue for once. She'd just allowed Ellis to see what it felt like without a condom one time because he was persuasive.

Apparently once was all it took, which didn't match up with what Ellis had told her.

Trixie argued that a fifteen-year-old pregnant girl didn't have a lot of good-paying job prospects to be able to afford a kid.

"I was seventeen when I got pregnant with you."

"But you were eighteen before I was born, and you were married to Daddy, and he owned a farm."

"He also owned a taste for beer, poker, and other women."

Trixie hadn't known about her daddy's infidelities before Momma dropped that bomb on her.

"So why ain't you gonna marry this Ellis? He's an idiot, but he's your idiot. The idiot that knocked you up. It's his kid. Hell, he's twenty-one years old. Ain't he got a job? You can live with him and his momma, come visit me on weekends. I ain't raisin' no kid again. I obviously didn't know what I was doin' the first time, and I still don't. At least you waited until after I turned thirty. If you'd made me a grandma in my twenties, I'd have beat your butt with that razor strop."

It was true that Ellis still lived with his momma. It was also true he could make good money sometimes, though sporadic and definitely not anything you'd want local law enforcement to hear tell of.

She'd also learned from her high school counselor that Ellis could go to prison for statutory rape. She didn't want him to go to prison. It wasn't rape, she told the counselor. "I've been seeing him since I was thirteen, and I always agreed to it. He didn't force me."

"Were you having sexual intercourse with him when you were thirteen?" the counselor asked, taken aback.

"Yes,'m, but we'd always been careful until the one time we weren't."

"That's not statutory rape, Trixie. That's child molestation."

Trixie didn't want anything to do with all that. She didn't love Ellis, she knew that, but he'd been part of her life for two years. She wasn't going to marry him, but she wasn't going to tell the counselor his name. She'd never initiated any of their sexual encounters, but she'd always gone along when he poured on the persistence. Or started pouting like a toddler if she said she didn't want to.

After a while, it just became routine. Something to do. Go shoot some pool and play the jukebox. Buy some beer and park out on a dark farm road somewhere in his pickup. Peel off the jeans and try to get comfortable on the vinyl front seat, avoiding the steering wheel and the stick shift. Never took long. Ellis always kept a box of Trojans in the glove box, ribbed to enhance the woman's stimulation, although she never noticed anything.

***

The waitress showed up with their lunches—Cobb salad for Shelby and a pork tenderloin sandwich with home fries for Trixie, the meat hanging out a couple inches on all sides of the bun.

"So where had you gone when I came back to ol' PW High?" Shelby asked. "I never saw you again. Did you move away for a while?"

"No, I just transferred to, um, well, I did some home schooling after that. Then I got pregnant with my boy and got my GED. Hard to go to high school when you got a baby to take care of. But I wouldn't trade him in for anything in the world."

"I want to have Austin's babies so bad I can taste it. They will be the cutest babies in the world. We've talked about having five or six of them."

"My advice, if I'm not overstepping my boundaries here, just speakin' from my experience, is to wait until after you're married to have any kids."

"Oh, of course. Austin and I both took purity vows when we were fifteen, and we've both honored those vows. I know, I know, hard to believe we're a couple of twenty-three-year-old virgins, but prayer and Bible reading help with that. Here, see." Shelby held out her left hand, a thin gold band around her ring finger where she wanted an engagement ring.

"You've both been able to keep up with that all these years?" Trixie wasn't sure how or why someone would do that, but something about it appealed to her, making her wish she'd kicked Ellis right in the nuts the first time he'd tried anything. That would probably have worked better than prayer. But if she'd done that, she wouldn't have Tyler, so she pushed that thought right out. What's past is past anyways.

"Yes, I'm proud to say," Shelby said. "Although some days it's not easy. I'll admit to burning with lust sometimes. Frequently. Often, even."

Trixie had never had one of those purity rings, but she'd seen one before.

***

After some back and forth, Sabine agreed that Trixie and the baby could live at home with her, and she'd watch him while Trixie did her GED coursework and worked at the McDonalds in town part-time. Got her license when she turned sixteen so she could drive herself to work.

Sabine had sold off all the beef cattle when her husband died to have enough money to live on. That lasted about a year. The working farm turned into sixty-three acres of overgrown pasture and collapsing barns.

There weren't many bills, but there wasn't much money either.

Sabine picked up odd jobs here and there, but mostly lived off a disability check and some assistance programs. Trixie was never quite certain what Momma's disability actually was. Of course, Sabine never told the assistance office about any jobs she landed, and never told her employers about the assistance. She just told them she didn't have a bank account and could they pay her in cash as an independent contractor. Less fuss, paperwork, and taxes for the business too, so it was a win-win.

When Trixie turned eighteen, Momma moved into town with Leon, her new boyfriend, who was just an unemployable as Sabine. Told Trixie to stay in the family home with Tyler. Wouldn't be no cost—the house was long paid for. Daddy had inherited it from his daddy, who got it from his daddy before him. Despite how hard times were, Momma couldn't bring herself to sell the place because of the family history.

Now the drafty old farmhouse was all hers, and the sixty-three acres too.

Nothing had been raised or grown or repaired on that place in five years. Trixie took on a second part-time job when she finished her GED, stocking shelves and cashiering down at the Dollar General. Sabine and Leon watched the baby during the day. Trixie was unsure of Leon at first—being a good twenty years older than Momma—but he won her over pretty quick.

Ellis had gradually disappeared once she told him she was pregnant. Offered to pay for an abortion, but Trixie was having none of that. Once she was showing, Ellis called on her less and less frequently. When she brought up child support, he tried claiming it wasn't his.

"Of course, it's yours. You're the only guy I've ever been with."

"How do I know that? You ain't been nuthin' but a little slut since I first met ya."

Fine. If that's how he wanted to play it, she'd cut that a-hole out of her life and out of the baby's life. Good riddance.

One regular customer at McDonald's was always flirting with her. A nice man who came in for lunch two or three times a week, old enough to be her daddy, telling her how pretty she was, how he liked what she did with her hair today, how her blue eyes really sparkled in this light. He was in line the day the staff sang "Happy Birthday" to her in front of the whole restaurant.

"How old are you?" he asked when he got to the counter.

"Nineteen today," Trixie answered. "What can I get for you?"

"How about letting me buy you supper tonight? Ya know, for your birthday."

Trixie had no idea why a "yes" slipped out before she even thought about it. She'd have to call Momma to see if she and Leon could watch Ty for another hour or two, and that would be a fight. But he was a decent man who, though a bit too familiar, always treated her politely, which wasn't something she could say about most patrons of the fast-food establishment.

It would be a nice dinner at an upscale place — Olive Garden, they called it — in Nacogdoches, where he said he had some business meetings going on for a few days, and she could meet him at the restaurant. Hour drive each way, at least an hour for dinner. Momma would have to watch Ty for maybe three or four hours. But Momma seemed thrilled to watch the boy for the evening if it meant Trixie had a date with someone who might have some money in the bank.

"It's gonna be late," Sabine said. "Whyn't you just pick Ty up in the morning? That way you don't have to rush back, and you don't have wake him up just to take him home. He'd be too fussy to go back to sleep."

She'd miss her boy, but one night without having to take care of a four-year-old sounded like a weeklong beach vacation in Galveston. Then she felt guilty for feeling that way. She'd never spent a single night away from Tyler since the day she brought him home from the hospital. But she took Momma up on the offer.

The man had a couple of drinks with his dinner. Trixie just drank Diet Coke. She didn't care for alcohol much, and they'd probably card her anyway. The last time she'd had anything to drink was four beers the night she got pregnant.

After dessert, and one of the finest meals Trixie had ever consumed, he asked if she wanted to stop by his room at the Fredonia Hotel for a nightcap. "We can have a little wine. I don't ask for ID."

Trixie had never had wine before, but she didn't really like the idea of going back to his room, so she politely declined.

He asked again. Said she'd be home before midnight if she was afraid she might turn into a pumpkin.

She declined again.

Third time was a charm when he told her a young woman needs to celebrate a birthday with a glass of wine. She really wanted to know what wine tasted like and what the inside of the Fredonia looked like.

Even two glasses in, she still had her wits enough to turn away from his attempt to kiss her. As they sat on the couch, she scooted farther away when he rested his hand on her knee. She was ready to get up and leave, even if it meant sitting in her car until the wine cleared out of her head enough to drive home, when he pulled out his wallet and started stacking twenty-dollar bills on the coffee table. With each bill, he laid out an offer.

"Twenty dollars just to see you without your clothes. You're so beautiful."

Trixie froze. *What the hell?*

"Forty to touch you."

Her mind was working through how to get up, grab her purse, and leave.

"Sixty for you to touch me."

She thought about patting him on the cheek and collecting her sixty bucks.

"Eighty for a little loving attention from your mouth, if you know what I mean."

It took her a moment to figure out he wasn't talking about a kiss.

He set the fifth bill down.

"A hundred dollars to crawl into that king-size bed and pretend you're my loving girlfriend."

Ellis had never paid her anything more than beer. She'd never done it in a bed.

"You got condoms?" she asked.

Trixie still got home before midnight, and with enough cash in her purse to buy some new jeans and something nice for Ty.

She felt guiltiest about not feeling guilty about nothing.

***

Lamar had called her the next day. She'd been foolish enough to give him her number. Asked her to come back to Nacogdoches again. Not for him, but for a business associate who needed a "date."

"Two hundred dollars," she said. She'd have to pay Momma to keep Ty a second night in a row.

It wasn't long before she had a list of clients from various financial institutions spread across east Texas, but she couldn't be driving all over kingdom come, so they started visiting the farmhouse.

She limited it to one client a week to start. Just a little extra spending cash to help make ends meet. Then two a week. Pretty soon she had to buy a calendar and start making appointments between shifts at her two jobs, always at times when Ty was at his grandma's or when she knew he'd be sleeping. One-hour limit. Never more than one customer in a day. Then sometimes two. Never on Sundays.

After she'd called out sick to work a few times in order to accommodate all her customers, she wondered why she was still slinging french fries for seven and a quarter an hour and gave her notice to both jobs. She made more in one hour than in three days at Mickey D's.

Her personal services business was booming.

***

Six months later, Lamar had set an appointment for ten p.m. He'd never taken her to Olive Garden again.

He showed up at the door, obviously intoxicated, with a terrified teenage boy in tow.

"Trixshee, meet my boy, Aushtin. He just turned eighteen and needs to become a man. He's taking my shpot tonight. Show him a good time. Rite of pashage. Boy says he's never been with a girl. Can't have that. Might turn out queer or something. I'll be back in an hour."

He stuffed a wad of cash in Trixie's cleavage and gave the boy a shove through the open screen door.

Trixie was dressed and had her hair and makeup done for her session with Lamar. She'd put a fresh cloth diaper, adult-sized, in her nightstand in case he was in that mood tonight.

Now she faced a boy about her own age. Someone who might have asked her to prom, if she'd done that sort of thing, which she hadn't.

The not-yet-man stood in the middle of the kitchen, feet glued to the spot, lip trembling, eyes about to bug out of his head.

"Austin? Is that what he said your name was?" Trixie tried to break the ice.

"Yes, ma'am."

"Whyn't you follow me back here where we can discuss my menu of services." She headed down the hall to the first-floor bedroom. It had been her momma and daddy's room. She'd kept her childhood bedroom upstairs for sleeping, across the hall from Ty's room.

When she didn't hear any footsteps behind her, she turned around. "You comin' or ain't cha?"

Austin didn't move. Austin didn't say a word. Austin looked like he'd just peed his pants or something. Maybe that diaper would come in handy after all.

"Your first time? Ain't no need in being nervous. We'll take our time—not too much time though. We only have an hour. Believe me, it all comes natural once you get going. I've been there too. I understand." Trixie figured this one would take less than sixty seconds.

She'd been petrified her first time in Ellis's pickup. It was dark, but to take clothes off in front of a boy? Mortifying that he might see her down there. No idea what she was supposed to do. How much was this going to hurt? Would she bleed? How long does this take? Would it be passionate lovemaking like in the movies, or more like when the bull mounted a cow in the pasture?

Mainly, she'd wondered if she could get her knee around that damn stick shift.

"I, I don't really want to do this, ma'am."

"Well, that's okay too. I'll just call your daddy to come get you and there'll be no charge."

"No, no, please don't do that. He can't know."

"Okay. Whyn't you just come on back here and we can sit and talk about it?"

"Is it okay if we sit here at the kitchen table and talk instead?"

Trixie kicked off her stiletto heels and pulled up a chair. "What's on your mind then?"

"My dad, he, uh, he means well. But he's pretty drunk. And I'm saving myself for marriage. I believe it's a sin to join together with someone you're not married to, especially with a prostitute. Um, uh, no offense intended."

"None taken. Some say it's a sin. Some say it ain't. Don't matter. We're all sinners, right?"

"Yes, ma'am."

"Please stop calling me ma'am. Making me feel old. Just Trixie."

"Yes, ma'am. Um, uh, I mean Trixie."

Trixie studied the young man—really just a boy, not even sure if he'd started shaving yet. If he had, probably only needed to once a week. Good-looking boy. He wore khaki trousers with a sharp crease in the legs and a pleated front. They were dry, so he hadn't actually peed himself. No sign under the pleats that his spirit was saying one thing while his flesh was saying another. A thin chain around the neck with a tiny gold cross, usually kept under that blue polo shirt, had come untucked. A watch with a black leather band. A gold ring on his left hand.

"Is that a promise ring? You have a girlfriend?"

"Sort of. Not exactly."

"What does 'sort of not exactly' mean exactly? You've got a girlfriend, but she doesn't know it?"

"It's called a purity ring. It's a symbol of my vow to maintain my virginity until my wedding night. So, it's like a promise ring, sort of. Only to the Lord, not a girl."

"Being with me would violate that vow then, wouldn't it?"

"Yes, m—Trixie."

"I may sin, and I may cause men to stumble, but I ain't gonna be causin' no nice young fella to break a vow to God. That probably wouldn't look good in my favor when the judgment day comes."

"Thank you for understanding."

"Would you like a Coke or some sweet tea or somethin'?"

"A bottle of water would be nice."

"I don't have any of that bottled water, but we got well water and it's even better." Trixie went to the cabinet to retrieve a glass. "You want ice?"

Austin swallowed hard to get out a yes.

"Does your daddy know about your purity vow?"

"Yeah, he knows."

"And he still brought you here?"

"He said I could take the ring off tonight, pray for forgiveness in the morning, then put it back on and I'd be a virgin again."

"I ain't sure it quite works like that."

"Like I said, he's pretty drunk."

Trixie and Austin talked about the weather, school, where Austin was planning to attend college this fall, what he wanted to do when he graduated. He wanted to be a musician. He played piano and guitar and loved to write music. Christian music. Like Christian rock songs, not like the kind they sing in church on Sunday mornings with a piano and a pipe organ and a choir of fifty in purple robes.

"So, what are you going to tell your daddy when he comes to pick you up? I suppose lyin' is a sin too, but I think God can wink at this one." Trixie wished people would take purity of the tongue vows and wear a lip ring as a symbol not to tell lies.

Austin took a long draw on the glass of well water and paused, thinking. "I'll tell him you're a beautiful woman and I had a really enjoyable time with you. That way, I won't be lying. If he asks me anything more, I'll say it's private and personal between you and me, and I won't discuss it any further. He'll respect that."

"That sounds like a real good plan. He'll be here shortly, so I should at least go muss up my hair and smear my lipstick a little bit. Wait, let me do this." She leaned over and kissed Austin on the lips. Closed-mouth, no tongues or anything. Just enough to smear her lipstick on her mouth and his. "Now, he'll believe whatever he wants to believe."

Austin's lipstick-stained grin stretched from one dimple to the other.

Trixie reached into her push-up bra and pulled out the cash Lamar had shoved there. She handed the money to Austin.

"This was a birthday gift from your daddy, so it's yours. Go buy yourself something nice. Or take some sweet girl out to dinner and a movie. You could probably afford Olive Garden with this."

"I can't take that. I took up an hour of your time. It's yours."

"I get paid for providing a sexual experience. I didn't perform any of my services."

"You gave me exactly the sexual experience I was praying for. I'm a satisfied customer. You earned it."

***

Trixie would never tell Shelby about her hour with Austin, of course. Weren't nobody's business. But would Austin tell Shelby about it? He must not have said anything yet. If Shelby knew about that night, she probably wouldn't want Trixie for a friend. *A friend might be a good thing for me too. Ain't had many of them.*

She would never mention the many hours with Lamar either. Business confidentiality rules. "I might be a whore, but I have ethical and moral standards," she'd said to herself more than once.

But what if they became best friends, then one day in a fit of transparent honesty, Austin tells his beloved bride about the time his daddy took him to spend an hour at Trixie's brothel? Even though he would explain that they hadn't done anything but talk, would Shelby feel her trust violated that her newfound bestie had kept it secret from her?

Just some things you don't go telling, not even your closest friend.

Shelby's ringtone started playing "Forever and Ever, Amen." Austin calling, Trixie assumed. She knew that song because Momma and Daddy used to dance around the living room to it when she was little, and then they'd both wave to her to join them. She'd stand on Daddy's feet while he danced and sang along with Randy Travis.

"She's right here, actually. You want to speak with her?" Shelby handed the phone to Trixie. "It's Marion."

"Trixie, I am so sorry I didn't reach you earlier. Seems I was misreading your phone number on your application. My old eyes—sometimes a four just looks like a nine. I was hoping to catch you while you were still having lunch with Shelby. The Ladies' Society Circle is thrilled to announce that one Victoria Burnet has been accepted as the newest member of our 142-year-old organization. We're proud to have you join us."

For one of the rare times in her life, Trixie was truly speechless, even though Shelby had already spilled the beans.

"You still there?"

"Oh yes, ma'am. Yes, I'm here. I'm very excited to join. Looking forward to helping out with all the wonderful projects y'all do for the community. When I get a new home, I'd be glad to host a meeting, but that ain't gonna happen for a little while and my house now just ain't really fittin' to hold the group and I don't really bake but I got a lot of clothes I can donate to—"

Marion started laughing. Trixie had rediscovered her words.

"I mean, I'm just happy to be a new member and I'll work real hard to make y'all proud of me."

"I'm sure you will, sugar. Now, you just go back to your lunch, and we'll see you next week at Cass's place. I'll email you the details."

Trixie handed the phone back to Shelby. "It's official. I'm in the Circle."

"You're in!" Shelby squealed like she'd just won the Powerball and bounced in her seat, shaking all the booths on that side of the diner. Most of the lunch customers barely glanced up this time, growing accustomed to Shelby's exuberance. "We're going to have such a good time."

"Why are you so excited? You already knew."

"I'm officially excited now. Let's work together on the Cast-Off Sale. Maybe we can attract a younger crowd so it's not just a bunch of old biddies."

Instead of donating her more erotic specialties for the used clothing sale, Trixie pondered if Shelby might be able to use some of them for her honeymoon.

CHAPTER 9

Mason wiped his head with a handkerchief and adjusted his glasses. "Well, let's see where we're at. We've got the foundation about set up paperwork-wise, just need to fund it. It'll all be invested very conservatively, as we discussed. You can be thinking about how you want to use that money—what charities or projects you want to support."

The window unit was blowing but Trixie couldn't feel it. A river of sweat trickled between her shoulder blades.

"I've been thinking on that. I've got two I want to get started on right away. I figure if I give a substantial gift to the First Church for the new building project, in return they might let Tyler go the Christian school through high school at no tuition. Tuition is $8,000 a year. He's got ten more years of school, so $100,000 ought to more than cover that. And maybe fund a scholarship to pay for a couple deservin' kids to attend whose folks couldn't afford it otherwise."

Mason didn't look up as he jotted notes.

"I also want to donate some to their African Children's Ministries. They send food and build schools and send missionaries to places so poor they ain't even got well water or flush toilets."

Mason looked up for a moment but went back to his note-jotting.

"Then there's the Ladies' Society Circle. They just voted me in as a member. They do a lot of good works in town—college scholarships, donations to the food bank, abused women's shelter, that sort of thing. If I gave them $10,000, that would be more than they usually bring in during a year's worth of bake sales and clothing drives."

Mason looked up, set his pen down, and wiped his head again.

"And," she continued, "maybe I could donate $10,000 for you to install some central air in this old building."

Mason chuckled. "Nah, another couple weeks and this heat will break."

Mason pulled his glasses down lower on his nose and studied some fine print.

"You know, you have other options with this foundation. Instead of giving money to the church and the women's auxiliary—"

"Ladies' Society Circle," Trixie corrected him.

"Society Lady Circle, whatever, you could cut out the middlemen. Directly fund the organizations you want to fund. The school donation would need to go to the church, of course, but you could find an organization helping poor people in Africa, or Texas for that matter, and give them your money directly instead of funneling through the church. My understanding is Pineywoods Church isn't operating any organization in Africa. They just send some money to a group that's already there.

"Same with the women's—ladies' group. Instead of giving them the money to give away to someone else, just give the money directly to the food bank and the women's shelter. Fund a scholarship on your own, if you want. The Victoria Burnet Scholarship—has a nice ring to it, don't ya think?"

"I figured these folks were already set up and are struggling to raise funds, so wouldn't it be easier to just give to them?"

"Yes, it probably would be easier. If that's what you prefer, we can do that."

"Maybe the first year. After that, we'll have more experience and time to research different groups that might be worthy. Then I can spread some of the Lord's blessings around a bit. But since ever'body in town knows I won the lottery, giving some back to local groups might go a long ways in, ya know, helping to establish good relationships with the community and all."

"Might go a long way toward helping you establish yourself in the power structure, that's for sure," Mason said. "And I suppose that makes sense too. But as the chief financial officer of the Burnet Foundation, I do have some requirements. You'll need to do some homework before I can sign off on any donations to any group."

"Homework. Ain't had none of that in a billion years."

Mason ignored her. "I'll write up a letter for your signature. No need to let anyone know I'm involved yet. The letter will let any group you send it to know you're considering a substantial gift, but it won't promise anything and won't mention any specific amounts. Just 'substantial gift.' That'll whet their appetite. Then the letter will spell out the requirements they have to meet in order to be considered by the foundation's board of directors."

"Do we have a board of directors yet?"

"Yes, in fact, we do. We're meeting right this very minute."

"Where? Who's on it?"

"Right here. You and me. You're the chairman and chief executive. I'm the financial officer. We'll need to add someone else later on, as we get established and funded. Maybe Lamar from the bank."

"I don't think Lamar is a good idea." Trixie squirmed in her seat a bit. She hoped she hadn't nixed that nominee so quickly that it would raise Mason's suspicions about any prior business relationship she'd had with Lamar.

"Or that lady that heads the United Way. Heck, you could put your momma on the board."

"Why'n the hell would I want to do that?"

"I'm just saying. Whoever you want. Need a third so we don't have any tie votes."

"It's my money, my foundation and I'm the chief chairman, so doesn't my vote count more?"

"Not per foundation bylaws that are set by the State of Texas and our good friends down at the IRS. But we won't have any tie votes as long as I know what you want to accomplish, and you follow my advice on how to get there."

"What do the groups need to do to be considered for this substantial gift? Sounds like homework for them, and I like that better."

"Quite a bit of homework for them. Make them earn it. We'll be asking for three years of financial statements, bank statements, and their budget. For the church building project, we'll need to see their budget, all their fundraising so far, their plans, bids and estimates from contractors, blueprints, building permits, the whole nine yards. That's us doing due diligence."

"Well, sounds like we need to do this do thing, whatever you said."

"Due diligence. Stop by tomorrow and I'll have two letters for you. Or maybe three. One for the ladies, one for the church building project, and a separate one for the church's Africa project. Do you know who should get the letters?"

"Lamar is the church treasurer, but Jasper Callahan is the chairman of the building committee. Treasurer for the Circle is Bee Callahan. Ya know, Mrs. Mayor."

Mason took a deep breath, held it for a second or two before exhaling loudly. "Those two got their fingers in every pot, don't they?"

***

The O'Bumpkin's cup was clean and set out by the coffee pot, which was already brewing. Clay had said he'd stop by to look over the real estate deal Mason had helped draw up, with assistance from his sister, the real estate attorney. Trixie still wore her jeans but had changed into a fresh blouse after the sweat had soaked through the first one at Mason's office. She might have to buy that man a good air conditioner.

Tyler was in his room, supposedly doing his homework. He'd lost two assignments—one math, one spelling—and had to redo them. If that boy didn't get on the stick, he'd have to repeat third grade. But it was still September, barely, plenty of time to for him to start acting like he was smart again.

Trixie would have to check on that boy every few minutes to make sure he was keeping his nose to the grindstone. He'd already been rewarded in advance with pizza for supper. She could splurge on that. No time to cook tonight. Trixie hadn't realized how many hours a day she'd have to work since she got rich.

Tires crunched across the gravel, followed by a pickup door slamming shut, then a light rap on the screen door.

"C'mon in, Clay."

Clay walked in, dust and bits of straw caked on his jeans and neck. A damp ring had soaked through his Stetson.

"Pardon my appearance, but I just came straight here from moving the cattle. Hope I don't smell too bad."

"I don't smell nothing." That wasn't exactly the truth, but it wasn't a bad smell. It was the smell of a man who'd spent twelve hours working in hundred-degree heat and high humidity, a dusty, musty smell mixed with a faint trace of machinery grease and manure. A manly cologne. Trixie kinda liked how he smelled, but she wasn't going to tell him that. He smelled like her daddy did when she'd crawl into his lap for a goodnight kiss.

"I could sure go for a glass of ice water before I dive into a cup of hot coffee."

Trixie bounced up for a glass of ice and topped it off with water from the faucet.

Tyler popped his head around the corner. "Hi, Mr. Garza."

"Hello there, scooter. I told you before you can call me Clay."

"I told him he has to address his elders proper-like," Trixie said.

"Then we'll listen to your momma, Mr. Burnet."

Ty giggled at being called Mister.

"And what are you doing down here? You ain't finished with your homework yet, I know. If you was, you'd have it in your hand to show me."

"Just wanted to say hi to Clay. Mr. Garza."

"Back to work, little man. You got an hour before bedtime and you still need a bath."

"But Mom—"

"Don't you but-mom me or I'll get that strop and show you the meaning of a but-mom."

"Fine." Ty waved and winked at Clay then headed back up the stairs, stomping with as much weight as he could muster.

"I don't know what I'm going to do with that boy. You want one? I'll make you a good price. Might toss him in with the farm just to sweeten the deal."

Clay looked deep in thought, like he was seriously considering the offer. "I could use an extra set of hands around this place. But his legs are probably too short to drive the tractor yet. Plus, I'd have to feed him, so he'd cost me more 'n I can afford."

Trixie couldn't keep the grin off her face. "I'll check back with you when he's a little taller. The way he eats, that'll be in a minute."

Trixie reviewed all the paperwork with Clay. A land-lease contract, with no payments due the first year, then a modest rent each month for the next two years, of which 50 percent would be applied to the purchase price. They'd agreed on a purchase price of 25 percent below fair market value because of all the work Clay had already done and all the work and repairs that were still needed: barns, fences, tractors, pastures, wooded areas that needed clearing, the house in a state of significant disrepair. Mason's sister had done her due diligence to find out what it might sell for on the open market in this economy, which was slumping once again in east Texas. Might not be any buyers out there anyway.

At the end of the three-year period, they could renew the lease one year at a time, or Clay could purchase it outright with Trixie holding the mortgage at 1 percent interest. Mason didn't like that. Said it was so far below market interest rate, and all that foregone interest might be considered a taxable gift. But just going to 2 percent interest made the monthly payment higher than Clay was comfortable affording with his best projections. Trixie suggested cutting the price in half to double the interest, but Mason didn't like that suggestion either. Mason could be a pain in the rear, but Trixie trusted him. Any financial adviser that wouldn't bother spending money on a new window unit because it's going to cool off in a month seemed like a frugal, honest person to handle her blessings.

Tyler popped up again with papers in hand. "All done, Momma."

"Let's take a look then off to the tub with you. You stink."

"Not as much as Mr. Garza."

Clay busted out laughing and grabbed Ty, pulling him onto his lap and rubbing his hands all over Ty's head. "Now you really need a bath. You smell like cows."

With homework checked and Ty ensconced in bubbles, conversation turned to Trixie's frustration with the school and her plans to move him into the Christian school along with her planned donation to Pineywoods First Church of the Risen Lord.

"You settling into that church yet?" Clay asked.

"Not yet. We've been three weeks in a row, but there's so many people and no chance to actually talk to anyone."

"Why don't you come to church with me next Sunday? Agape Community Church."

"Agopp-what?"

"Ah-GAH-pay," he sounded it out for her. "Greek for love. Just a small group, nothing fancy. We meet in the old Radio Shack on Main Street. I think you'll really like our pastor, Brother Kent. We got better music too. Young guy for our music director, guitars and drums and such."

"I need to be seen at First Church if I'm going to be contributing to their building project."

"Why do you feel the need to be seen?"

"I don't know. Just want to be accepted as a part of this community. I lived here all my life and always on the edges. I want people to see me, who I really am, not what I did..." Trixie trailed off. She wasn't quite sure what Clay knew—or suspected—about her previous vocation.

"Thankfully, the Lord sees us for who we are, not what we've done in the past. We'd all be in a world of hurt if that was the case. Besides, I always figured I didn't need to be seen at church. I need to see who's there. Might be someone who needs a helping hand, whether it's a damaged roof or a broken heart. But you're welcome anytime you just want to try something different. We all stand around chatting for an hour before the service starts. We have coffee and doughnuts too."

CHAPTER 10

Mason had signed and mailed the due diligence letters. Trixie met with Ty's teacher again, which didn't go any better than the first time and ended with another request for a donation to the PTA to fund teaching assistants and supplies. At the same time, Ms. Lipscomb seemed to discourage Trixie from attending an actual meeting. "We don't really want your kind there, just send a check," seemed to be the message.

Then she took Momma and Leon to look at another house. Met Clay down at the bank to sign all the land contract paperwork in front of a notary, and then off to deliver the paperwork to Mason's sister to file with the county clerk. Then back with the Realtor to look at two houses for her and Ty.

First up was one of the old Victorians downtown. Beautiful dream home on the outside, a gingerbread-looking dollhouse, but inside, it probably needed more work than the farmhouse. Then off to a new-construction ranch-style home in a subdivision of half-acre lots and fenced-in backyards—so new, hardly anyone lived there yet and there weren't any trees. Most of the houses were still in various stages of construction. Sidewalks looked so fresh she wasn't sure she should step on them. Every house looked the same. Functional but no character. Trixie wanted character.

She still beat Tyler home from school by about fifteen minutes and collapsed on the sofa to kick up her bare feet on the ottoman for a moment. She'd have to start thinking about supper in a little bit, but not until her arches stopped aching. She wasn't used to doing this much work standing up.

She never heard Ty come in as she dreamed about hosting the Circle in her gingerbread house as Bee and Cass gushed over the donation she'd made, which Reagan had announced on their social medias.

***

Ty took advantage of his sleeping momma to pad quietly up the stairs, taking his shoes off first so as not to wake her. He went in the bathroom and held a washcloth under the cold water until it was soaked through, then held it gently to his eye. It felt good, but the mirror told him the red and blue bruise wasn't going to wash off. He wondered if he could sneak into Momma's bedroom vanity and get some makeup to cover it.

He needed to get out in front of this one, tell his momma what happened. The teacher was going to call her anyway. Maybe she'd be proud he'd stood up for himself, and that Carson looked a lot worse than he did. Maybe he got a shiner, but Carson had blood pouring from his mouth and was light by at least one tooth.

Momma'd always taught him fighting was a last resort. Avoiding a fight was the first option. Walking away was second. Talking your way out of it, third. Or maybe talking was second and walking third. He couldn't remember. Fourth—when you had no other options and no way out—throw the first punch when your foe least expects it. And make it count.

Ty had exhausted all options, surrounded by three boys, all bigger than him, as they'd waited for the bus in front of the school. He and Carson stood nose to nose. Ty balled his fist at his side, trying to decide if it was time to throw that first punch. That's when Franklin sucker punched him in the eye from the side.

It stung, it watered, but all Ty could see was a wave of red. Franklin had thrown a punch then backed away laughing. Walker was high-fiving Franklin. Carson, the ringleader, was the only one within reach.

As Carson glanced at his friends, laughing with them at Franklin's boldness and the surprised look on Ty's face, Ty saw an opportunity and went for it with gusto. Not one punch. Not two. Not even five or ten. Ty had no idea how many punches he threw. They just flew, one fist after another after another, over and over, all on Carson's face until he dropped to his knees screaming. That's when Ty gave him a knee to the chin, and Carson slumped to the ground, spitting blood.

Ty didn't stop there. It took a teacher and the bus driver to pull Ty off as he pounded on Carson's face, his head bouncing off the sidewalk with each hit.

Carson was bloody, crying like a two-year old, snot and blood mixing together on his shirt, while Franklin and Walker stood back with the rest of the crowd, like they'd had nothing to do with it and didn't even know Carson. Other kids cheered for Ty.

The teacher led Carson inside the school and told the bus driver to take Ty home. She needed to see if Carson needed any medical attention and call his folks to come get him. She'd call Ty's mother after that.

Ty climbed the steps onto the bus and another cheer went up from all the kids that had watched from inside.

"You okay, son?" the driver asked.

"My hands hurt."

"I can imagine. Did your daddy teach you to fight like that? You're pretty good."

"My Uncle Leon's been giving me boxing lessons. He used to be a perfessional."

The driver had smiled and told the rest of the kids to sit down and be quiet as he closed the door and dropped the bus into gear. The driver told Ty to sit in the first seat.

Franklin and Walker sat as far to the back of the bus as possible and never said a word.

Ty didn't know if the teacher had already called his momma or not. He doubted it since she was sleeping. She'd be pacing back and forth fuming if she'd known.

***

"Momma, you gonna wake up? I'm hungry. And I got to tell you something 'portant you ain't gonna like."

Trixie had silenced her phone so she could get a few minutes of rest. The teacher had left a voice mail, but she was happy to hear it from Ty first. She'd call the school in the morning.

Trixie fixed up an ice bag for Ty to hold on his eye. When he said it was too cold and pulled it away, she gave him a stern look. He put it back.

"It's so cold it hurts."

"Getting in a fight hurts, don't it?"

"The ice hurts worse than the punch."

She allowed him to set the ice pack down while they ate supper, then he finished his homework and took a bath. No TV. No video games. No bike riding for a week.

She never threatened to get the leather strop off the wall though, and she never yelled at him. All she said was, "This is why you avoid fights any time you can. Even if you win, it can still hurt, and you will still be in trouble. Not as much trouble as if you'd started the fight. But I understand sometimes you got no choice. You just try to keep yourself out of those situations."

With supper done and dishes put away, homework completed, bath over, Ty sat on the couch in his PJs reading for another half hour before his eight o'clock bedtime. Trixie, in her lightest cotton nightgown, sat in her daddy's old recliner, going over foundation bylaws and financial documents from Mason. She eventually set it aside and slipped in her earbuds to listen to music and think about nothing.

The second song had just started when Ty pulled on her shoulder.

"What? Can't I get a moment of—"

"Momma, that jerk is here again."

"Go to your room. Almost bedtime anyway."

"I got ten more minutes."

"Read a little longer then lights out." She planted a quick kiss on Ty's cheek and sent him up the stairs with a pat on the butt. "Love you, little man."

"Love you too, Momma."

"You know I don't approve of fighting, but I'm proud of you. Just remember that."

Trixie threw the screen door open so fast, Ellis didn't have time to get out of the way. "Why are you here again? You don't leave, I'm calling the cops right now."

Ellis shoved a boot inside the door so Trixie couldn't shut it on him. "Don't be acting like that. Just needed to talk to you."

"Talk then. You got thirty seconds."

"Can I come in?"

"No."

Ellis's breath practically steamed whiskey. His red eyes had trouble focusing on Trixie. She thought if she shoved him hard enough, he'd go right down.

He stumbled forward and pushed Trixie back a step or two. By the time he regained his balance, he was in the mudroom, resting a hand on her shoulder for stability.

She knocked his hand off. "I mean it, Ellis. You get in that truck and get out of here."

"I just wanted to see my boy."

"He ain't your boy. You signed all the papers. Gave up all rights and responsibilities. Then I had to get that restraining order 'cause you kept stopping by even though you'd been legally disinvited. You will go to jail, ya know."

"Don't matter what papers I signed. He's my boy too, and you know it."

"He don't need to know his sperm donor is a worthless piece of shit."

Ellis took a step and fell flat on his face at Trixie's feet. He tried to stand but only made it to his hands and knees.

Gravel crunched and headlights flashed up the driveway. *Did that boy call Clay again? He really wants his butt whooped, don't he?*

But it wasn't a pickup this time. A sedan. She didn't recognize it.

"Get your butt in a chair and don't open your mouth. I got a visitor."

"I thought you retired."

"Shut up. It's some woman."

"Didn't know you were into that."

"You really want me to call the cops, doncha?"

The woman knocked on the screen door and called out "hello" as Trixie approached.

"Can I help you?"

"Are you Victoria Burnet?"

"Who's asking?"

"Lynn Roberts, Texas Department of Family and Protective Services. Are you the mother of Tyler Burnet?"

"Yes, ma'am, I am. He's gone to bed. Now's not a good time. If you call, I can set an appointment to come see you at your office."

"I'm afraid not. I've been asked to do a welfare check. I need to see your son, now."

"I have company that was just leaving. Can you come back in ten minutes?"

"No, ma'am. May I come in now? Or should I call the police? We can do this the easy way or the hard way."

Trixie wondered if she shouldn't let the old biddy call the police, who could haul Ellis away on violating a court order. But the panic about protective services showing up rose in her throat. Had the teacher called them because she hadn't heard her phone ring earlier?

She opened the screen door and escorted the social worker through the kitchen, past Ellis, who rested his head on the kitchen table, into the living room and offered her a seat on the couch. She didn't offer any coffee or well water.

"Never mind my guest in there. He just showed up uninvited and too drunk to drive home."

"You often have uninvited guests show up?"

"Never. Then two in one night. Imagine that."

"Do you think that's really a good environment for a young boy, where intoxicated men just show up randomly?"

"I was about to call the cops to come get him when you showed up."

"I'll be glad to assist with that. Then I'd have an official police report to add to your file."

"My file?" Trixie's mind went through the list of people she might call for help. Clay? Mason? Momma and Leon? No, that wouldn't be a good idea. "What exactly do you want?"

"I want to see your son first. Then I have a few questions for you."

"I'll get him. He's upstairs. He should be asleep, but I doubt he is yet."

Trixie climbed the stairs and met Ty on his way out of the bathroom. She pulled him into his bedroom and shut the door.

"There's some lady downstairs asking questions. Prolly about your fight today. You be on your best behavior, just say yes ma'am and no ma'am and don't say nothing else. You smile and act happy. I don't like her, but she could cause us trouble. This is important. You understand?"

"Yes, ma'am."

"Perfect."

"Is that jerk still here?"

"Yeah, he's passed out at the kitchen table, which ain't helpin' matters none. We'll just ignore him like he's not even there, got it? Don't say nothin' about Ellis."

"Yes, ma'am."

"That's my little man." Trixie held Ty's hand and led him down the stairs.

"You must be Tyler."

"Yes, ma'am."

"I'm sorry to wake you up. My name is Ms. Roberts, and I'm doing what's called a welfare check. It's to make sure you're okay, that you're safe. Do you feel safe?"

"Yes, ma'am."

"How'd you get that shiner?"

Ty looked to his momma since he couldn't figure out how to answer that with a yes ma'am or no ma'am. Trixie nodded at him.

"A boy hit me at school."

"Why'd he hit you?"

"I dunno. He's mean."

"Who hit you?"

"Franklin."

"Did Carson hit you too?"

"No, ma'am."

"But you hit Carson?"

"Yes, ma'am."

"If Carson didn't hit you, why did you hit him?"

"He was gonna hit me. Him and Franklin and Walker were all gonna beat my—they were going to beat me up 'cause I wouldn't give them three dollars."

Trixie interrupted. "I've already talked to the teacher twice about these boys bullyin' Ty, but she hasn't done anything to stop it."

"Well," Ms. Roberts said, "Carson had some stitches in his tongue and has a mild concussion. Lost two permanent teeth."

"Maybe that'll stop it then," Trixie said. She had to suppress the proud momma moment.

"His parents wanted to file charges for assault. Chief Hale talked them out of it."

"How could they file charges against my boy for defending himself against three bullies?"

"That was the chief's point too."

"Then why exactly are you here?"

Ms. Roberts ignored Trixie's question and turned to Ty. "Do you know that man in the kitchen?"

"Yes, ma'am."

"You've seen him here before?"

"Yes, ma'am."

"Okay, young man. Thank you. I have a few questions for your mother, but nothing more for you. You can go back to bed. I'm sorry to have to disturbed you."

Tyler glanced at his momma, who gave him the nod of approval to head back upstairs.

A light popped on in the kitchen. "Hey, girl, you got any beer in this fridge?" Ellis was awake.

"Ellis, you need to leave or this here lady from the State of Texas is going to call the police before I do. If you're too drunk to drive, go get in your truck and stay there 'til you sleep it off. But I want you out of my house now."

Ellis stood in the entryway between the kitchen and the living room, swaying slightly. "Did I hear you say you're with Family Services?"

"Yes, sir, I am."

"As the boy's father, I have a right to know what's going on."

"Get your ass out of here right now, you bastard!" Trixie screamed at him.

And there stood Ty, her little man who'd been halfway down the stairs listening.

Trixie grabbed her phone and dialed a nine and a one before Ellis said, "Fine, I'm outta here." The social worker sat on the couch looking like she'd crapped herself. Tyler stood rooted to the spot, tears brimming, breathing in short gasps to suppress a sob.

Ellis staggered a bit then righted himself and headed out the screen door.

Trixie turned to Ms. Roberts. "I would appreciate it if you'd give him time to leave, then follow him on out of here. I've got a private family issue I'm needin' to discuss with my boy. Not a conversation I wanted to have for at least a couple more years, but looks like there's no more puttin' that off."

"Would you like me to stay for that conversation?"

"I most certainly would not. I think your bid'ness here is through."

Ms. Roberts stood and collected her purse, then watched through the kitchen window as Ellis drove away. "I'm leaving, but I can assure you, my business here is not through."

***

"Is that jerk really my daddy?"

Trixie and Ty sat at the kitchen table, Trixie with a cup of coffee and Ty with a mug of hot chocolate with tiny marshmallows floating and melting on top. Way past his bedtime, but she'd write him an excuse note and let him sleep in tomorrow.

"I'll answer you in a minute. But let me tell you a story first."

"That means he is, or you'd have just said no."

"Don't matter. I need you to listen to me."

"Yes, ma'am."

"You know how you got in a fight today, even though you know you're not supposed to fight, but it wasn't really your fault. But you're still getting into some trouble over it, right?"

"Yes'm."

"When I was a kid, not really a whole lot older than you, I was barely a teenager, I made a mistake too. Everybody does. That's how we learn sometimes. Sometimes you can make a mistake, and nothing bad happens. You just try to remember not to do that again."

"Like when I fall off my bike but it don't hurt."

"Yeah, like that. But sometimes, when you make a mistake, there are consequences. Maybe not too bad—just a skinned knee or a black eye. But you can make a mistake that is really bad. Like if you were shootin' the gun with Leon, and you didn't follow the rules and you hurt someone, all because you made a split-second mistake. And you can never take it back."

"I'm always careful with the gun like you and Uncle Leon taught me."

"And I'm proud of you for that. But then, sometimes, you can make a bad mistake, and something really awful happens, but then somehow, not because of anything you did to deserve it, something good comes out of it. Do you understand?"

"I'm not sure."

"Well, here goes anyway." Trixie had really wanted to postpone this conversation until, well, maybe until it didn't matter anymore. She took a deep breath. "When I weren't much older than you are now, I had a boyfriend. He weren't a good boyfriend either, but my daddy had just died and I was hurting and lonely and angry. So having a boyfriend who was kinda mean sometimes suited me just fine. I could be mean too. I wanted to get back at my momma for letting my daddy die, even though it wasn't her fault. I was angry at daddy for dying, even though he couldn't help it none. I was mad at God for taking my daddy away. I didn't understand. I still can't say I understand it all, but things just happen, sometimes for a reason, sometimes for no reason at all. But it made me so angry, I took up with a boyfriend who was a real piece of work."

"Was that Ellis?"

Trixie paused and took another breath. She was trying to keep her words under control, say just what needed to be said and not a word more, but Ty could figure things out too quick and kept jumping ahead in the story.

"Yes, sir, my little man, that was him. And then when I was fifteen years old, I got pregnant. That's way too young to have a baby, you understand?"

"Yeah."

"But I was pregnant and that was that. There were consequences. I had to drop out of school."

"Maybe I should get priggant so I don't have to go to school no more."

"It don't work like that." The grin that spread across her boy's face told her he knew better, and she started laughing. A good chuckle helped break tension, but she wanted to keep this talk serious, not get distracted by Ty's jokes. "But anyway, I had to get a job, take care of a baby, and I was still just a kid myself. It was real hard. But I did what I had to do. You know why?"

"Why?"

"Because that baby was you. The best thing to ever happen to me in my whole damn life. Don't say damn, okay?"

"Yes, ma'am. I mean, no ma'am, I won't."

"So, I made a really bad mistake, and something terrible happened, and then the most beautiful thing in the world came out of it all. You. You are my life. I wouldn't change a thing."

"So that jerk is my daddy?"

"Not exactly. He's your biological father. He's what got me pregnant with you. But I'm not ready to talk about how that happens just yet."

"You mean you had sex with him?"

Trixie nearly swallowed her tongue. "Um, yeah, that pretty much sums it up. How d'you know about that stuff anyways?"

"Everybody knows that stuff. And I seen the cows and bulls. Sounds gross."

"It is. Don't ever do it."

"Yes, ma'am."

"So, yeah, he's your father. But he's not your daddy. I'm sorry, I wish I could change things, but you don't have a daddy. You only have me. Me and you against the world. A daddy would be living with us, and would love you, and take you places, do things with you, teach you things, tuck you in at night. Take you hunting and fishing and show you how to drive the tractor and work on cars. Play ball with you."

"Like Uncle Leon, 'cept he can't play ball 'cause of his bad leg."

"Yes, like Uncle Leon. A daddy would be like a younger Uncle Leon who lives with us and loves you all the time. Ellis ain't never been your daddy and never will be. He don't know how to love nobody. It ain't in him."

Tyler sat silently, staring at the table, looking lost in thought. Without raising his head, he asked, "Is that why I've been in trouble at school?"

"What do you mean?" Trixie lifted Ty's chin to look him in the eyes.

"Like why them boys don't like me and the teacher yells at me all the time."

"What does that have to do with Ellis?"

"If he's my father 'cause he had sex with you, then I'm part you and part Ellis. Is his mean part coming out in me? Am I always gonna be an a-hole like him?"

The tears Trixie had held in for the better part of half an hour threatened to burst like a thunderhead before she was able to reel them back in. She grabbed Ty and hugged him and never wanted to let go.

"You're nothin' like that a-hole, and you never will be. You'll always be my little man, even when you're bigger 'n me. And I told ya not to say a-hole no more."

Ty hugged her neck so tight she could barely breathe. He shuddered to hold in that first sob, then it overwhelmed him. Trixie hugged him tight enough to squash him and let him cry. She figured he'd earned a good cry about now, and she'd rubbed the back of his neck while he let it all out. She wanted to do the same but needed to be strong for him.

CHAPTER 11

The next meeting of the Ladies' Society Circle convened at Cass and Lamar Reeves's house. Trixie had trouble viewing it as a home for people to live in. It was the largest house in all of Pineywoods, and nothing about it seemed to fit with east Texas. Something between a Sheraton Hotel and a European estate — several acres of manicured lawns, flower beds, and sugar maples planted in rows as perfect as corn. A low rock wall that seemed to stretch for miles encompassed not just the huge lawns but the surrounding pasturelands and woods too. An arched gateway, with an electronic security gate, announced the entrance to the long, straight, blacktop driveway lined on both sides with tall, skinny juniper trees standing sentinel and framing the portico and double front doors to the home.

Marble statues and fountains filled the front yard, if it could be called a yard. Cobblestone walkways meandered in and around the gardens and more flower beds. A waterfall about three feet tall spilled into a tiny creek that weaved in and out, filled with some carp-looking fish of brilliant colors that Trixie had never seen before. Trixie wondered if they'd taste better fried or baked. A couple of elderly Hispanic men in coveralls watered and trimmed.

Trixie figured if you're the richest man in town and you own the bank, you're probably entitled to whatever house you can afford. *I could probably afford this, but who'd want it?*

And it seemed a bit too large for a family that only had two children — Austin and his older sister.

Cass gave Trixie the big tour of the first floor. The inside looked like a museum of stuff children should never touch — vases, paintings, large statues in the corners, small statues on antique tables. Crystal cigar ashtrays that had probably never seen a cigar. Another fountain inside, for crying out loud. Curved staircases on each side of the entry foyer that met at a landing at the top, a space large enough to hold two couches, two easy chairs, and ornate coffee and end tables. A reading nook, Cass called it. Trixie didn't think it looked like anyone ever sat there with a book.

A stuffed grizzly bear stood on its back legs in the alcove between the bottom of the two sweeping staircases, guarding the upper floor from intruders.

The tour didn't include going upstairs, the residential quarters, Cass called it, which held seven bedrooms. Altogether, the house had eleven bathrooms. Maybe Lamar and Cass had thought they'd have more kids. Why else would they need a place this size? Maybe they were planning for lots of grandbabies or had a large extended family that came to visit frequently.

A team of caterers brought hors d'oeuvres and pastries from the kitchen, coffee and hot tea in silver serving pots along with trays of dainty little cups hand painted with roses and bluebonnets, matching saucers, and tiny little silver spoons. Trixie had four cups at home and only used one of them for herself and the O'Bumpkin's mug for Clay. The other two might get hot chocolate for Ty now and then.

Marion called the meeting to order then welcomed Trixie as the newest member. Cass read the three lines of minutes from last week's meeting. Bee noted there was no treasurer's report because there'd been no financial activity since last week other than a donation from the dry cleaners that had taken twice for the check to clear the bank.

"Reagan," Marion said, moving the agenda along, "as our membership director, do you have anything to report?"

Reagan cleared her throat. "I've got posts up on local social media pages promoting our group, and getting a lot of reacts, but no comments or inquiries yet. Maybe y'all could give me a list of names of ladies you think might be interested and I can reach out to them."

Bee shifted in her chair and raised her hand but didn't wait for Marion to call on her before she started talking. "Maybe we're growing the group too fast. We should take it slow and careful."

No one said anything in an awkward moment of silence, so Marion ignored them both. "Any updates on the clothing sale?"

With no updates, Marion adjourned the meeting. It all took about six minutes.

Then it was time to sip coffee and eat tiny little pastries of flaky dough with a small dollop of fruit or jam or cream cheese in the center. Trixie studied one of the pastries, trying to decide if it was too big to pop the whole thing in her mouth at once. If she tried to bite it in half, the fruit might tumble onto her lap or get all over her lips.

Marion pulled up a chair next to Trixie and leaned in to whisper. "Cass always goes all out when she hosts a meeting. Sometimes I just grab a couple dozen doughnuts from Krispy Kreme." She winked at Trixie then moved on to talk to someone else.

Shelby filled the vacant spot next to Trixie in a flash. "How you doing, girlfriend?" She giggled and leaned over to give Trixie a side hug.

Trixie hadn't had a girlfriend in, well, maybe since grade school. Her and Lorna were inseparable from kindergarten through fifth grade. Then Lorna's parents got divorced and her momma took her and moved to Fort Worth. They'd promised each other to write letters, but that had only lasted about two letters each. Trixie wrote three more letters after that but never got a reply. The third one came back as undeliverable, no forwarding address on file. Now, Trixie couldn't even remember Lorna's last name. Didn't know where she was or if she was married and changed her name. If she was dead or alive even. She'd searched for anyone named Lorna on the internets, but there were thousands. Trixie had no idea there'd be that many people named Lorna in the whole wide world.

She gazed around Lamar's home, thinking she should have charged him a lot more. He could've afforded it. He probably spent more on fish food for those carp every month than he did for his special requests in Trixie's bedroom.

"Austin has band practice tonight," Shelby said. "You want to go see a movie with me?"

"Austin's still—" Trixie caught herself. "Austin plays music?"

"Oh yeah. That's what he wants to do for a living, but don't breathe a word of that around here. His parents would hit the roof. Cass tells him it's a pleasant hobby but you can't make a living at it. Lamar tells him to put down the guitar and pick up a golf club for the good of the bank—networking and business deals and such. But Austin has no interest in golf. Says it's boring."

"I always figured a boy needs to follow his dreams," Trixie said. "Girls too, for that matter. But I'm afraid I'll have to pass on the cinema tonight. I got my boy to take care of and some business stuff I have to go over." Trixie hesitated, hoping she didn't come across like she was brushing her off. "But another time? Maybe this weekend?"

"You got my number. Text me and let me know what works for you. My schedule is flexible. I always forget you have a kid to take care of."

Bee sidled up next to Trixie and Shelby like she wanted to join the conversation or maybe join them at the movies, but she didn't say anything, just hovered.

Shelby took the hint. She winked at Trixie. "I'm going to get some more of these wonderful little Danish. And those chocolate thingies look tasty too. Might have to try one or five of them."

"How are you this morning, Bee?"

"I'd like a quick moment of your time, if you want to step over here out of earshot."

Trixie flushed, the heat rising in her face. Did Bee hear something about Trixie's previous line of work? Want to ask about Jasper ever being a client? Why was she being so secretive?

"Sure, I guess."

Bee walked to the foyer with Trixie at her heels, away from the sitting room, into the shadow of the bear.

"I don't like discussing financial matters where prying ears like to tune into what's none of their business yet," Bee started. At least it didn't sound like she was going toward Trixie's personal services bid'ness.

"I can understand that," Trixie said.

"I've received your letter asking for financial records. I do appreciate your willingness to boost this group's finances. I'm not going to lie, it's been a little tight the past few years as membership dwindled, especially when we lost two of our most generous, longtime members. So sad, but they were both in their nineties, so it wasn't like it was unexpected."

"I'm so sorry for the loss of your friends."

"I really thought Fanny would've left us something in her will, but she didn't. Most of us put a gift in our wills for the group after we're gone, you know, like an honorary eternal afterlife membership. But Fanny didn't even have a will, which was stupid of her considering she had more money than God and the Reeves put together. Her boys had to fight that out in court, and neither of them thought she might have wanted to leave something to the group that she'd practically been a founding member of."

Trixie still needed to set an appointment with that estate planning attorney Mason had recommended to get her will together. She'd keep in mind that eternal gift to the Circle.

"Fanny's grandmother was a founder of the Circle. Her mother had been president back when we had more than fifty members. But Fanny never had any girls, just two boys, and neither of them had kids. One is gay as a three-dollar bill, and the other is just too ugly for any woman to consider, so that was the end of a long line of Glasscocks in the Circle."

Trixie hoped she hadn't grinned too hard at that last name.

"And then there was Velma," Bee continued. "That nursing home she was in for twenty years with Alzheimer's took every dime she had. Sad. Just sad. So of course, she didn't leave us anything."

"Have you had time yet to pull together the financial records so's my foundation can consider a substantial gift?" Trixie tried to get Bee back on track. Mason wouldn't approve no gift without the due diligence.

"Now see, a few things I need to explain. First of all, there are annual membership dues from all of us. You're joining late in the year, so I will pro-rate your dues to half for this year."

It was almost October, so Trixie figured it ought to be pro-rated down to about a quarter, but she wasn't going to quibble.

"The dues are only $250 a year, so $375 will take care of you through next year. I'll be glad to take a check from you today, if you have that on you. Otherwise, just bring it to next week's meeting."

"I'll be sure to bring that next week."

"And we all donate our time and resources as we are able—whether it's volunteering time, holding meetings at our homes, baked goods, on and on. And those of us who are able to contribute financially, over and above the annual dues, do so on a regular basis. But no one has ever asked for all these records before to make a donation. We're just a small group, and there aren't a lot of records, nothing formal like what you were asking for."

"Oh, I will certainly be volunteerin' my time and payin' my dues and donatin' clothes—I'm not much of a baker, I'm afraid. And I'll put in some extra money now and then to help out. The recordkeeping stuff isn't for me—it's for the foundation. That's the requirements of the board of directors."

Mason had anticipated Bee might have some pushback on all the due diligence, and Trixie had rehearsed her little speech that Mason had coached her on. Make sure they know this is the foundation, and the board, that requires this. That way she could take the personal out of it, sidestep the responsibility. Blame the board. They're a bunch of stiff old coots who don't like to give out any money they don't have to.

"I'll do what I can," Bee said. "We don't keep real formal records as such. Not sure we have three years' worth like you're asking for. We don't even do a budget or anything that fancy."

"I'm sure Lamar can have the bank print off all the statements, and you can just make copies of your monthly treasurer's reports for the past few years."

"It's usually just handwritten notes, nothing typed up, and after I've read the report each week, I don't keep copies. I have a folder in my bureau at home with receipts and such."

"Just pull together as much as you can and maybe write a letter explaining why you don't have the other stuff. I'm sure the board will take that into consideration."

"I'll do my best. Sorry to be such a pain, but we're just a small group of women trying to do some good works in our community, not a big, formal organization like the Rotary Club or such. I've been the treasurer for ten years, and no one's ever asked for anything like this before." Bee hesitated and glanced around. "And, if you don't mind my asking, exactly what size donation are you, or this foundation, looking at? The letter just said 'substantial gift.'"

"That'll be up to the board," Trixie said, not quite a lie since she was half the board. "It may depend on how much of the due diligence you're able to provide."

"I was just curious. Not sure if they're talking about a thousand dollars or a million." Bee cracked a rare smile to let Trixie know she was joking, sort of, while still fishing.

"I'm guessing it will be somewhere between those two substantial numbers," Trixie said with a chuckle. "Now let's get back to the group and I'll buy you one of those delicious tiny pastries."

Bee smiled nervously, but she'd stopped sniffing quite so much. Even made an attempt at eye contact a few times.

CHAPTER 12

Trixie didn't relish the idea of getting cornered on Sunday morning by Jasper and Lamar peppering her with questions about the foundation paperwork, like Bee had done at the Circle.

"Clay," she said when he answered, "what time is service in the morning? Maybe I'll join you."

"Ten a.m., but we're not real sharp on the time. We start showing up for doughnuts about nine, and when it looks like everybody's about had their fill, the band starts playing softly until everyone wraps up their conversations and takes their seats. How about I pick you and Ty up about quarter 'til nine and y'all ride up with me? I have to make one stop on the way. It's my week to bring doughnuts."

"That'd be great. I'll see if I can make Ty presentable, but he won't stay that way long. I picked up a new dress just for church tomorrow, so I'm set."

"That's fine, if you want, but you'll be the only woman there in a dress. Jeans is fine. As hot as it's been, some folks have been wearing shorts and flip-flops. Told ya we're pretty casual."

Trixie had been taught from the age of three that ladies wear dresses, or at least a skirt and a blouse, to the Lord's house on Sunday mornings. Sign of respect and worshipfulness or something like that. Wearing jeans to church sounded nice, but she wasn't sure how comfortable she was with that. She was pretty sure that had been a sin at the church Daddy used to take her to. Pretty much everything was a sin there.

"Ty, you need to get in the tub and get to bed."

"Momma, it's only seven o'clock. Not a school night."

"We're going to church in the morning."

"Again? Ain't we gone enough yet?"

"You haven't learned to obey your momma yet, so apparently not. Maybe you can pray for the Lord's forgiveness for beating the crap out of that boy. And don't you say crap. Ain't a nice word. In fact, don't say ain't either. It's just not proper."

"Do I have to wear a tie?"

"You don't have to get dressed up at all, but you need to not stink. I'll throw some jeans in the wash for you tonight."

"I can wear jeans to church?"

"Yeah, we're going to visit a different church. With Clay. So you be on your best—"

She didn't bother finishing the sentence because Ty had left the room, running up the stairs for the tub.

"Momma?" he yelled from the top of the stairs. "Can you wash my John Deere shirt for me too?"

"Yes, sir, my little man."

Clay had given Ty a green and yellow t-shirt for his birthday with a John Deere logo embroidered on the sleeve. She'd practically had to pry him out of that thing to get it in the wash or he'd wear it every day.

It landed at her feet when a nude boy threw it from the top of the stairs.

"Get your nekkid butt in that tub."

Ty's giggle was followed by the bathroom door slamming shut and the water kicking on. Trixie gathered the t-shirt, which smelled like sweaty boy, a few pairs of jeans and a couple of her more casual blouses from the hamper, then remembered to wait until the tub was done filling up before starting the washer.

***

"If we grow too much, we might have to move our service next door." Clay balanced three boxes of doughnuts in one arm and held the door to the former Radio Shack, which was right next to the vacant Piggly Wiggly. "So we've got room to expand."

Trixie and Ty walked into the large open space where a few dozen metal folding chairs were arranged, as well as a lectern up front, but no stage or altar or anything like that. Behind the lectern, a set of drums stood on a small platform behind a Plexiglass screen. Various speakers, guitars, electronic keyboards, and microphones were set up with a mass of wires spread on the floor connecting them all.

Ty also carried one box of doughnuts, and Trixie carried two.

"Set these down over here." Clay nodded toward two folding tables against the wall with a coffee pot, Styrofoam cups, paper plates, and napkins.

Trixie glanced around the room, where maybe a dozen people scattered about in clusters of twos and threes, busily chatting and laughing.

"About time you got here," another cowboy said. "We were wondering if the Lord had forgotten to provide us our daily bread."

"Trixie, let me introduce you to our pastor. This is Brother Kent. Kent, this is my neighbor and employer, Trixie Burnet."

The pastor, maybe still in his twenties, wore jeans, boots, a belt buckle the size of a small dinner plate, and a cowboy hat. His thick, bushy mustache hung down past his upper lip, bright red like the flips of hair that rolled out from under his hat and around his ears and collar in unruly waves.

He stepped forward with a noticeable limp and held out a rough hand to greet Trixie. "Kent Sterling, ma'am. We're so blessed you joined us this morning. Clay has told us a lot about you."

As Trixie clasped his hand, the temperature of her face rose a few degrees. Just what had Clay told them? Who is 'us?' The whole congregation? Maybe he'd put in a prayer request for the hooker who'd just won the lottery?

"And this fine young fella must be Tyler." Kent reached out and shook Ty's hand. Ty gave it a manly shake while staring at the belt buckle.

Trixie took a deep breath. "I sure hope Clay didn't talk about me too much. My ears might've been burning."

Kent had a hearty, full laugh that, for some reason, put Trixie at ease.

"Oh no, just that he's been working your land, and that he invited you to join us. But he mentioned you've been attending First Church, and I told him we don't need to poach people who've already found a church home. If the Lord wants you here, he will lead you here."

"Oh, he didn't poach us at all. We've been visiting First Church but haven't joined up officially yet. Clay just extended an open invitation, and this felt like a good day to take him up on it."

"Can I have a doughnut, Momma?"

"Go right ahead. But just one."

Brother Kent started to say something else when the door opened and a shriek pierced the air, stopping every conversation and turning every head.

"Trixie! Trixie! Trixie!" Shelby squealed and ran across the room to throw herself on Trixie in a bear hug. "What are you doing here? I mean, I'm glad you're here, as if you couldn't tell."

"I was about to ask what you're doing here."

"This is my church. Austin is the music director. I sing in the band. Here, let me introduce you." Shelby waved Austin over. "Austin, this is my friend Trixie I was telling you about."

Seemed everyone was talking to everyone else about Trixie. It had been four years or better, but she recognized the handsome, frightened teenager. His eyes weren't bugging out this time, but he still looked like he didn't need to shave but once a week.

Trixie took his outstretched hand and saw the recognition form in his eyes. Apparently, he hadn't put two and two together before. Like maybe there were as many Trixies as there were Lornas.

"Um, hello. It's nice to meet you. Again. Welcome to Agape."

"Have y'all met before?" Shelby asked.

Before Trixie could think of what to say, Austin said, "Briefly. In passing."

"Maybe down at the bank or something," Trixie added, though she didn't like the idea of telling a lie in church, even if it was an old Radio Shack.

Austin held onto Trixie's hand and placed his other hand on top with a gentle, welcoming pat. The thin gold band still adorned his finger. Untarnished.

Clay walked up and handed Trixie a Styrofoam cup of coffee. "Trixie's my guest this morning. How do y'all know each other?"

"We're in the Ladies' Circle together," Shelby answered before Trixie could take a sip, "where we're gonna shake things up, aren't we, Trixie? Better question is where do you two know each other from?" Shelby gave Trixie a not-so-sly wink.

"Trixie's my employer," Clay said. "She owns the farm I've told you about, where I've been working."

"Business partner now," Trixie corrected him. "Not employer."

Shelby squeezed Trixie's forearm and gave her a conspiratorial look. "Well, that's quite the coincidence, isn't it?"

Austin excused himself to go plug everything in and turn on the amps. "It's wonderful to have you here, Trixie. I hope you'll find us as welcoming as family."

***

The service was a little different than anything Trixie'd experienced before. As a kid, there was the Pentecostal Holiness church. Small, out in the country, a lot of shouting and amens and praise the Lords as the preacher yelled. Occasionally someone would start jabbering in tongues. Once that Trixie recalled, a lady fell down and rolled around in the aisle like she was having a seizure, but the preacher waved everyone away from helping her. It was just the Holy Ghost moving through her, he'd said. And sure enough, after another hymn and prayer, the lady sat up, wiped the spittle off her chin, and shouted, "Praise Jesus!" before she returned to her seat as if nothing had happened. Trixie used to pray that the Lord would keep the Holy Ghost to Himself and never send His Spirit down on her. She wouldn't be able to withstand that kind of attention.

Then came a ten-year hiatus from attending the Lord's house. Now, the giant First Church with announcements, prayers, a choir, a pipe organ. Burgundy carpet, oak pews with burgundy cushions, stained-glass windows behind the choir and down both sides. Everyone in a suit and tie or a dress. Older women wore hats like they was the Queen of England. Everyone sat still and listened quietly. Spirit-led delirium wouldn't likely be tolerated in First Church.

In this empty storefront with commercial vinyl tile flooring and a few missing ceiling tiles, the band sounded like a rock concert, not that Trixie had ever been to one. She didn't know any of the songs, but they projected the words on a screen. Seemed most songs had one verse, two at the most, and then they all sang the chorus over and over, like eight or ten times. By the third time, Trixie could sing along as people clapped and swayed and held their hands up with eyes closed. Wild compared to First Church. Sedate compared to the Antioch.

They stood to sing, and they sang one song after another after another. Trixie finally slipped her shoes off. They were short heels, not high, but they were rubbing blisters on her feet and her arches throbbed. She'd never been to a church where they stood for this long at a stretch.

On about the third chorus of "Our God is an Awesome God," a woman slipped into the empty seat in front of Clay. Straight, waist-length, jet black hair with green and blue highlights, pulled into a ponytail. She had full sleeve and neck tattoos, and Trixie assumed there were probably more hidden under her black Harley-Davidson tank top. Studs and rings hung in her ears, nose, lips, and chin. Even one in her cheek. Trixie didn't want to think about what else she might have pierced. Kind of a criminal tough-girl look that Trixie wasn't accustomed to seeing in church.

The woman turned and leaned back while Clay leaned forward and kissed her on the cheek. They held hands a moment and she patted his forearm. Girlfriend? Ex? Seemed too friendly for an ex. She wore black leather pants and black boots that laced up to her knees. Clay hadn't ever mentioned a girl, but the subject had never come up. *Maybe they're just friends*. Not that it mattered, of course, other than she figured Clay deserved better than a biker chick.

By the twelfth or twentieth repeat of the chorus—Trixie hadn't been counting—about the time she was wondering if it would be rude or sacrilegious to sit down, the song ended and Kent limped to the podium, motioning everyone to take their seats. He removed his hat and hung it on a guitar behind him, exposing a mass of red hair that was thinning on top.

He talked about the woman caught in adultery that all the leaders of the community were going stone to death, but Jesus told them they could only throw a rock at her if they'd never sinned in their whole lives, so they all dropped their rocks and went home sad. Then Jesus told the woman, "Go on now and don't do that no more."

Trixie wondered just who put the pastor up to this—preaching a sermon about the fallen woman on the day she decided to visit.

But Kent didn't focus on the woman. Barely mentioned her again. He talked about the people who showed up ready to kill her. How they'd judged her. How they looked down on her but didn't think on their own sins. How maybe some of them went home angry that they didn't get the chance to toss a few rocks at the riffraff. Maybe some of them went home and thought about it, decided they probably shouldn't be quite so harsh to judge in the future, even if they believed they'd never done anything as bad as what that woman was accused of. And, maybe, just maybe, two of them went home, dropped to their knees in prayer and cried out to God for forgiveness. The next morning, one of those two went back to work, hung out with the same people he'd always hung out with, did the same things he'd always done, and by the end of the day had forgotten all about it.

But one, maybe more but maybe just one out of that whole mob, changed. Went out the next day to make amends to those he'd judged before. Took the adulterous woman a sack of groceries and asked for her forgiveness, and she hugged him as they cried together. Went to the homeless beggar on the corner, the one he'd always crossed the street to avoid. He didn't give him some spare change but invited him to come to his home for dinner. Went to the old, bitter woman who lived in a shack, the one who sat out front and cursed and spat at everyone who walked by. But he didn't walk by. He walked up to her and asked what she needed. He fixed her leaky roof. Gave her a new coat. Stopped by every day to see how she was doing and if she needed anything. Told her he loved her. Some days she told him she loved him. Some days she cursed and spat at him. He still went back the next day.

None of that was in the Bible, of course. That was just Brother Kent surmising what might have happened if only one person listened to what Jesus actually said. One changed life. Countless lives touched by the one. Judgment lifted one soul at a time. Hope restored one life at a time. Love restored one heart at a time.

Kent had tears in his eyes by the end of his ten-minute sermon, whispering about how he wanted to be that one. "Please, Lord, let me be this one today. Help me be this one."

Trixie had to admit she'd never heard any preacher talk like this. She felt some relief that the sermon didn't focus on the fallen woman. That would have felt a little uncomfortably close to home.

She glanced around, and there wasn't a dry eye in the place. Except Ty. He wasn't crying. But he was listening, not sleeping. Staring at the pastor, engrossed in the story. Or maybe just staring at that belt buckle.

She just hoped he wasn't thinking about filling his pockets with good throwing stones before school in the morning.

***

After the service ended, the fifty or so folks in attendance didn't head for the door to shake the pastor's hand and hurry to beat the Methodists to Denny's. Everyone just hung around. Grabbed another doughnut or cup of coffee. A couple of men stepped out front for a quick smoke before coming back in to fellowship a bit longer.

The biker chick met Clay at the end of the row for a big hug. Her face lit up when they talked. So did his. Trixie wasn't sure what to make of the bite of jealousy that rose up in her throat.

Clay finally motioned to Trixie to come over and meet his friend.

"Trixie, this is Harris. Harris Sterling, Trixie Burnet."

Sterling? Where had she heard that name before?

Before Trixie could reach out to shake hands, Harris grabbed her shoulders and pulled her in for a hug. "So wonderful you could join us."

Trixie wasn't ready for a hug, and felt a bit flat-footed, arms in the wrong position, standing too far back and leaning too far in. Harris held the hug for just a moment until Trixie relaxed into it. Comfort.

Harris stepped back and sized Trixie up with her eyes. Mesmerizing, light blue eyes. A smile that could serve as a lighthouse on a rocky beach. "Clay has told us all about you."

How many people has he been talking to about me? What the hell has he been saying?

"Sorry I had to slip in late this morning," Harris said to Clay. "Had the late shift and just couldn't get moving this early."

"I'm sure the pastor will forgive you," Clay said, and they both laughed as Brother Kent walked up, his limp becoming a bit more obvious, like he'd been standing way too long.

"She has to forgive me a lot more than I need to forgive her," he said, then leaned in for one of those comfort hugs and kissed her full on the lips.

Sterling. Brother Kent Sterling. Harris Sterling. The pieces started to fit together. He didn't look like any preacher she'd ever seen before, and Harris certainly didn't look like any preacher's wife she'd known. A sense of relief replaced the moment of jealousy, but Trixie didn't like that feeling either. She had no reason to feel either and pushed them away.

Clay asked the group if they'd all like to go to brunch. Those doughnuts just weren't filling the void. The diner served breakfast all day.

"I'm afraid we can't," Kent said. "I'm due at Winn-Dixie in an hour for my shift, and Harris promised to have lunch with her folks. We'll catch you next time though." He turned to Trixie. "We'd love to spend some time with you, get to know you better. I hope you felt the Lord's Spirit here this morning, and that you'll find the church home He leads you to. Selfishly, I hope it's here. But that's between you and Him. You two go on to breakfast without us."

"Three," Ty said.

"Five," added Shelby as she walked up. "Austin and I are coming too. We're always up for breakfast at Roy's."

Another round of hugs to say goodbye to the pastor and his wife. As Trixie hugged Harris, less awkwardly this time, the pastor's words ran through her head again. Here she was, a single mom who'd had a baby out of wedlock at fifteen, a recently retired prostitute with a boy who was getting out of control, yet she'd judged Harris from the moment she'd seen her inked and pierced skin, biker-chick clothes, and neon-streaked hair.

Trixie wasn't the immoral woman they'd wanted to stone. She was a member of the mob with a fist full of rocks. He'd preached directly at her after all.

She hugged Harris a little tighter, held on for a moment longer, not wanting to let go of that comfort that seeped straight through her bones.

CHAPTER 13

Trixie had only one doughnut, more than an hour ago, and something more substantial sounded good. Ty wasn't hungry. He'd had his one doughnut she'd allowed, then another when he thought Trixie wasn't looking. Then another after the service. She made him eat a fried egg and drink a glass of orange juice just to get some nutrition in that boy.

Clay and Trixie sat next to each other on one side of the table for four, with Shelby and Austin facing them, and Ty pulled up a chair at the end that waitresses had to maneuver around.

As the waitress cleared away their mostly empty plates and refilled coffees and waters, Shelby picked up the conversation right where she'd left it when the food had been served.

"I still can't believe I've been your friend for several weeks and had no idea that Clay worked for you. We've known Clay from church for nearly a year. I knew he worked a farm outside of town. He'd told us he worked for a single momma with a little boy, but I never made the connection when we met. To think you've known him as long as we have, and we'd never crossed paths before just blows my mind."

When Trixie was nervous, she could prattle on too much. Shelby talked like that all the time. The more she talked, the more excited she'd get about whatever the topic was.

Once in a while, Austin would discreetly reach over to trace a finger over the back of her hand, and Shelby would bring her thought to a close and let someone else have a chance to speak.

When Clay and Austin started chatting about the high school football team, Shelby grinned at Trixie, like she was up to something. Her eyes grew wide with a smile, then she glanced at Clay and back to Trixie with a wink.

Trixie acted like she didn't know what Shelby was getting at, then shook her head and directed her attention to whatever the guys were talking about. The last thing she needed was Shelby trying to hook her up with her foreman and tenant.

Clay was different than any man she'd ever known. No way a man like Clay would be interested in her, especially if he knew what she'd been doing the past few years. A man like Clay deserved someone special.

"Shelby," Trixie jumped in during a lull in the conversation. "Tell me about your family. Any sisters?"

***

After brunch and saying goodbye to Clay when he dropped them off at the farmhouse, Trixie told Ty to keep his clean clothes on. They had somewhere to be.

"Can I ride my bike?"

"No, you'll get all dirty. We have to leave in about twenty minutes, so just go sit on the couch and read for a bit so you don't mess yourself up too much."

"Why do I have to go?"

"'Cause you ain't old enough to stay home by yourself yet."

"Don't say ain't, Momma. And where we gotta go now?"

"There's a house I want us to go look at."

"Why we wanna look at a house?"

"Maybe we'll like it and move there."

"I ain't movin' nowheres."

"If I move, you're movin' with me. When you're eighteen, you can move somewhere else all by yourself if you want. Until then, you live where I live."

"But this is home."

"This is a house. And it's fallin' apart. Home is where we live, doesn't matter which house we put it in. We could move our home into a nicer house."

Ty huffed and stomped to the living room, and flung himself onto the couch in a pout. He didn't pick up his book.

***

The open house was from one to four. Trixie wanted to get there a little early, be the first one to see it in case she liked it, maybe put down a deposit to hold it. If not, they'd get back home sooner so Ty could ride his bike and burn off some of that rebellious attitude.

It wasn't one of the old Victorians, but it wasn't in the brand-new subdivision with no trees or people. A nice neighborhood built about twenty years ago, so the houses were much newer than her old farmhouse and the trees had all come in nicely. Kids were playing in front yards and riding bikes up and down the sidewalk and street. The house was in a cul-de-sac, which Trixie wasn't sure if she liked or not. Less car traffic, so it was safer, but only one way in or out. It was only about five minutes to First Church and the Christian school. Even closer to a grocery store. A city park and playground were just around the corner, an easy bike ride for Ty. They had tennis courts and a baseball field too, along with a bandstand for summer concerts.

Trixie imagined sitting on a blanket and listening to music on a warm summer evening while Ty rode his bike around the park with friends. Maybe Shelby would sit on the blanket with her during the concert. Maybe Austin and Clay would join them too. And Kent and Harris as well. Might need two or three blankets. Pack some drinks and sandwiches.

The house was a two-story, like her farmhouse, but it also had a full, finished basement that would make a wonderful playroom for Ty. He could have friends over. Maybe put a pool table and a pinball machine or set up a big screen TV with video games. The three-car garage would provide extra storage since she couldn't imagine needing more than one car no matter how much money she had in the bank.

A tall, wooden privacy fence surrounded the large backyard with a perfectly green lawn even though it hadn't rained in nearly a month. The back patio was built with flagstone, and a stainless-steel gas grill was built into a matching flagstone counter. She could grill burgers and hot dogs for Ty and his friends, maybe toss on some steaks for Clay, Shelby, and Austin.

She could picture herself living here. She could picture life here.

The three bedrooms upstairs were each bigger than her boudoir. The master bedroom on the main floor felt bigger than the whole first floor of the farmhouse. King-size bed, huge dressers, walk-in closet, and a full bathroom that would be just for her. The bedroom had so much space, a couch and loveseat sat in one corner, like that reading nook at the top of the stairs in Cass's home. Trixie knew she'd actually use this spot for reading, not just show.

Much, much nicer than where they lived now. Not so big or ostentatious that it would be too much for her to keep clean or be drawing attention, flashing her money around.

"Okay, we seen it. Can we go now?"

"What do you think? You like this house? It's nice, ain't it? Isn't it?"

"There ain't no trails to ride my bike."

"There's sidewalks and that park around the corner. Maybe you could take tennis lessons."

Ty rolled his eyes. "There's no barns to play in."

"Those barns are getting dangerous. There's a backyard. And trees. We could build you a treehouse. There's kids around. You could have friends to play with. You could have a sleepover."

"I don't like none of these kids."

"Do you know them?"

"Nope. Don't want to, neither."

"Your attitude is going to get adjusted one way or another, little man."

Another couple walked in to see the house, and Trixie didn't like the idea of looking at the same time as someone else. She'd have to work on Ty, but he'd come around. She grabbed the information sheet and told the Realtor thank you. Ty was already out the door and headed to the car.

Trixie drove from the open house to the now empty parking lot of First Church, pulled in and drove around to the school building.

"See how close this is to that house."

"I don't like this church. I like Mr. Garza's church. They got doughnuts."

"See this building here?" Trixie pointed Ty's attention to the single-story brick building behind the church. "That's the Christian school. You'd like this school better, and you wouldn't have to ride the bus no more. You could ride your bike to school when the weather's good. When it ain't, I can drop you off and pick you up 'cause it's so close."

"Why would I want to go to school here? I hate it."

"You hate your school now. Don't like your teacher. Don't like the kids. Got Carson and his gang threatening to beat you up every day."

"I hate this school even more. I ain't movin' and I ain't changin' schools."

Trixie quit arguing with him. Weren't doing no good. He was just in a mood to argue about everything. Even if he liked it, he wouldn't admit it now. Let him sleep on it and catch him in a better frame of mind. But it couldn't wait too long. Before they'd pulled away from the open house, two more cars had pulled up. Someone would buy that place before she could get Ty's attitude right.

***

Monday around noon, Trixie finished her errands and ran home for lunch. She ate a quick sandwich and some chips, drank a Diet Coke, and sat on the couch for a few minutes to prop up her feet.

The next thing she knew, someone was knocking on her screen door, calling out, "Ms. Burnet, are you home?"

Trixie roused from her too short of a nap, not quite sure what day or time it was for a moment. Glanced at the clock. Only ten minutes had passed.

"Just a minute. I'm coming." She yawned and ran her hands through her hair to smooth out the flat spot she'd been lying on.

There stood Lynn Roberts again, clipboard in hand, representing the interests of the people of the State of Texas in maintaining safe and protective homes for children.

"Tyler's still at school, ma'am. You'll need to come back around four when he gets off the bus if you want to speak with him."

"I'd like to speak with you while he's not here. Do a quick inspection of your home."

"Why do you need to inspect my home?"

"To ensure Tyler is in a safe and suitable home environment."

Trixie wanted to get that razor strop off the wall and chase Ms. Roberts back to her car, but that probably wouldn't help the situation. She unlatched the screen door.

"House is a bit of a mess. I've been out all day on bid'ness. But it's just clutter. House is old, but we keep it clean."

"Why don't you give me a tour?"

Trixie led her through the kitchen. The woman had the audacity to open the fridge to see what was in it. Plenty of food, juices, vegetables, a six-pack of Diet Coke and a six-pack of grape soda. "He's only allowed one can a day," Trixie assured her.

Trixie never offered her anything to drink.

Ms. Roberts opened the pantry, some cabinets.

"Do you keep any guns in the home?"

Trixie hesitated a moment to think about it. The Ruger was still in the glovebox. "No, ma'am."

Trixie led her upstairs to the two bedrooms and shared bath. She made her bed every morning. With Ty, it was hit and miss if he remembered to do it. She opened his bedroom door and there it was — covers pulled into place and pillows on the bed. It didn't look great, but it looked like an eight-year-old boy had at least made an effort. A few toys were on the floor, and his dirty clothes from the day before, jeans and the John Deere shirt, were in a pile on the floor at the foot of the bed, not two feet from the clothes hamper where he was supposed to put them.

The woman walked in and looked around, made a few notes on her clipboard, opened a closet door, behind which Ty had a few clothes on hangers and a shelf full of books.

"He likes to read," Trixie explained.

"That's what his teacher said too."

"You've talked to his teacher?"

"Yes, I've visited with his teacher and school officials. They had some concerns."

"Precisely what concerns do they have? Are they concerned about the bullies shaking him down for money every day? They concerned that he's so far ahead of the other kids in his class that he's bored?"

"Just questions about what his home life might be like given his behavioral issues at school."

"His home life is fine."

"That's what this report will help determine."

Trixie grew more irritated but managed to hold her tongue. Opened the door to her bedroom across the hall from Ty's. The bathroom at the end of the hall.

Back downstairs to the living room, and Trixie led her back to the kitchen, where they stood in the middle of the room. Trixie didn't invite her to sit in the living room or offer a chair at the kitchen table.

If she's got more questions, she can stand here and ask. There was a time for hospitality, but this weren't one of them.

"What's down that hall?"

Trixie hadn't shown her to the boudoir. She hadn't been in it in a month. She hadn't even gone in to dust.

"That's the guest bedroom. Never gets used."

"I'd like to see it, please."

Trixie didn't move. She always kept it tidy, everything put away, but if Ms. Roberts started opening closet doors and dresser drawers, she might be in for a bit of a shock. Or maybe not—who knows what goes on in someone's private life?

Ms. Roberts waited a beat, but when Trixie didn't move, she headed down the hallway on her own. Trixie quickly followed.

"I'll need to unlock it." Trixie reached for the key on top of the door frame. "I keep it locked just so Ty doesn't go in and mess it up. Mainly used for storing stuff I'm going to be donatin'."

Trixie unlocked the door. The bed was made, with a frilly comforter and extra pillows with matching shams. A four-poster queen-size bed. One nightstand with a lamp, one small dresser, and a double closet. A full-length mirror on the back of the door aimed right at the bed when the door was closed.

Ms. Roberts looked around the room.

"You have any overnight guests use this room?"

"Was my momma and daddy's room. I just kept my room upstairs to be close to my boy."

"When was the last time a man stayed the night here?"

"Last man to spend the night in here was my daddy before he died ten years ago." Trixie never let a client spend the night. One hour maximum. Then they had to leave. She had to get up in the mornings to get Ty ready for school.

Ms. Roberts opened the closet door to a full array of dresses that looked like Trixie might hang out in fancy nightclubs. "Beautiful dresses. Where do you wear these in this town?"

"I don't. All stuff picked up at yard sales and such. Momma used to resell them at the flea market to make a few dollars, but not much market for such in Pineywoods, so she stopped. It's all going to charity. My clothes are all in my bedroom closet upstairs."

Ms. Roberts had already inspected the handful of modest dresses, skirts, and mostly blue jeans in the upstairs closet.

Trixie was trying to figure out how she'd explain the massagers, the warming lubricants, the crotchless panties, and the adult-sized cloth diapers if Ms. Roberts opened a dresser drawer or the nightstand. But she seemed to lose interest until she saw the shoes at the bottom of the closet.

"Oh my, these are beautiful," she said, picking up a pair of black pumps with four-inch heels. "Jimmy Choo's? These are pretty pricey. You're just going to donate them?"

"You want them? I'll make you a good price."

"No, they're not the right size. My feet are way too wide for these. Not sure where I'd wear them anyway."

Ms. Roberts set the shoes back down carefully between the clear acrylic six-inch platforms and the red stilettos. "Interesting collection. Let's go chat in the other room for a moment, then I'll let you get back to your day."

Trixie breathed a sigh of relief as she locked the door behind her. Ms. Roberts led the way and pulled up a chair at the kitchen table without being invited.

Ms. Roberts reviewed the notes on her clipboard and then began what felt like an interrogation, except the woman just read the questions from a form and checked boxes. She seemed bored.

"Do you cook? How often do you cook at home versus going out to eat or bringing in fast food? Do you have any concerns about your food security? Do you ever worry about having enough money to buy food? Does Tyler ever complain about being hungry? When was the last time Tyler saw a doctor? Dentist? How much time does he spend at home alone? What is your daily routine in the morning before school? After school? What is your religious or faith preference, if you have any? Do you attend any religious services on a regular basis? Does he have friends? Does Tyler visit with any extended family in the area? Are you on any kind of government assistance? How do you generate an income?"

Ty always complained about being hungry but had never missed a meal in his whole life. That little man was a bottomless pit, like most growing boys. She fixed him breakfast every morning and packed his lunch and cooked supper most evenings. They'd splurge on Golden Corral or order pizza once a week. She never fed him fast food after her experience working in that industry. They had a family doctor and dentist she took him to once a year for shots and checkups, but he'd rarely missed a day of school due to being sick. She always saw him off to the bus in the morning and was home when he got back. They attended Pineywoods First Church of the Risen Lord. She was going to enroll him in Sunday School this coming week, although he didn't know that yet and was certain to put up a fuss about having to get to church an hour earlier.

Trixie hadn't taken a dime of government assistance since Lamar had wined and dined her at Olive Garden and the Sheraton four years ago. She certainly didn't need it now. She skipped over that part to talk about the farm, that she'd hired a foreman to run it for her, was planning to sell it to him and buy a new home in town.

The questions went on for about fifteen minutes. Trixie used every bit of her willpower to keep her answers to "yes, ma'am" and "no, ma'am," or as brief a response as possible. She wanted to bubble over and start interrogating Ms. Roberts, but she didn't. She didn't mention the lottery winnings, just that she had some investments and was financially secure.

"That's my last question. I thank you for your time and cooperation."

"I have one question." Trixie couldn't hold back any longer. "Why are you here? Did someone file a complaint? Is this about Ty gettin' in that fight at school? Those boys were pickin' on him, they hit him first, and he defended himself. I hope you're visiting their homes too, the little snakes. What happens next?" Trixie realized that was more than one question and tried to corral her words again.

"Any concerns someone might have reported are strictly confidential. I'll be talking to a few more people and then I'll submit my report to my higher-ups. After that, there might be a follow-up visit, or even a hearing in family court if there are any serious issues, or the case might be closed if it's determined there are no issues of concern."

Court? Like with a judge?

Trixie bit the insides of her cheeks and said nothing more. She stood and waited for Ms. Roberts to get the hint. This conversation was over.

CHAPTER 14

When Trixie told Mason the matter was urgent, he said his calendar was clear and to come on down.

She filled him in on the social services visit. Wanted to know if he had another sister who was a family law attorney.

He pulled a business card from an ancient Rolodex file and handed it to Trixie. "He's not my sister, but he's the best. Sounds like someone has it in for you, wants to cause you some trouble. I have no doubt it's due to your recent change in circumstances. Someone wants to see if they can squeeze some money out of you. Did this start before or after we sent those letters to the church and the ladies' group?"

"Let me think. It started after Ty got in a fight at school. Yeah, as a matter of fact, that lady showed up right after those letters went out."

"Give me that card back."

Trixie handed over the attorney's business card, and Mason dialed the number.

"This is Mason. Is DeWitt available? Well, have him give me a call at my office. Tell him it's important please. Thank you, honey."

He handed the card back to Trixie. "If you don't hear from him today, you call him first thing in the morning and tell Madison—she'll be the one answering the phone—that I referred you and it's urgent. If you talk to him before I do, tell him to call me. I'll fill him in on the financial situation. You don't need to get into that with him. Just let him know social services has been badgering you and you're a client of mine."

As Trixie backed her car out of the angled parking on Main Street in front of Mason's office, she spotted Ellis's pickup parked across the street. He sat in his truck smoking and glancing in his rearview mirror.

Trixie pulled away and circled the block to make sure he wasn't following her, and she dialed Mason on her cell.

"Can't talk right now, but there's another possibility. I'll call you later and fill you in on one Ellis Shackelford. He might be tryin' to cause me some trouble too."

***

She still had a couple hours before Ty would get home from school, so she drove over to Momma and Leon's place.

Leon was sitting on the deck, cigarette dangling between his lips while he fiddled with a block of wood and a set of carving knives, making a mess of shavings by his feet and on his shoes.

"Hey, little missy. What brings you down here to the slums?"

"Hey, Leon. Momma home?"

"Where else would she be? She's inside takin' a nap in front of the TV. Go ahead and wake her up. She'll pretend she hadn't been sleepin' anyways."

Trixie pulled up the chair beside Leon. "Let her sleep. What're you working on?"

"I ain't sure what it's going to be yet. I just start chiseling some stuff away that doesn't look like it belongs and see what's hidin' underneath. Keep whittlin' until it reveals its ownself."

Trixie filled Leon in on Ty's fight. "I don't want him fightin', but a boy's gotta protect himself when he's attacked, so I wanted to thank you for teachin' him how to do that. No tellin' what them boys would have done to him if he hadn't coldcocked the ringleader."

Leon's pride showed through a smile so wide the cigarette fell out of his mouth. He picked it up before it could set the wood shavings on fire.

"Although I'm a little concerned," Trixie added. "He didn't stop once the kid was down. He could have really hurt him."

"Sounds like he did hurt him pretty good. Now normally, in a fair fight or in the boxing ring, when your opponent goes down, you step away, see if it's over or not. But if there's three of them, well, can't say I blame him much. You let that kid get back up, you're at a severe disadvantage. But I'll chat with him. Sounds like he lost control of hisself, and that's never a good thing. Always stay in control, even when you're outnumbered."

"Thanks. That'll be good advice for him."

"That's good advice for anyone, in a fistfight or just in the daily struggles Satan sends our way. Stay in control. Throw punches that accomplish the goal, but don't wear yerself out, and don't get so focused on the enemy in front of you that you don't see what's sneakin' up behind you."

The screen door squealed as Sabine stepped out, lighting a cigarette and rubbing the sleep from her face. "What are y'all doing out here? All this gabbin' disturbed my beauty sleep."

"It's obvious from lookin' at ya that you've had more than your fair share of that." Leon patted Sabine on the butt.

"Not in front of my kid, you dirty ol' man."

"I ain't a kid no more, Momma."

"Honey, you ain't never been a kid," Sabine said. "You were always just too growed up for your own good, or mine. So, you here to take us house hunting again? Cops raided the place at the end of the street yesterday. Shots fired, the whole thing. Leon and I agreed we need to find a place with no steps, a dishwasher, and no meth labs."

"I'll call my agent this evening, see what we can set up. Y'all need to get out of this mess."

Trixie filled Momma in on Ty's fight, social services, and Mason finding her a kick-ass attorney.

Then she broke the news.

"I'm gonna buy a house in town and sell the farm. I know it's been in the family for generations, but I need to get Ty in a better environment. I weren't sure how you'd feel about that though."

"I should have sold that place off years ago," Sabine said, "but then where would you have gone? It's served its purpose. Time for a new leaf."

Leon agreed. "Although a farm is a fine environment for a boy. You'll have to keep a closer eye on him in town."

"There'll be more kids his age to make friends," Trixie said.

"More kids for him to beat the shit out of, if you ain't careful."

"I got him in church now. I figured that can't hurt. Gonna put him in that Christian school. Maybe they can teach him some manners."

Sabine laughed. "As long as they don't turn him into one of them holy rollers like yer daddy was. I was always waitin' for the Sunday when the preacher would pull out the snakes, and that's when I was gonna call it a day and go back to bein' a Catholic, if'n they'd have me."

"I seriously doubt they would," Leon deadpanned.

"So who you gonna sell the old place to? Can't imagine anybody'd want it."

"I'm selling to Clay."

"Who's Clay?"

"You've met him. The guy leasing the land and living in the trailer."

"That Mexican boy?"

"He ain't Mexican, Momma. He's as American as you and me. And he sure ain't no boy."

"Mexican American, then."

Leon huffed. "Why's everybody gotta be hyphenatin' everything these days? Had a form down at the clinic asking if I was African American. I said no. Ain't never been to Africa in my life. Don't plan on it neither."

"Good-lookin' fella, but what's he know about running a farm?" Sabine asked. "Shouldn't you find someone who knows what they're doing? Someone a little older."

"He grew up on a farm. That's all he knows. Well, that's not all he knows. He knows a lot of stuff. But he knows how to raise cattle, fix a tractor, build a barn, run a business. He can fix a roof. He goes to church and does charitable work. He's a fine man, smart, and he'll make a good go of it. And all that money goes to you 'cause it was yours and daddy's place. You've let me live there rent-free."

"I gave you that place. It's yours to do with as you please."

"You just signed it over to me 'cause you couldn't make the back taxes."

"And where's he gettin' the money?"

"He's going to lease until he's profitable enough to buy it. He's got big plans for expanding the herd, clearing some land, fixin' up those barns. He's already got that ol' tractor going again."

"Why you lookin' like that?" Sabine asked.

"Like what?"

"You talk about this Clay fella and you stare off in the distance and get all doe-eyed."

"Do not."

CHAPTER 15

Mason suggested Trixie and the lawyer meet in his office rather than being spotted walking into a law office, especially since this lawyer worked from home. She'd had an hourlong intake interview over the phone with Madison, his receptionist/paralegal.

DeWitt Armstrong was an imposing figure. Well over six feet tall, cowboy hat and boots, suit and tie even though it was still over ninety degrees outside, nearly that in Mason's office. His perfectly manicured nails suggested he'd never done any ranching, just liked the costume. Well north of sixty years old. Maybe older.

"I've been doing battle with overly aggressive social workers for a decade. I've got a pretty good track record. Of course, there are cases where there's no winning—abused kids, neglected kids, malnourished kids. Kids where, quite frankly, the state needs to step in. And they miss a few, as can be expected. They can't possibly save every child from a bad situation or evil parents. But about twelve years ago, they had a couple of cases that went horribly wrong. This was back when their philosophy was to keep children with a parent or immediate family member if at all possible. Give the parents counseling. Get them settled down, give them advice, make sure they have food, anger management sessions if that was called for, drug and alcohol counseling. Put the kids in a foster home or shelter for a few days until things are under control, then put the kids back with Mom and Dad. Or usually just Mom, or Mom and a boyfriend. But at home, with family, where they belong."

Armstrong stopped and sipped on a bottle of water. Trixie wondered if the city water was no good and if she bought a house in town, would she have to start buying water instead of just turning on the spigot.

"Mr. Armstrong," Trixie said, "my boy is well taken care of. I don't drink, never have done drugs, never have even spanked my boy. Maybe I should've a few times, but it just don't seem right. I do threaten him with the razor strop that hangs on the wall, but I'd never do that."

"I'm quite certain you take very good care of your son. But like I said, they had two cases, back to back, where that approach of keeping kids with the family didn't work out. Down in Beaumont, one kid, eight years old, had been picked up by protective services four or five times due to complaints from the neighbors and reports from his teacher. Every time, they'd take the kid back to his momma and her live-in boyfriend, a heavy drug user and everyone knew it. He'd been in and out of jail. Did a couple years in the state pen for assault. But social services never thought to say the boy can't live there with this guy and give the woman a choice — your son or your boyfriend, but you can't have them both in the same house.

"The next call was for an ambulance. The bastard had beat that boy black and blue, and then he stopped breathing. Paramedics got him breathing again, but he died the next day from brain swelling."

Trixie nearly swooned from the thought of a boy the same age as Ty getting beaten to death, or maybe it was just the heat, or the combination of the two. The room tilted a little to one side and her vision closed into a tunnel. Her mouth was as dry as dirt in August.

"Mason, could I get one of those bottled waters from ya?" she managed to choke out. While she opened the bottle and tried to get the blood back to her head, Armstrong continued with his story.

"While the entire state was investigating what happened, what social services could have or should have done differently, it happened again. This time in Houston. FPS had called on this home more than twenty times in two years. Had taken the kids out of the home for a few days now and then. They eventually put them in foster homes for six months. Then they brought them all back, and a week later, three dead kids, a dead momma, and a dead daddy. He shot all the kids, his wife, and then himself after barricading himself in the home with their corpses for eight hours while the police tried to get him out. PTSD from the war and opioid addiction."

Trixie took a long draw on the water, fighting to remain conscious.

"After that, FPS immediately put out all new procedures and a whole new philosophy. Get the kids out. If you have any doubt, keep the kids out. Err on the side of not losing another child. Foster homes and shelters swelled overnight. Of course, when they went this direction, a lot of perfectly fit parents in perfectly fine homes got their kids taken away. That's when my practice took off."

"You don't think they can take my boy away from me, do you?"

"That's what I'm going to fight to make sure doesn't happen. But I can't make any promises. Those folks can be like the Gestapo if they choose, and they can do whatever they want. All they have to do is say, 'It's for the child's safety,' and nobody wants to cross 'em. Nobody, no judge, wants to be the one who says, 'Send this kid back home,' and then the kid winds up in the coroner's office."

"What should I do?"

"Hiring me is the first and best thing you can do. I'm also going to put a private investigator on the case to find out what, or who, is behind this. There's no evidence of abuse or an unfit home or malnourishment or any of that. No boyfriend in the home. A good student with perfect attendance. A recent scuffle, but what eight-year-old boy doesn't have at least a couple of those? Medical care is good, health is top notch."

Trixie looked to Mason, but he was staring out the window at some thunderclouds rolling in on the horizon, and she couldn't catch his eye.

"Mason filled me in on your financial circumstances. First of all, congratulations are in order for your good fortune. And I think he may be onto something—some folks might be jealous or thinking they can extort you. I mean, if money is no object, any mother is going to pay whatever it takes to not have her child taken away by the system."

Trixie hadn't thought about how much an attorney would cost. He was right. She'd pay whatever it took, and she'd rather pay him than pay somebody who's trying to push her around.

"Should I ask about your fees now, before we go any further?"

"Well, that's interesting. I have my standard rates, plus expenses. But frankly, I rarely get paid much. Sometimes nothing. Most of the parents I represent don't have much money. So you get some poor momma with no money going up against the entire government of the State of Texas. But this became about more than money to me years ago. I'd had a successful practice—divorce is much more lucrative. I sold that practice to a big law group out of Dallas for even more money than I'd made from it. I guess you could say I hit the lottery too.

"I retired for a couple of years, and then decided to take on this line of work as a labor of love. Now, it appears you could probably afford me. But I don't want your money. That private detective will want to be paid, of course, and I'll bill you for that. I pay Madison out of pocket. She's my daughter, so I take good care of her. There could be court costs you'll have to take care of, if it gets that far."

"You don't want any money?"

"Nope. I'm retiring again. I want to go out with a case that really exposes a couple of these folks. Don't get me wrong. The vast majority of social workers do a tough job in impossible conditions, usually dealing with the worst of the worst. Often, their hands are tied by the bureaucracy and the state. They love kids, and they want to help. That's why they went into this line of work.

"But there are a couple of 'em right here in our region that just don't need to be in this job. And one of them happens to be Lynn Roberts. I've had my share of run-ins with her. And I've won every single time. She has it out for me, and I've got it out for her."

"You don't even know me," Trixie said. "Why's this so important to you?"

"Got my first taste of this when Madison went through an ugly divorce. Got uglier when her ex filed for custody of my granddaughter. He made up all kinds of stories and got FPS involved. That's when I came out of retirement. And that was when I first laid eyes on Ms. Roberts."

Trixie sipped her water and wiped her lips. "This is personal for you then."

"As personal as it gets. My first goal, of course, is just to make this go away before it ever gets ugly. But if it gets ugly, then I'm bringing my ugly stick. There is one thing I need you to do though."

"Anything."

"You got a smart phone?"

"Yes, sir."

"You know how to use it to record conversations?"

"No, sir."

"I don't either. Give Madison a call and she'll walk you through it. I want you to record everything that FPS worker says if she calls or comes to visit. But don't let her know you're recording. Keep it on the downlow. Then you text that recording to Madison immediately. Every time."

"Ain't that illegal?"

"We are blessed to live in the wondrous State of Texas, which is single-party consent. That means if you consent to recording your own conversations, you don't have to tell the other party. It's only a crime if you record it without giving your own consent. Don't think anyone's ever been charged with that."

Trixie took another sip then cleared her throat to get Mason's attention away from the window. It didn't work.

"Mason," she said, snapping him back to the conversation. "Have you filled in Mr. Armstrong about my, um, situation?"

"I told him about you winning the lottery and that I'm handling your finances. I told him we sent out those letters just before this started with protective services. And, um—"

Armstrong jumped in. "We don't have any proof of anything like that, of course — that's what the PI is for. But I thought it was an interesting thread we need to follow. There's even been rumors, never proven, that this Roberts woman has tried to shake down any parents who were well off enough to have a tree to shake. Just gossip, but where there's smoke, ya know. And she probably knows you've got a tree worth shaking."

"Did Mason fill you in on my previous career?"

"Yes, ma'am, he informed me you were a sex worker, but that's behind you. Never understood why that's illegal anyway. A woman can give it away, no problem. A voluntary exchange between two consenting adults? Shouldn't be nobody's business."

"I just figured if word had gotten out about that, child services might think that's not a suitable home for a boy, or I'm not a fit mother."

"Our approach to that topic is it's all in the past and not worth discussing. Maybe you used to do drugs or you used to drink too much. They'd be hard pressed take your boy away for something you used to do. And it could be some of both. Someone out to get money from you, so they're using your past to prod FPS. You think any of your former clientele would do something like this?"

"I don't think so. I was very selective. Any of my old customers would have as much to lose as I do by making it public. That was one of my requirements."

Mason finally joined the conversation. "And there's also this Ellis Shackelford character you've alluded to."

"The ex-boyfriend?" the attorney asked.

"I guess you'd call him that. Back when I was thirteen to fifteen. He's the father of my boy. He was already a legal adult back then. But we reached an agreement before Ty was born. I wouldn't give up his name to law enforcement, and he'd sign over all parental rights and responsibilities and never bother me again. Then he kept showing up at my place, usually drunk, and I got a restraining order. Told him if he didn't stop, I'd file charges for statutory rape. Statute of limitations ain't up yet."

"Yeah, you can file a criminal complaint against him for twenty years after your eighteenth birthday, so you're holding a pretty big sword over his neck."

"Hadn't really bothered me too much in a while, but since I won Powerball, he's showin' up real regular. He was there, drunk as usual, when the social worker visited the first time. He told her he was the father, and Ty overheard him. I had to explain all that stuff to my boy."

Armstrong wrote in his little leather-bound notebook that fit in a jacket pocket. "That's good to know. He basically admitted to committing child sex crimes in front of an officer of the state."

"If Ellis is behind this, I know he just wants money."

"He won't be getting any," Armstrong said, "but he might find himself a guest of the State of Texas in one of their fine hospitality suites. I'll have the PI check on him. Might even pay him a visit, have a little conversation."

"Ellis is as stubborn as a dead mule."

"My detective can be a very convincing fellow."

CHAPTER 16

Another week gone by, no problems with Tyler at school as long as he remembered to turn in his homework, no visits from a social worker or Ellis, and no responses to the due diligence letters. Another Ladies' Society Circle meeting, this time at Reagan Hale's house.

Chief Hale and Reagan, along with their four stairstep boys, from infant to six years old, lived in a modest home, comfortable but tight quarters given the size of their brood. Certainly nothing to compare to the Reeves's McMansion, or even Marion's Victorian museum. The ladies all congregated in the living room with extra chairs brought in from the kitchen. Trixie decided she'd need to start arriving a few minutes early to get one of the comfortable seats for a change.

Surprisingly, or maybe not, Bee changed seats to sit next to Trixie and patted her arm like they were best buds.

What's she up to this time?

Trixie had hoped Shelby would sit next to her, but she came in a moment too late and had to take Bee's previous seat, the comfortable easy chair on the other side of the room. Trixie had thought about moving there when Bee had sat beside her but decided that would look rude.

Marion called the meeting to order, and it went through the normal and prompt routine, except Bee asked to save her treasurer's report for last.

Reagan updated everyone on the social media campaign to promote the Cast-Off Clothing Sale, which had generated forty-three interactions, including three people promising to donate clothing — folks who'd never donated before, two of whom said they'd never heard of this annual sale, now in its sixty-third year. The Circle was duly impressed.

Trixie let the group know she'd be donating a closetful of stuff she never wore anymore, along with a couple boxes of stuff Ty had outgrown.

Shelby and Angelina each had a list of names of local women they thought should be recruited to join the Circle. They read through the list, giving a brief bio of each one, to see if anyone had any objections. Apparently, it required unanimous consent to even approach someone.

Bee sniffed at a few of the names but didn't object to any of them. Cass was concerned about a couple of them, pointing out so-and-so was on her fourth marriage and was flighty, ditzy, and unreliable, and the other was rude to her in the grocery store once. When questioned by Marion, Cass couldn't recall exactly when that rude behavior was exhibited, but somewhere around the time of the big ice storm that took down some power lines and collapsed the roof at Walmart. Marion pointed out that was seventeen years ago.

The list of prospective members included members of First Church, a couple of Methodists, a Baptist, and one from Agape Community Church. Angelina asked if anyone knew any Catholics or Mormons they should be recruiting. Bee sniffed that their charter called the Circle a "a Christian women's organization," so that excluded Catholics and Mormons.

Marion pointed out that Catholics and Mormons were Christian. Bee wasn't convinced but let it go.

"One thing we have to keep in mind," Marion added, "is that this group was founded in an era when most women did not work outside the home. They kept house, raised children, and did volunteer work. That's not true anymore. The vast majority of women in this town have jobs outside the home. That makes it more difficult to find new members who have the time and resources to commit. A few of you are fortunate enough not to have to work."

"You always worked," Cass said.

"Yes, Fred and I had that newspaper to run. Some years, I worked part-time, especially when the children were small. But my hours were always flexible and being in a civic group was considered part of my job."

Marion looked around the room. "So is Shelby the only one here who has a full-time job?"

Angelina looked offended. "Being a pastor's wife is a full-time job. I'm executive assistant down at the church, plus all the services and events I'm expected to attend. At least Shelby can work whatever hours she wants to, and all from the comfort of her home."

Reagan wasn't going to be diminished by not working outside the home. "Raising four boys is a full-time job. I'm homeschooling the oldest two. Plus, I'm social media director for the church and the Circle, both volunteer positions. We made the financial sacrifice to live on Travis's salary so I could fulfill the duties of a full-time wife and mother."

Reagan hadn't quite been fulfilling all the full-time wife duties since the chief had hired a part-timer to assist with at least one of those chores, but Trixie immediately felt guilty for even allowing such a thought to cross her mind, and in Reagan's home, no less.

"Being married to the bank president comes with a lot of time-consuming obligations as well," Cass said.

The meeting momentarily spun out of control as everyone talked at once, each trying to sound busier than the next. Marion's face turned red and she waved her hands, trying to get everyone's attention. She looked unaccustomed to veering from the orderly agenda to disorderly chaos.

"I wasn't saying y'all aren't busy little beavers," Marion said just loud enough to be heard over the commotion. "I'm just saying that historically in this group, and most of you today, don't have a forty-hour workweek or more and then go home to take care of your house and raise children and take care of your husband and business-related obligations on top of that. This group has usually consisted of the wives of local businessmen and community leaders in the past. For funding, we relied heavily on donations from the businesses owned by our husbands. But the world has changed. That makes recruiting new members and fundraising more difficult today than it was a hundred years ago. Bee, don't you agree with me?"

"How old do you think I am?"

Trixie wasn't sure if Bee had just made a joke or not.

Reagan said, "We let Trixie join, and she doesn't have to work for a living. But I guess we don't have a lot of Powerball winners in town we can approach."

The room fell silent. The unspoken had been said out loud.

After an uncomfortable moment, Trixie said, "Yes, the Lord has definitely blessed me in a wholly unexpected way. But I also run a farm, raise a boy—just one, not four, mind you—and I run a philanthropic foundation. So that all keeps me pretty busy, to say the least, but I'm still excited enough about this group to find the time to contribute."

Bee fluttered her hand at Marion to get her attention. "This might be a good time for me to jump in with the treasurer's report, don't you think?"

"I think it's a perfect time for someone to jump in with something," Marion agreed. "Bee, the floor is yours."

For the first time in the few meetings Trixie had attended, Bee stood to give her report. She reached into her oversized purse and pulled out a manila folder.

"Since our last meeting, we've had no income and no expenses, so nothing to report there. However, we have a request from the Victoria

Burnet Foundation..." Bee paused and nodded to Trixie with a smile, "to provide some financial information in order to apply for a grant. I want to thank Trixie for this wonderful opportunity for the Ladies' Society Circle."

"Exactly how big is this grant?" Angelina asked.

Shelby couldn't have wiped the grin off her face with a belt sander.

Before Trixie could reply, Bee answered. "The amount is still to be determined by the foundation's board of directors. But they indicate in their letter that it would be 'substantial.'"

"Whatever that means," Reagan said.

Trixie was pretty sure Reagan rolled her eyes like a teenager. She really wanted to give her a good slap, but fortunately was out of arm's reach.

"As the foundation states in their letter, the size of the grant may be partially determined by the transparency and accountability of our response to their due diligence request. I've spent the better part of the past two weeks trying to piece together the information they've asked for. We don't have all the detailed records they've requested, but I've done my best. It's all here in the folder—bank statements, income, expenses, donations, projects, scholarships—everything I could retrieve from my files, from the bank, and from our scrapbook."

Bee looked downright pleased with herself.

"With the group's approval, I would like to submit this packet of materials to Trixie to take back to her board of directors. And I'd like to thank Trixie for her generosity and charitable heart to consider our little group."

"Why go through all this rigmarole?" Reagan wasn't through yet. "If she wants to donate to the group, she can just write a check like the rest of us."

Marion said, "I think this might be a bit more substantial than what any of us donate with a check. I don't know how much we're talking about, but maybe even an ongoing sustaining gift, if that's possible. Think of how much good we could do in the community if we were more fully funded."

"I don't want to mislead anyone into thinking this might be an ongoing thing every year," Trixie said. "It's one year at a time. The foundation may want to spread it around to different groups each year."

"Oh, of course," Marion said. "I didn't mean to overstep."

Marion looked a bit chastised, which made Trixie feel guilty. She hoped she hadn't corrected her too sharply.

"But an annual gift is a possibility, I suppose," Trixie added to soften the moment. "We just haven't gotten that far out yet."

Reagan wasn't ready to let it go. "I'm not sure how comfortable I am with the Circle accepting a large sum of money from ill-gotten gains."

Marion quickly rejoined Trixie's defense team. "How is being fortunate in the lottery ill-gotten gains?"

Reagan looked chastised now. She shut up but looked around the room for support.

Cass came to her rescue. "What I think Reagan means is that the lottery is gambling. I know our pastor preaches against gambling, against the lottery. Would we accept a large donation if one of our members was a drug dealer? A mafia godfather?"

"Oh, this is such bullshit," said the pastor's wife. "Comparing winning the lottery to being in the mafia? Seriously, Cass."

"Your husband is the one who preached against it. Told us we should vote against back when they put it on the ballot."

"Well, it passed anyway. It's run by the State of Texas. It's perfectly legal. And I buy a ticket every week."

Reagan found her tongue again, behind quivering lips and a red face. "We all know what she did for a living before she won Powerball."

"That's enough, Reagan," Marion fired across the room with a blaze in her eyes.

But Reagan didn't let it go. "How do we know she's not donating her whore profits?"

There it was.

Trixie swallowed the lump in her throat but couldn't stop the blood rushing to her face. All she could look at was her lap, where her hands wrestled with each other. She wanted to grab her purse and run out the door, but her feet wouldn't move. Her butt was glued to the seat. The silence descended with as much weight as if a cement truck had filled the room with concrete. It didn't sound like anyone was even breathing.

Trixie glanced across the room to her new friend.

Tears welled in Shelby's eyes, her face like she'd just seen a horrific car accident. She stared at Trixie, mouth open, stunned. Unmoving, like everyone else in the room.

Shelby turned slowly to face Reagan, who looked like she'd just swallowed a frog, like she really hadn't meant for those words to slip from her mouth. At least Trixie could relate to that.

Shelby held her fiery glare until Reagan turned to look at her. "How dare you, you stupid bitch. That's not true."

"Shelby," Trixie quietly interrupted, her voice quivering more than she wanted it to. "I ain't denyin' it."

Marion broke in before more words could fly. "Reagan, at next week's meeting, after you've had time to cool down and evaluate your hurtful words here today, you need to offer a heartfelt apology to Trixie in front of our group. Either that or submit your resignation from the Circle. I will not tolerate that kind of hatefulness from anyone, not even from someone I cherish as much as I do you."

Now it was Reagan's turn to cry.

While everyone's attention had turned to Trixie, she decided it was as good a time as any to clear the air. For good or bad, she'd say her piece. She quickly pledged to herself that she'd get through it without shedding a single tear. She wasn't a crier like Shelby and Reagan, and she wasn't going to start now.

"What Reagan said is true. Was true. I was in a bad spot several years ago. Made some bad decisions." Trixie hesitated, trying to keep her words under control. *Think first, figure out what you're gonna say before you say it.* She gradually lifted her face up to look around the room at the women, all sitting in a circle and staring at her. Except Reagan, who was now the one with her head down.

"All my own fault, I know." Trixie sat up a bit straighter and cleared her throat, willing her voice to speak without shaking. "I ain't blamin' nobody else. I knew it was wrong too. My momma raised me better 'n that. But I did it, I ain't proud of it, but I ain't gonna be ashamed of it neither. And it's one of those things that once you start, you can't get out of it. I prayed to the Lord for a way out. And He heard my prayers. He provided me that way out. Now all I want to do is help others who need help, like I did. The Lord blessed me with more than I can ever use, so I figured it could be used to bless a whole lot more folks."

When Trixie paused, Marion asked, "Trixie, why are you here? Don't get me wrong. I'm glad you're here. But you don't need us. Why did you ask to join this little group of women, and then subject yourself to this kind of reception?"

Trixie took a moment to look around the circle and meet each woman's eyes. Shelby's, which looked heartsick. Cass, aloof. Bee, worried. Reagan wouldn't even glance up to acknowledge she was in the same room. Trixie thought Angelina might come over to give her a hug any moment. Marion had the kindest eyes Trixie'd ever seen.

"I'd heard of this Ladies' Circle all my life," Trixie said, "and how much good a devoted group of society women could do in our community. My momma looked up to you people like you was a bunch of saints. When I was little, I dreamed of being in this group, to sit around and sip tea from hand-painted china and dole out money to worthy causes and needy people. But I knew better than to think I'd ever actually be here. But here I am. I've changed my life and now I'm here tryin' to help change other lives too. If you'll let me."

The room went silent again, other than Reagan and Shelby both sniffling and trying to restrain sobs.

"Marion," Angelina said, "I believe we were considering Bee's proposal to submit the paperwork to Trixie's wonderful foundation."

Marion shook her head and looked down a moment, like she was praying or trying to shake off the cobwebs after getting punched in the back of the head.

"Yes, let's set this ugliness aside. We'll deal with that later. Do I hear a motion to accept Bee's proposal and submit this paperwork to the Victoria Burnet Foundation?"

"So moved," Angelina said.

"Seconded," Shelby said, her voice shaking, tears flowing.

"Trixie, you will need to recuse yourself from voting on this since it's related to your donation. All in favor, raise your hand."

Four hands went up. Only Cass and Reagan kept their hands firmly on their laps.

"By my count, the motion passes four to two. Bee, you are hereby authorized to submit our paperwork as requested by the Victoria Burnet Foundation. Cass, please duly note the vote in the meeting minutes."

Bee handed the folder full of due diligence to Trixie.

Cass jotted the vote down in her notes, then said, "I want to add for the record that I'm still not comfortable accepting tainted funds."

Marion nearly came out of her chair.

"Cass Reeves, you think we should only take good, clean, pure, sinless money? We shouldn't be taking lottery money, or drug money, or mafia money, right? Well, maybe we shouldn't be taking money that was generated by the slave trade and handed down generation after generation through a family of bankers. No one's ever complained about that before. Maybe we shouldn't be taking any of Bee's money since our good mayor inherited his wealth from his great-grandfather embezzling from the railroad. Or maybe this group wants to return every dime I've given since Fred's grandfather bought that newspaper ninety years ago with profits from running moonshine during the Prohibition.

"And Reagan, your money is good and clean. Your husband is paid with tax dollars. Taxes paid on lottery winnings and profits from businesses that were started with money from immoral activities, money we all married into or inherited. Every one of us in this room won the lottery, one way or the other, ill-gotten gains all."

Trixie had seen a deer in the headlights before, but the Circle looked like a whole herd caught in the lights of a Friday night football game.

"Seeing there's no other business, do I hear a motion to adjourn?"

"So moved," everyone said at once.

"Seconded," they all said.

"Adjourned," Marion said. "I know we all like to sit around and gab after our meetings, but I'm too tired and pained by all this mess." She stood and brushed the wrinkles from her skirt, then headed out the front door, looking much frailer than Trixie had ever noticed before.

Reagan sat paralyzed in the La-Z-Boy, forgetting her hostessing duties to show her guests to the door or offer some coffee cake.

With Marion in the lead, it was a mad rush to the door. No one wanted to be the last one in the room with Reagan. Especially not Trixie. She'd hate to have to explain to Tyler how she got in a fistfight with the police chief's wife at a Ladies' Society Circle meeting.

***

Shelby and Angelina stood by Marion's car, talking to her through the open driver's side window. Shelby waved Trixie over.

Trixie hesitated. She just wanted to go home, maybe curl up in bed with a good book. She walked over tentatively. What would Shelby think of her new best friend now? Or former best friend. Trixie was just getting accustomed to the idea of having a best girlfriend again.

Shelby immediately embraced Trixie in a sobbing hug.

Angelina rested her hand on Trixie's back, patting it like a mother whose child had hurt feelings from bullies at school.

Marion reached out the car window and gripped Trixie's upper arm. "I'm so sorry you had to endure that vicious attack. That was so uncalled for. For the first time in my life, I am ashamed of the Circle."

Shelby pulled back a bit to end the hug, started to say something, then burst into tears again and fell into another embrace.

"Look," Angelina said, "we can't stand out here in Reagan's driveway blubbering all over each other. Let's go somewhere."

"Y'all come to my house," Marion said. "Right now."

Trixie peeled away from Shelby, who released reluctantly and wiped her face.

Trixie climbed into her car and followed the others, bringing up the rear. She'd held it together in the face of being attacked by Reagan and, to a somewhat lesser extent, Cass. She kept her emotions in check while Shelby got snot all over Trixie's new blouse. But a block from Reagan's house, she had to pull over. Her vision blurred as the tears poured. She hadn't had a good cry since before Daddy died. She couldn't cry at his funeral, and she'd never allowed herself to cry since. *If you can't cry when your daddy dies, then there ain't much else worth cryin' over.*

She would have preferred to unleash this torrent at home alone, not parked in a neighborhood where people might look out their front curtains and wonder why this hooker was sitting in a Corvette having a complete breakdown.

***

Marion opened the door as Trixie reached for the doorbell. "I was about to come looking for you. Shelby tried calling but you didn't answer. You were right behind us. What happened?"

"I had to make a stop." Trixie hoped her eyes weren't too puffy and red. She didn't need anyone making a fuss over her.

Marion had saved the comfiest chair for Trixie as they gathered in the same room where the Circle had met a couple weeks earlier. Marion asked who wanted coffee then wandered off to make a pot before anyone answered.

Shelby pulled her chair closer to Trixie and reached over to hold her hand. She'd apparently made a trip to the bathroom to wash off the makeup that had bled all over her face.

"Before you got here," Angelina said while Marion was in the kitchen, "we chatted a bit, and we all want you to know we've got your back. We're here for you. We support you. Don't let those witches bring you down. You're better than them."

Marion walked in with four cups on a tray. "I just assumed everyone needed some. Cream, sugar?"

With the four of them seated, sipping and stirring, stirring and sipping, it felt like a Circle meeting before everyone had shown up.

"First of all," Marion broke the ice, "I want to apologize for earlier."

"You've got nothing to apologize for," Angelina said. "You can't apologize on behalf of those two idiots."

"Not apologizing on their behalf. For me. For how I handled it. I was so stunned, I didn't know what to say, and I didn't say something fast enough. Then I lost my cool. I'm supposed to be running that meeting, and I lost control."

Marion turned to Trixie. "Please forgive me for taking too long to put a stop to that mess. I just don't know what to do about Reagan."

"Angelina's right," Shelby said. "You have nothing to apologize for. You handled it better than any of the rest of us would have."

"I might have punched her in the throat," Angelina said. "Not very Christian of me, I know, but I'm thankful you were running the meeting, not me. I can't remember the last time I was this angry."

Trixie pulled free of Shelby's hand and walked over to Marion. She leaned down and gave her a hug. "They're right. You didn't do nothin' that needs forgivin', but if it helps you feel better, I forgive you for not punchin' Reagan in the throat."

The laughter broke the tension. Shelby laughed through a few more tears.

"It doesn't surprise me greatly that Reagan would act like that," Marion said. "She's always trying too hard. She thinks she has to act all high-class around us, trying to fit in with whatever it is she thinks we are. We've been fortunate, lucky, blessed, whatever you want to call it, so we've dedicated this group to helping people who need a hand. Not because we're better than others. Because we're the same, and one small change in life's circumstances, and any one of us would be on the other end, needing help rather than having the resources to help."

"And Cass," Shelby said. "She might be my future mother-in-law. She's always been rather aloof, but I've never seen her treat anyone like this."

"Mother-in-law?" Angelina said. "Is there something you haven't told us?"

"Shh. It's a secret. We haven't told anyone yet, so please don't let that leave this room. Well, I told Trixie. But now I'm wondering if it's the right decision. Do I really want to become a member of that family?"

"You're not marrying her," Marion said. "And like you, I've never seen Cass be quite that rude. I'm not sure why she was supporting Reagan. She doesn't even like Reagan. We had to talk her out of blackballing her membership. I'm extremely disappointed in Cass, given what I know about her."

Another moment of silence fell on the room until Trixie finally asked the question the rest were thinking. "What is it you know about Cass?"

"No, I've said too much already. Just suffice to say I'm surprised she would act this way given her youthful indiscretions."

Angelina laughed. "Well, if you're not going to tell us, quit dropping breadcrumbs to whet our appetite. You know you want to. Spill it, girl."

"It's just, well, it was a long time ago. And I don't care. I never did care, and even if I had, I would have gotten over it thirty years ago. But it's just surprising that Cass would take such a hard line against Trixie for having been a, uh, in the...um. Trixie, what do we say that won't be taken as offensive, because I certainly wouldn't mean it that way?"

"I referred to it as my personal services bid'ness."

The room erupted in a laughter as healing as it was raucous. "That's pretty personal," Angelina said. "I like that."

"Sounds better than sex worker," Shelby said. "Wait, are you saying Cass used to be in the sex... personal services industry?"

"Now keep in mind, this was a long time ago. Times might have been different then, but men weren't much different than they ever are. And Cass was quite the looker in her heyday. Came from a poor family. Her father abandoned the family, then her mother wound up in an asylum — drugs, alcohol, mental illness. Cass went to live with an aunt, who was apparently quite a stern woman."

"I've heard some of this, but not all of it," Shelby said. "I don't know if Austin knows all of this."

"Oh, I'm sure Austin doesn't know the half of it," Marion added. "Cass wanted to move out but had no money. She found some jobs, but there was no opportunity in this little town for a poor seventeen-year-old girl who dropped out of high school."

Trixie was confused. Were they talking about Cass still, or about her?

"So," Marion continued, "Cass took a job dancing at the gentleman's club just north of town. The one they shut down a few years back, but it did a great business back in the day."

Shelby's shocked face was getting a workout today. "Cass Reeves? Wife of bank president Lamar Reeves? Was a stripper?"

"She was indeed. And I remember enough about her from those days to know she was drop-dead gorgeous. Any man would pay a dollar to see her take her clothes off, no doubt about it. And that's where she met Lamar."

"What?" Shelby's mouth wouldn't shut.

Angelina started laughing hysterically.

"Now y'all swear none of this leaves this room," Marion said. "I'm not gossiping here. I'm just providing the back story so you can understand why Cass's behavior concerned me so."

"Kettle, meet pot," Shelby said.

"Lamar's friends took him to the strip joint to celebrate his engagement. That's right, he was engaged to be married. Daughter of the plastics company owner. Can't recall her name. A nice enough girl, a bit plain and not too bright, but a marriage made in the financial reports, that's for sure. Then he sees Cass on stage and goes ga-ga over her. His friends pooled their money and paid for a private dance, where the girl takes the guy in the back room and gets totally nude. They always had to wear a little something on stage. Supposedly nothing else happened back in those rooms, just dancing, but I doubt it was all on the up-and-up."

"Cass Reeves, pole dancer." Angelina managed to get out one sentence and she lost it again.

"I know she's got two kids," Shelby said, "but it's hard to even imagine that woman agreeing to make love with her husband with the lamp on, let alone take her clothes off on stage in front of an audience."

"Lamar was smitten," Marion said. "Asked her out that night. And the next. Broke off his engagement six months before the wedding and two weeks after the engagement announcement had published in the paper. Lamar and Cass eloped to Vegas and got married on the same day he was supposed to wed that plastics gal."

"No wonder Lamar's momma never accepted her," Shelby said.

Angelina pulled herself together enough to ask, "How do you know all this?"

"Honey, Fred and I ran that newspaper for half a century. We know all the stories that weren't fit to print."

"Bee is the one who surprised me the most," Angelina said. "For such a stiff old coot with her nose in the air, she suddenly gets downright cozy with Trixie. I'm glad, but that's the one I thought might be the biggest problem."

"That's because Bee is all about the money," Marion said, then turned to Trixie, who'd been listening to this whole conversation without much to say. "Bee is trying to butter you up because she wants that donation from your foundation. Of course, we all do. It would be a wonderful thing, and we could do so much good with whatever amount they see fit to provide us. But as treasurer, that's Bee's whole focus. As it should be, I guess, but her attitude toward you shifted once she learned about the possible donation."

"I just want to do something good and be a part of something good. Y'all are something good. And I thought a donation might help everyone accept me, especially given my background. If the money helps change someone's attitude about me, that's fine. Then I can win them over as time goes by."

Marion sipped her coffee and thought for a moment. The rest of the room could see the wheels turning, Marion being her thoughtful self, trying to think of the right words, so everyone stayed quiet and gave her space to think.

"I understand why you might feel that way," she said. "But be careful. Some people will accept you for you, as we in this room do. Some people won't accept you no matter what. Maybe that's Reagan. Some might come around, and I'm hoping that's Cass. She's better than this. And then some will pretend to come around just because of your money, like Bee. Proceed with caution with that one. Don't try to win people over with a donation. Don't you think that sounds suspiciously like being on the other side of one of your personal services arrangements? Guy offers to pay a girl some money so she'll pretend to like him for a few minutes, but she doesn't really. Did any of those men ever win you over because they paid you? You don't really want to be them, do you?"

That one hit Trixie right between the eyes. Marion had a way of saying just the right thing after she thought about her words a moment. Trixie wanted to learn that skill.

Everyone seemed to take a breather to absorb Marion's wisdom, to let the tension of the morning fade away, to enjoy each other's company in silence.

Then Shelby started giggling. She tried to suppress it when everyone looked at her.

"Go on and share," Angelina prodded. "You picturing Cass in a g-string?"

"Oh Lord, no. I have to have lunch with Austin today and that image would put me off my food."

"Then what?" Angelina pushed a little more. "Can't have secrets among this group. That should be obvious by now."

"You know," Marion said. "I agree with Angelina. If it was funny enough to make you laugh in the middle of this garbage, we could all use a chuckle. Your turn to spill."

Shelby giggled again like a schoolgirl. She struggled to find the words. She glanced nervously at Trixie and giggled again.

"It's just... I was wondering... I shouldn't ask though..."

"Spit it out," Angelina demanded.

Shelby turned to Trixie. "You mentioned you've got a lot of clothes to donate to the Cast-Off Sale. I was just wondering, exactly which clothes are you talking about?"

Marion exhaled an audible gasp and started shaking in her chair, trying to hold in the laughter. Angelina didn't even attempt to hold it in. Shelby lost it at that point.

And so did Trixie.

The four of them laughed long and loud for a minute or two. Once they'd mostly calmed down, Angelina turned to Trixie. "Well?"

"Yeah, okay, I have a closet full of, uh, um... personal services attire."

Marion said, "I want to see Bee's face when she sorts through that stack."

Angelina slipped off her chair and sat on the floor, doubled over, barely able to breathe.

"I wasn't gonna donate the crotchless panties," Trixie said, "but I'm reconsidering that decision now."

"You know," Angelina said to Trixie after the group became a bit more subdued, "I'm so jealous of you. And I don't mean about the money. I mean, even before, and I understand why you gave it up after the lottery, but what a life. Men come to you, they pay you, then they go home. How desirable you are. I'm forty-five years old, and I try my best to take care of myself and be desirable to my husband, but, well, the good reverend's just not interested anymore. He's older, pushing sixty, but shouldn't that make me look young and attractive to him? What's wrong with me?"

"There's nothing wrong with you," Marion said before Trixie could answer. "There's obviously something wrong with him if he's not attracted to you."

Trixie added, "You're beautiful. Any man would be interested in you. I think sometimes something happens after a couple are together for a number of years. They grow so accustomed to each other, they just don't see each other that way anymore. From my experience, it seems it's more often the wife that loses interest, which was good for my bid'ness. But sometimes it's the other way around, or it's just mutual. I don't know why."

"I can't imagine that ever happening to me and Austin. We can barely keep our hands off each other now. Our purity vows are sure on thin ice some days."

"Your what?" Angelina said. "You guys still doing that? Or should I say, not doing that?"

"We've talked about it. Decided we've both waited this long, let's just keep on. Maybe one more year. Although some days, I don't know if I can hold off any longer. It gets harder every time."

"Oh, I bet it does." Angelina started cackling again. "Harder and harder. You made a promise back in high school. That was to get you to adulthood without getting pregnant. I think you can safely set that aside now."

Trixie didn't think that was the right advice, especially coming from the preacher's wife. "I think it's sweet. And if they've waited this long, they can go a little longer. That will make their wedding night so incredibly special. I never had that special night. I was thirteen, in a pickup truck."

"Thirteen?" Marion and Shelby said in unison.

"You and Austin aren't thirteen anymore," Angelina said. "You're both adults. You're in a committed relationship and plan on getting married. Get it while you can as often as you can. It won't last forever. You push out a couple of babies, add thirty pounds and some cellulite, and Austin will suddenly get very busy down at the bank. Too busy to come home on time, too tired to do anything when he gets home. You'll be so exhausted from taking care of the babies, you'll be relieved he's not interested. But then, those kids grow up and move out, and you're staring at a middle-aged guy who forgot why he couldn't keep his hands off you."

Marion disagreed. "It doesn't have to be that way. It wasn't with me and Fred. Well, we went through periods, sometimes long stretches, where intimacy wasn't as important as it was before. But we'd find ways to rekindle that romance. I'm proud to say we had an active love life well into our seventies, until Fred got sick."

Angelina smiled at Marion. "That's sweet. I wish I had that, but I don't. I wouldn't have the nerve to actually do it, but having men find me so attractive they'd pay me to spend the night with them with no further obligations sounds kind of ideal."

"I can't believe you're jealous of me," Trixie said. "All I ever wanted was what y'all have. A home and a family. Ever since Daddy died and Momma kinda lost her shit, our family was gone. I'll never have that. I wouldn't even care if sex wasn't part of it anymore. It ain't all it's cracked up to be. I just wanted a family again. And I have that with my boy. No, there ain't no daddy in the picture, and I don't care. It's me and Ty against the world."

"You do have a family," Shelby said. "But it's not just you and Ty anymore. You've got us too."

CHAPTER 17

"Why do I hafta go to school on Sunday? I go to school all week."

Getting Ty up and ready for Sunday School, an hour earlier than for the worship service, proved more of a battle than she had energy for. "Fine," she told him. "But we're still going to church, so get your butt out of bed."

"We goin' with Mr. Garza again?"

"No, we're going back to our church this week."

"It's boring."

"Sunday School would be fun, but you don't want to get movin' fast enough. Don't make us late to worship service too."

***

Trixie brought a pad of paper and pencil for Ty to doodle on during the sermon. Figured that was better than him fidgeting or falling asleep.

After the service ended, Trixie looked for a side exit to avoid standing in line to shake the pastor's hand, but the crowd funneled her and Ty into the line like loading cattle into a truck. No avoiding it.

"Good morning, young man," Rev. Webb said, shaking Ty's hand. He placed his other hand on Trixie's shoulder and pulled her a little closer. "Our trustees met this week to consider your generous proposal and have agreed to apply for a grant. I am so pleased that we're included in your plans. You should hear from Lamar and Jasper this week. We're so pleased to have you join our flock and support the Lord's work here."

Trixie gave her memorized spiel about the decision being up to the board and moved on as quickly as she could, thankful this time for Ty pulling her hand to leave.

***

Sunday evening, Clay joined Trixie and Ty for supper. Ty suggested they invite him. Trixie served chicken fried steak with mashed potatoes and gravy, and a can of green beans that she doctored up with some seasonings. After the dishes were washed and stacked, Ty went to his bedroom to watch TV for an hour before bath time. Trixie and Clay sat in the living room with their coffee rather than their usual spot at the kitchen table. Trixie sat on the couch and let Clay take her daddy's recliner. She should've got rid of it years ago but just couldn't. The fabric was worn clean through in spots, the frame collapsing on one side, the seat so flattened she'd set a throw pillow on it to provide some cushion. She'd never wanted to part with it because it had smelled like Daddy, but his scent had faded years ago.

"I'm going to go look at that house again. I think it would be perfect for Ty."

"What does Ty think?"

Why's he always ask about Ty's opinion? He's just a boy — he ain't got no say in this.

"He said he didn't like it, but he was in a mood. There's a park he can ride his bike to, the Christian school is close — and yeah, he hates that too. He's just that age to hate anything I suggest. He'll adjust. But what are you planning once I get moved out?"

"I'll probably pull the trailer up here next to the house to have a place to sleep while I fix this place up. I've got to get underneath and see what the foundation and floors look like."

"What if that's no good?"

"Then it might be easiest to tear the house down and start over."

"You know how to build a house?"

"Done it a couple of times. Got a few friends to help me out when I need a hand. Will take some time, just doing a little bit as I have time and money."

Trixie felt an unexpected sadness at the idea of the house being razed. She wouldn't blame Clay one bit if he just wanted to burn it to the ground, but still. There had been happier times. When Momma and Daddy danced in the living room to the stereo. When she and Daddy watched the Cowboys play on Sunday afternoons. She didn't have any interest in football, but sharing popcorn and a Coke while Daddy yelled at the TV was a good time. Helping Momma make supper and learning to cook from her.

"Ty, time to get in the tub."

Of course, he didn't get in the tub immediately. He ran downstairs to tell Clay goodnight before he bounded back up for the bathroom.

"That boy is enamored with you," Trixie said.

"I'm kind of taken with him too."

It had been a nice evening. A relaxing evening. No more drama. Just a nice supper, relaxing conversation, a good cup of coffee. But Clay was ready to head out, go get comfortable, and put his feet up in his trailer.

"Everybody missed you at church this morning," he said as he slipped on his hat and headed to the door. "Said to tell you hello. Shelby really wants to poach you from First Church. Brother Kent and Harris still want to have you out for lunch or supper one day. Maybe you'll have time this week."

"That would be great. I've got a few meetings, but I know I can work y'all in. Let me know what day works best."

Trixie walked him to the door. They stood just outside the screen in the dark, only one porchlight to create a little visibility, the evening air starting to take on an early fall chill for the first time. October tomorrow. About time the heat broke. In knee-length jean shorts and a t-shirt, barefoot, a shiver hit Trixie.

"You better get back inside. Coolin' off out here. And thank you again for a nice meal. I don't get a lot of home-cooked suppers."

He patted Trixie on the shoulder, and she reached up to give his hand a squeeze.

"You're welcome, anytime. You should join us more often rather than eating fast food out in that trailer."

Clay leaned in and left a soft kiss on Trixie's cheek, a friendly thank you peck, gentleman-like. She returned a kiss to his cheek while she could still reach it, before he stood back up to full height. Their hands hadn't let go. They stood there a couple of seconds, or maybe it was a couple of years. Trixie couldn't tell.

Clay kissed her again. On the mouth, holding both her hands. A gentle, sweet kiss.

She responded, kissing him back and squeezing his hands. A shiver ran up her back from tailbone to neck — from the cool breeze or the feel of his lips on hers, she wasn't sure. Then the thoughts started up.

Why was he kissing her? Why was she happy about it? Would he expect something more than just a kiss? She'd never been kissed by anyone other than Ellis and her customers, all of whom expected more than just a kiss.

Clay pulled away slowly, his eyes staying closed a moment after Trixie had opened hers.

"Well, I didn't mean to do that," he said. "I hope you're not mad."

Trixie hesitated, trying to be like Marion and think about what to say before she started talking. But no words would come to her.

"I did make you mad then."

"No, not mad at all. Just..." She'd never been kissed that way. Or that unexpectedly. She'd have to figure out how to tell him what she used to do for a living. She couldn't hide that, and if there was something going to come of this, she needed to tell him upfront. But if she told him, just how fast and how far would he run?

They still held hands, so Trixie just stretched up on her tiptoes to kiss him again.

"Ms. Burnet." A woman's voice from the dark startled them both.

Lynn Roberts from social services.

In the living room with Clay, Ty's TV echoing down the stairs, they hadn't heard her car pull in or seen the headlights come up the drive.

"What are you doing here this time of night?" Trixie yelled. "Scared me to death. That's a good way to get shot 'round these parts."

"I thought you said you didn't have a gun. And it's only eight o'clock. I need to speak with you."

Clay let go of Trixie's hands. "We'll talk tomorrow. Or call me later if you need to chew me out for that. I'll apologize, if need be, even if I ain't all that sorry." He tipped his hat toward Ms. Roberts. "I was just leaving, ma'am."

Trixie stepped inside but didn't hold the door or invite Ms. Roberts in. "I'll be right back."

"May I come in?"

Trixie didn't answer. She retrieved her phone from the coffee table in the living room and followed Madison's instructions to start recording. Then she went upstairs, checked on Ty, and slipped on a hoodie with a large front pocket to hold the phone.

Trixie stepped through the screen door and joined Ms. Roberts outside. "My boy is taking a bath, so let's talk out here. What can I do for you?"

"Who was this gentleman caller?"

"Is that really any of your business?"

"To ensure a healthy home environment for a child, everything is my business. Every time I've stopped by, you've had a different man here."

"That ain't true. I was here alone once. And one of them wasn't invited or welcomed."

"My mistake. Two out of three visits, a different man in your home, one highly inebriated and starting a rather loud argument, and tonight, you're making out with a man while your son is upstairs in the tub. Seems to fit with the allegations we've received about your line of work.

If those reports are true, the state will take immediate steps to remove your son from this environment."

Armstrong had told her to not take the bait. But could this woman really take Ty away from her. Another shiver ran over her whole body, a different kind of chill than the breeze or Clay's kiss.

When Trixie relented and held the door open for her, Ms. Roberts made herself at home at the kitchen table. Trixie stood, refusing to offer any hint that she was welcome.

Ms. Roberts pulled out her notebook and had two more questions, innocuous questions about Ty's school and friends, like she'd come up with any excuse to just pop in unannounced. Trixie gave the briefest of nonresponses she could without being accused of being uncooperative.

Ty walked in, hair dripping, a towel wrapped around his waist. He froze for a moment then ran back upstairs, looking mortified that a strange woman had seen him nearly naked.

"I have a boy to get ready for bed and a big day tomorrow. If there's nothing else, let me show you out."

Ms. Roberts stuffed her notebook back in her bag and headed out the door.

"Do be careful," Trixie said. "Been a couple of bobcats roaming around out here at night. They've been getting braver about coming up to the house."

Trixie'd never seen a bobcat around here, but that little lie was worth the look of terror on Ms. Roberts's face as Trixie latched the screen door behind her and turned off the porchlight before she made it to her car.

She got Ty into bed, then remembered to stop the phone from recording. She sent it to Madison with an apology about the bobcat story and recording her goodnight song to Ty.

Trixie sat in the recliner and leaned back, looking at her phone. Her daddy's scent might be long gone, but Clay had left a trace of himself on the chair and on her lips. She pulled up his number but had no idea what she even wanted to say.

Instead, she texted Shelby, *we have to talk tomorrow*. She added emojis for a heart and a pair of puckered lips and a cowboy hat.

After thinking about what to say to Clay for a good half hour, she texted him.

good night sleep tight dont let the bedbugs bite

CHAPTER 18

Mason had turned off the useless air conditioner and cracked open a couple of windows, creating an enjoyable cross breeze, but any papers on the desk needed to be anchored down with a stapler, a pair of scissors, the Rolodex, or the desk phone.

"It's been an interesting few days going over the due diligence materials from these folks. You haven't made promises to anyone, have you?"

Trixie agreed to kill two birds with one stone, meeting first with Mason at his office at two o'clock, then meeting with Armstrong in Mason's conference room.

"No, I've been careful. Told everyone it was up to the board."

"That's good. This isn't going to be easy, but you need to hear it."

Mason pulled out a manila folder stuffed with random papers. The pages had paperclips and sticky notes attached that weren't there when Bee had handed the folder to Trixie.

"Let's start with the messy one. Ladies' Society Circle." Mason had finally gotten the name right. "Not just a messy folder. Horrible recordkeeping. I had to put everything in order, attach notes to figure it all out. Once I'd done that, I put together a spreadsheet to get it all onto one page where I could see it."

Mason pulled two sheets of paper from the top of the stack that was spilling onto his desk. "Here's a copy for you to follow along." He handed one to Trixie and kept one for himself.

"Mrs. Callahan has been the treasurer of the Circle for more than a decade," Mason said. "During that time, she's never produced formal weekly or monthly treasurer reports. Her attached letter of explanation was that it's a very small, informal group, so she would just give verbal reports at each meeting to update the group. If anyone needed or requested additional information, she would provide that. She called herself 'an open book' in her cover letter but noted that she isn't a professional accountant so records might not be all tidy like we'd want them. She offered to answer any questions we have by phone."

"I've seen her do her reports," Trixie said. "Not much happening though. They don't have a lot of money."

"No, not a lot there. I reviewed all their bank statements, deposits, and checks written over the past three years. There are annual membership dues. Three years ago, they had fifteen members. Back in its heyday, they had more than fifty. Down to six now."

"Seven," Trixie corrected. Her membership dues check wouldn't show up until the next bank statement. "I heard they'd lost a couple of members recently, but I didn't know it had gone down that far."

"I went through the membership rolls. In three years, they've had two members pass away, one moved into a nursing home. One moved away due to husband's job transfer. One moved out-of-state to be near her children when her husband died. Six just dropped their memberships — didn't renew, no reason given. They're still alive and still live in town. They've added two new members — Shelby Wheeler a few months ago and Reagan Hale last year. And now you."

"And they may be about to kick one out, so we'd be back to six again." Trixie related an abbreviated version, without all the details, of how Reagan had been rather rude at the last meeting and Marion gave her the ultimatum to apologize or resign. "I think it was all kinda traumatic for Marion."

"I can imagine. Marion is sweet as can be on the outside, tough as a drill sergeant on the inside. Can't picture her putting up with any nonsense. She's the one who made sure the newspaper made a profit while Fred wrote opinion columns and played a lot of golf. Surprises me she'd allow Bee to be so lax in her fiduciary responsibilities."

"Bee can be difficult. I think Marion just doesn't want to create any waves."

"Not the Marion I know, but she's got to be pushing eighty now, so maybe she's just not on top of stuff like she used to be."

"Eighty? She can't be that old." Trixie would have guessed Marion was late sixties, maybe early seventies.

"Close to it anyway. Got my first job out of college in the business office at the paper. They had to be in their forties back then, and that was thirty-five years ago."

"So back to this due diligence stuff," Trixie said, pulling Mason back to the present, away from his moment of nostalgia. Armstrong was due in less than an hour.

"Right. According to their bank statements, in the past three years, they've brought in about $33,000 in income through membership fees, donations, and their four annual fundraising events. They do the Cast-Off Clothing Sale every October."

"That's coming up the end of the month," Trixie said.

Mason reviewed the other events. Two bake sales, one in February, one in August. And the big one: the Annual Chili Cookoff at the county fair every June.

"Contestants pay an entry fee—these are mostly sponsored by local businesses. Customers buy a ticket to sample the different chilis, then they can donate to the bucket for their favorite chili. A panel of judges—local restaurant owners—vote on the best chili. The team that wins the judges' vote gets the trophy. The team that raises the most in donations gets a special certificate as the people's choice. Just a popularity contest, for the most part. But it can bring in a chunk of change, so it would seem."

Trixie followed the numbers on the spreadsheet. There were all the membership dues, with the names of each member for each year. There were the corporate and business donations, topped by First National Bank, which gave $5,000 a year—almost half of the Circle's total income.

"I would have thought they'd be bringing in more money than this," she said.

"As would I," Mason agreed. "Now skip down to the expenses."

Trixie looked over the scholarships—two at $2,500 each per year. Abused women and children shelter—$1,000. Another $2,000 each year to the food bank. Marketing expenses. Bank fees. County fair vendor fees. Church rental hall for the bake sale.

"That one ain't right," she said. "They said at the meeting that the church lets them use the hall at no charge."

"Good eye," Mason said. "But look back up at donations. You'll see a donation from the church for the same amount. It's an in-kind donation, so it's just an in-and-out entry. No money actually changes hands."

Trixie was a little embarrassed she didn't catch that herself.

"Overall," Mason said, "when you add it all up, balance the bank statements to the records, everything matches up. Deposits are all there. Their bank balance fluctuates greatly as money comes in and they give it away. They about break even every year, which is fine since they're a non-profit. Means they're giving everything away after expenses. Everything appears on the up-and-up. Until..." Mason paused as he flipped through more pages and newspapers clippings in the folder.

"Until? That don't sound good."

"It's not. Now keep in mind, some of this is a guess. But it's an educated guess. She included copies of these newspaper articles from the group's scrapbook, I guess to show all the good work they do. But something doesn't smell right."

Mason looked through some more papers, pulling out a page now and then.

"All the significant donations from businesses are by check. Those all match up with the bank statements and deposit slips. It's the cash deposits that concern me. A lot of donations—such as the clothing sale, the bake sale, the chili cookoff—are in cash. Small denominations. You stop by a bake sale and buy a cake for ten bucks. You go to the used clothing sale and buy a pair of shoes for five dollars. You're probably not writing a check or using a credit card. And there aren't any receipts. Someone hands over a ten-dollar bill for a pie, the money goes in the till, the treasurer counts up the money at the end of the day and makes a deposit."

"So how would anyone know if some of that cash didn't make it to the bank?" Trixie asked.

"Exactly. But if you read through all the newspaper articles, they talk in generalities about how much money they raised. They claimed the chili cookoff raised nearly $3,500 last year. Checks were deposited totaling $2,000. Cash deposits were only about a thousand."

"Where's the other five hundred then?"

"Maybe they rounded up a few hundred to make it look more impressive in the newspaper. But the article also talks about how many people bought tickets to the chili tasting, and there was a photo of a line of people waiting to put a donation in their favorite team's bucket. I've been to the chili tasting myself a few times. There will be hundreds of people paying five bucks each to get a small taste of six different chilis. They're all paying cash."

Mason stopped to rummage in the folder for another spreadsheet page. "I pieced it together as best I could, and I estimate there should be a cash haul in the range of $2,000 to $5,000. It's a guess, but like I said, it's an educated guess. Enough to raise questions we need to ask."

"Maybe there's some explanation, Bee just didn't keep good records."

"Maybe. But my fraud detection alert started ringing. I've seen this before."

"Really. With who?"

"Now, Trixie, you know enough not to ask about confidential information on my clients. Former client, in this case. I don't ask about yours."

"Sorry. But what did you do?"

"I reported it to the board of that organization. They brought in an outside audit firm that proved it. Their treasurer went to federal prison for three years."

"I don't really want Bee going to prison."

"I doubt she would. This is really small potatoes compared to what that guy did. But if this could be proven, she might have to pay restitution to the group, at the very least."

Trixie took a few minutes to review the spreadsheets and absorb the bombshell. Bee? Defrauding the Circle? More like defrauding the women's shelter and the food bank. Taking food from the mouths of babes. Complaining about the newspaper charging for their services, or the bank charging fees like everyone else has to pay. No written treasurer's report. Not everyone liked Bee all that much, but they all trusted her completely. Mayor's wife and well-known socialite in town.

"What do we do with this?"

"I need to stew on it for a few more days. Maybe I send some pointed follow-up questions in writing, on behalf of the foundation, and copy all the officers of the group—Marion, Mrs. Reeves, and Mrs. Hale as membership director, assuming she's still in the group. That might even help make sure Chief Hale hears about this. See what shakes loose."

"As long as that comes from you. I gotta sit in a circle and have coffee with these women, and there's already one about to get the boot because of me."

"You ready for the complicated one?"

"I think I need a break first."

***

With an empty bladder and a new bottle of water to refill it, Trixie settled in for the next round, keeping an eye on the clock for her appointment with Armstrong.

Mason pulled a thick three-ring binder from the credenza behind his desk. The binder was neatly organized with different color tabs, and a full-color cover with an artist's rendering of the planned expansion of Pineywoods First Church of the Risen Lord and Christian School.

"We actually have two different packets from the church. Let's start with the easy one first."

If this was the easy one, Trixie thought, there was no way they'd finish before her lawyer showed up. And she had to be home by four when Ty got off the bus.

"There's a lot here, but it's all the plans, architect's renderings, market research on the needs of the community, a lot of info that's more of a promotional nature. Fundraising promotion. More than half of this document is their fundraising packet. They include an overall projected budget, how much they need to raise, and how much they will finance. There's an addendum that they just voted to increase the amount they need to raise in advance."

"Yeah, I was there for that meeting. The law changed or something."

"Some lending regulations tightened up. But the most interesting thing I've found is they haven't raised much money yet. They set up an account at the bank to deposit all donations, and there's some there."

"They said they'd raised $200,000."

"Donations and *pledges* of $200,000," Mason corrected her. "Less than twenty grand actually in the bank. Half of that is a bank loan to pay for an architect. The rest is money people have promised to donate in the future. And two of those people have died. I'll have to find out if they left their estates obligated for the pledge or not. I mean, I could pledge a million dollars and then never write them a check. There's no legal obligation unless someone signs a promissory note. Some of those pledges are for annual donations. Let's see..." Mason flipped to the yellow tab. "Here's one who pledged to give $2,000 a year for ten years, so that counts as a $20,000 pledge. They haven't actually given a dime yet, and that money won't be in the bank when it comes time to pony up a down payment on the financing."

"But these are church members who have promised to give the church money. Even if it's in the future, don't you think they'll keep their promises?"

"Most will, but some will always fall off. You always want at least one-and-a-half times more in pledges than you actually need. People change their mind. Circumstances change or people are too optimistic about their future finances, and they pledge more than they can afford when it comes time to write a check."

"I s'pose some want to look good, or think if they promise to give a lot of money to the Lord, He might bless them so they have enough to meet that promise with a bunch left over."

"I think you're spot on in your analysis there, Ms. Burnet," Mason said formally with a grin. "There's also a bit of nepotism buried in here."

"Neppo-what?"

"Family connections. They've contracted JC Construction as the contractor. You know who owns JC Construction?"

"Jesus Christ," Trixie swore.

"No, but close. Jasper Callahan. And the architectural firm they've retained?"

"JC Architects?"

"No, Kaufman and Ochiltree, out of Dallas."

"That's a relief."

"Not quite. The president and CEO is Jack Callahan, Jasper and Bee's boy. Jasper is the chairman of the board. Seems he and his son bought K&O recently."

"You said this was the easy one."

"Let's move on. This one concerns me even more. The regular finances for the church."

"Someone's stealing from the church? Don't they know they'll burn in hell for that?"

Mason chuckled. "Well, I'm not sure I'd use the word stealing, although some might frame it that way. Just not from a legal standpoint. Not like what Bee might be up to. It's all legal, and it's all in the church's budget, duly approved by the trustees and voted on by the congregation in their regular business meetings. But it doesn't quite match their marketing."

"What do you mean?"

Mason pulled a second binder off the credenza, much thinner than the building project binder. He flipped through various tabs to find the one he wanted.

"First of all, with Lamar Reeves as treasurer, their financial reports and due diligence are in as good a shape as I've ever seen. Everything is there. Everything is clear and transparent. Now, not many church members are going through all this each month, or even once a year, to see what all the church spends money on."

"How much does Rev. Webb make?"

"You're reading my mind." Mason laid open the binder and flipped it around for Trixie to read. "He's paid an annual salary of $80,000."

"That sounds like a lot for a preacher."

"Not really. It's a large church. There's a large staff. A lot to oversee. It's a decent paying job for a town this size, but it's not out of the ordinary for a church this size. And he's got a doctorate degree, so that's worth something."

"The pastor down at Agape doesn't get any salary at all. He works at Winn-Dixie."

"But Webb gets a few perks on the side. Again, these aren't out of the ordinary in businesses, or in larger churches and organizations, and it's all spelled out here. They aren't hiding anything. He gets a housing allowance of a thousand a month, a car allowance of five hundred a month, an expense account that averages about a thousand a month."

"How much does all that come to?" Trixie asked.

"That's another $30,000 a year. Plus his wife."

"Angelina?"

"She's listed as the executive assistant to the senior pastor. Fifty K a year. Plus car allowance."

"That's really startin' to add up."

"It's a part-time job."

"Heck, that's about the same as my personal services bid'ness."

"I'll pretend I didn't hear that. I don't want to know if you've properly filed all your taxes or not."

"That was before I hired you as my accountant, so we'll just keep you in the dark. So, you're saying the pastor is getting paid quite a bit more than it looks like."

"We're just getting started. The youth pastor. That's Webb's son-in-law. Married to his daughter. The daughter is also on the staff as a part-time receptionist. The facilities director? That's Webb's son."

"What does a facilities director do?"

"Normally, a facilities director is in charge of all the buildings, grounds, and maintenance. Repairs, cleaning, all that. They've contracted out the janitorial service to a local firm. Any repairs are contracted out. They have a lawn maintenance company that takes care of the grounds. The facilities director would normally be in charge of all that, doing some things himself, supervising a maintenance person or two, contracting and overseeing outside companies to do anything they can't do themselves."

"So what does *this* facilities director do?"

"For a salary of $40,000 a year, a full-time job, plus a car allowance, this facilities director is a sophomore in college. In Colorado."

Trixie sat back and pondered. It didn't fit with her perspective of the church's mission. She didn't begrudge a pastor a living wage, or even hiring his wife as secretary with a fancy title. But this seemed a little bit of taking advantage of the situation.

"The gift shop," Mason said, flipping through more pages in the binder. "They promote that the gift shop proceeds are all donated to charitable works overseas, specifically the Africa Children's Fund. But the money is deposited directly into the church's operating fund. That money is used to pay salaries, electric bills, choir robes, whatever. They track it separately as an obligation but haven't written that check in three years. Maybe longer, but that's all the records we asked for. It's like a pledge they haven't followed through on."

A rap on the door, and Armstrong stuck his head in. "Am I interrupting your high finance?"

"Now's as good a time as any," Mason said. "I think we've covered everything. A lot to chew on here, and I'll pull together my notes for how to follow up. At this point, I think you need to look for other options for the foundation to support. But don't breathe a word of any of this to anyone. I'll handle the communications when the time comes."

"When will that be?"

"As soon as I figure out who I need to talk to and what I need to say."

"I need another break," Trixie said. "Mr. Armstrong, can I meet you in the conference room in about five minutes? I hate to make you wait, but I gotta make a quick call."

She needed to reach Clay. She hadn't talked to him since Sunday night—three days and only the one text message she'd sent him. He'd only replied with a sleepy face emoji. But she might not make it home by four. She needed Clay to meet Ty at the bus.

CHAPTER 19

"Pineywoods First Church of the Risen Lord, emergency meeting of the board of trustees, is now in session." Jasper Callahan, as chairman of the trustees, sat at the head of the table and called the meeting to order. Lamar Reeves, treasurer, sat to his right, the Rev. Parker Webb to his left. The other four members were scattered around the conference room table built for sixteen, each with a coffee, soda, or bottle of water and a notepad in front of them.

"As this meeting concerns financial matters that have not been approved by the church body," Jasper continued, "I call this meeting into executive session. As a reminder, that means all discussions are confidential and not to be shared outside this room. We can't vote to take any action until we adjourn the executive session and call a regular meeting of the board, which is announced in advance to the church so any members so inclined may attend. I do ask that everyone push their notepads and pens out of reach and that any recording or electronic devices be turned off."

"Why all the secrecy?" Chief Hale asked.

"Standard procedure to discuss confidential matters that we aren't ready to take to the full church for a vote yet," Jasper said. "We agreed years ago to follow the standard protocols that the city council has to follow, to enhance transparency and accountability."

The chief pushed his pad and pen away. "Not sure how a secret meeting enhances transparency."

"You know firsthand how the city council works, Chief," Jasper said. "This is for background information and discussion purposes only. Now, let's get started. Lamar, why don't you update everyone on the latest?"

Lamar pulled a letter from an envelope. "I could just read this to you, but I'll pass it around to anyone who wants to see it. Jasper recommended we not make any copies of it at this time. But I'll summarize the high points. It seems the Victoria Burnet Foundation—"

"Is that the young lady, Trixie?" Rev. Webb asked.

"Yes, one and the same," Lamar said. "It seems she has acquired the services of Mason Brooks as the financial director of her foundation, and he is on their board of directors. I'm not sure yet who else is on that board. We submitted the due diligence package with our grant request for the building project. Mason has come back with some follow-up questions that feel a bit accusatory. I think we'd like to smooth this over and answer his questions as best as possible, even make a few adjustments to our plans to appease them, if necessary, given the potential size of the grant."

Jasper slammed his pen to the table, which then bounced to the floor, where he left it like he'd intended to do that. "What kind of changes?"

"The foundation doesn't seem too fond of the idea that we've hired Jasper's construction company as the general contractor for the project, and that Jasper's son has been hired as the architect. Wanted to know if we got competing bids, and if so, they want copies."

Rev. Webb looked at Jasper. "I didn't know your boy was an architect."

Chief Hale jumped in again. "We didn't hire Jack. We hired that K&O group out of Dallas. What's Mason going on about?"

Lamar looked at Jasper, deferring to him to clear the air.

"Jack and I bought K&O a couple of years ago. He runs the place, I just fronted him some money to help with the acquisition."

"Was that before or after we hired K&O?" Hale asked.

That question went unanswered as Lamar pressed ahead. "The foundation is also asking about the pledges we've received versus the money actually paid in, how confident we are in all our pledges coming through, if we have plans to generate an overage of pledges, and if we have fallback plans in case not all pledges pan out."

"Exactly how much money are we talking about in this grant?" Rev. Webb asked Jasper. "Is it worth all this headache?"

This time, Jasper looked to Lamar to answer.

"They haven't specified any amount," Lamar said. "Just that it would be substantial."

"Didn't I read that she won $200 million?" the pastor asked. "I mean, if she wanted to tithe that—"

"No," Lamar corrected him. "The whole jackpot was around that, but there was more than one winner. She might've gotten ten or twenty million or so, maybe."

"Still. A tithe on that might pay for our whole project. I think we need to address any concerns they have."

Jasper just shook his head.

"That's not all, Pastor," Lamar said. "Mason had also asked for the church budget and financial reports to consider us for Ms. Burnet's regular tithes and offerings—above and beyond the grant from her foundation. Mason is also raising questions about church operations."

"What the hell?" Jasper pounded his fist on the table. "What's that little—"

"Jasper," the pastor cut him off. "Let's keep calm here. I know it might be frustrating, but let's be sure to keep a Christlike attitude in all things. So let me ask the question. What sort of questions is he raising about church operations? We've taken great measures to be good stewards of the Lord's gifts, open and accountable to the whole church. Right, Lamar?"

Lamar agreed, then went through the list of Webb family members on the payroll that Mason had questioned.

"None of that is secret," the pastor said. "Every time, we've gone through the board, the church's personnel procedures, and asked for approval from the whole church before offering a position. We interviewed other candidates for most of these positions. All the salaries were checked against other churches of similar size, and against comparable private sector jobs."

"I completely agree, Pastor," Lamar said. "If you recall, I cautioned that some of these hires might look a bit like nepotism, and we took extra steps to make sure everyone was treated fairly and above board. I think what Mason is saying, what the foundation is saying, is that from the outside, it still looks a little questionable, so he's doing his job to ask the questions. I believe we can address all of these to his satisfaction."

"Remember we didn't hire my son-in-law as youth director. My daughter married the youth director. Be sure you let Mason know that. It's not like we're going to fire him because he fell in love with my princess."

"The bigger issue will be how to explain that our full-time facilities director lives in a college dorm in Colorado," Lamar said, but received no reply from the pastor.

"I apologize for my outburst earlier," Jasper said, "but I'm not comfortable with all these questions, attacking our decisions and our motives. Our integrity."

"I understand, Jasper," Lamar said. "But if they truly are looking at a substantial gift, like in the hundreds of thousands of dollars, maybe a million or more, then they're asking all the right questions. It would be remiss of them not to. The more upfront and direct we are with them, the more likely it will be approved."

"We can't look defensive," Rev. Webb added. "We must be fully and openly cooperative. And if we need to put my boy on an unpaid sabbatical for a while, he'll be fine with that."

Chief Hale agreed. "If we get defensive, it looks like when I'm interrogating a suspect. The more defensive they get, the more suspicious I get. But what are they asking we do about the contractor and architect for the building project?"

Jasper looked ready for another outburst, but Lamar cut him off with a look.

"We answer the questions," Lamar explained. "We contracted with the largest local construction company, experienced in projects of this size, who fully understands what we are trying to accomplish and the needs of our growing church. He bid the job at a fair price, plus pledged to return a portion of any profits back to the project. Any other general contractor we could have hired—someone experienced with projects this size—would be from out of town. We felt an obligation to the community to use a local contractor to create jobs and contribute to the Pineywoods economy."

"And the architect?" the chief asked.

"They're one of the top firms in the state," Lamar said. "A whole team of architects and engineers and designers that we will have access to, all in one group. There's no local firm with those resources. The fact that Jasper's boy is president of the company now should have no bearing. And if Jasper wants to invest in his son's business, that shouldn't have any impact on our choice."

"We're getting friends and family discounts, too," Jasper added. "Jack grew up in this church, and he considers it his home."

The meeting ended with unanimous agreement that Lamar would write up the responses to the foundation.

Jasper walked to his car with Lamar then waved over the chief to continue the conversation.

"Lamar, this is all well and good," he said. "But I need to warn you. They're up to something over at that foundation. The Ladies' Society got a similar letter."

"Yes," Lamar said. "I know."

"How do you know? They sent the letter to Bee."

"Cass was copied on the letter," Lamar said.

"So was Reagan," the chief added. "She showed it to me. Marion would have gotten it too, since she's president of the group."

Jasper looked ready to put a fist through the hood of his own car. "That little weasel sent a letter insinuating Bee was doing something unsavory, and he copied other members of the club? This ain't right, I tell you. It's not right, and I'm not going to stand for it. All sorts of accusations against my wife? Against the Ladies' Society, for crying out loud. Why would this little slut go after a bunch of old women who sit around to gossip and have bake sales?"

Lamar and the chief stood, hands in pockets, staring at the ground, not ready to deal with Jasper's temper.

"We need to do something," Jasper said when no one responded.

"What do you think we should do?" Lamar asked. "I think you're reading too much into these due diligence requests. I didn't read that letter to the Circle as accusing anyone of anything, just asking pertinent follow-up questions for clarification."

Jasper turned to the chief. "Isn't there something you can do? You're supposed to be the law around here. Can she and her accountant just harass everyone and accuse them of things now that she suddenly has money? Isn't that slander or something? You know what she's been up to out at her farm. Maybe you should pay a visit out there, get some dirt on her. Then we can play tit-for-tat."

"Sorry, Jasper. That farm is outside the city limits. Not my jurisdiction, even if I was inclined to investigate, which I'm not. And how's that going to convince the foundation to give us a grant? Lamar is right—just answer their questions and keep calm. If there ain't nobody doing anything wrong, nothing to worry about. Maybe the church and the Circle will get some money. Maybe we won't. If not, we're no worse off than we are right now, so no damage done."

"Agreed," Lamar said.

Jasper climbed into his car and rolled down the window. "I don't agree. But I'll sit tight for now, see if you're right. But if she makes any more accusations against me, my wife, my son—I'm not going to sit tight for long. I'm going to do something about it."

The chief had to step back to let Jasper drive away, a little too quickly for a church parking lot.

"I hope he calms down and doesn't do anything stupid," Lamar said.

"Me too," the chief agreed. "He's been stupid once or twice before."

***

For the second time in a week, Clay had agreed to meet Tyler at the house when he got off the bus, but there'd been no need this time. Sabine didn't like the house Trixie and the agent showed her. Turned and walked out in the first five minutes. "Ain't nowhere in that yard to put up the martin house Ty and Leon built."

Trixie beat the bus home by about five minutes.

Clay was sitting on the tailgate of his pickup when she pulled in.

"Thank you," she said. "I didn't know if I'd get home before he did. Sorry to interrupt your work again." Neither of them addressed the topic burning in Trixie's brain, and she assumed in his too. At least it better be.

"No problem at all," Clay said. "I needed a break about now."

"You got something that needs doing or you got time for a drink? I got Diet Coke and water. I could fix some iced tea or coffee too."

Clay slipped from the tailgate. "I might just call the day done if you think Ty has a spare grape soda."

"C'mon in, then. Been trying to teach that boy about sharing."

Trixie wasn't sure whether or how to bring up the subject of the lingering goodnight kiss. Pretend like it never happened? Ask what he thought he was doing, just assuming he could kiss her? Ask if he'd do it again? Maybe just kiss him this time, see how he likes being caught off guard. Nearly a week had passed, and neither had mentioned it. But she knew there was another talk she needed to have with Clay before she could kiss him again, and she still hadn't thought of the right words for that conversation.

She fumbled for her keys, then paused. One pane of glass was broken, and door wasn't quite shut all the way. She pushed the door open and stood there for a second.

Clay grabbed her by the elbow and pulled her back, shoving his way in first. "Stay here."

He stepped into the mudroom and the kitchen. He pulled the chef's knife from the block on the counter.

Trixie didn't stay put, but followed him in.

"Anything look out of place?" he asked without turning around to look at her.

"No, not yet."

"What's down that hall?"

"The guest bedroom. It should be locked."

Clay gave the knob a turn. Locked.

"Key on top of the door," Trixie said.

Clay unlocked and opened the door. "Doesn't look like anyone's been in here." He looked around as Trixie stepped into the doorway. He glanced under the bed and opened the closet door, searching for someone hiding. "All clear. Upstairs. Can you please stay here? Ty might show up."

Trixie listened this time and parked herself back in the mudroom to keep one eye on the inside of the house and one eye out for Ty. She thought about getting the .22 out of the glovebox, but it didn't appear anyone was still here.

"Nobody home," Clay said as he came down the stairs. "Nothing looks out of order, but you'll need to go through and see if anything is missing. They didn't mess anything up, at least. Maybe they broke the glass and opened the door, then got spooked and left. I didn't pass anyone on the way in."

Trixie walked around, looking to see if anything obvious was missing. TV was there in the living room. All the knives were in the block, other than the one Clay still gripped.

Ty walked in before Trixie could check upstairs.

"Hey, little man."

Ty ignored his momma. "Hi, Mr. Garza. Momma, did y'all see the broke glass all over out there?"

"Yeah, we saw it," Trixie said. "Just checkin' around to make sure everything's okay. Looks fine. Maybe a bird flew into it."

Ty went to the fridge for a grape soda. "Mr. Garza, you want one?"

"Don't mind if I do, if you don't mind letting me have one of them?"

"I got plenty. Momma'll buy more."

Ty grabbed two sodas, handed one to Clay, and sat down at the kitchen table, tossing his backpack on the chair beside him.

"Who's this letter from?" Ty asked, holding up an envelope.

"That come out of your backpack?" Trixie asked.

"No, it was here on the table."

"Give that to me right now."

Trixie borrowed the chef's knife from Clay to slit the standard letter-size envelope, a bit of overkill, and pulled out the single sheet. She read it over a couple of times, then handed it to Clay.

"Who's the letter from? What's it say?"

"Ain't from your teacher this time, so none of your business. Why don't you go ride your bike for a bit while you got daylight? You can do your homework after supper."

"Okay."

Didn't have to tell that boy to go outside more than once, unlike any chore she might assign.

Clay read over the letter until Ty was outside and headed down the path on his bike. "You need to call the sheriff on this one."

"Maybe I should call Chief Hale."

"You're out in the county. This would be for the sheriff." Clay read the letter again, then handed it back. "We're probably getting our fingerprints all over this."

Trixie held it by the edges and refolded it, inserting it back in the envelope, which was hard to do with her hands trembling and trying not to get her fingers on it.

Clay rested a hand on her shoulder. She thought maybe she should take offense, but she didn't.

"You think Ellis is behind this?"

"Could be, but looks too clean." She sniffed the envelope. "Doesn't smell like cigarette smoke neither. It's typed. All the words are spelled right. If Ellis did it, he had help."

"I'm not trying to cause any alarm here, but maybe Tyler shouldn't be out there by himself right now."

"Yeah. Can you call him in? He won't argue with you. Think of some excuse."

"What are you going to tell him? Be hard to hide when the sheriff shows up."

"I don't know. Let me chew on that. I don't want to scare him. And I really don't want the sheriff's posse out here snoopin' around."

Trixie bit her nails and pondered a moment, then picked up her phone and punched in a number.

"Hey, Madison. I need you to have that investigator come call on me. Like, right now."

After she ended the call, she invited Clay to stay for supper again. "Ty might even let you have another grape soda."

"One of those every six months is my limit. But I'll definitely stay for supper. I wasn't planning on leaving anyway, not with this mess going on."

***

Ty was fed, homeworked, TV'd, bathed, and asleep by the time the car rolled up the drive.

Two men got out. Armstrong came with the PI on the drive down from Dallas.

Trixie had already swept up the glass, and Clay had cut a board to cover the missing pane, but she'd taken photos of everything with her phone and texted them to Madison, per her instructions, including photos of the letter and envelope.

"Ms. Burnet, this is my investigator. We're just gonna call him Dick Tracy for now. He's not officially on this or any other case until he gets his licensing thing cleared up with the state."

"Pleasure to meet you, ma'am," the mystery detective said.

"Please, call me Trixie."

"Please don't call me Dick. Let's go with Lee instead."

They all moved to the kitchen table. Holding the envelope by the edges with her fingertips, Trixie held out the letter to Lee. "Do you need to put on some rubber gloves or something so's not to contaminate the evidence? We both already handled it pretty good before we realized what we had."

The detective smirked, grabbed the envelope with his bare hands and pulled out the sheet of paper. He smoothed out the unsigned letter on the table and read it out loud.

"Die, bitch."

Reading the words herself had mostly made Trixie mad. Hearing them read out loud gave her a shiver. "At least whoever wrote it don't mince words."

Lee pulled out a notepad and started asking questions. Armstrong wandered around the kitchen and living room aimlessly, looking for clues and evidence in Trixie's spotless home with nothing out of place or missing.

"Any idea who would have sent this?"

"First off, they didn't send it. They hand-delivered it. Special express service. And no, no idea."

"Is there anyone angry enough at you to send—break in and drop this off?"

"There might be a bunch of people who are a bit jealous, but I can't imagine. The only one who might be a natural suspect is Ellis Shackelford, but he ain't smart enough to do this."

"Ellis? I've been getting acquainted with him."

"You've met him?"

"Not officially. Just stopped at a local tavern for a beer the other day, and imagine my surprise when I found myself sitting next to him at the bar. Now, there's someone who should have been named Dick. But why are you so sure this isn't from Ellis?"

Trixie explained her rationale.

"He might have gotten someone to do it for him."

"He ain't got no friends that can type."

"You'd make a good investigator. If you ever decide to get in this business, I'd be glad to take you on as an apprentice."

"I'll pass."

Lee asked a few more questions, asked if he could look around, unlike Armstrong who just seemed nosey. Trixie gave him a tour of the first floor, opening the guest room but not the closet, mainly to show him nothing was messed up or ransacked. She declined to show him the upstairs because Ty was sleeping.

He took a few more pictures of the door, even though it had already been cleaned and patched.

"Not sure why they went to the trouble of breaking in to leave you a letter. Could have just stuck it inside the screen, or taped it to the door, or shoved it in your mailbox for that matter. That might just be anger. Wanting to do some damage."

Armstrong's cell rang. He excused himself to the living room to take the call.

He wasn't gone thirty seconds. "Lee, that was Mason. They were a little harder on his place. Turned the place upside down. He's got Chief Hale and half the police force down there now. You done here yet?"

"Is he all right?" Trixie didn't mean to yell, but it came out with a bit more volume than she intended. "Is he hurt?"

"He's fine," Armstrong said. "He was home having an adult beverage after supper. Silent alarm went off and notified him on his phone and the cop shop at the same time. Whoever did this isn't too bright. He's got his place wired with more security cameras than a bank."

Lee gathered his stuff to leave.

"You gonna be all right here alone, ma'am?" Armstrong asked. "I surely don't expect anyone coming back, but do you have any personal protection?"

Clay responded, "I'm staying here for now."

"That's well and good," Armstrong said, "but I was talking about firepower."

Trixie said she'd get her .22 out of the car.

"That BB gun would prove more irritation than stopping power."

"I'll bring my 12-gauge in," Clay said. "It's in the truck."

"That's more like it."

"Clay," Trixie said, "I truly appreciate the concern, but like Mr. Armstrong said, ain't nobody coming back. No need in putting yourself out like that."

"I'll sleep on the couch or the guest room. The kitchen floor. You won't know I'm here other than I'll probably make coffee before you're up."

"It's really not necess—"

Armstrong interrupted. "You might not think it's necessary, but I do believe it would be prudent. I mean, Mason's office has been ransacked, and you got someone who went to the trouble of breaking into your house and saying they're going to kill you."

"Momma, who said they're gonna kill you?" Ty stood in the entry between the living room and dining room. He ran to her and buried himself in her side.

"It's just somebody playin' a mean joke, nothin' to worry about, my little man. Besides, I've got you here to protect me." Trixie figured she might need to sew some bells on his PJs so he'd quit sneaking up on adults having conversations.

Ty looked up at his momma, then over to Clay. "I think Mr. Garza should stay with his shotgun."

"Smart boy," Armstrong said.

"How long you been standin' there eavesdroppin' anyway?"

Armstrong and Lee headed for Mason's place. Clay and Trixie retrieved their weapons.

"Ty, you need to get back to sleep. You want to sleep in my bed tonight?"

"I'm not a baby. I can sleep in my own bed."

"I know, but maybe I'd feel safer knowin' you was in there to protect me."

Ty shook his head and headed up the stairs.

Trixie turned to Clay. "You want some coffee? I don't think I could handle any. My nerves are already shot—I'd never get to sleep."

"You got anything stronger?"

"No, sorry. I don't allow alcohol in my home."

"Me either. Wasn't for me. I thought maybe if you had something, a little bit might help you get to sleep."

"I think I've got some decaf around. It's instant."

"That'll work fine."

Trixie and Clay settled into the living room with their microwaved instant decaf. "Don't quite taste the same," Trixie said, "but it'll do, I s'pose."

Clay blew across the top of the O'Bumpkin's mug and tested the temperature. "About the other night," he said, testing the temperature of that topic.

"Yeah, about that. You make a habit of just goin' around kissin' every girl that cooks you supper?"

Clay thought about it a moment. "I guess the answer would have to be yes."

"Seriously?"

"Well, you're the only girl that's ever cooked for me since my mom died. I always gave her a thank you kiss and hug."

"I hope you didn't kiss your mother like that."

"Of course not. Just a peck on the cheek, like I did with you. To start. Then it just seemed like... it felt like..."

Trixie let him suffer for a moment.

"Like I said," Clay continued after swinging in the breeze a moment, "if I was out of line, I'll apologize. But since you kissed me back and didn't push me away or slap me, it might not be a very sincere apology."

"You kissed me and didn't even bother to call me the next day. Or for five days since. That's what you should be apologizin' for."

"I was a little afraid of what you'd say."

"You're scared of me?"

"A little, yeah."

"But you're here to protect me from the boogeyman tonight? Lord, help me. You need more coffee yet?"

Clay stood and moved from the recliner to the couch next to Trixie. "The coffee can wait. And yes, I'm here to protect you tonight. There was no way I was leaving you and Ty alone with whatever's going on."

"You didn't bother to ask if I wanted you to stay. You just sort of invited yourself. Kind of like that kiss. I'm beginnin' to see a pattern here." Trixie could feel the grin on her face and tried to restrain it.

Clay reached over and held her hand. "I guess I've always been that way."

"What way is that?"

"When I see something that needs doing, I just do it."

"So you just thought I needed protectin', and you just thought I needed kissin'?"

"I guess so."

Trixie leaned her head against his shoulder. "You're a pretty good guesser."

***

After finishing a bland cup of decaf and letting her nerves settle a bit, Trixie set out bedding for Clay to sleep on the couch. He preferred that over the guest bedroom, so he'd be able to hear anyone coming in the front door or kitchen door.

Trixie said goodnight, gave Clay a peck on the cheek, which turned into another simmering kiss on the lips, then she climbed the stairs to bed, where Ty was safely ensconced sideways.

CHAPTER 20

Trixie made one of the hardest phone calls she'd ever had to make. She was surprised when Reagan accepted her invitation to meet for lunch at Roy's Diner. They'd meet at one, after most of the lunch crowd had gone back to work, and they could get the back corner booth for a semblance of privacy.

"I wanted to clear the air between us," Trixie started after the waitress took their orders. "I don't want you leavin' the Circle on my account. Maybe we won't ever be best buds, but maybe we can be civil and work together, not make everyone else uncomfortable because there's bad blood between me and you."

Reagan sipped her sweet tea, looking real awkward, not making eye contact, fidgeting.

"You do good work for the Circle, helpin' them grow and get the word out." When Reagan hadn't said anything, Trixie felt the need to fill the gap and keep talking. "I know the other ladies adore you, and I'm the newbie in the group, and people have questions given some of the life choices I've made in the past. But it's in the past."

"In the past now that you've got money." Reagan finally found her words.

"You're right."

Trixie just let that sit there. No arguing about that. Reagan didn't seem to know how to respond when Trixie agreed with her.

"You think winning the lottery now gives you the right to just barge in and flaunt your money, and everyone fawns all over you? I've been here, working hard to be a part of this group, and no one pays any attention."

"I'm not tryin' to flaunt nothin'. Just tryin' to change my life. I prayed to the Lord for some way to get out of what I'd been doin', to make a good life and be a good momma to my boy. I made some bad choices when I was pretty young, and I felt stuck with no way out."

"Well, it sure looks like the Lord answered your prayers. I pray too, but He never saw fit to give me a million dollars to change my life. Maybe He expects people to change their lives on their own."

"I agree. That's why I want to make sure I give back from what He blessed me with. See if I can't make up for some of the, uh, other stuff." Trixie thought back to Brother Kent's talk about the woman caught in adultery. "All I know is, He told me I was forgiven and don't sin no more. I'm tryin' real hard, and I know some things I ain't gonna do no more, but I'm sure I'll still mess up sometimes. Like I ain't got no room to be judgin' anyone else. You got room to judge me, that's for sure, and I don't blame you."

The waitress showed up with their burgers before Reagan could reply. Trixie shoved a couple french fries in her mouth to stop the words from rolling out of her face. Fresh from the fryer, they would leave a blister to remind her to keep her words under control.

Reagan picked the tomato off her burger, which she had asked the waitress to hold, and added some ketchup. Trixie didn't understand why someone would take the fresh tomato off and then pour on liquid tomato from a bottle, but she was tryin' not to judge.

"So, what do you propose we do about this?" Reagan cut to the chase, then shoved an oversized bite of burger in her mouth.

Trixie took a bite to think about her answer. Wiped her lips with a napkin and took a sip of Diet Coke.

"I know Marion said you needed to apologize for what you said. Maybe that's not in your heart right now to do, and that's fine. But if we can agree to get along, treat each other with respect in front of the Circle, we can both let the other ladies know that we've made amends. They'll take that as you've apologized, and apology's been accepted, without you havin' to stand up in the front of the group and grovel. Then maybe, eventually, we can work together on some project just to show them all is good between us. I don't know what I can do to help. I don't have any skills really. Not like you. I don't know about all this social media stuff like you do. But I want to work, do something. Not just give money."

Reagan chewed on her lunch and on whatever was going through her mind as the two ate in silence for a few minutes.

"I shouldn't have said what I said," Reagan finally replied. "I know that. I wished I hadn't said it out loud the moment I said it. I can't help thinking it, but I didn't mean to say it. Made you, me, and everyone else uncomfortable."

"If that's an apology for saying it out loud, apology accepted. I don't blame you one bit for thinkin' it. It's true. It was true. It ain't no more. If we had to say we was sorry for every thought that crossed our minds, I'd be walkin' around saying sorry all day long."

Reagan smiled, almost laughed, for the first time. "Yeah, me too. But I have one question. Maybe it's what's been bothering me the most. Maybe why I keep thinking about this and why those words popped out."

"Shoot."

"Was my husband one of your customers?"

Trixie didn't have to think about her answer to this one. She'd thought about this question many times over the years in case it ever came up, but it never had. Until now.

"I will never answer that question for anyone, about anyone. I won't say yes and I won't say no."

Reagan's eyes filled with tears. "Then I think you just answered it."

"No, that's not what I said."

"If he wasn't a customer, you'd just say so."

Trixie gathered her words in the right order while she washed down the last french fry with a sip of Coke.

"Let me explain. It's like this. Let's say you come to me with a list of ten names and ask me to tell you if any of them were clients of mine. You read through each name. If I said, 'no, not him' to the first name, and 'no, not him' to the second name, then 'I won't answer that' to the third name, then you'd have a pretty good idea that guy number three was a client. But if I say 'I won't answer that' to every name on the list, then I haven't compromised the confidentiality of any of them, and you don't know if all of them, some of them, or none of them were customers.

"So, I'll repeat my previous answer about the chief. I won't say yes and I won't say no, and that's the same answer I'll always give no matter who's asking or who I'm asked about."

"You can't just lie to me and put my mind at ease?"

"I've done a lot of stuff I'm not proud of, but I don't like lyin'. Sounds like your mind ain't at ease to start with. You got a beautiful family and a well-respected husband with a good job. Why would you be thinkin' things like this about him?"

"Because even if he's never been with you, there have been others that I know of."

"Why are you still with him if he can't keep it in his pants?"

"I got four boys with him. A home. Trying to make my place in this community, but that hasn't been easy. It's like everyone in town knows about him and feels sorry for me, but they won't say anything. I've caught him twice. He denied it at first. Then asked me to forgive him and swore he'd never do it again. Suspected he was still out with other women and confronted him again. He wouldn't even deny it that time. Just said, 'A man has needs.' Expects me to stay home and raise our boys and make a good home while he can say he has to go out on a call anytime day or night, and I'm supposed to believe him."

Trixie was real glad she'd always made him wear a condom.

"Maybe some men just can't be civilized after all," Trixie said. "You just gotta decide if it's something you can live with, or if it's just going to eat you up."

"Not like I won the lottery and can just pack up and leave."

And there it was.

"I wasn't his first wife, you know. First wife divorced him for having an affair with a younger woman."

"I s'pose that should have been your first clue," Trixie said.

"I was that younger woman. Then I had four babies and wasn't as young as I used to be."

"He ain't exactly a spring chicken."

Reagan laughed. "You speak the truth. I thought he'd settle down as he got older, had boys to be a role model for. Lord, I hope they don't take after him that way. I'm trying to raise them better than that. Teach them some respect and some morals. They're not old enough to get into that kind of trouble yet, just trying to teach them to treat girls as human beings, not strange creatures."

"Well, we are strange though, ain't we?"

The waitress interrupted their laughter with the check, which Trixie grabbed.

They were still laughing as they walked out to the parking lot.

"If you ever need to talk about it some more," Trixie said, "I'll listen."

"I've never had anyone I could trust enough to talk to about this. But you seem to be able to keep things confidential."

"That's one job skill I do have."

Reagan reached over for Trixie's hand. "I know I said some pretty awful things to you, and we're just starting fresh here, and I'll understand if you'd rather not, but is it too soon for a hug?"

***

Trixie was home cooking supper for Ty. Clay wasn't joining them this evening. That burger still weighed heavy on her stomach—Roy's world-famous half-pounder—so she was frying up some eggs and bacon for something a little lighter. Ty loved having breakfast for supper since morning was usually a bowl of cereal.

"Ty, can you get that?" she called out when someone knocked on the screen door at the mudroom. Probably Clay stopping by to check on them. Ty ran to the door like he assumed it was Clay too.

"It's some man for you, Momma."

Trixie turned down the stove so as not to burn the bacon and wiped her hands on a dishtowel. Maybe Lee or Armstrong stopping by unannounced.

"Can I help you?"

The man wore dress pants and shirt, a tie. No jacket as it had warmed up again. Indian summer, her momma had always called it.

"Are you Victoria Burnet?"

"Who's asking?"

"I have a letter for Ms. Burnet. I have to deliver directly to her."

He didn't look like he worked for the post office, but she didn't figure anyone was going to send a young man out in a tie while the sun was still up to deliver another death threat.

"I'm Trix—Victoria."

He handed her the envelope. "You are hereby summoned to appear before Judge Archer in family court next Tuesday at ten a.m."

CHAPTER 21

"You wanna swing by and pick me and Ty up for church in the morning?" Trixie was glad her ten p.m. Saturday night phone call to Clay didn't wake him up.

"You're not going to First Church anymore?"

"Just gonna skip it until all this grant stuff is settled. I can't deal with any more stress." After the break-in, the death threat, the summons for family court, and sorting through the tension with Reagan, Trixie just couldn't handle sitting in church looking at Jasper, Lamar, Chief Hale, and a few hundred other people who probably all knew what she used to do for a living and that she'd won the lottery.

Made Ty excited to go to church too. "Ask if they got Sunday School or something for us kids."

"Not yet," Clay said, having heard Ty over the phone. "It's in the works though. Soon."

Clay called back five minutes later.

"Brother Kent doesn't work tomorrow. Wants to know if we can join him and Harris for lunch. He's grilling chicken at his place."

"Tell Harris I'll bring potato salad."

***

"Might be the last day warm enough to grill outside for a while," Trixie said. Everyone looked at her like she'd lost her mind.

"That man will grill in an ice storm," Harris said.

The grill was an old 55-gallon barrel, cut in half, hinges attached, smokestack welded on, all spray-painted black but now about half rust on the outside.

"He made that grill himself," Clay said. "He's got two more, even bigger, out in the shed. One he can do a whole hog on."

Kent and Harris lived in the country, in an older but well-maintained doublewide on five acres, mostly woods and thicket, but an acre or so was cleared around the house. A dozen or more chickens ran around the yard, in and out between Kent's feet while he tended the grill.

"You'd think they'd know better since one of their cousins is sitting up here smokin' right now."

"Maybe they're comin' to pay their last respects," Trixie said.

Newspaper was taped down on top of the old picnic table as a tablecloth. Paper plates and plastic cups were set out beside a pitcher of iced tea. Trixie's green Tupperware bowl of potato salad sat next to a Corel Ware casserole dish of green beans and a stack of fresh corn on the cob Kent had grilled alongside the chicken.

Everyone took a seat, Kent and Harris on one side, Clay and Trixie on the other with Ty between them.

"Clay," Kent said, "would you do us the honor of blessin' this meal?"

Everyone bowed their heads and closed their eyes. Well, Trixie peeked to make sure Ty was following instructions and not reaching for the wishbone while everyone else was praying.

Clay gave a soft and brief prayer, like he couldn't wait to eat or he didn't trust Ty to keep his hands out of the chicken for long.

"How'd you cook this chicken so fast?" Trixie asked. Church hadn't let out an hour ago.

"I smoked it for six hours last night, then put it in the fridge. Just heated it through and crisped it up now."

"You haven't lived until you've had his brisket," Clay said. "Melt in your mouth."

Kent looked like he belonged on a ranch or in an Old West movie. Harris looked like she'd be most comfortable on the back of a Harley. No, in the driver's seat.

"How'd you two meet?" Trixie asked.

"It's a long story," Kent said. "Short answer is God put us together."

"Longer answer," Harris said, "is I had to shake some sense into him. Still do now and then. And when he gets mad at me, I just say, 'God told me to do that so get over it.' He can't argue with God."

"But I still do."

"You never win either, do ya?"

"I never win an argument with Him or you."

"You'd think you'd learn." Harris poked Kent playfully on the shoulder, and he leaned in for a quick kiss.

"Why don't you tell Trixie your story?" Clay said. "I told her you would."

"Let's finish eating first or the food will get cold," Harris said.

***

"Just dump all the scraps in this bucket," Harris said, "and I'll toss them in the compost pile for the garden."

Everyone pitched in to clean up, even Ty and without being told. Then Ty ran around chasing chickens while the adults moved to the Adirondack chairs on the deck, looking out over the hill that dropped off into the woods.

"Watch out for that rooster," Kent told Ty. "He'll chase you back."

"Let me hear this story now," Trixie said.

Kent and Clay puffed cigars to life. "My only vice," Kent said. "She lets me keep one."

"I like the smell," Harris said. "But not in the house."

Blowing a thick, blue cloud into the air, Kent paused and thought a moment. "Did Clay tell you I used to rodeo?"

"No, he hasn't told me much of nothin'."

"Well, I did. Started when I was sixteen. At nineteen, I rode bulls in Vegas at the national championships. Didn't do too well, but just to make it there was quite an honor. Highlight of my life at that time. Of course, that meant I was hanging out with guys a lot older than me. Some real professionals. Some wild ones too."

"Naturally," Harris interjected, "he drifted to the wild ones."

"Look who's talking. But yeah, I took up with some who weren't the greatest influences. The next year, I was back at the nationals again. Stayed out all night long drinking, which wasn't unusual. But I didn't normally do that the night before competition. I wasn't drunk when it came time to ride, but I was a bit fuzzy and pretty hungover. Not sharp. Not on my game. Made a stupid mistake. Got my boot hung up in the rope, wrapped around a ton of angry beef. Underneath it. Then he was down, on top of me. Broke my leg in three places, shattered a couple vertebrae and fractured my pelvis. Not to mention the danged thing planted a hoof in my thigh.

"The next thing I remember was a month later, still in the hospital."

"That's awful," Trixie said. "Is that why you have that limp?" She regretted saying that as soon as the words escaped.

"Yeah, that and a few other aches and pains. It hurt real bad back then, and docs finally discharged me from the hospital with a scrip for pain meds and an order for physical therapy. I did the therapy a couple of times but didn't much care for that. With the pills, I didn't see the point. And that was the beginning of a long slide down."

"And he was starting at the bottom," Harris said.

"That I was. I couldn't ride anymore, of course. I couldn't work anywhere. Other than ranching or riding, I didn't really have any job experience. When the scrips ran out, I found someone to supply my needs who didn't require a doctor's orders. But I'd have to pay for them. So he agreed to let me do some work for him. Driving down to Mexico to pick up some boxes, then driving back. He wouldn't tell me what was in the crates, and I didn't want to know. He paid me, part in cash, part in pills.

"Driving wasn't easy, between the pain and the pills, but at least it was sitting-down work. I didn't have to load the crates, just drive the truck. No problem until the day the Mexicans I'd been working with started shooting at me. I got out of there, made it back, told the guy I couldn't do it anymore. He threatened to shoot me too, but he didn't."

Kent paused to relight his cigar. Harris refilled Trixie's iced tea.

"I couldn't figure out what to do. I had to have my pills, but they weren't worth getting shot and buried down Mexico way. Looked up a rehab center near Lufkin. Figured if nothing else, they could help calm my nerves for a few weeks and the cartel might not know where to find me, if they were still looking."

"And this is where I came into the picture," Harris said.

"You were in rehab too?" Trixie asked.

"I was a counselor there. I'd done the rehab thing years ago, back when I was sixteen. Got clean, finished school, went on from there."

Kent said, "She's being modest. She's got a master's degree in addiction and substance abuse counseling."

"And it was pure hate at first sight," Harris said. "Surliest client I'd ever had."

"Six weeks later she agreed to marry me if I was still sober after a year."

"One year later we got married," Harris added. "He's stayed clean and sober, but he's still surly."

"I thought Harris could be tough, but then God got ahold of me and said there's a church that needs a pastor. Harris agreed with God, but I had other ideas. I didn't know anything about that. I was raised in a Christian home but never paid no attention to that stuff. But the Lord said to just go there and tell my story, and He'd do the rest.

"And here we are."

"Speaking of degrees," Harris said, "Kent only has two more semesters left. Getting his degree in Biblical Studies at LeTourneau, online."

"I've been thinking about goin' back to school myself," Trixie said. It had crossed her mind, anyway, so that wasn't really a lie.

"I'm taking some online classes in ranch management," Clay said.

"You never told me that," Trixie said.

"Not looking for a degree. Just a few classes to help me run the farm better."

"What's your story?" Harris asked Trixie.

"I'm not sure I'm ready to talk about all that just yet."

Trixie's cell phone interrupted the awkward moment, which gave Clay and Kent time to relight their cigars once more.

"I'm afraid I'm going to have to cut this short," Trixie said. She looked at Clay. "That was Chief Hale. Wants to know if I can meet him down at the police station. Just to talk. He didn't really want to drive out to my place. Can you watch Ty?"

"You need me to go with you?"

"No, he just wants to discuss the break-in at Mason's."

Clay tossed his keys to Trixie. "Take the truck. We'll be here waiting for you. You call if you need anything. And call Armstrong before you go."

***

She hadn't needed to call Armstrong. He was already at the police station waiting for her, along with Lee. They went into the chief's office, not into an interrogation room, which was a relief.

"I just want to update y'all on a few things, keep you informed," the chief said. "Mr. Armstrong here informs me he's your attorney, not that you need one. He also informed me that you had a break-in at your place, and someone left you a love note, same day that Mason's place was trashed."

Trixie looked to Armstrong. She hadn't known he'd filled the chief in. He just nodded to her.

"That's right," she said. "Knocked out a pane of glass in my door and left the letter on the kitchen table for my boy to find."

"We've got all the surveillance video from Mason. I'd like you to watch it, see if you recognize anyone. Fair warning, the video is black and white, a bit grainy, and they're wearing hoods and masks. But maybe just from stature, or the way someone walks or moves, maybe you can spot something."

The chief turned the monitor on the corner of his desk to where Trixie could see it and hit play.

Trixie watched the four-minute video three times. Nothing about either of the guys looked the least bit familiar. She would have recognized Ellis. They both appeared to be younger men, just from the way they moved and tossed file cabinets around. One was tall, like Ellis, but heavier set. The other one was small and wiry. Nobody she recognized.

"That confirms what we were thinking," the chief said. "Neither look like Ellis, but who knows if he wasn't sitting out front as the driver. We know a couple of guys who could possibly fit the descriptions, a couple lowlifes in town that have been known to hang around Ellis some, but they both have solid alibis. It wasn't them."

The thought that these two creepy looking thugs had been in her kitchen gave her the willies. Maybe she should upgrade that little peashooter .22 for something with a bit more oomph.

"They didn't steal anything," the chief said. "They didn't even look for anything. They just threw shit around, pardon my French. It was just malicious vandalism."

"Just sending a message," Armstrong said.

Lee cleared his throat and spoke for the first time. "Somebody's mad. Big mad."

***

Armstrong met Trixie in the waiting area outside family court at 9:45 a.m. sharp.

"Today is nothing to be alarmed about. Just an initial or preliminary hearing. It's mainly just the judge checking on the situation, making sure there's no child in imminent danger, and then scheduling a hearing. I'm going to ask for thirty days out. There's no trial or anything like that. You probably won't have to say a word. If the judge does ask you anything, you answer 'yes, Your Honor' or 'No, Your Honor.' Leave the rest to me."

"Why do we have to wait thirty days? Can't we get a hearing sooner and get this behind us?"

"More time is better for us. See if Lee can get some info on what's driving this."

The only folks in the courtroom were the judge, Armstrong sitting next to Trixie at a table, some kid fresh out of law school in a suit and tie that didn't fit right, sitting next to Ms. Roberts at a table across the aisle, and a sheriff's deputy sitting in the corner who looked like he was sleeping. A woman sat at a weird-looking typewriter at a folding card table next to the judge's bench.

The judge called the preliminary hearing to order and read a bunch of stuff. Trixie couldn't concentrate. Nothing about her and Ty, just legal mumbo-jumbo.

The kid in the suit stood and requested an emergency hearing to determine if the child needed to be removed from the home for his safety.

The judge looked up for the first time, peering over his reading glasses to eyeball the kid. "You have any evidence whatsoever that would justify that request?"

"Your Honor, we believe the child is not in a home that is conducive to his emotional well-being and development."

"Do you need me to repeat my question?" Judge Archer asked. "I don't like having to repeat myself. Makes our clerk here do twice the work. She's paid by the word, so that starts wasting taxpayers' money."

"No, Your Honor."

"No, you don't need me to repeat myself, or no, you don't have any evidence?"

"No need to repeat yourself. We believe—"

"Did I ask what you believe? Your beliefs cannot be submitted into evidence. You might believe the world is flat." The judge looked down at papers in front of him and muttered, "Where do they dig up these idiots?" It was loud enough for Trixie to hear, so she assumed the idiot kid heard it too. Did the clerk type it into the record?

The kid and Ms. Roberts whispered to each other, and she helped him find the paper he was looking for in his folder.

"Your Honor, if I may, the state would like to submit this report from the child's school administration about bruises, cuts, abrasions, and a black eye the child sustained recently."

"Let me see." The kid took the paper and some pictures to the judge then returned to his seat.

"How did the child come to sustain these injuries?"

"An altercation at school with another student."

"So this didn't happen at home, and it didn't happen due to any negligence of the parent?"

"No, Your Honor, that's correct."

"Then maybe you should be hauling the school administration before this court to ask how they allowed this to happen. Was the boy seen by a doctor?"

"No, Your Honor, not to our knowledge."

The judge looked to Trixie.

"No, Your Honor," Armstrong answered for her.

The judge looked back to the kid lawyer. "Is the boy back in school?"

"Yes, Your Honor."

"Was he disciplined by the school for fighting?"

"No, Your Honor."

"Why not?"

"They deemed the other boys started it and it was self-defense."

"Other boys? More than one?"

"Three, Your Honor."

"Did any of the other boys sustain any injuries?"

"One was treated in the emergency room for severe injuries."

"Were the other boys disciplined in this matter?"

"I do not know, Your Honor."

"Is the state bringing any case before this court on the suitability of these other boys' homes?"

The kid looked to Ms. Roberts, who shook her head.

"No, Your Honor."

"So let me get this straight. This child was attacked by three boys at school, and you're questioning the suitability of his home but not of the boys who attacked him. Do I have that correct?"

"Yes, Your Honor. But there is more."

"Then you better get busy."

"We are in receipt of reports that the mother, Victoria Burnet, runs a house of prostitution at her home where the boy lives."

The judge removed his glasses and looked up. "You should have led with that one."

Archer put his glasses back on and flipped through the papers in the folder. "I don't see any police reports in the file I was provided."

"Not police reports, Your Honor. Verbal reports."

"Verbal. No written affidavits even?"

"No, Your Honor."

"Who made these reports?"

"They were anonymous, Your Honor."

Armstrong raised his hand. "Objection."

The judge glanced at Armstrong. "This isn't a trial, so I'm not accepting any objections. But young man," the judge redirected to the kid, "if this was a trial and you pulled that, you'd never see the inside of this courtroom again. You understand me?"

"Yes, Your Honor."

The judge read through some more papers, then turned to Trixie, glaring at her over his glasses.

"Ms. Burnet, do you conduct prostitution or any other illegal activities in your home?"

"No, sir. Your Honor."

"Have you ever done so?"

Trixie looked to Armstrong. He nodded.

"Yes, Your Honor, I used to."

"How long ago is 'used to'?"

"I retired more than two months ago."

"Well, that's not that long ago. How can this court be assured you won't come out of retirement?"

Trixie looked to Armstrong again. He just nodded again.

"Your Honor, I have recently been blessed financially and no longer need to work."

"How did you become so financially blessed that you can retire at..." he looked down at his papers again... "at twenty-three years old? I've been on this bench and practicing law longer than you've been alive, and I can't retire yet. Somehow this doesn't seem fair to me." Judge Archer chuckled but looked to Trixie for an answer.

"I won the Powerball, Your Honor. The Lord blessed me and provided a way out of that life."

"He sure did bless you."

The judge turned back to the kid and Ms. Roberts. "Tell me, when did this action begin at Family Protective Services?"

Ms. Roberts flipped through some paperwork and handed a sheet to the kid. "September the ninth, Your Honor."

"Just over one month ago. A month after Ms. Burnet was blessed with the winning numbers, and a month after she had retired from her previous vocation that could have provided grounds to remove a child. Do I have this timeline correct?"

Ms. Roberts whispered to the kid, whose voice grew shakier as the hearing went on.

"Your Honor, it wasn't until around this time that FPS was made aware of these issues and began looking into matters. It came out when they were following up on the fight the child had in school, since there were injuries that required medical attention at the emergency room, and during that follow-up, a concern was raised by the school about the child's home environment."

"Understood," Archer said.

He read some more papers and took some notes. He leaned over and said something to the clerk, who looked through a spiral-bound calendar and whispered back to the judge.

"Your request for an emergency hearing is hereby denied. We will schedule a regular hearing next Tuesday. Any objections, counselors?"

"None," said the kid. "Your Honor."

"Your Honor, we would like to request the hearing be scheduled thirty days from now, if it pleases the court."

"Why?"

"I was just retained as counsel by Ms. Burnet last week and would like more time to prepare."

"From the looks of how things went today, I'm not sure you'll need to do much preparation unless the state gets their act together."

The judge looked through papers once again, whispered to the clerk again, then moved his glasses to the top of his head.

"A hearing will be held two weeks from today. Same day, same time, same channel. Until then, Ms. Burnet is to meet with Ms. Roberts twice per week, at Ms. Burnet's home at least one of those times each week, and at any other mutually convenient time and place as Ms. Roberts determines. This preliminary hearing is adjourned. Oh, and young man, you either need to be prepared for the next hearing or you don't need to show up at all."

The judge rapped the gavel so loud Trixie came out of her chair.

Out in the parking lot, Armstrong told Trixie, "Well, that went almost as good as we could possibly have hoped for. This is not a judge who likes his patience tried. And I don't think he cares for Ms. Roberts any more than I do."

"He's kinda scary, ain't he?"

"Oh, he tries. I play golf with him at least once a month, and he's the nicest guy in the world. Now I can't play golf with him until your case is settled. But I have a request. Actually, Lee has a request that he asked me to pass on to you. I don't think he felt comfortable being the one to ask. Might not be something you want to answer, but it could be important."

"Anything if it helps me with my boy."

"I don't want to see it. Just Lee."

"See what?"

"A list of all your clients."

CHAPTER 22

The Ladies' Circle meeting with an appropriately contrite Reagan went off without a hitch and ended in a hug-a-thon. Bee, of course, wasn't a hugger. She kept her distance from Trixie this time, once again unable to make eye contact, sniffing like she suffered from hay fever. Plans for the Cast-Off Clothing Sale were finalized, and Trixie remembered she still needed to sort through that closetful of work uniforms to see what would be appropriate to display on clothing racks in the First Church fellowship center.

Shelby wanted to have lunch at Roy's again after the meeting.

"I need to talk to you," Trixie said, "but can we meet somewhere to talk in private?"

"Come to my place," Shelby offered.

Shelby lived in a two-bedroom apartment, top floor walkup, three stories up.

"Pardon my mess," Shelby said as she moved piles of laundry from the couch to the floor — Trixie wasn't sure if they were clean or dirty — to create a spot to sit. Shelby tried to shoo the cat off the pile of clothes, to no avail. The lone coffee table was covered with soda cans, water bottles, and an empty pizza box.

"Here, let me show you my office." Shelby led Trixie down the hall. One bedroom door was open, bed unmade, a path from the door to the bed cleared of the surrounding piles of clothes, boxes, and shoes. Worse than Ty's room had ever looked. The sulfuric smell of a litterbox burned Trixie's throat, but Shelby didn't seem to notice.

The bathroom vanity didn't have a spare inch of countertop space underneath the makeup, hairbrush, curling iron, and various bottles of skin treatments. The second bedroom door was shut. Shelby opened the door with a "ta-da," revealing a neat, organized office: one small desk, a matching file cabinet, and shelves lining one wall filled with medical books and three-ring binders meticulously arranged. The lone window overlooked the complex's swimming pool, covered and closed for the season. Two large monitors and a keyboard sat on the desk, a printer on the file cabinet. Not a paperclip was out of place.

"I keep the door shut to keep the cat out."

"I still don't understand what your job is exactly," Trixie said.

"Medical coding. Work from home. I enter all the treatments and billing information into the computer for six different doctors and dentists in town, and that all gets filed with the patients' insurance providers or Medicaid or Medicare. Work whenever I want as long as I get it done in a reasonable time. That allows me time to be in the Circle and the church band and anything else I want to do."

Trixie figured it must not leave much time for housekeeping.

Shelby sat in the standard office chair behind the desk and pointed to the small side chair. "Pull up a seat and tell me what's on your mind that's all private-like."

Trixie was relieved to sit in the office rather than the living room that looked like a tornado had come through. Austin might have to forgo his music career to keep that bank job just to afford a maid.

"There's just some stuff goin' on that I wanted to tell someone, but I can't. Nobody other than my lawyer."

"Lawyer? Gracious, girl, must be serious. You in some kind of trouble for, ya know, what you used to do?"

"Not exactly, but it might be related. You can't breathe a word of this to no one."

Shelby mimed zipping up her mouth, locking it, and throwing away the key. "You know me enough to know I wouldn't do that."

"I know. I just felt like I had to say it. It seems child protective services is snoopin' around, tryna find something on me so's they can take my boy away. I would die if that happened."

"No way. That will never happen. You love that boy. Why in the world would they want to do that anyway?"

"My lawyer thinks someone is puttin' them up to it. Somebody who's mad at me or jealous, maybe wants money or wants revenge. He's got an investigator working on it. I can't give you any more details than that. It could be my ex-boyfriend, Tyler's father. It might be a former customer of mine who's worried I'm going to blackmail them. And..." Trixie trailed off, wondering if she'd said too much already. But she needed to say it out loud to someone.

"And what?"

"And someone broke into my house and left a note threatening to kill me."

"Oh my God." Shelby was stunned nearly speechless, as rare an event for her as it was for Trixie. "Oh my God."

"I know it all has to do with me winning this money. What good is all this if I lose my boy? I thought the Lord had blessed me. But it's not a blessing. It's a curse. Punishment for my sins."

Shelby was up in a flash, leaning over and hugging Trixie. The deluge came again, the second time Trixie had cried in more than ten years.

"Sorry about all that," Trixie said as she regained her composure. "I didn't mean to blubber all over your nice blouse."

"That's what I'm here for. And this can go in the laundry."

Trixie wondered which room's floor the blouse would land on.

"Is there anything I can do to help? I could ask around. Maybe Austin or Lamar or someone has heard something. Just poke around, not let anyone know what's going on."

"No, the lawyer's on it. Chief Hale knows."

"I don't know if I trust Hale," Shelby said. "That dude gives me the creeps. 'Accidentally' brushed his hand over my butt one day at Walmart. Just the way he leers at me." Shelby shivered and sat at her desk again. "Poor Reagan."

"Probably not a good idea to say anything about any of this to Lamar. Or Austin."

"Oh my God!" Shelby yelled as a light bulb practically appeared over her head. "I just read in the paper that your accountant's office got broken into. Is that because of you too?"

"Yeah, it appears that's my fault too."

"I didn't mean your fault," Shelby said. "Of course it isn't. But there's more you need to tell me." She stared at Trixie expectantly.

"Ain't much more I can tell you. It's all confidential and such."

"I don't mean about this. I mean about Clay. What is up, girl?"

But Trixie had to excuse herself and promised to call later. Two more showings on the schedule to look at houses with Leon and Sabine. Those two couldn't make up their minds about anything. And Trixie wanted to let her agent know to make an offer on that two-level cul-de-sac with the three-car garage. She held her breath down the hallway, but it didn't do no good at keeping the litterbox fumes out of her lungs.

CHAPTER 23

"I'm just not comfortable giving out these names," Trixie told Lee. "How do I know you're going to keep this confidential? They are good men, family men, pillars of the community kind of folks. They're human so they ain't perfect, but they don't need their secrets let out. Ever'one has a secret. And that would make things even harder on me."

Lee stroked his chin in thought as they sat in Mason's conference room.

"Maybe you don't put it in writing. Just tell me a name, we'll discuss that gentleman, and if there's no reason to suspect him, we'll move on to the next and I'll forget the name."

"How do I know I can trust you? I mean, you got kicked off the Dallas police force for unethical behavior, then you lost your PI license, and now you're doing detective work without a license. Not a good track record for me to trust."

"I always keep confidences. Always have. Can't prove that to you. I've done this type of work for twenty years, never gave up a confidential informant or inside operator. As you said, no one is perfect, but the most I've ever been accused of is being a bit overly aggressive in getting the job done for my clients. And how did you know I used to be with the Dallas police? Besides, I didn't get kicked off the force. I resigned."

"You resigned because they asked you to."

"I could have fought it. But when the establishment is out to get you, you can't win, and I'd have lost my pension. And how did you even find out my real name?"

"They got this new thing called the internets. Doesn't take a detective to use this thing called Google, ya know."

"You sure I can't hire you as an investigator?" Lee stopped talking and stared out the window at the street below.

Trixie couldn't tell if he'd lost interest in their conversation or was thinking hard about her case. But her gaze followed his down to the street below, where Ellis sat in his pickup, smoking, parked across from Mason's office.

"He's been following you a lot." Lee scratched the back of his head. "Or maybe he's following me. Either way, probably not a good idea to let him see the two of us together. I was planning on bumping into him for a beer again this evening."

"He ain't hidin' very well, is he?"

"It's amazing how many people think they're invisible."

Lee stared for a bit, then returned to the conversation with Trixie.

"Let's do this instead. You don't tell me if anyone is a client of yours."

"Was. Was a client."

"Was. You just give me names. People you think I might ought to check into. Maybe they were clients, maybe not. Anyone who, however remotely, you think might have some reason to shake you down for money, blackmail you, or might want to protect their own reputations because they think you might know something that could be damaging to their, uh, pillarhood."

Trixie thought for a bit.

"I guess we should start with the obvious," she said. "Ellis out there in that truck. He was my boyfriend, if you can call it that, when I was thirteen. He was already nineteen and should've knowed better. He got me pregnant when I was fifteen and he was twenty-one. He signed papers giving up all parental rights in exchange for having no parental obligations, no child support or nothin,' and in return, I never gave up his name as the boy's father so he wouldn't go to jail for statutory rape of a minor. Never told my boy that was his father until a couple weeks ago when Ellis came over all drunk and obnoxious and blurted it out. Tyler overheard it, so I had to explain somethin' I never wanted to explain. He used to come sniffin' around wantin' to visit me for free when I was in bid'ness, but I always said no. Wanted nothin' to do with him anymore. I finally had to go to court to get a restrainin' order, and I told him if he didn't abide by that, I'd file charges on the rape thing and he'd go to prison. He steered clear of me until after he heard I won the lottery."

Lee jotted a couple of notes on a pad of paper. "Yeah, he's a prime suspect. But you said before you didn't think he left the death threat, and that he didn't appear to be one of the gentlemen who paid a visit to Mason's office."

"No, but maybe he's still involved somehow. But it doesn't really seem like him. He's more the type to get drunk and show up askin' for money."

"He has a criminal record. Pretty substantial."

"Yeah, that's the only career he's ever been able to hold down for more 'n a month."

"Who else?"

"Mr. Armstrong said this Ms. Roberts from FPS has been known to push people around unless they paid her off."

"I've checked into that," Lee said. "There was one formal complaint, about eight years ago, where someone alleged that. There was an investigation, and the parents recanted their accusation. No evidence. She was cleared. A few rumors after that, but that was most likely gossip that got started because of the one false allegation."

"Maybe she got to them, threatened them or somethin'."

"These folks were a real piece of work. No credibility. Like Ellis, they were career criminals. Drug addicts and small-time dealers—husband-wife team. Kids running around the house with crack pipes and drugs scattered all over the kitchen table."

Trixie knew she had no right to judge any parents for being unsuitable considering what she'd been doing. But she hadn't had a choice, had she? She had to provide for her boy. When she started, it was only going to be a few times to get them on their feet. Just for a little while. But then it kind of grew. Got impossible to stop. Maybe like being addicted to meth or something.

Trixie rolled a tissue in her hands. "So even if they were tellin' the truth, no one would've believed 'em anyways." She paused. "Kind of like if the momma was a hooker or somethin'." It took her a moment to realize she'd said that out loud.

Lee didn't react other than to glance out the window again. "Besides Ellis, who's obviously a person of interest here, and this social worker, who might or might not be, who else should I be interested in?"

"There's a couple. Husband and wife, I mean. Jasper and Bee Callahan. He's the mayor and heads up the church building committee that has applied for a grant from my foundation. Bee is the treasurer of the Ladies' Society Circle, and they're up for a grant too. Mason's got suspicions that they both might be skimmin' a little off the top."

Lee pulled his attention away from the window and back to Trixie. "How would harassing you help them get the money?"

"I don't know," she said. "Seems like they out to be goin' out of their way to be nice to me."

"Unless they think Mason's onto them. And this Jasper was a client of yours." It wasn't a question, just a statement of fact.

"How'd you know that?"

Lee jotted notes and didn't look up. "I didn't until just now."

Trixie didn't know whether to be furious or impressed, so she decided to ignore it.

"And then there's Lamar Reeves," Lee continued. "President of the bank, church treasurer, another client of yours, and he might be upset that you brought your financial business to Mason rather than to him."

"Why do you think he was a client of mine?"

"You can tell me if I'm wrong. Let's just say he has a long, well-established history of visiting professional women, so again, I just made an assumption. Usually in Las Vegas or at banking conventions in Miami, Chicago, Dallas, Phoenix. He's also in deep financial trouble. Bank is on shaky ground. His personal finances are even worse."

Trixie thought about that massive estate where Lamar and Cass raised two kids with eleven bathrooms. She also thought having more money than God didn't protect you from losing all of it. Or worse.

"Not sure why you need me to tell you anything since you already know."

"If I'm going to do my job for you, you've got to learn to open up and trust me. Even if you don't trust me. Yet. You will."

Trixie looked out the second-floor window, down to the street where Ellis's truck still sat, with Ellis still in it, still smoking, flicking ashes out the window. She looked around the conference room. Old paneling on three sides, all windows on the other, one door to the hallway and one door to Mason's office. A conference table with a speakerphone in the middle. A few pictures hanging on the walls that looked like they'd been pilfered from a Motel 6.

"I got one more name," she said. "Might be nothin'. Might be somethin'. Maybe he was a customer, maybe he weren't. I ain't sayin.'"

"Are you thinking who I'm thinking?" Lee asked.

"You first then," Trixie said.

"I'm thinking the thin blue line, Pineywoods' finest, protecting and serving."

"We do seem to be on the same page now," Trixie said.

"About time. If word got out that he wasn't always on the upper side of the moral equation, he could stand to lose his job, his wife, his kids, his house, his reputation. Not that his reputation is all that shiny anyway. But his contract with the city includes a morals clause. He wouldn't be as fortunate as I was, able to resign and keep my pension. He'd lose that too. And what's he got? Five or six kids?"

"Four."

"And you seem pretty tight with that young wife of his. He might be worried you're going to say something to her."

"How much time do you spend followin' Ellis and how much time followin' me?"

"I only follow you to keep an eye on who else is following you." Lee glanced out the window again. "What is this bastard up to now?"

Trixie looked in time to see Ellis crossing the street toward Mason's office, glimpsing his hat just before he disappeared under the building's awning.

Lee stood and stuck his head out the conference room door. "Mason, looks like we might be having an uninvited guest heading our way."

Lee motioned Trixie into Mason's office as cowboy boots thumped up the flight of wooden stairs. "I'll be right on this side of the door listening. He doesn't need to see me, but if necessary, I'll show myself. If I do, you two drop to the floor."

Trixie sat in her usual chair across from Mason's desk, her back to the door, the hairs on her neck prickling at the thought of Ellis coming in behind her any second. Neither spoke, pretending to be reviewing paperwork as boots came down the hall then stopped. After a moment of silence, the footsteps retreated, then clomped back down the stairs in a hurry. Out the window, Ellis crossed the street and climbed into his truck, nearly backing into a minivan as he pulled out of the parking space, then left in a huff of blue smoke and burning rubber, fishtailing down the street.

Lee stepped through the door between the conference room and the office, a gun in his hand that looked three times the size of Trixie's, which he immediately slipped into a holster under his sports coat. She wasn't sure how it seemed to disappear as soon as he put it away, not leaving any protruding bulge. The thing was as big as a small car.

Trixie rejoined Lee in the conference room, and they got Armstrong on speakerphone to fill him in.

Then Trixie headed to yet another showing with Sabine. Leon couldn't make it this time. His knee was acting up, Sabine said, which Trixie knew was code for he'd been medicating himself with Beefeater's gin since lunch.

CHAPTER 24

With his momma's blessing, Ty headed out to the cow and tractor paths in the pasture on his still almost new bike, the one with knobby tires for the trails. A few hills, some short up-and-down rises that were perfect for catching some air.

He followed his usual path — climbing the hill up the right side of the pasture so he could get more speed coming down to the jumps. Had to avoid an occasional rock or cow patty, but he knew where they all lay. Mr. Garza had moved the cattle to the other pasture, so no new obstacles got in the way of his route.

He always made three trips around the pasture trail, working his legs harder on each pass to gain more speed, more air on the jumps, hissing through his teeth to create the sound effect of the audience cheering. Pumping a fist in the air to celebrate when he hit a particularly clean landing. Dusting himself off when the front tire hit first and tossed him into the dry grass. Maybe have to scrape some manure off his jeans.

Once, he'd gotten a mouthful. He'd learned to keep his face up and his mouth closed when he left the bicycle seat.

He had his marker. Two stones stuck out of the ground a few inches, one on each side of the trail, right before the first jump, about four inches of space between them. If he split the middle between those two rocks, he'd nail the first jump and be aligned just right for the second jump immediately following. He'd hit it so many times, he'd carved a small rut exactly where he needed that front tire to track.

There was only time to pump the pedals twice to regain some speed for the third and final jump, the tallest of the three. That's the one where, if he did it just right, he could get both tires off the ground at the same time.

He hadn't been able to get as much lift from his new bike as he did from his old one, even though it was faster. It was bigger, heavier, lots of extra chrome.

First pass was a bit slower today, as always, a trial run, making sure no new obstacles were in the way.

Instead of heading into the second pass, he pulled the bike to a stop at the shed near the barn closest to the house, where Mr. Garza kept his toolbox. Ty walked in and called out, but no answer.

Ty found a screwdriver and a pair of pliers. *Need to lighten the load. All this fancy looking stuff is weighin' me down.*

He removed the chrome fenders from both wheels. Not only lighter, it looked tougher. No need for that rearview mirror mounted on the handlebars. Not like he ever needed to look behind him. The chainguard had to go next. And the decorative piece of chrome across the handlebars. Looked cool but served no purpose other than adding excess weight that prevented him from getting the lift he needed.

Ty carefully stacked all the extra parts in an empty crate and admired his renovated creation. A new bike, still shiny, but stripped down like a monster ready to hit the trails.

Another easy pass. Ty could feel the weight lifted.

A second pass to add some speed, see if he could get both tires off the ground on the jumps. Then he'd really pour on the gas for the third run. The crowd held their breath in anticipation.

He aimed for the rut between the two stones that marked his perfect launching point, but the bike didn't want to go there. It pulled to the right, heading straight toward one of the rocks. He yanked the handlebars left. The tire wobbled, the bike jerked to the left, the front tire meeting the rock on that side head on.

The jolt from the tire to the handlebars knocked one hand loose as the bike got some air — more than he'd been accustomed to on that first easy jump. Instinct to hit the brakes kicked in, but pulling the brake lever doesn't slow you down when you're in midair, leaving the trail, and headed toward the pasture.

"Don't use the front brake," he recalled Mr. Garza's instructions, but that was the only hand still holding on. And it was too late.

The bike landed at an awkward angle, nose down, front wheel first with the brake squeezed tight. The tires didn't roll forward like a good landing. They didn't bounce like a rough landing.

Ty lay there in the grass and dirt and rocks, looking up at the blue sky through the chrome frame of the bike that landed on top of him by the time they stopped rolling. His jeans were torn — the nicer ones he'd worn to school and Momma had twice told him to change before going out for a ride. His head rested on a crunchy, dried cow patty.

"Momma's gonna kill me."

***

Clay stared into Trixie's fridge. "Ty around? I'd like to see if he's willing to share another of those grape sodas. I'll buy him some more."

"He's out ridin' his bike somewheres. Take one."

"I'm not one to take advantage of his generosity," Clay said as he popped the top. "Or yours."

Trixie poured a cup of coffee and sat at the kitchen table with a stack of papers.

"What are you working on now?"

"The offer on that house. My Realtor just sent all this over for my signature, then she'll submit it to the sellers' agent. It'll be a cash sale, but it still takes a few weeks, maybe a month or two, for closing, assumin' they accept my offer. I don't know why my agent wants to put in a low bid and make them negotiate. I'd rather offer what they're askin' and be done with it."

"You never know," Clay said. "They're probably asking for more than it's worth just as a starting offer, knowing they'll get offered less and they'll take less. It's a weird game. But always offer less and negotiate if you need to. I'm not trying to tell you how to manage your money — you got that under control — but that's how a lot of people with money lose it. They just think they can afford whatever and spend more than they need to."

Trixie looked at Clay and thought about it a moment. "How do you know so much about real estate negotiations?"

"One of my online classes walked us through all the ins and outs of buying, leasing, and financing a farm. That's how I know you're giving me way too good a deal on this place. But you make me a lowball offer, then you pay too much for that house, and you buy a sports car, give a chunk of change to this group or that group, and next thing you'll know, everybody will be taking advantage of your generosity, and your money won't last as long as you thought it would."

"You can be pretty smart for a farm boy."

"You can be pretty smart for a farm girl. And that's why I'll be replacing those grape sodas."

"Speaking of grape sodas, that boy should be home by now. He better've changed out of his good jeans before he went out there."

Clay tried to suppress a grape belch, then said, "I'll go flag him in."

Clay left to call Ty in, and Trixie took the time to go through a few dozen sheets of paper to initial at the bottom of each page and sign in the fourteen places her Realtor had highlighted, remembering to print her name and date each line.

About the time she'd found the last signature line, the engine on Clay's truck roared to life and spun across the gravel.

What in the world? Out the kitchen window, Clay's pickup bounced across the rutted pasture on an old tractor trail.

She ran out the screen door and across the gravel driveway to the edge of the pasture. In the distance, she could just make out a crumpled bike, chrome reflecting the late afternoon sun.

"Ty!" she screamed and started to run down the tractor path, then stopped. She ran back inside and grabbed her phone in case she needed to call an ambulance. She watched as Clay peeled the bike off Ty and helped him to his feet. After a few steps, he picked him up and laid him in the cab, then one-armed the bike into the bed.

Clay drove much slower on the return trip.

Must be okay or he'd still be hurryin'. Or maybe he's hurt so bad he doesn't want to bounce him around.

Clay pulled up next to Trixie.

"Do I need to call 9-1-1?"

"Just get in. This'll be quicker."

Ty looked up at his momma. "Sorry about my jeans."

Trixie slid into the seat, pulling Ty over to rest his head on her lap. An unnatural warmth spread on her thigh as the blood seeped from the back of his head onto her new jeans.

***

Clay lifted Ty off Trixie's lap. He was still conscious, not talking much, but not crying or whining. More sedate than Trixie had ever seen him.

Trixie ran into the emergency room as the automatic double doors swooshed open, rushing to the registration desk to let them know.

A nurse immediately ran to Trixie's aid, held her arm and tried to escort her to a gurney waiting in the hall. "Let's get you off your feet. The doctor's on the way. Can you tell me what happened? How are you feeling?"

"Not me," Trixie said as the nurse stared at her blood-soaked jeans. She pointed behind her as Clay walked in carrying Ty. "My boy."

Clay walked over and laid Ty on the gurney. The blood immediately spread across the white pillow.

The waiting room—with an elderly couple, young parents with a crying baby, and a mom with a teenage boy holding his arm in a homemade sling—stared as Ty was rushed back to a room while they had to continue waiting. Trixie went with Ty and the nurse, and Clay stepped back out of the way.

The nurse set to work as she turned Ty this way and that, getting a gauze bandage on the back of his head to stem the tide, checking him for any other injuries besides the obvious gash. Some smaller cuts on his arms, a swollen and red cheekbone, a cracked tooth—one of his adult teeth, so that would need to be fixed. A deep, softball-size bruise on his back that glowed an angry red and purple. He could wiggle his toes and move his arms. He grew sleepier by the minute, but the nurse kept asking him questions to keep him awake and talking.

"What grade are you in?"

"Second. No, third. I think."

"Do you remember what happened?"

Ty's words weren't coming out right. Something about jumping cows.

"Can you tell me where it hurts?"

He said nothing hurt. He just wanted to go to sleep.

That's when Trixie knew he was hurt bad 'cause that boy never wanted to go to sleep.

"What's your favorite TV show? Do you like sports? What do you like to eat? Do you have a girlfriend?" The nurse was grasping for any topic of conversation that would keep Ty talking.

A man walked in.

"You the doctor?" Trixie asked.

"No, I'm a nurse practitioner. Name's Cameron. Just call me Cam. The doc will be here in just a moment."

Trixie never knew the ER in this little town's hospital could be so busy.

Cam checked the first nurse's work and asked her a few questions, then turned to Trixie. "Can you tell me what happened?"

"He was out riding his bike. Took a tumble. He's lost so much blood."

Cam looked at Trixie's jeans. "Are you hurt, or is that all his blood?"

"All his."

"We're getting the bleeding stopped. Head wounds always look awful because there's so much blood. Not as bad as it looks. Lots of little blood vessels and capillaries on the scalp. They bleed like crazy. He's going to need a few stitches. Hope he doesn't mind too much if we shave some hair. Then the doc will probably order an x-ray."

"Why's he so sleepy?"

"That can be a normal symptom of a bump to the head. We want to keep him awake. Could be a concussion. Doc will check that out too, of course."

The curtain flew open. Trixie turned, expecting the doctor. It wasn't the doc. It was Leon and Sabine.

"How's my baby boy?" Sabine asked, her face turning white as she saw the blood on Trixie and all over the pillow and sheet surrounding Ty.

Cam turned to Sabine. "We're getting him all taken care of, ma'am, but we will need to ask you to sit in the waiting area. Not enough room back here for everyone, and only one visitor allowed."

"Go on, Momma. I'll come fill you in in a few minutes. And how'd y'all get here anyway?"

"You called us."

Trixie didn't remember calling her momma. The drive from the farm to the ER was a blur. She remembered singing to Ty. "Amazing Grace" and "The Old Rugged Cross," one verse of each. That's all she could remember from her youth at the Pentecostal church, so she repeated them both a few times. More to sooth her own nerves and fill the silence as Clay drove.

Leon held Sabine's arm and gave her a gentle tug to step out. Trixie walked into the hallway with them.

"How'd y'all get here anyway? You ain't supposed to be drivin'."

"I drove," Leon said. "Thankfully the car started."

"You don't need to be drivin' neither." Trixie glared into Leon's eyes, looking for signs.

"I'm fine. Ain't had nothin' to drink in three days. Somethin' told me to quit drinkin'. Maybe this was why."

Leon escorted Sabine back to the waiting room to sit with Clay, and Trixie pushed through the curtain to wait for the doc and hold her boy's hand. She needed to keep talking to him, keep him awake, alert as possible. Don't let him fall asleep, the nurse had said. Don't let him slip away. Don't ever let him out of sight again.

Oh please please please Lord let my boy be okay please don't take him from me please please oh Jesus I'm so sorry for ever'thing I ever done please don't take my boy I can't live without him I'm so sorry I'll be better I'll go to church I'll give all that damn money away I don't want it no more I'll never have sex ever again with nobody ever please oh Lord please fix my little man...

"You know, sweetie," the first nurse said. Trixie never caught her name. "We've got some spare scrubs back here if you want to go wash up and get into clean, dry clothes. Those are probably ruined, and that's going to start getting real sticky as it dries."

Trixie didn't want to leave. She didn't want to let go of Ty's hand. She stroked his hair, still short from his last haircut. At least they wouldn't have to shave much.

Another woman walked in, a tall woman with black hair and piercing, raven eyes. "This must be Tyler. I'm Dr. Castro. Let's have a look, shall we?"

Trixie nodded hello but couldn't get any words past the lump in her throat. She wasn't going to start bawling again. She'd done that twice recently, and Ty needed to see her calm and collected.

Dr. Castro turned Ty on his side and peeled the bandage back to look at the back of his head. She pulled the sheet down and examined the bruise on his back. Checked his arms and legs again, his split lip and cracked tooth, felt around his neck and throat. Listened to his heart and lungs with the stethoscope. Looked in each eye with a penlight. Poked and prodded his belly, then covered him back up to his neck.

"We're going to get some pictures, make sure nothing is fractured or going on inside that we can't see. A radiology tech will be down in just a few minutes to take him up. Should only take twenty minutes or so, then we'll have a better idea. I don't see any obvious signs of anything, but this is to rule out anything more serious, just to be safe. Right now, I'd say he took a pretty good bump to the head, and that's going to hurt for a few days. Might have a mild concussion. Hope he doesn't mind staying home from school a few days."

The doc rested a hand on Trixie's shoulder. "Are you injured? Or is this all his blood?"

Trixie still couldn't get her voice to work, so Cam said, "All his. We're going to get her into some clean scrubs when they take him up to radiology."

Then everyone left the room, leaving Trixie alone with Ty with instructions to keep him talking, or at least awake.

She got him a sip of water. Just a tiny sip through one of those bendy straws. She looked around to see if there were any more of those straws she might be able to take with her. He'd like to drink grape soda out of those. She patted his arm and gently rested a hand on his cheek.

Ty flinched. "That hurts."

"You look worse than after your fight with that boy. You look more like he did, I think."

"Cool."

"You remember what happened yet?"

"Yeah. That bike's too big for me. I hate it. I want my old bike back."

If Trixie hadn't won the Powerball, she wouldn't have had the money to buy that new bike, and Ty would be home having supper about now, then finishing up his homework if he'd remembered to bring it home, then an hour of TV or video games and then bath and then bed and then do it again tomorrow. He wouldn't be lying here on a blood-soaked hospital gurney.

Did the Lord answer her prayers for a way out of what she'd been doing? Or did He do this to teach her a lesson? Or maybe it wasn't God that gave her the numbers to Powerball. She'd never been much for believing in Satan like the preacher at her old church used to rant about, but she'd never fully gotten that out of her mind either. When you're eight years old and the preacher is yelling about how the Devil is going to come to you looking like something good and beautiful to trick you, that never really leaves you.

She'd always pictured Satan looking more like a dirty cowboy with dangerous-looking homegrown tattoos, fiery green eyes, and a scar on his face. When she met Lucifer face to face the first time, she knew. He introduced himself as Ellis, but she knew, and she climbed into the pickup truck with him anyway.

God had taken her daddy. What worse could Satan do?

The first nurse came back in with an armload of new linens for the gurney and a stack of clean nurse's scrubs for Trixie.

"When they take him to radiology," she said, "I'll change this bed out. And that would be a good time for you to clean up too. Then you can go visit with your husband and parents out in the waiting room."

"I'm not..." Trixie trailed off. Wasn't worth correcting her.

***

When Trixie walked into the waiting room, everyone looked up. The parents with the baby were gone. Another elderly couple had taken their place. Clay, Leon, and Sabine all glanced at her then went back to reading.

Clay was the first to look up again. "Trixie? I thought you were a doctor."

All the blood washed off, the blue scrubs fit loose and comfortable, and she'd rinsed some blood out of her hair and tied it up in a rough bun.

Sabine leaped from her chair and hugged her, stifling a sob. "How's that boy?"

Trixie led her momma back to the chair and sat beside her. She leaned forward to see everyone.

"He's gonna be fine. Took a pretty good thump to the head. Lots of blood, but they'll stitch him up. Might have a concussion. They're doing a scan to make sure ever'thing inside is okay. He chipped a tooth pretty good, got some bruises. We'll know more in a bit."

Sabine sobbed in relief. Leon wiped his eyes.

Clay stood and moved to the empty seat on the other side of Trixie. He put his arm around her shoulders. "I called Brother Kent and Harris. They set the prayer chain in motion. The whole church is praying for him right now."

Clay pulled out his wallet and a few bills, handing them over to Sabine. "Why don't you two run get us some fast food somewhere. We may be here a while."

"Not McDonald's," Trixie said. "Anything but McDonald's." The sun was setting, but Trixie hadn't even thought about supper. She didn't know if she could get anything down or keep it down.

"And get me a Diet Coke," she added as Leon and Sabine shuffled out the double doors with a whoosh. "I don't think they heard me."

"There's a drink machine here." Clay walked over and slipped a dollar bill in the vending machine. "Diet Pepsi okay?"

"How 'bout a Dr. Pepper instead."

Clay handed the can of soda to Trixie and sat beside her again.

"Your whole church is prayin' for Ty right now?" she asked after taking a swig, not realizing how parched she was until the cold bubbles hit her throat.

"Yup. We're all praying for you too. Ya know, for strength and comfort. Harris said she'd come down and sit with you, if you want. I told her to wait a bit. Seemed like there was enough of us here."

"Don't want to take up all the seats here. You've been prayin' for me too?"

"I've been praying for you for years."

"You haven't even known me for years."

"I've been praying for you since before I knew you."

"What are you talkin' about?"

"I figured God had someone special out there, someone He intended for me to be with. I just prayed He'd introduce us when the time was right. First time I saw you, I knew. But God said the time wasn't right yet."

"What's He sayin' right now?"

"I think He's saying the time is right. Either that, or I just got impatient and jumped the gun."

Trixie looked away. Looked to the reception desk. Down the hall. At the drink machine. Anywhere but into those eyes. Clay couldn't be after her farm. She'd already worked out that deal with him. He never seemed to care about her money, so that wasn't it. Didn't even want her to be out the cost of a grape soda. They'd kissed a couple of times, and he'd never pressed her for anything more on that front either.

Why in the world would any man want her if not for her body or her money?

CHAPTER 25

Trixie rediscovered her appetite when Leon and Sabine returned with hot sandwiches from a local sub shop. Ty would be back from radiology any minute, so she needed to eat fast. That, and she had no idea how hungry she was until she unwrapped the shrimp po' boy with extra hot sauce, just how she liked it. Her momma knew how she ordered it.

She wasn't three bites in when her phone rang. She had no intention on answering—if it was important, she'd call them back—but she glanced to see who it was. Ms. Roberts. Family Protective Services.

"Oh crap," she said, shooting a piece of shrimp from her mouth to the lap of her clean scrubs. "She's probably been up at the house waiting on me and getting mad as a wet hornet." Trixie picked up before it went to voice mail, figuring that would just make her madder.

"I'm so sorry, Ms. Roberts. I'm up at the ER in town with Tyler. He fell riding his bike, needs a couple of stitches. Can we reschedule?"

Trixie paused. "There's no need for that, ma'am. I'll be home all day tomorrow, or any other time. Or I can meet you wherever you'd like that's more convenient for you."

Trixie listened some more. "Well, I'm a little busy here takin' care of my boy, but I guess that's fine, if you want to drive down here. Not sure how much longer we're gonna be."

Trixie hung up and shook her head, wrapping up the remaining three-quarters of her po' boy. Her appetite disappeared as quickly as it had reappeared.

"What's wrong?" Sabine asked.

"I had a meeting with that social worker this evening, but with all this goin' on, I completely forgot. I should have called her to reschedule, and now she's pissed off. She's comin' down here. To document his injuries probably. Try to make me out to be negligent and unfit and all that."

Clay stood and paced. Leon stood and stretched, then joined Clay in pacing, albeit a bit slower because of his knee. Sabine patted Trixie's thigh.

"You don't worry about it none. She's just doin' her job, but she ain't got no reason to blame you for any of this. You're a good momma. Better 'n I ever was to you."

"You were a good momma. I know I was a mess after Daddy died. Too much of a mess to deal with."

"Me too, child. Me too. I mean, your daddy died, but my husband died. Love of my life. I fell apart, and I shouldn't have. I had a kid that needed me, but I wasn't there for you. That left you to deal with losin' your daddy without a momma to lean on. I wish I could take it back, wish every day I could go back and do it over. But I can't. I can't."

"I know, Momma, I know. It ain't your fault. Despite it all, I always knew you loved me."

"More than my own life, child. As much as you love that boy in there."

Trixie put her arm around her momma's shoulders and pulled all her strength together to hold her while Sabine sobbed. Everybody else needed to cry, but Trixie needed to just keep it together — for her momma, for Ty, and to not fall apart in front of Ms. Roberts. That would be no good. No good at all.

***

The radiology tech wheeled Ty back into his cubicle in the ER. Cam waved Trixie over, but she was already up and on her way. Ty was cleaned up, head bandaged but waiting on the stitches. Clean sheets and pillow on his gurney.

"Hey, Momma. Look what I got." Ty held up a stethoscope. He plugged the earpieces into his ears and listened to his heart. "I don't hear nothin'."

"That means you're dead," Cam told him. "So you don't need those stitches after all."

"Fine with me, but if I'm dead, how am I still talkin' to ya?" He moved the scope around a bit. "Ah, there it is. I can hear it. I'm still alive." Ty grinned at Trixie, his chipped tooth front and center.

"Don't even joke about that, little man. You die, you're grounded."

"Sorry, ma'am," Cam said. "Didn't mean to upset you. He's got quite a sense of humor though, doesn't he? Now, let's get you ready for sewing class. We're going to numb this up and you won't feel much of anything. If it hurts, you just raise your hand to let me know."

Trixie sat next to Ty and held his hand while Cam and the other nurse worked on the back of his head. Shaved a spot and rubbed some solution on it. Trixie had to turn away for a moment when they pulled out the syringe to numb it up.

"This might sting for about two seconds," Cam said, "so close your eyes, take a deep breath, hold it, hold it, now exhale real slow."

Trixie found herself breathing along with Ty. When he squeezed her hand extra tight and his eyes flew open wide, she inhaled deep and hoped she'd remain conscious. Then he relaxed his grip and fought off the tears that had formed in his eyes.

"All done with the hard part," Cam said. "Good job. We'll wait a couple minutes for that to kick in, and you won't feel anything when we stitch that up. Just one question, young man."

"What's that?" Ty asked.

"Do you want stitches, or would you prefer we put in a zipper? Then your mother could unzip it now and then to make sure your brain didn't fall out."

Ty grinned and giggled. Trixie exhaled the breath she'd been holding.

The receptionist stuck her head through the curtain. "Ms. Burnet, there's a woman here to see you. A Ms. Roberts, said you were expecting her."

"Tell her I'll be out to see her as soon as they're done stitching up my boy. She can chill in the waiting room with everyone else." Trixie didn't want to be rude to the woman, but this wasn't the time for it, and she was in no mood.

She also wanted to take a few more minutes to calm her nerves so she could deal with Ms. Roberts. *What was her first name? Lynn. That's right. Lynn.*

It didn't seem like two minutes elapsed before Cam said, "All done. Looks great. The doc will be in shortly to look it over and let you know what the scans show. He's obviously looking a lot better now than when he first came in."

"Can I see?" Ty said.

"I don't think you can see it in the mirror," Cam said.

"One sec," Trixie said. She pulled her phone out and handed it to Cam. "You take it and show him. I don't think I'm ready to see it yet."

Cam took a couple of shots then showed Ty.

"Cool. A zipper would have been cooler though."

"Maybe next time," Cam said.

"Ain't gonna be no next time," Trixie said as Cam handed the phone back to her and she dropped it into the deep front pockets of her scrubs.

She wondered if she would be charged for the clothes, or if she was supposed to bring them back or what. Her bloody jeans and blouse were in a garbage bag in the waiting room at Sabine's feet. "You stay here and rest. I've got to go out and talk to this lady. Cam, will someone let me know when the doctor comes back?"

"You go ahead. We'll find you."

Trixie kissed Ty on the forehead and took a deep breath on her way to the waiting area. She spotted Ms. Roberts—Lynn—sitting on the opposite side of the room from Clay, Sabine, and Leon, the only ones left in the waiting room. Trixie glanced at her but walked straight to her family first to give them an update before walking over to the social worker.

Swallowing her pride, she went the apologetic route first.

"I'm so sorry to have missed you, Lynn. I didn't mean to stand you up, but as you can see, we had a bit of an emergency. I should have called but I just forgot with all this going on."

"I understand," she replied, looking a little off guard at the first-name basis and the immediate apology. "I have a few questions, but let's talk in private. I checked with the receptionist here, and they've been kind enough to offer us a room to chat." Lynn stood and headed to the reception desk, where the lady pointed her down the hall to the right. She turned and looked at Trixie.

Trixie didn't budge. "This is my family here. No one else around. I'm waiting for the doctor to come give me an update, so let's just talk here. I need to be here when she comes back."

Lynn hesitated, looking perplexed that Trixie didn't follow her or follow instructions. She looked like she wasn't used to being questioned. "I'd really prefer to speak privately."

"I'm agreeing to meet with you right here. Whatever you have to say, you can say in front of my family." Trixie realized she was including Clay in 'my family.' And he didn't get up to politely excuse himself.

"Okay," Lynn said with a deep sigh. "If you insist." She came back to the waiting area and sat down again.

Trixie didn't sit, just hovered near her.

"Let's start with you telling me what happened. How's your boy?"

"He's gonna be fine. Fell on his bike. Bumped his head. Needed a couple of stitches. It happens."

"Yes, those things happen, especially with young, active boys." Lynn pulled out her pad and started jotting notes, then pulled out a sheet of paper and handed it to Trixie. "This is to notify you that we have the right to see all medical reports on this incident. I'll be filing this with the hospital administrator first thing tomorrow morning."

Trixie had never seen Leon move that fast before, but he was up from his chair and across the room in a flash, next to Trixie, hovering even taller over the seated social worker.

"What gives you the right to see private medical information?" Leon demanded.

"Uncle Leon, it's okay. Don't worry about it. Go sit down. I'll handle this."

Lynn pulled her FPS ID card up, which hung on a pink lanyard around her neck. "This, along with state laws protecting children and a judge's orders give me the right."

Leon didn't say anything else, but he didn't back off. Trixie put a hand on his shoulder to encourage him to take a step back. He was looking a little aggressive — something she'd never seen in him before, but she wasn't sure she'd ever seen him completely sober either. Maybe the gin took the edge off that side of him.

Lynn stood, going face to face with Leon, as close to face to face as she could given his height advantage, her chin jutted out like she was daring him to punch her.

"Leon, go sit down. I got this."

Leon shook his head and exhaled, then turned to go back to his seat. The pop of his knee echoed across the waiting room, and Leon crumpled to the vinyl floor.

Trixie couldn't reach out to grab him fast enough, not that it would have helped. Probably just pulled her over with him.

Sabine screamed. Trixie dropped to his side as he held his knee and writhed, groaning. Clay and Sabine both were at Leon's side within a breath.

"Did you push him?" Sabine screamed in Lynn's face.

"No, of course not," Lynn said, looking a bit chastised and anxious.

"Nurse!" Trixie called.

Cam came running.

"He's got a bad knee, I heard it pop," Trixie told the nurse.

"I didn't hear no pop," Sabine said. "I think she pushed him. Knocking down a crippled old man. Who does that?"

Clay and Trixie stepped away to allow Sabine to kneel beside Leon on one side while Cam worked on his other side, asking questions, manipulating the knee. "Let's get you into a wheelchair and get you back to have the doc take a look at this. Did you hit your head or anything when you fell?"

"Nope," Leon said with a grimace. "I've fallen enough, I've learned how to land."

"This is getting to be more excitement than I can take for one evening," Trixie said, then turned to Lynn. "Can we pick this up tomorrow? You do whatever you want with getting his medical records. Ain't got nothin' to hide."

Lynn gathered her papers and shoved them back into a folder, then put the folder back into her briefcase. "I'll call you tomorrow." She headed toward the ER parking lot.

Trixie followed. "Ma'am?"

"Yes?"

"I do apologize for my uncle. He's just very defensive of family. He's not a violent or angry man. Never seen him lose his cool before. I think this was just a lot of stress for him. He'd never lay a hand on ya, and he's a good man. I'm just sorry tonight has been such a mess and an inconvenience for you."

Lynn stopped and came back to Trixie, standing on the sidewalk just outside the ER doors. She reached out and patted Trixie's arm like an old friend.

"I know you've been going through a lot lately. But I have a job to do. And that includes writing another report to detail the injuries to your son, and how they occurred."

"You said yourself that these things just happen with boys. They're rough and tumble."

"Yes, they can be. As a parent, your responsibility is to help protect him. My job is to make sure a child is getting adequate supervision to mitigate the frequency and severity of injuries. Now, there are two ways this report might go. I might find that it was a normal childhood accident—a boy being a boy, taking a fall on his bicycle. No big deal, not a concern. Or, I might write the report up noting that this is the second time he's suffered significant injuries in the past month, that his teacher and school officials have expressed concerns about his behavior at school, that something seems off. And I do have a witness willing to go on the record about that business you were running out of your home, sometimes while your boy was upstairs sleeping. Maybe we have an issue of parental neglect or negligence here at the least, maybe worse. How do I know he fell off his bike? How do I know someone didn't intentionally hurt him?"

"You know that's not true," Trixie snapped. "You know I'd never hurt that boy."

"Maybe you wouldn't, maybe you would. Maybe one of the men always hanging around your place would. Maybe that hotheaded colored man you call your uncle hurt him. I think a judge would be interested in seeing more investigation into this, maybe moving the boy into protective care for the duration of the investigation."

"Please don't take my boy. Please don't do that. There's no need."

Lynn looked around at the nearly empty parking lot. "Like I said, it all depends on what I find and how I decide to write up that report. Might be something serious that needs state intervention. Might just be typical childhood injury through no one's fault and you sought immediate medical attention as a good mother should."

Lynn stepped closer to Trixie and leaned in, like she was confiding to a friend. "I think we both know how we can work this out to everyone's satisfaction. A win-win for everyone."

Trixie leaned back to get her personal space out of Lynn's face. "What do you mean?"

"What I'm saying is, you could save yourself a lot of grief and help make sure this report goes your way. I mean, you just came into enough funds to really help yourself out of this situation. Would just be between you and me."

"I'm not following you."

"I could be putting my job at risk to write something up that isn't true."

"I'm not asking you to write anything that ain't true."

"I'm not willing to take that risk unless you made it worth my while."

Trixie stared at Lynn, unable to comprehend what was happening. Was Armstrong right? Had this woman been shaking down moms and dads for years? She caught her breath, held her words for a moment.

"How much?"

"Fifty."

"Fifty dollars?"

"Thousand."

"A thousand dollars?"

"Fifty thousand. It would take $50,000 to ensure this report goes your way, with the whole situation dropped and an all-clear from me to the judge."

"That's a lot of money," Trixie said.

"Not for you, it isn't. You're not trying to negotiate for your child, are you?"

"It ain't like I can write you a check tonight. I'll have to move money over and—"

Lynn started laughing. "Oh no, dear, no checks. Cash. Twenty-dollar bills. As long as I have it all before court next Tuesday. We have two more appointments. I advise you keep them both. Bring $25,000 to each meeting. I'll have two different reports written and ready to file. Your cooperation, or lack thereof, will determine which one the judge sees and which one goes through the shredder. Understood?"

The ER doors swooshed open, and Clay stepped out.

"Not a word to anyone, not even your Latin lover there," Lynn whispered to Trixie. "Understood?"

"Trixie, the doc is ready to see you."

"I'll be right there," she called over her shoulder. She faced Lynn and leaned closer, then repeated in a firm voice. "Fifty thousand dollars and you'll write a good report for the judge. Cash. All twenty-dollar bills. Understood. How do I know you're going to keep your end of the bargain?"

"I always keep my word, honey." Lynn turned and walked toward her car. "See you day after tomorrow, four o'clock at your place. Be there this time and have the down payment with you so I'll know you're serious about wanting to keep your boy."

Trixie walked to Clay. She tried to catch her breath, on the verge of hyperventilating. Every nerve in her body was firing. Every muscle shook. Her teeth chattered like she was cold.

"What was that all about?" Clay asked. "You okay?" Clay gently rested his hand on the small of her back as they walked into the waiting area.

"Yeah, I'm gonna be fine. Would you ask the doctor to wait one more minute for me please?"

CHAPTER 26

Trixie stepped around the corner into an empty hallway as Clay went to find the doctor. She wiped her sweaty palms on her once-clean blue scrubs. Her hands trembled, her fingers jittered. She had trouble getting her eyes to focus on anything.

All the shaking made it a difficult chore to pull out her phone. She had trouble making out the buttons through her blurry vision. But she found them.

She hit the 'stop recording' button, then hit 'share,' clicked on Madison's name, and hit 'send.'

She took another deep, calming breath, or maybe two, then walked into Ty's room, checking to make sure the file transmitted okay before putting the phone away.

"So how is he, Doc?" she said with a steady voice and a smile.

"They're gonna ampimitate my head, Momma."

Dr. Castro laughed.

"Have you had a chance to look at my uncle's knee yet?"

***

Dr. Castro wrote a note for Ty to miss three days of school to stay home and rest, no strenuous activity for a week, and a follow-up visit to the family physician. He'd be tired and have a headache, but it was a mild concussion, no fractures, no internal injuries. Nasty bruises on his cheekbone and back. Everything else was minor abrasions like he'd get every day anyway.

Trixie drove Leon and Sabine home. Clay followed and made sure Leon got up the stairs okay. Nothing broken there either. However old he was, he seemed much older and frailer in some ways, but in other ways, she could still see the younger version of him, the version in stories he would tell Ty—the tank driver from the Gulf War and the boxing champion of Fort Hood. That shrapnel in his knee ended what he'd planned as a career in the Army that he could retire from at age forty.

Trixie climbed into Clay's pickup with Ty in the middle. Clay had pulled a horse blanket from behind the seat to throw down over the blood Ty had left behind.

"I'm sorry about your car seat," Trixie said. "I'll try and get that out tomorrow."

"What happened to his car seat?" Ty asked.

They pulled into Trixie's driveway. Clay pulled Ty's bike out of the pickup bed.

"You can throw that away," Ty said.

"Nothing wrong with it we can't fix," Clay said.

"I don't want it no more. I ain't ridin' it. Ever."

"You know what they say about falling off a horse?"

"Don't do that?"

"Well, that's the first thing they say. Don't fall off. Second thing they say is when you do fall off, because you will, you get right back up again. Otherwise, you get spooked. You get scared. You wait too long, you'll never do it again. You also learn why you fell off and learn not to do that again."

"I ain't scared. I just don't want to."

Trixie intervened. "Well, you have to wait a bit anyways. Doctor's orders. No bike riding for a bit. Then, we're going to get you one of those helmets. And a smaller bike. Maybe one with three wheels."

"Sheesh." Ty stared at his momma until they both burst out laughing, then Clay joined in before a round of goodnight hugs sent Ty to bed.

Clay and Trixie's goodnight hug lasted a bit longer under the front porch light.

"I meant what I said before," Clay said, "but I shouldn't have said anything. I hope I didn't scare you off."

"Take more than some ol' farmer to scare me off. But there's something we need to talk about before you decide to take this any further." This time, Trixie kissed Clay.

***

Shelby had texted Trixie about five times the night before, so Trixie called her the next morning and filled her in on Ty's injuries. She didn't mention the visit from FPS.

"I heard from Harris. We were praying for him."

"He'll be fine, so y'all's prayer chain must've worked," Trixie said. "But I'm gonna have to miss the Circle today. I have to stay home with him, and I'll have to drag him around to a couple meetings with me today. He'll be so bored, he'll be happy to go back to school. Tell ever'body there I should be back next week. And if you want to come over and help me sort out clothes for the sale sometime, just let me know."

Shelby could barely contain her enthusiasm for that, a chore that Trixie had kept putting off, and now the sale was in a week.

Mason wanted to meet today. And Armstrong and Lee. And her real estate agent had a counteroffer from the seller that she needed to review.

And she had a voice mail from Chief Hale.

Maybe she'd better drop Ty off with Momma and Leon. He could lie on their couch and watch TV rather than sit in waiting room while she was in meetings.

First, she called the chief back. He wanted to meet with her, Mason, and Armstrong all together. Yes, he was willing to come to Mason's office. She could kill all those birds with one stone.

***

Chief Hale was direct and to the point. He'd met with Marion Schleicher yesterday, and she'd asked him to open an investigation into Bee Callahan's handling of the Circle's finances. Based on information from Mason's audit of their books, Marion had suspicions. But the chief didn't want to open that can of worms—investigating the mayor's wife and the women's charity group. He hadn't promised Marion anything, but was willing to defer the lead to another law enforcement agency—the state, the FBI, whoever. Anyone but him. He had to go to church with these people, serve on committees and boards with Jasper. The mayor and city council had the authority to hire and fire the police chief. This was just too tangled and too many conflicts of interest wrapped up in a nest of vipers.

He could contact the state attorney general.

"Maybe the FBI," Mason suggested.

"Unless there's been some federal aspect to this," Armstrong said, "like crossing state lines, using phone lines and computer systems to commit fraud, there's no jurisdiction for the feds. And we're talking small potatoes here. The FBI isn't going to commit resources to investigate some little old lady who might've stolen a couple thousand in cash."

"I don't want the Circle to get shut down," Trixie said. "A big investigation is going to kill them. And I don't really want to see Bee sent to prison."

Everyone stared at the floor silently for a few minutes, pondering the next move, until Mason had another idea.

"What if Marion hired me to conduct a full financial audit for the Circle? I'd give the audit report to Marion, she could convene a meeting of the officers and confront Bee with it. Demand her quiet resignation and payment of restitution in exchange for not filing any charges. Based on everything I already have, I could get this done in less than a week. And the burden of proof wouldn't need to be as strong as for any criminal charges—just a strong suspicion with enough evidence to justify it, make it real uncomfortable for Bee to deny, letting her know it would all go public with a criminal investigation if she doesn't agree."

Armstrong and Hale looked at each other and nodded.

Trixie said, "I knew there was a reason I put you on my board."

The chief said he'd call Marion later this morning, after the Circle meeting had concluded, and run that by her. He was sure he could convince her to go that route. Then he excused himself because he had to go meet the fellas down at Roy's Diner for coffee and the latest gossip.

Armstrong took the lead on the next meeting.

"Mason, do you think it's possible for Trixie to get $25,000 in cash, all in twenty-dollar bills, by tomorrow afternoon?"

"First off, why? Second, I don't know how that would even be possible."

"Good," Armstrong said. "I thought that's what you'd say. Trixie, you need to stall at your meeting tomorrow with Ms. Roberts. Just let her know you're working on it, but it takes a week to get money wired out of investment accounts, and then the bank needs a few days to verify the deposit, and probably a few days to come up with that kind of cash. And forget using your phone to record the meeting. Lee here is going to set you up with a wire."

"Like in the movies?"

"Just like in the movies."

"I'm supposed to meet with her twice next week too. How long do you think I can keep stalling her?"

"I doubt you'll have to meet with her next week." Armstrong turned to Lee. "What's the latest on the break-ins and threats? Anything more on Ellis or Jasper?"

Lee cleared his throat and flipped through a tiny, leather-bound notebook.

"I just happened to be sitting on Ellis's favorite barstool when he came in yesterday. He seemed a bit put out but took the seat two down from me. Struck up a conversation with him, and eventually he moved over next to me. He's always looking for an angle to make a buck. I told him I knew a lawyer's office that needed to be trashed just to send a message. He started laughing and wondered what was going on. Said that was the second time in two weeks he'd been approached about trashing somebody's office. He was offered five hundred bucks to do that to some accountant's office, but he'd turned it down."

"Who approached him on that?"

"He didn't know. Some guy from out of town, just like me. Wondered if we knew each other. I think he got suspicious that I was an undercover cop trying to set him up, said he was real glad he'd turned down that other job too. But I asked if he knew anyone who'd be interested, maybe whoever it was that did the accountant would be interested in doing it again. He said he didn't know, but he gave me a name of someone who might know someone who might know someone. Then he swallowed his beer and excused himself, laughing his ass off all the way out the door."

"I ain't never knowed Ellis to turn down cash before."

Armstrong said, "Maybe he thinks he's working on a bigger payday with you."

The group chatted about various leads that went nowhere for the next few minutes, then Armstrong and Lee excused themselves. Lee would stop by the farmhouse tomorrow at two to get Trixie wired up, then he'd be parked down the road, around the corner where he was in range to listen, but Ms. Roberts wouldn't see him when she came to visit.

Mason had one more piece of business to discuss after the attorney and the investigator went their separate ways.

"We got a response from the church on their grant request, answering all our questions. Not to my satisfaction, but they at least are trying. This decision will be up to you. I have my doubts that they're running things as up-and-up as they should, but it's also very transparent. Doesn't appear to be any room for fraud here. Just a bunch of good old boys who are connected to everything in town, and now they're connected to this church building plan. Jasper especially. I think with Lamar as church treasurer, he's doing his best to ride herd on the whole thing to keep it all accounted for, legal, and open. Just not how I'd like to do business, especially for a church. I think their eyes are bigger than their stomachs. Big dreams and plans, more ego-based than reality."

"But you said it's my decision."

"Yes. It's your money, your foundation. As the director of your foundation, I recommend against it, or at least recommend holding off. It's not going anywhere. We could tell them their request is being put on hold for six months and will be reviewed again at that time. But I also understand your reasons for wanting to donate to their fund, be a member of the church, get your boy into that school. It's a good school. Fully accredited and they get high marks from the state. So, like I said, this one is your call."

"Write that letter. Tell them we are putting their request on hold for six months. I got too much to deal with right now. I need to pick up my boy and I got clothes to sort."

CHAPTER 27

"Oh my God!" Shelby said for what seemed like the hundredth time. "Look at this. It is so cute. But wherever would you wear something like this?"

"Roy's Diner, maybe," Trixie said with a grin.

"I'm so sorry. I keep forgetting you didn't wear these out, you wore them in."

"Never for long either. They're all practically brand new. You think anyone shopping at the Cast-Off Sale is going to buy things like this?"

"They won't be able to resist. Reagan's bringing in a younger crowd. These look like things you'd wear to a fancy nightclub in Houston or something like that. Girls will buy this stuff just to have it. Maybe they'd wear it for line dancing at the Winchester just to liven things up a bit."

One item would go in the box to donate to the sale. Another item would go into a box for donating to Goodwill. Maybe a trip to a Goodwill in Dallas would be in order. Occasionally an item would go in a plastic trash bag or back in the drawer.

"Why are there adult diapers here?"

"Oh, um, might be from back when my daddy was real sick, before he died." Trixie didn't like lying, but she wasn't telling that story about Shelby's future father-in-law.

"That's so sad. What should I do with them?"

"Toss 'em."

The stack of adult-size cloth diapers hit the plastic bag.

"Ooh, this is definitely something you don't wear out in public." Shelby held up a see-through teddy negligee, pink with lots of frills and matching see-through panties. "It's beautiful, but how could you sleep in this? I'd be freezing."

"You don't sleep in it, silly."

"Well, you can't just get rid of all this," Shelby said. "Might not work for the Cast-Off, too nice to throw it away. But I never felt right about donating used underwear, I don't care how good a shape they're in."

"Throw it back in the drawer then. I'll figure out what to do with those things later."

Shelby really wanted some of the shoes, but her feet were too wide to fit any of them. Then she held up a pair of clear acrylic platform shoes, at least six inches high, with gold straps. "These look like something Cass might have worn thirty years ago when she was pole-dancing." Shelby burst into hysterical cackling at the thought.

"Whyn't you give 'em to her as a Christmas gift?" Trixie said, then joined in, lying down on the floor next to Shelby, surrounded by piles of clothes, laughing until her sides hurt.

***

The meeting with Lee wasn't nearly the same barrel of laughs. He went over how the wire worked, held it up for her to see, then told her to take her shirt off.

"Why?"

"So I can put this on you?"

"I can put it on."

"No, I have to tape it on you, and make sure it works and that it's not going to be visible. A loose t-shirt would work best, if you have one."

Trixie went upstairs to get a t-shirt rather than the powder blue scoop-neck blouse she had on. She checked on Ty, who was napping.

Back in the kitchen, she hesitated again to remove her shirt in front of the investigator.

"You have a bra on, right?"

"Yeah, so?"

"Then I won't see anything. Didn't expect you to be quite so modest."

"I'm paying you, you're not paying me."

"I'd take my shirt off, but that's not going to help us any."

Trixie peeled off her blouse, and Lee held the microphone end to her sternum. Cold like a doctor's stethoscope.

"Hold this right here."

As she held it, he peeled off some medical tape and put on three strips to hold it in place. Then he wrapped the wire around her waist and taped it in the back, then connected the transmitter, about the size of a book of matches, and taped it in place. Then he taped the wire down in about five more places.

"How am I supposed to move with all this tape? I'll rip something loose."

"No, you won't. It's fine. You'll forget it's there. Now put your shirt on. Not that one."

Trixie slipped the t-shirt on over her head, a little awkward with the tape pulling at her skin as she stretched her arms over her head.

"Now," Lee said, "let's check it all again. Make sure everything is in place and hidden."

"Thought you said it wouldn't come loose."

"I've been known to lie."

But it hadn't come loose. Trixie was sure she'd have to soak in the tub to get that tape off.

Lee pulled out a small box with switches, buttons, and a set of headphones attached. "This is the receiver. I'll be listening to the whole conversation in real time, and this box will be recording it. If anything goes wrong, and I'm not expecting anything, I'll call your cell phone to interrupt you. If I'm not hearing anything, or the sound is too bad to make it out, I'll call you. If I call you, and I probably won't, I'll ask for Lee. You say wrong number and hang up. That way I know you're okay and we're just having technical issues. If that happens, just keep the meeting as brief as possible and don't worry about getting her to say anything. Just tell her you're working on it and you'll contact her, or have it for the next meeting, something like that."

"If everything is working?"

"If everything is working, let her do most of the talking. Just tell her you haven't been able to get access to the cash yet, just like Armstrong was telling you. You don't have to try to draw anything out of her or ask anything. Don't say more than you have to. No need to raise her suspicions by trying to get her to say anything. Just let her talk."

Lee put the receiver in his briefcase and headed out.

"That's it?" Trixie asked.

"I'm going to drive to the end of the driveway, then I'm going to turn this on. Give me one minute, then start talking so I can make sure it's transmitting clearly."

"What should I say?"

"Anything. It's just a test. Say, 'testing 1-2-3, testing 1-2-3,' if you want. Oh, and make sure no TV or stereo or anything is on."

The test worked perfectly. Lee drove about another hundred yards down the road, around the curve, and tested again. Still perfect.

***

"I thought you were prepared to be much more cooperative about this," Ms. Roberts said.

"I am. I'm trying. Just my funds are tied up in investments, and I have to go through a financial manager to sell off some stocks and transfer the funds to the bank. That takes a few days. I'm sure you're familiar with how all that works."

"Momma, can I get a snack?" Ty had come downstairs, finally waking up. He'd slept for nearly three hours.

"I'll be right back with you, Lynn." Trixie walked to the fridge to get a fruit cup and a glass of juice for Ty.

"Can I have a grape soda?"

"Not until after I get to the store to buy more."

"Did Mr. Garza drink them all?"

"Seems like it. You told him he could."

"Yeah, that's fine. I don't mind."

"Then take your snack up to your room and read. No TV just yet. And don't spill."

Ty headed back upstairs, and Trixie sat at the kitchen table again.

"Will there be anything else?"

"I told you before. This goes whichever way you decide. Not keeping your end of the bargain means you won't like the report I submit to the judge. Just keep that in mind. I'll see you Monday at four, and I expect to see some progress if you expect this to go well for you."

"We'll be fine. I promise."

After Ms. Roberts left, Trixie sat at the kitchen table and exhaled loudly right in Lee's earbuds. Within two minutes after Lynn's car had pulled out, Lee pulled in. He let her go in the bathroom to remove her shirt and peel off the tape and wires. She brought the piles of electronics, pieces of tape still stuck to it in several places, and likely a few layers of skin still attached to the tape.

"We'll do this again if there's another meeting with her. Sound came across great, everything's recorded. I'm taking this to Armstrong right now."

"He said I wouldn't have to meet with her again."

"Maybe, maybe not. Never know how these things go."

CHAPTER 28

Thank God it was Friday, and the last day of Ty's excuse from school. Still had to face Saturday and Sunday with that boy home and not allowed out to play or ride bikes. He was driving Trixie crazy. Felt like the last week of summer after three months at home and it had only been three days.

He'd read, but that gave him a headache. "How come TV don't give you a headache? It's givin' me one."

She played board games with him. Caught him jumping from the couch to the coffee table to the recliner once. "It's hot lava down there, Momma. I can't touch the floor."

"I'm gonna get that strap and hot lava your butt if you do it again."

"Then I'd have a buttcussion too."

Hard to hold the angry momma face long enough to be taken seriously when your kid's a riot.

"Go get out of those PJs and get real clothes on. We're goin' to the store."

"Why do I have to go? I'm sick, remember."

"You ain't sick. You're injured."

"Then I shouldn't be walkin'."

"Oh, you can jump on the couch but you can't walk. Your brain is injured—your legs are fine. Besides, you can help carry the grape soda."

Trixie had already learned the hard way that the Corvette wasn't really designed for major grocery trips. More trips into town with smaller hauls. No room in the tiny back seat, and hard to get to. Trunk space was basically useless. Another reason to move into town—the store would be a lot closer to make several trips a week rather than just one.

"I need to stop by Mason's for just a minute too."

"Boring."

"I won't be long. You can wait in the car if you want." Trixie remembered Ellis hanging around Mason's office. "On second thought, you'll need to come up with me. But I promise it's just for a minute."

"Then why do I have to come in?"

"'Cause I said so and I'm the momma."

After the groceries and stopping by Mason's to sign some paperwork for the bank, she hit the drive-through teller to drop the forms. She kept checking her phone every few minutes to make sure she hadn't missed a call or text from Armstrong. She expected to hear from him after he got the recording from Lee, but no word yet. She wondered if she should call him.

While waiting in line at the bank drive-through, she texted Madison. She replied almost instantly.

he's golfing today. be in touch monday

She texted Lee.

did you get that stuff to armstrong

She hadn't received a reply by the time her turn at the teller came up. "Just droppin' this off. Can you pass it on to Austin for me please?" Austin had volunteered to be her personal banker.

"Sure thing, sweetie," the teller said.

"Can we go home now? I'm gettin' hungry." Ty was getting whiny too, and they hadn't been gone an hour.

"Yes, we're goin' home now. How 'bout a bologna sandwich and mac 'n' cheese?"

"Cut the crust off?"

"The crust is the best part."

"You can have mine then since you like it so much."

Fifteen minutes later, Trixie pulled the Corvette into the gravel driveway alongside the house. As they pulled around back, the gravel and dirt area where she parked was full of vehicles.

There were three sheriff's deputy squad cars. Two sedans. Clay's pickup parked behind them all. Trixie pulled to the side as far as she could to find a place to stop.

"You stay right here. Don't you move." Trixie jumped out and raced toward the group of people gathered at her screen door, wondering if they'd caught someone breaking in this time.

"What's goin' on?"

Clay took a couple of steps toward her when a scrawny deputy stepped in front of him and put a hand on his chest to stop him. Clay could have broken him like a twig and tossed him aside, but he stopped in his tracks.

Out of the crowd, Lynn Roberts stepped forward.

"Victoria Burnet, I have orders here to take your son into protective custody until the hearing on Tuesday."

Ms. Roberts continued walking toward Trixie. Trixie stood still, feet planted in the dirt and gravel, her legs gone numb, her brain overloaded with all the cars and people and words.

A female deputy walked over to the Corvette. Ty locked the doors. She rapped on the window and motioned for him to come out, talking sweetly to him. "Come on out, you're not in any trouble, we just need to talk to you. C'mon, open the door."

Ms. Roberts stepped up beside Trixie and put a hand on her shoulder. She leaned a little closer and said, out of earshot of anyone else, "This is to show you how serious I am. Maybe you'll take it a little more seriously by the time I visit on Monday."

"Don't you take my boy. Don't you dare take my boy. I'm callin' my lawyer right now." She reached for her phone, but it wasn't there. It was still in the console of the car. "Clay, you got your phone?"

"You can call whoever you want," Ms. Roberts said, now loud enough for everyone else to hear. "But first, you need to convince your son to get out of the car and go with this lady here, or the sheriff here will cut the doors off that nice, new vehicle of yours."

"Where're you takin' him?"

"He'll be in protective custody where we can keep him safe. Safer than you do. You don't even make him wear a bicycle helmet."

Trixie sized up Lynn's neck and figured she could get both hands around that fleshy blob and choke the life out of her before a deputy could peel her off.

"Don't make this a big scene," Lynn said. "Just be calm. You don't want your boy to see these officers slam you and your boyfriend to the ground and cuff you. That would be traumatic for him. And if the boy is upset and fighting us, we'll have to restrain him for his own safety."

Clay pushed through two deputies who tried to restrain him. The scrawny deputy pulled his Taser, but Lynn motioned him to be calm.

"Trixie, just do what they say," Clay said. "Don't make this harder on Ty than it needs to be, and we'll get him back."

Trixie tried to tamp down the anger that boiled inside. She wanted to yell out for all to hear, *"She's only doing this because I haven't paid her blackmail money yet."* She wanted to punch that woman in the nose, but knew the cops would throw her to the ground. She didn't want Ty to see she resorted to fighting. She was glad she didn't have her gun on her, or she might do something really stupid.

Her gun was in the glovebox. In the car. With Ty.

She pulled away from Lynn and walked over to the car.

"Ma'am," she said to the deputy who was still trying to sweet talk Ty out, "I got this."

The deputy stepped back.

"It's okay, little man. Ever'thing's gonna be fine. I need you to get out now. Just unlock the door and come to me."

Tears streamed down his face, eyes wide with fear. Trixie couldn't show fear or weakness or anger. She had to plaster on a face of calm and cool, that *ever'thing's gonna be fine* face, before that boy did something really, really stupid.

Ty hesitated and wiped the tears off his face.

"That's my little man, just come out here and give me a hug."

Ty looked to the door lock button. His eyes shifted to the glovebox. He reached toward it.

Trixie rapped on the glass hard enough to make him jump. "Don't you even think about it. Unlock the door and come to me."

She could almost see the wheels spinning in his head as he slowly reached for the unlock button. When it clicked, she yanked the door open and wrapped him in a quick hug to make sure he didn't reach for that glovebox. She lifted him out in a momma-bear hug.

A tiny, meek, older woman stepped forward with a teddy bear in her hands. "You must be Tyler. I've heard so many wonderful things about you. I'd like you to come with me for a little while. We'll have some fun, I promise."

Ty gripped his momma even tighter, refusing to look at the little elf.

Trixie didn't know if she'd ever be able to let go or if they'd have to get a crowbar to pry her arms away from her little man.

She turned to Lynn and the teddy bear woman, Ty facing away from them with his head buried in Trixie's neck.

"If y'all will step back and give us a moment, let me talk to him. I'm cooperatin' here but all of y'all are scarin' him."

Clay stepped up beside Trixie and wrapped one of his granite arms around them both.

"You have two minutes," Lynn said. "Don't make this hard on everyone, especially not your boy."

Everyone stepped back. Trixie kneeled down, still wrapped up with Ty. Clay took a knee beside them.

"Looky here, little man. There's some big mistake, some misunderstandin.' We'll get this all straightened out and you'll be back home in no time. But for now, just for a little while, you're gonna need to be strong. You're gonna need to go with the nice lady with the stupid bear. You need to be the big man for just a bit—not my little man. Stand up proud and strong like the man I'm tryin' to raise you to be. Like Uncle Leon. Like Clay here. You might not like it, you might be scared, you might be mad. Don't matter. You be a man for a little bit and don't let 'em see nothin' else. You'll be home before you know it. When you're back home, you can go back to being my little man. To bein' a boy again. It ain't time yet for you to be a big man all the time, but I need you to be that man for a little while. For me. I need you to be a man for me right now. I ain't strong enough to do this on my own. But together, we can do it. It's you and me against the world."

Ty sniffed and tried to stuff a sob inside, but it escaped anyway. His grip around Trixie's neck relaxed just a shade.

Clay put a hand on both of their backs and leaned in. "How about a quick prayer?"

Trixie nodded. They bowed their heads. Before she closed her eyes, she caught all the deputies removing their hats and bowing their heads.

"Our Father in heaven," Clay started, "we don't know what all is going on here, but we trust that You are in control. We ask for your peace in our hearts, peace that surpasses all understanding. We all need that right now, Lord. More than ever. Be with Ty and give him courage. Be with Trixie to give her strength. And be with me so I don't punch that ugly-ass woman in the face. Amen."

"Amen," Trixie said.

"Amen," Ty sniffed with a giggle.

Trixie wiped Ty's face on her shirt tail, gave him another hug, and pointed to the woman with the stupid bear. "You go with her. I'll see you in no time."

Ty latched on for another hug, then crawled into Clay's arms. Then, making his momma proud, he stood tall and walked up to the woman. When she held out the bear, he looked at it and said, "What? You think I'm like three years old or somethin'?"

"Mind your manners, young man," Trixie scolded him with a smile she couldn't suppress.

The little lady reached down to hold Ty's hand. He refused to take it but walked with her to her car.

"Ms. Burnet, I need a word with you privately." *Ms. Burnet.* Lynn was getting all formal again. "Can we step inside?"

"No, Ms. Roberts, we cannot. You just took my boy for no reason. You ain't welcome in my home."

Lynn took a few steps away from everyone, and they all took the hint. The car with Ty in the back seat made a about a six-point turn in the parking area and headed down the drive, Ty waving to his momma.

"I told you I was serious, but apparently I needed to get your attention. I'll call you on Monday and tell you when and where to meet me. And the price just went to $100,000 if you ever want to see your kid again. Just for all this extra trouble you've caused me and the great State of Texas."

***

The house was dead quiet, not two minutes after the last deputy pulled out. Clay sat next to Trixie on the couch, arm comfortably around her shoulders as she leaned tight against him.

She pulled her phone out and texted Madison again.

they just took my boy. get armstrong off the golf course. NOW!!!

She set her phone down on the coffee table and buried herself in Clay's side. She didn't know how she'd stand the quiet in this old house with no Ty underfoot.

She couldn't sit still any longer. She unraveled from Clay and walked to the kitchen. "Coffee? Or if you want a grape soda, they're still in the car. I need to get those groceries in before that milk turns sour."

"I'll get them," Clay offered and headed out the screen door.

The door slammed and the house got even quieter. Trixie wasn't sure how that was possible.

That just made her phone ring louder than a school bell between classes.

She ran to the living room and grabbed it.

"Did you say social services took your boy?" Armstrong on the line, the wind audible in his phone. Still on the golf course.

"A whole bunch of cop cars, Ms. Roberts, and some other lady. She had papers to take him. Says I'm unfit, negligent, failure to provide a safe environment, and the boy's exhibitin' behavioral issues and physical injuries that are suspicious in nature."

"Well, that's interesting timing."

"And she upped her price to a hundred grand. By Monday or she'll go full-bore with this story to the judge, take my boy away forever. You got to do somethin'. You got to do somethin' right now. I want my boy home this very minute."

"I'm working on it right now, I promise you. This will all work out. I know it's hard, but it will take more than a minute. I need you to be strong." Armstrong was talking to her like she'd talked to her eight-year-old.

"You ain't workin' on it right now. You're on the damn golf course. I'm callin' Mason and I'll have that cash for her on Monday. If you ain't done nothin' about this before then, I'll pay her. I will pay that bitch to get my boy back."

CHAPTER 29

Clay slept on the couch again; he'd refused to leave Trixie alone. Trixie went to bed and tossed and turned for a couple of hours, unable to turn off the parade of fears that marched through her head, blaring trombones and fire engine sirens and scary-looking clowns honking bicycle horns.

She eventually got up and moved to Ty's single bed. It smelled like boy, but clean boy since he always took a bath before bedtime. It smelled like the baby shampoo he still used, and Ivory soap and that sparkly, purple toothpaste he used every night. She couldn't decide if his scent calmed her or inflamed her anxiety. He'd been gone half a day and it felt like forever. Could she even get through a night without him? What if it was several days before Armstrong could get him back? What if the worst... she couldn't even let her mind go there.

About three a.m.— maybe she had dozed off for a little bit of fitful sleep, maybe she'd never gone to sleep at all, she wasn't sure—she got up to go to the bathroom. As she passed the top of the stairs, the light from the kitchen illuminated the bottom of the stairway. Did Clay forget to turn it off? Did he prefer to sleep with a light on?

Might as well make some coffee, but she didn't want to wake him. Then the smell of fresh-brewed coffee wafted up the stairs and reached her nose. *Guess he can't sleep either.*

She went to her room and slipped a fluffy robe over her nightgown, then padded down the stairs barefoot. She stood in the entry between the living room and kitchen, watching Clay sit at the table, staring into a cup of coffee gripped in both hands. A second cup already sat next to the pot.

"Mind if I join you?" she said as quietly as she could. She didn't want to startle him into spilling his coffee.

He didn't look up for a moment, like he'd fallen asleep sitting up. When he did, his eyes were damp, and Trixie realized he'd been praying. Maybe she should try that more often. Had to be better than worrying herself half to death. But God had taken her daddy. Would He take her boy too?

She'd called her momma earlier that day to fill her and Leon in on Ty's whereabouts. And she'd called Shelby. Clay had called Brother Kent to start the prayer chain. There was no one else to call, and she was all out of words. She couldn't have told it again.

Trixie filled her cup and sat next to Clay. She patted his hand.

He set his cup down and held her hand in both of his giant hands, callused, yet somehow clean and soft. The warm comfort from his touch flowed into her like an electric blanket on a winter night when the furnace went out.

They sat with no words for the better part of twenty minutes.

"I wonder if lawyers answer their phone at..." Trixie glanced at the clock on the stove... "three-thirty on Saturday morning."

"I kind of doubt it," Clay said.

"Did you have trouble sleeping too?"

"Not really. I slept like a baby for a few hours. Then just woke up. Not too much earlier than I always get up. I was wide awake and knew I wasn't going back to sleep, so I just made us coffee. Had my daily solitude time."

"Sorry if I disturbed that."

"Not at all. It was kind of nice sharing that quiet time with you."

"Yeah, you won't get a lot of quiet time with my mouth runnin' all the time."

"That's a'ight. I usually get more solitude than I need or want."

Trixie needed to get moving. There wasn't anything to do, she just needed to be busy. Wiped up imaginary spots on the countertop by the coffee pot, drips Clay had already cleaned. Pulled out the last load of laundry she'd thrown in the dryer the night before, a load of jeans—hers and Ty's. She put the folded jeans by the stairs for the next trip up. Looked around the living room for anything that needed doing, but Clay had already folded all the bedding and stacked it, so she grabbed the jeans and carried them up. She put them all away except a pair she slipped into. She was up. Might as well get dressed.

At nearly seven a.m., sunlight breaking over the horizon, she decided it didn't matter if it was Saturday morning. She called Armstrong.

She was prepared to leave that scathing voice mail before realizing, as she waited for the beep, that it wasn't a recording. Armstrong had picked up.

"Lee is still tying up a few loose ends, following a couple more leads. Madison has transcribed all the recordings. It's all just going to take a little bit more time. Try to relax. Not going to get the court do anything over the weekend, and we have a hearing already scheduled for Tuesday, so I doubt the judge is going to move it up to Monday. Just be patient."

"You mean I won't see my boy until Tuesday?" Trixie practically screamed at him. "That is unacceptable."

"Your boy is being taken good care of. He'll be treated well."

"He ain't home in his own bed bein' taken care of by his momma, so no, he's not bein' treated well."

"Just be patient. You've done great. Hang in there a little bit longer. We've got to do this right. No panicking allowed."

"So what do I do on Monday when Ms. Roberts calls and wants her cash?"

"I'll let you know Monday. But whatever you do, don't pay her a dime. She would try to turn that into you bribing her and use it against you."

Trixie tried sitting at the table with Clay, but her legs were restless, bouncing up and down. If she concentrated on not bouncing, they'd stay calm for about thirty seconds, then jerk like they'd do sometimes right before falling asleep. She finally stood and paced around looking for something that needed doing.

"I've got an idea," Clay said. "I've got to go check on the cattle, and there's a section of fence that needs tightening. It's not down, but I need to ratchet it up. Could use a second set of hands. Why don't you go with me? Get out of the house. You can't sit here all day."

Trixie thought that sounded like a fine idea. "Let me get my boots."

"You have gloves too?"

"Somewhere in the mudroom."

***

Helping Clay around the farm was the best idea she'd heard in a while. They stayed out all morning, making sure the cattle were fed and watered, tightened up some loose barbed wire fencing, including adding a few new t-posts for strength. Then they mucked out the barn and tossed more straw around.

As they covered one end of the sixty-three acres to the other, Clay pointed out each area and his plans. Clearing more pasture here to add more head to the herd next year. Shoring up that barn to use for equipment storage. Tearing down that barn because it was too rotten to save. The foundation was solid, so he'd rebuild it, but maybe a metal pole barn instead of wood. There was an old field, once used for hay and alfalfa, that had lain fallow for years, now overgrown with weeds. He hoped to plow that under before too long, before the weather got too cold, then plow it again in the spring and plant alfalfa.

"What about the house? You gonna tear it down and start over?"

"Not sure yet. Hate to tear down an old farmhouse. That house has stood strong for more than a century. Maybe it's worth shoring it up and updating it, get another century out of it. I'll probably be done with it by then."

"You just going to live in that old camper until you get it fixed up?"

"Maybe. Might pull the camper up next door to it. But there's a great view out where I'm at now, top of that hill, all trees on one side and looking down at the pastures the other way. View stretches halfway to the county line. Maybe I'll live in the farmhouse and build a new house out there, then decide what to do with the farmhouse. Just trying to figure out how many houses and bedrooms I really need just for me. Not like I'm opening up a bed and breakfast out here."

The few chores that needed doing turned into five hours, followed by a sandwich at Clay's trailer.

They sat in lawn chairs outside the trailer, taking in the view after they'd finished eating. Taking a few minutes to rest before heading back out for the rest of the chores.

Trixie kept trying to find the words she needed to say, and waiting for the right moment to bring up the topic. If there was to be any relationship with Clay, she had to tell him. And that would probably mean there wouldn't be any relationship with Clay. But he'd hear about it from someone eventually, so better for him to hear it from her now before things went any further between them. If it hadn't waited too long already. But this was such a peaceful moment, she didn't want to bring it up now.

"So, what was this thing you wanted to talk to me about?" Clay asked, like he was reading her mind or her face.

Trixie stayed silent a few moments. Maybe a minute. She sipped her sweet tea from one of those 32-ounce plastic cups Clay had stocked up on with drinks from 7-11. She stared off into the distant view of pastures and hillsides and woods.

Without looking at Clay, she fumbled around for a place to start.

"Well, things seem to be happening between us that I don't know what to do about. And Ty really worships you. I'll admit I'm drawn to you too. I just don't know."

She paused, hoping he'd say something, but he didn't. Just gave her space to think until she continued.

"I mean, I never really had a boyfriend before. Yeah, there was Ellis, but that wasn't really like a boyfriend-girlfriend thing. That was me lashing out after Daddy died. Huge mistake, I know. But Ty came out of all that mess, so it's hard to regret it too much."

"He's a fine boy," Clay finally said. "The Lord can take any bad situation and make good come out of it." Then he shut up again, but he reached over and held her hand.

"And then, ya know, I was a teenager, a stupid teenager, but working two jobs and tryna raise a boy, and then Momma moved out and left us in this house. She had to go on with her life, I know, but it was all so overwhelming. So overwhelming. And I made some more really bad decisions. Bad decisions seem to be the only thing I'm good at."

She took a couple of deep breaths, still not knowing how to tell this fine Christian man who was interested in her that she'd slept with men for money for four years. She could just picture him high-tailin' out of Dodge.

"We've all made bad decisions," Clay said. "For all have sinned... you know that verse."

"Maybe I've sinned a whole lot more than most."

She took another deep breath, and a shudder ran through her. She reached over with her other hand and put it on top of Clay's. She turned sideways in her lawn chair and met his eyes straight on.

"Clay," she said and cleared her throat. "I've got to tell you somethin' and I don't know what you're gonna think about it, but I have a pretty good idea you won't want much to do with me after that. And that's gonna hurt me real bad because I'm havin' feelings about you I've never had about anyone before in my whole stupid life."

She tried to blink back tears but was unsuccessful.

"Whatever you've done, has God forgiven you?"

She sniffed and thought about it. "Yeah, I believe so. I've asked Him to. And I'm not doing it anymore. Ever."

"If God has forgiven you, what right would I have to hold it against you?"

Trixie thought about it a moment. "Well, you might forgive me too, but that don't mean you'd want to hang around me anymore neither."

"I can't think of anything you might have done that would scare me off that easily."

Trixie decided she'd just go ahead and try to scare him off.

"I've been with more men than just ol' Ellis. I've been with a lot of men. For money. That's how I made a livin' the past few years. I didn't like it. I didn't want to. But I had to provide for Ty, and it kind of fell in my lap and then I didn't know how to get out of it. I prayed every day for the Lord to forgive me and give me a way out. After a while, though, I stopped prayin' because He didn't seem to be hearin' me."

"Yeah, I know all that part. But what was you gonna tell me that s'posed to scare me off? I thought maybe you were gonna tell me you'd buried that Roberts woman out in the south forty somewhere."

***

Clay had held her and kissed her passionately, with more caring and tenderness than Trixie had ever experienced. But eventually, after maybe ten minutes or an hour, she wasn't sure, Clay said they had a few more chores they had to do so they couldn't sit there and make out until dark, which was still hours away.

They climbed back into the pickup and bounced across another pasture to check.

Trixie eventually stopped checking her phone for messages.

***

As the dark closed in that night, Trixie knew she'd never be able to sleep with Ty not home. But she was wrong.

When she woke up, the sun was up, the coffee was made. She was lying on the couch, where she'd drifted off in Clay's arms the night before. He'd covered her up with the sheets and blanket she'd set out for him.

"Where'd you sleep?" she asked.

"That recliner works quite nice."

Trixie stumbled to the bathroom, then after splashing water on her face and running her fingers through her hair, shuffled to the table where Clay had already filled her cup.

"You think you'd be up to going to church with me this morning?"

"I don't think I'm up to seeing nobody yet. You go on without me."

"You sure you're up to being here alone?"

"Maybe I need some of that quiet solitude for a bit. Tell ever'one I said hi and thank them for the prayers and all. But I just don't want to face nobody."

"I'll bring you a doughnut."

***

But Clay didn't bring just a doughnut. He brought a cardboard box large enough to hold a set of pots and pans. Trixie held the screen door for him, and he set the box on the table.

"Be right back. There's one more."

Two boxes. No doughnuts.

Fried chicken. Mashed potatoes. Gravy. Vegetables. Casseroles. Desserts. Potato salad. Macaroni salad. Five-bean salad. Salad salad.

"Where did you get all this?"

"The church. Most of the women—and a few of the men—cooked up stuff for you so you wouldn't have to worry about food right now. Kent stayed up all night smoking a brisket for you."

"I can afford food. Why did they do this? I mean, besides Harris and Shelby, I don't know none of them people. They don't know me."

"It's what they do. Someone's hurting, they cook."

"I can't eat all this."

"I'll help. It doesn't get much better than church lady cooking. And most of this stuff will freeze. You can just pull something out and defrost it every day for a couple of weeks."

"A couple months probably."

"Well?" Clay asked.

"Well what?"

"What do you want for lunch?"

"How about that brisket?"

"I was hoping you'd say that."

***

Monday. Ms. Roberts was going to call. Armstrong said not to answer. Ignore her. But what if she just showed up at the house? Armstrong said go somewhere else. Don't be home.

She spent another day out with Clay doing chores. Another day listening to his plans and dreams to make this a working—and profitable—farm. It would take a few years to get everything done he wanted to get done, and by then, there'd be a new list of projects.

About two o'clock, the social worker called. And called again ten minutes later. And again. Trixie let them all go to voice mail, but after the fourth call, she blocked the number. She forwarded the voicemails to Madison without listening to them herself.

When the day's work was done, they went to the house and gathered up food from the box for a meal, then took it out to his camper to eat in case the social worker showed up uninvited.

Trixie spent the night. She had to insist on taking the couch. She wasn't going to make Clay sleep on his own couch while she took his bed, which was really just a single-wide cot. The couch looked more comfy anyway.

***

Trixie tried on three different outfits, modeled them all for Clay. A flower-print new dress she'd bought to wear to First Church, but she hadn't gone since she bought it, which made her look like a churchgoing mother. A skirt, blouse, and jacket combination that looked very businesslike, professional, like she belonged in court as a lawyer rather than an unfit mother. She also tried on the pantsuit with matching jacket and immediately regretted buying it. She'd toss that in the Cast-Off Sale box with the price tag still on it.

Clay was no help. Just said she was beautiful in every outfit. Even the ugly pantsuit.

Should she called Armstrong and ask whether she should look like a momma or a businesswoman? He was a man, and men usually wouldn't know or care. But he spent a lot of time in court and maybe had some psychological angle that her wardrobe might play with the judge.

She put the dress back on and handed her phone to Clay to get a picture. Changed into the business suit again, another photo. Texted them to Madison.

you'll kill in that skirt/jacket

Trixie hesitated. Killing someone wasn't a good idea, but it wasn't completely out of the question either. She hung the church dress back in the closet and went to fix her hair. She'd rummage through the donate box to find those black pumps that would look perfect with this outfit. Maybe she'd have to keep those, not that she planned on spending any more time in court than she had to.

***

She met Armstrong at 9:45 in the parking lot and climbed into his Range Rover for their pre-court meeting. His law office on wheels.

"I hope you got all your ducks in a row," Trixie said.

"I do believe all the ducks, geese, and chickens are aligned," he said. "Here's what I'm going to need you to do." He pulled a sheet of paper from his briefcase and handed it to her.

Trixie held the single page and stared for a moment, then flipped it over. Flipped it back and turned to Armstrong. "This is blank."

"That's right. And that's what you need to do. Nothing. Nada. Zip. This is out of your hands now. You ready?"

"I guess so."

"You look perfect, by the way. Love the shoes."

Armstrong stepped from the big SUV and came around to give Trixie a hand down, then held her by the elbow and escorted her up the steps to the courthouse, down the hall to the family court, and to a seat on the wooden bench in the vestibule. Wooden benches lined both sides of the vestibule, could probably seat ten or twelve people, but Armstrong and Trixie were the only two there.

"We wait here until we're called. Just like last time."

Trixie pulled a tissue from her purse for soaking up the sweat in her hands rather than wiping it on her new skirt.

Armstrong pulled out his phone and read.

Trixie glanced over his shoulder to see if she could learn anything about what he planned in court. He was looking at pictures of little kids on Facebook. "Who's that?"

"My grandkids. Madison's boys." He looked up at Trixie. "I've never been in your shoes. Well, obviously those heels wouldn't fit me. But I can't imagine being in your position. I look at these pictures to imagine in my mind how I'd feel if someone tried to take them away. I do know what it's like to lose one though. My boy died in a car accident when he was nineteen. Drunk driver killed him."

"I'm so sorry."

"It was a long time ago. He'd be forty this year. The pain changes, but it never goes away. I'm not going to let you go through anything like that. I promise."

Trixie glanced at her phone. 9:57.

Lee walked in and handed a folder to Armstrong, then turned and walked out. Not a word was spoken between them. Lee barely acknowledged Trixie's existence with a slight nod as he walked past.

Armstrong never looked inside the folder. Just went back to scrolling through photos on Facebook.

10:03. The door opened and a Hispanic couple walked out, holding each other around the waist. The woman was quietly sobbing, the man trying to comfort her in Spanish. The door closed behind them.

10:09. Armstrong and Trixie hadn't said a word in nearly fifteen minutes. Trixie tried looking at her phone, but there was nothing that could hold her interest or concentration more than a few seconds.

10:17. The door opened, and a deputy called out, "Burnet."

"It's showtime," Armstrong said. "Don't forget your lines."

The assistant DA who didn't shave yet sat at his table, Ms. Roberts beside him. Judge Archer was already seated behind the bench, the court clerk fiddling with her machine.

No sooner than Trixie and Armstrong sat down, the bailiff called out, "All rise. This session of Pineywoods County Family Law Court is now in session, the Honorable Judge Nolan Archer presiding. Be seated."

The door behind them squeaked open, and a man in a suit and tie slipped in and sat on the back row of the otherwise empty courtroom. The kid DA turned, and they nodded to each other.

No one else was allowed in during family court. She jotted 'who's that' on her notepad and turned it to Armstrong.

He wrote underneath 'the DA.' Then leaned over and whispered, "Probably checking to see how this kid is doing."

Judge Archer finally looked up and around the room. "Well, what business are you bringing before me today?" he said to the kid.

"We have here the case of the State of Texas, Family Protective Services, versus Victoria Burnet. The state had wished to make the case that the child in question, an eight-year-old boy, was in an unsuitable environment."

"What do you mean by 'had wished'?" the judge asked.

Ms. Roberts shot the kid a death stare and mouthed, "Yes, what do you mean?"

"We are withdrawing this case and ask for summary dismissal."

Ms. Roberts's mouth bobbed open and shut like a fish that just landed on a boat.

"Counselor," the judge directed to Armstrong, "may I assume your client has no objections?"

"You'd be assuming correctly, Your Honor."

To the kid assistant DA again, the judge asked, "Do you have any other business to come before the court this morning?"

"Yes, Your Honor, we have one more piece of business. I will defer to our district attorney who has joined us." The kid sat down.

The DA walked forward with a stack of papers. "May I approach the bench, Your Honor?"

"Nothing would please me more."

"I have here for your signature the search warrant I previously briefed you on."

The judge slipped on his readers and glanced through the paperwork, then signed at the bottom. "Do you have anything else?"

"I do, Your Honor. I have a duly authorized arrest warrant for Ms. Lynn Roberts, who has been indicted for multiple counts of blackmail and fraudulent use of state funds, among other various pending charges still under investigation. Since we are in your courtroom, Your Honor, I would like your permission to ask your bailiff to take her into immediate custody."

"Permission granted. Bailiff."

Ms. Roberts was frozen in place, unable to speak or move, her eyes darting back and forth.

"Ms. Burnet," the judge said. "A representative from Family Protective Services will be in touch shortly to arrange for the immediate return of your child. On behalf of the State of Texas, I am truly sorry you had to endure something like this. I would also, on behalf of the State of Texas and of this court, like to thank you for your cooperation in this effort to root out corruption in what should be the most compassionate and honest efforts of this state to ensure the well-being of our children. Your services are truly appreciated."

Trixie was as lost for words as Ms. Roberts.

"Case dismissed. You are excused."

Armstrong stood quickly and nearly dragged Trixie out of her chair and out the door, whispering, "You remembered all your lines perfectly, my dear."

He escorted her to the double doors and opened one side with a flourish.

The vestibule was overflowing. Standing room only.

She saw Clay first, taller than the rest plus the Stetson to top it off.

He stood with Brother Kent, Harris, Shelby, and Austin.

Seated on one bench were Marion and Angelina. At the end of the next bench, Cass sat, with Lamar standing next to her, his hand on her shoulder. Reagan stood next to Chief Hale.

And Mason too.

No Mayor Callahan. No Bee.

A half dozen more from Clay's church—people she recognized, and may have been introduced to briefly, but she couldn't recall their names.

Armstrong stepped forward facing the crowd and, without a word, gave the two-thumbs up sign.

As the whole group cheered and applauded, Clay rushed forward and lifted Trixie into the air to meet her face to face and plant a kiss on her lips in front of God and everyone.

Clay set her feet on the ground but didn't let go.

Another man stepped forward, someone Trixie'd seen somewhere before, with a camera around his neck. The newspaper. She didn't want her picture in the newspaper again. He'd taken the picture when she'd won the lottery. She didn't want any more publicity. Nothing about Tyler in the paper. He's just a kid. *Don't they have laws about this?*

She turned to Armstrong, but he pulled her and Clay to the side as the reporter walked past them without a glance in their direction. He stopped and pointed his camera to the opening door, getting the obligatory perp walk photo of a handcuffed Ms. Roberts for tomorrow's front page of the *Daily Progress* as she was escorted out and walked across the street, in broad daylight, to the county jail.

"The judge could have had her escorted through the underground walkway," Armstrong told Trixie, "but looks like he wanted her on parade just a bit."

Crossing the street in the opposite direction at the same time were Leon and Sabine.

"When do I get my boy?"

"They're about an hour away," Armstrong said. "They should be on the way shortly. They couldn't be given any advance heads-up, but they know now. Let me buy you lunch. Madison sends her best. I invited her, but one of her boys has some program at school."

"What about Lee?" Trixie asked.

"I don't know who you're talking about." Armstrong winked.

"Roy's Diner?"

"Are you kidding?" Armstrong said. "Look at you. Look at those shoes. Just look at them. Those shoes only eat at the Pineywoods Country Club. I'll meet you there in twenty minutes. There are some people here who want to see you. I'll tell FPS to drop your boy off there and he can get something to eat too."

Armstrong patted Trixie on the back and shook Clay's hand, then headed down the hall.

The crowd immediately converged on Trixie, Shelby leading the way and hogging all the hugs until Sabine walked up.

***

Trixie had never had lobster before, but Armstrong insisted. "If you don't like it, I'll eat it and you can get a something else."

She liked it. Like fish but less fishy. She was tempted to pick up the little bowl of melted butter and take a swig.

"You gonna tell me when you got all this done?"

"When could I possibly have had time to do all this as I whiled away the hours on the golf course? Is that what you mean?"

"Pretty much."

"You think golf is just a game? Depends on who you're golfing with."

"Archer?"

"You catch on quick. It was a foursome. The DA and the head of FPS joined us."

"What about the break-ins? Did the detective who can't be named figure that out too? Who left me that death threat?"

Armstrong dipped another bite into the butter and took his time chewing, wiping his lips on the cloth napkin and taking a sip of sparkling water before answering. "All due to one Ms. Roberts. Unfortunately, in her line of work, dealing with kids from some pretty bad home situations, she gets to meet a number of lowlife parents. Most of them don't have the money to make it worth trying to shake them down, so she extracts favors in other ways. Like breaking and entering, vandalism, leaving threatening letters, whatever needs to be done."

"Why? What was she trying to accomplish?"

"Best I can tell, just to rattle you. Maybe she thought that would stress you out and soften you up when it came time to shake your money tree."

They were ordering cheesecake and coffee when a voice cut across the room.

"Momma!"

Trixie's napkin hit the floor when she jumped out of her seat. She took two steps, then stopped to kick her heels off and run barefoot across the carpeted dining room to meet Ty halfway.

She hugged him tighter than when they'd taken him away. Buried her face in his neck. He smelled different. He was clean, but she wanted to take him home and bathe him in baby shampoo and Ivory soap.

A few steps behind, the little pixie lady finally caught up. "I'm so glad I'm able to bring your young man back to you. I just wanted to tell you what a fine gentleman he is, obviously a tribute to how he's being raised."

She held out the teddy bear. "Here, don't forget this."

Ty took the stupid stuffed bear and pulled it close. "Thank you, ma'am."

Then, without prompting, Ty pulled away from Trixie and gave the little woman a hug.

CHAPTER 30

Despite all the excitement and disruption, or maybe because of it, Trixie pushed Ty to get up and ready for school the next morning to get back into the routine. His doctor's note had expired, and Trixie had a Circle meeting that morning. She had final details for the weekend's Cast-Off Clothing Sale to nail down.

Trixie had four large boxes to donate. She wasn't sure how all of it had fit in that tiny closet.

The meeting was moved to Marion's at the last minute. She had called all the members the day before to let them know it was moving from Bee's house, even though it was Bee's turn. Trixie was just glad she checked her messages in time rather than be the only one to show up at the Callahans' place.

Marion called the meeting to order.

"Shouldn't we give Bee five more minutes to get here before we start without her?" Reagan asked.

"No, Bee isn't going to make it today. I have her weekly treasurer's report here." Marion pulled out a small stack of papers and handed them over to Angelina. "Take one and pass it around."

Trixie took her copy and passed the remainder to Shelby. She skimmed the numbers, down to the bottom line, which contained a lot more digits than usual.

"First order of business is this treasurer's report and a quick explanation. Bee Callahan, bless her heart, has regretfully submitted her resignation from the Ladies' Society Circle due to personal reasons that she has requested remain confidential and private."

"She's resigning as treasurer?" Angelina asked.

"No, she is resigning from the Circle completely."

"Oh no," Shelby said. "She wouldn't say why?"

"She asked that I keep her reasons in the strictest confidence, and I promised her I would do so."

"Is this a typo?" Trixie asked. "We had about twelve hundred dollars. Now it's over twenty grand."

"That's no mistake. To show her gratitude, her dedication, her love for this group that has meant so much to her over the years, she made a $20,000 donation, a parting gift, if you will."

"What a beautiful soul," Cass said.

"This Circle loves Bee as much as she loved this Circle," said Angelina.

"Think of how much good we'll be able to do with this," Shelby said.

"Her gift will change lives for years to come," added Reagan.

"Maybe we could set a portion of this aside for a new scholarship, and name it the Bee Callahan Scholars Award," Marion suggested.

The whole group *oohed* and *aahed* then broke into applause.

"What a fitting memorial for Bee," Cass said.

"She's not dead, Cass, for crying out loud," Marion said. "But it will be a nice tribute to honor her years of hard work."

Cass made the formal motion, and Trixie seconded. The vote to approve the Bee Callahan Scholars Award, initially funded with $15,000 from Bee's donation, was approved unanimously and enthusiastically. The other $5,000 would go to the group's general funds.

"That brings me to the next order of business before we get to the fun stuff. With Bee's resignation, we need a new treasurer. Do we have any volunteers?"

The room quieted down instantly. Nobody moved. Nobody spoke. It felt like everyone was afraid to twitch.

Trixie quietly raised her hand.

"Trixie," Marion said. "Are you volunteering to be treasurer?"

"Oh, no ma'am, I wouldn't be no good at that. But I'd like to recommend someone."

"Go ahead then."

"If she's willin' to do it, I think Shelby would make a fine treasurer."

"Shelby?" Cass seemed a little doubtful.

"Yes, Shelby," Trixie answered. "She's got mad computer skills. She handles finances and billing and insurance forms for six different doctors. That's complicated stuff, and she keeps it all straight. Makes sure people get billed the right amount, not too much or too little. Makes sure the insurance companies pay what they're supposed to pay and not try to weasel out of something. She makes sure the doctors get paid for the work they do so they don't have to worry about that side of the business, so they can spend all their time treating patients."

The room went quiet. Trixie looked to Shelby, who was twisting a napkin to shreds and looking at her feet.

"Shelby," Marion said, "is this something you'd be willing to do?"

Shelby looked up at Marion, then to Trixie. A smile pulled at the corners of her mouth as her chin came up. "Yes, ma'am, if the group is willing to give me a chance, I know I could do it. I can computerize the whole thing. I can put everything into an accounting software program that will generate weekly, monthly, quarterly, and annual reports for the whole group, balance the bank statements, track all invoices and payments, dues and donations. We could move most of our payments online and automate them. Even set up membership dues to be automatically renewed and drafted from bank accounts—"

"Whoa, hold on there," Marion interrupted with a laugh. "Most of us old women here don't know what you're talking about, but I like how you're thinking. Maybe one step at a time though."

Shelby smiled at Trixie and held her head a little higher.

"I nominate Shelby Wheeler to be treasurer of the Ladies' Society Circle," Trixie said.

"Second," Angelina and Reagan said at the same time.

"All in favor, say aye."

Once again, the Circle was in complete harmony with a unanimous vote. Even Cass.

***

After everything was settled with the Cast-Off Sale, who was doing what, making sure there were always at least two Circle members there to assist, working in shifts, that the room was set up in advance and cleaned up after the sale, and that any remaining unsold merchandise was gathered and boxed to be donated to Goodwill, the group sat around with coffee and doughnuts. Marion apologized repeatedly for not having baked something like coffee cake or cinnamon rolls, but it was such short notice. Nobody seemed to mind as the dozen and a half doughnuts disappeared within minutes between the six of them.

Eventually, one lady after another stood to excuse herself to leave, but conversations continued until all six of them stood near the front door, no one making the first move to actually depart.

Trixie took that opportunity to sidle up next to Cass. "Before you leave, may I have a word?"

Cass agreed and stepped away from the cluster at the front door, back to the sitting room with Trixie.

"First, I want to thank you and Mr. Reeves for being at court yesterday to support me and my boy. That really means a lot to me."

"Certainly, dear. That's just awful what they tried to do to you. Nobody deserves that."

"I'll never forget it, and I'll always remember you were there. But I have another question for you." Trixie hesitated a moment.

"Go on."

"What do you think of Shelby?"

"Well, she's young and enthusiastic, and I think she'll make a fine treasurer. Maybe drag us into the twenty-first century kicking and screaming."

"I'm not talkin' about her as treasurer. What do you think of her as a person?"

"Oh, she's as sweet as they come. I don't know her all that well, but I don't have anything to say about her but good."

"I'm glad to hear that," Trixie said. "She's become my best friend. Maybe the only best friend I've ever had. She has a heart bigger than the moon. She'd do anything for the people she loves."

"I'm sure she would, dear."

"And she loves your son."

Cass chuckled. "Yes, she's been hanging around him quite a bit. I'm sure she'd find him quite a catch. Marrying up, as they say."

"And Austin loves her."

The silence descended before Cass found her tongue. "Yes, he's mentioned that. I told him that's wonderful, but he shouldn't rush into anything. Make sure he's met a lot of the young ladies out there who could make a wonderful wife for a future bank president."

"They've been in love since middle school. I don't think they're rushin' into anything here. Besides, even if they were rushin', that works out for some people too. My momma and daddy got married three months after they first met. They stayed married until daddy died. 'Til death did they part, ya know. How long did you date Mr. Reeves before you married?"

"Well, not that long really. Probably should have been longer. But we knew. We knew immediately—"

"Austin and Shelby have known since they were fifteen."

"But Austin is so young. He's only twenty-two. Just graduated college. He should be a little older, a little more mature before he makes such a life-changing decision."

"How old were you when you met Mr. Reeves?"

"I was nineteen, Lamar was twenty-three. But that was a different time. Things were different then. I don't want Austin to get taken advantage of or make a decision he regrets later."

"He's old enough to make those decisions, don't you think? You won't find a young man with a better head on his shoulders, thanks to how y'all raised him."

"Why are you saying all this to me?"

"I already told you why. Shelby's my best friend. And she doesn't want to do anything that would create problems between you and your boy. Because no matter how much they love each other, that's the kind of woman she is. She knows how important it is that you give your blessing to them. She won't push Austin to defy you. She'd walk away before she made him choose between the two of you. You don't want her to do that, do you? You know what it's like for the momma to not accept you. And your husband stood up to her to stand by you. Isn't that what you'd want Austin to do? Don't do that to Shelby. Or to your boy. They both deserve to be happy."

Trixie had said a lot more than she intended, but she knew enough to stop. She leaned in to hug Cass before Cass had time to maneuver out of the way.

"Just think about it, okay. And listen to your heart."

Trixie hugged Marion and Angelina and Reagan before heading out the door.

Shelby waited for her on the porch. "What was that all about?"

"All what?"

"Don't all what me. All that top-secret whispering you had with Cass back there? Should my ears have been burning?"

"Girl, your ears should have burst into flames."

***

On the drive home, Trixie pulled the car over in the vacant Piggly Wiggly parking lot and dug her phone out of her purse.

"Mason, on that grant to the Ladies' Circle. We're going to increase that. Make it $20,000. Designate ten grand for operating funds and ten to the Bee Callahan Scholars Award Program. Let's go ahead and approve it."

Trixie drove down the road another mile, just outside the city limits, then pulled over in the RV and camper sales lot. She was going to have to learn how that Bluetooth thingy worked so she didn't have to pull over to call someone.

"Mason, one more change. Make that a $19,000 donation."

She didn't want to steal Bee's thunder.

CHAPTER 31

Trixie finally had a moment to sit down and do nothing. Ty wasn't due home from school for half an hour or so. Clay was out doing Clay stuff, said he'd stop in later to share a grape soda with Ty, then probably help eat some church lady leftovers for supper before heading to his camper to call it an early night.

The house was clean. Laundry was all done and put away. She'd reviewed the latest counteroffer from her real estate agent, which was generally just frustrating her that it had to be such an involved process. *Ever'body would starve if we had to buy groceries this way.*

Trixie kicked off her shoes and propped her feet up on the coffee table as she sat on the couch, wondering if she dared close her eyes for a quick rest or at least a few minutes of that quiet solitude Clay seemed to like so much. If she fell asleep, she'd hear the screen door slam as soon as Ty got home.

Just for a few minutes. Some peace and quiet. Why did the empty house feel so comforting knowing Ty would be home shortly compared to the same empty silence when she didn't know when, or if, he'd be home? She shifted from sitting up to lying down and stretched her legs out on the couch.

She never heard the screen door.

She never heard his footsteps cross the kitchen's vinyl floor.

She slowly came to as he stroked her hair and her cheek. She nuzzled into him, his face scratchy, unshaven. His breath smoky and reeking of Jack Daniels.

Her eyes flew open.

"Ellis, what the hell are you doin'? Get off me this second!"

Ellis raised up and spit in her face. Her hand flew up and clawed across his cheek. The fist to her cheekbone nearly sent her back under.

"We can play rough if that's how you want it," he said in a low growl.

Trixie fought off the cobwebs. Dreaming? "I said get off me and get out of here right now or I'm calling the cops."

"How're you gonna do that?" He slapped her, open palm this time rather than a fist.

She lashed out again, but he caught her wrist and twisted until she screamed. She tried to get up, but his full weight pressed against her. His knees dug into each of her thighs. He let go of her wrist and pressed down on her throat as she gasped for the next breath.

With his other hand, he unbuttoned her jeans, tugging them lower on her hips.

She managed to wrangle her left arm free and landed a useless jab to his shoulder. He slapped her again, stinging her cheek, bringing tears to her eyes.

He sat back on his knees, resting his weight on her thighs, digging into her muscles like shovels in soft garden soil. She screamed again and thrashed from side to side, trying to shake him off, to no avail, as he unbuckled his belt and unsnapped his Levis. His hand left her throat as he pulled his jeans down to his knees, and she gasped air.

With both hands, she pushed him back as hard as she could while he tried to get his jeans down, but he barely moved. The next hit wasn't open palmed, but another fist, this time to her eye. Light exploded with the pain. The only relief was when he stood, letting off the crushing pain to her thighs that had pinned her down.

Ellis stood and shoved his jeans down the rest of the way to his boots. He stood over her, white boxer shorts partially covered by the flannel shirt tails, jeans resting on top of his boots. He reached down for her waistband and yanked, but her jeans barely budged, wedged between her hips and the couch.

She kicked at him, but he just caught her ankle. Again with the other foot; again, the same result. He scraped at the denim for a grip to give them a tug, but she pulled both knees to her chest and kicked out with as much strength as she could muster, both feet landing against his chest and sending him backward over the coffee table.

She could barely shake off the throbbing in her head long enough to sit up as Ellis dragged himself to his feet, hobbled by his jeans.

"You always were a feisty one," he said.

Trixie managed to pull herself up to her unsteady legs. Her phone was on the kitchen table. She took three steps that direction when Ellis lunged just far enough to grab her by the hair and yank her back, tossing her to the floor like a ragdoll.

"Stop it!"

Trixie and Ellis both froze and looked toward the kitchen. Ellis stood in his white boxers and jeans pushed down to his boots. Trixie lay on the floor, raising her head high enough to look through one eye. The other eye was useless, filled with fluid — tears or blood, she couldn't tell.

"I said stop it!"

"Hey now, boy. You just need to set that thing down real gently on the floor and step away before you hurt yerself." Ellis was frozen in place.

Trixie focused as best she could. Ty stood in the kitchen pointing at Ellis. Pointing both hands at Ellis. Pointing that .22 at Ellis.

Ellis reached down for his jeans.

Ty flipped off the safety. "Don't move or I'll kill you dead."

Ellis played statue, bent halfway over, hands aiming for the top of this jeans but stopping a few inches short.

"Now, you don't want to shoot nobody. You might accidentally hit your momma. Just set that thing down, let me pull my pants up, and I'll leave. No more trouble. I'll leave. Just let me pull my pants up."

"You move, I'll shoot."

"Ty, walk over to the table and get my phone to call 9-1-1. Don't set the gun down, don't listen to him, but take your finger off the trigger. Remember trigger control like Uncle Leon taught you."

"He said don't put your finger on the trigger unless you're ready to shoot someone. I'm ready to shoot this a-hole."

"Do what I tell you. Go get my phone."

Ty hesitated. He kept his aim straight at Ellis's core. His stance was perfect. Left hand providing support. His trigger control was nonexistent. He glanced at his momma.

"Do what I tell you."

"He hurt you."

"Yes, he did. But you showed up and saved me. I'm okay now. He's going to leave, but you're going to call 9-1-1."

"He hurt you bad."

Trixie had no idea what she looked like. The pain had all gone numb. Maybe she had a shiner that would match the one Ty gave Carson. She didn't try to move. Just lay on the floor. Wasn't sure if she could move, and she didn't want to startle Ty.

"I'm gonna pull my pants up now." Ellis's boxer shorts pointed forward as his previous enthusiasm quickly waned.

"Hands in the air!" Ty yelled. "Where I can see 'em."

Ellis followed directions immediately, his jeans dropping back down again. "You watch too many movies."

Ty never budged from his stance or his aim.

"Look, I'm gonna try this one more time. I'm going to reach down and pull up my pants so I can leave."

"Don't move."

"I'm moving slow. Just pullin' up my—"

The gunshot cracked across the room with a snap over Trixie's head and a thump on the wall.

Trixie screamed.

Ty held his stance, ready for a second shot.

Ellis stood there, half bent over, staring at Ty. He looked down then doubled at the waist and dropped to his knees.

"That little sumbitch shot me." His hands went to his crotch.

Trixie watched the blood spread between his fingers, then fan out across his white boxer shorts, turning them red within a moment.

"That little sumbitch shot my dick."

The screen door slammed shut, and Ty spun around, aiming the gun behind him, directly at Clay.

"Whoa, whoa, put that down!"

"Ty, no!" Trixie screamed.

Ty immediately dropped the gun, which clattered on the vinyl floor.

Clay grabbed the gun in one hand and scooped Ty up in his other arm, looking at the living room scene, bewildered.

"He shot me in the dick! Call 9-1-1. Call an ambulance! Please!"

"That's pretty good shootin' to hit a target that small," Trixie said as she cleared her head.

Clay rushed to her side, still holding Ty and the gun. He set Ty in the recliner and kneeled beside Trixie, brushing her hair out of her face to look at her cheek and eye. "Are you all right?"

"Call me an ambulance now!" Ellis screamed.

Clay pointed the .22 at Ellis. "If I'm calling an ambulance for anyone, it's for her. You can sit there and bleed out."

Ellis fell to his side, clutching at his boxer shorts.

Trixie looked at Clay. "I hope you were plannin' on replacin' this old carpet anyway."

"Please call me an ambulance."

"You're an ambulance," Ty said, completely deadpan.

Ellis moaned. He pulled the waistband of his boxers away from his skin to take a look.

"Is it still there?" Trixie asked.

"I think so," Ellis whimpered.

"Too bad."

"I can fix that," Clay added.

"Ty, go get me my phone like I asked you to."

Ty ran to the kitchen table and ran back with Trixie's phone.

Trixie dialed 9, then 1, then... then she hung up. "We're in a bit of a pickle here, ain't we?"

Ellis whimpered again. "Please. I didn't mean nothin'. I'm sorry. Please."

"There's a couple of ways I can see this goin'," Trixie said calmly, sitting up and leaning against Clay, who still held the .22 on Ellis. "I could call an ambulance for you, and the sheriff is gonna show up and want to know what happened. You tell 'em my little man shot you, and even though he might have been defending me, social services is gonna get all involved and ask how he had access to that gun. I don't want my boy to go through that mess again. I'd rather just sit here and watch you die, tell the cops I shot you in self-defense."

"Oh God, no, I won't tell them nothin', just call." Ellis writhed from one side to the other, doubled at the waist, trying to apply pressure to the wound with both hands.

"Then we better get our stories together," Trixie said. "Hmm. Maybe, yeah, that might work. Here's what happened. You came over to buy my gun from me. You slipped it into the waist of your jeans, and it fired. You shot yourself. Ty and Clay weren't even here. Just you and me, and we'll both stick to that story."

"Yes, yes, that's what I'll say. Please call."

"How do I know you'll stick to that story? I can't trust you for nothin'."

"I will, I promise. Just get me to a hospital before it's too late. I don't want to lose it."

Ty said, "Maybe they'll have to ampimitate."

"I could do that right now," Trixie said. "Save all those medical bills. Let me go get that knife."

"No, please, please call. I'll say whatever you want me to say."

Trixie thought about it a moment longer. "Okay, here's the deal. You stick to that story, so will I. You say anything different, you even mention my boy was in the house, and I'll tell the cops you was violatin' a restrainin' order and assaulted me. I'll tell them how old I was when you sexually assaulted a minor and got me pregnant. Then that damaged pecker of yours will be on a sex offenders registry for the rest of your life. After you get out of prison, that is."

"Deal. Deal. Please call."

Trixie dialed 9, then 1, then hung up again.
"Are you sure you're gonna stick to our story?"
Ellis moaned and passed out.

***

Clay helped clean Trixie up before the ambulance arrived. Didn't want her bruises bringing any unnecessary questions to the story. She'd gotten pinned between a heifer and a fence earlier, which would explain the bruises.

Ellis regained consciousness, and Trixie made him review their story again. When the siren headed up the road, Clay handed the .22 to Trixie, loaded Ty in his pickup, and drove across the pasture to park behind a barn.

They'd come back just after the ambulance arrived, wondering what all the commotion was about.

CHAPTER 32

Trixie had put the extra leaf in the kitchen table to make room for Sabine and Leon. She'd pulled a casserole out of the freezer and heated up some vegetables for sides.

"This is delicious," Sabine said for probably the twentieth time.

"You never compliment my cooking so much. But some church lady cooks, and you can't stop raving about it."

"Well, you don't usually make anything this delicious."

Even Ty liked it. Leon and Clay both went back for seconds. Clay took thirds, polishing off the casserole after making sure no one else wanted any more. Then Sabine took a bite off his plate.

"I'm full, I just wanted to taste it one more time," she said.

"There's also apple pie and ice cream for dessert, so leave room."

"Now you tell me," Sabine said.

Trixie's cheek was back to its regular skin tone, and the makeup almost but didn't quite cover the bruise under her eye. It had faded in two weeks but wasn't gone.

With coffee served along with dessert—even Ty got a half cup of coffee topped off with milk as a special treat—everyone went quiet again. Only the clinking of forks on the plates and the occasional "mmm, mmm" broke the silence.

When everyone had finished, pushed back from the table, and loosened a belt buckle a notch or two, Trixie stood to gather the dirty dishes.

"Whyn't you sit down a moment, missy?" Leon said. "I've got somethin' I wanna say."

"Oh, Lord," Sabine moaned. "Ever' time he has some announcement, it costs me money."

"You jus' hush now, woman. This time it's important."

Leon pushed back from the table and groaned as he stood, whether from a full belly or a sore knee, Trixie wasn't sure. Or maybe just a bid for sympathy. He cleared his throat and looked around the table at each person, like he was collecting his thoughts.

"First, I jus' wanna say how much I 'preciate every last one of you. How much I love you, and I wasn't raised in an environment where anyone ever came out and said that out loud. I know my momma and daddy loved me, but if I'd asked, they'd have both said, 'I put a roof over your head and feed you, don't I?' So it don't come natural to me stand here and say I love you. But I do. And I jus' wanted to say that to each of you. That includes you, young man," he directed to Clay.

"I love you too, Uncle Leon," Ty said.

Trixie waved Leon over for a hug and wrapped her arms around his waist while he stood next to her chair.

"Young lady, you lost your daddy too young. I know that I can never replace him, and I don't mean to even try. But I want you to know that if you need a father kind of person to talk to, get advice from, whatever you need, I will always be here for you."

"And you, little fella," he said to Ty, "are the apple of my eye."

"Apple pie of the eye?" Ty asked.

"Apple pie of the eye," Leon repeated. "With ice cream."

He walked to the other side of the table next to Sabine and put a hand on her shoulder. "And I love this woman. Some days I wonder why, but most of the time, I know exactly why."

Leon rested a hand on the back of Sabine's chair and put his other hand on the table.

"Miss Trixie, your momma and I have reached a major life decision."

Trixie couldn't believe it. "Y'all are gonna get married?"

"Oh, hell naw," Sabine said. "Who in their right mind is gonna marry that ol' coot?"

Leon laughed. "Well now, we've been together long enough the state considers us married by common law already. But back to business. We've decided we will take that new doublewide trailer on the half-acre lot south of town. It's a mighty fine home, and plenty of room to put up that purple martin house."

Trixie bounced up from her chair to hug Leon and her momma at the same time, one arm around each of them. "We'll call the Realtor right now and get an offer in."

Clay cleared his throat. "Just give me a minute first here. Seems everybody has some big announcement they'd like to make, and now it's my turn."

Trixie kissed Leon and her momma on the cheeks, and returned to her seat.

"Before you go callin' that real estate lady, hear me out. Maybe there could be a change of plans."

"What are you plottin'?" Trixie asked.

Leon lowered himself delicately back into his seat. "Yeah, what are you goin' on about?"

"Just hear me out." Clay turned to Leon and Sabine. "What if I fixed up this old farmhouse and you moved in here?"

Trixie looked around the table and thought about it. "Ya know, that's not a half-bad idea. Ty and I will be movin' into that house in town in a couple months or so."

"I don't want to move to town."

"You hush. You'll like it there."

Clay raised his hand again, like a polite third grader trying to get the teacher's attention. "I wasn't done yet."

"First, before I fix up the farmhouse, I'll build a little house out where I've got the trailer. On top of that hill with the view. Then Leon and Sabine can move into this house, and you and Ty can move in up there. With me. Assuming you would agree to marry me."

The words didn't sink in. Trixie replayed them in her head a couple of times. She must have misheard Clay. Her brain must have gotten the two conversations crossed. Maybe Leon had asked Sabine to marry him and she just got confused. She stared at her empty dessert dish and nearly empty coffee cup. *What did he say?*

"What did you say?"

Clay dropped to one knee at Trixie's side. "I said, Victoria Burnet, will you marry me?"

"Of course she will," Ty said.

"Of course she will," Sabine said.

"I-I-I, I don't know. I mean, it's so sudden like. I weren't expectin' this. I need to think about it."

"Thinking about it is better than a no. I might have to take that for now and we can talk about it more. I've been praying about it, and it feels like the right thing."

"So, the Lord told you to marry me without checking with me first?"

"The Lord said to ask. He didn't guarantee me the answer I wanted. That's seems to be how prayer usually works."

"You gotta say yes, Momma. Mr. Garza said I could get a pony if you said yes."

"You nearly kill yourself on a bicycle and you think I'm puttin' you on a horse?" She turned to Clay. "And you're bribing my boy now?"

TURNING TRIXIE

"Not a bribe. Just a reward if he helped convince you."

"Look, I'm just gonna have to think on it, okay? I'm not saying no, but I'm not saying yes just yet either."

"I'll be here when you're done thinking on it."

THE END

INTERVIEW WITH THE AUTHOR

Q. Do you ever worry about writing a female character, specifically about being true to character, as a male author? Given Trixie's specific struggles, those that come with prostitution and parenting, did that cause you any kind of concern about not being able to get in her head?
A. My simple, flip answer to this is that JK Rowling was never a boy wizard, and she did all right. My longer answer is that female characters come to me more naturally. Maybe because I find women more interesting, I don't know. Men can be dull and uninteresting.

As far as understanding women enough to create female fictional characters, while I'd never claim to understand women (or men, for that matter), humans are human, and in many ways not that different from each other. Besides, I've had a lot of experience in living with women at all stages of life. I lived with a mother (and father too) for the first sixteen years of my life. I was raised with a little sister. I've been married for nearly forty years to the same woman. I raised a daughter. Have been a surrogate dad to many of her friends when she was a teenager. I've worked with women throughout my career, including as my boss.

While I don't base my characters on real people, all those real people inform my writing with a general understanding of human nature and how the world's most remarkable creatures think.

And yet they can surprise me — in real life and on the written page — constantly.

Q. How did you research to create a woman who has turned to prostitution? Did you speak to any real sex workers?
A. I did not go out and find sex workers to interview them about their careers and lives. But over the course of a lifetime, I have known women who had been sex workers at an earlier point in their lives, and I've listened to their stories. None were exactly like Trixie's situation, and Trixie was not based on or inspired by any particular person.

I've also known men who made life choices early on that they had to struggle to overcome. Men or women, maybe they regretted these choices later, or just moved on with an attitude of "no regrets but I'm glad it's over and don't recommend it." I think we all have that to one degree or another.

When I wrote about Trixie in that situation, I could imagine how she might feel, act and react, and think about herself. Like I said above, human nature is not that different, even though we each might make different choices given similar situations.

Q. All of your main characters seem to have, shall we say, quirks. What is it about these quirky characters that draws you to them? Do you look for the quirks, then write about them, or do you start building a character and then think, "Hmm... what quirks can I instill in them?"

A. The characters more or less come to me with their quirks fully intact. I just have to get to know them to learn about their personalities, including any oddities. I don't think about what kind of traits to give them — not consciously, at least. I think every person is this way in real life. Except me, of course. I'm perfectly normal.

Q. Your novels aren't in the Christian fiction genre, and with some of the situations and language you include, wouldn't be considered for publication or marketing in that genre. Yet your novels often feature Christian characters. Why is this important to you? Do you ever get pushback from readers, from either side of that equation?

A. For starters, no, I don't write in the Christian fiction genre. I write secular fiction. My publisher calls it contemporary southern lit. I go for realism in characters. Many real people are people of one faith or another. My stories are set in the south, where faith, Christianity in particular, and church are cultural touchstones. I find it much odder to read an entire novel set in the south that never mentions faith or religion or church. It's like writing about Texas and none of the characters drives a pickup or a novel set in Maine that never mentions lobster boils. It's part of the landscape and it's an innate, inseparable part of many people's lives.

And just like in real life, there are devout, compassionate people of deep faith and there are hypocrites. There are people who try but fall short of the standards set by their beliefs, and people who just go through the motions because it's a social expectation. Maybe it's just good for your business to be seen in church every Sunday.

All of those people appear in my stories because this is real life. It was part of my upbringing and is an integral part of my life.

And yes, I have had pushback from both sides on various novels, such as, "How can you write Christians into the same book as a sex scene and foul language?" Or, "Your book has too much religion in it so I just couldn't finish it." I've had reviewers say, "I thought it was great the way you made those fundamentalists look so stupid," and, "I thought it was great how you portrayed what a true Christian is supposed to look like."

Those were comments about the same book, so I felt like I'd succeeded in capturing a realistic slice of the culture and human nature.

Q. Another tactic you often employ in your writing is that the story isn't always neatly tied up at the end. In *Turning Trixie*, for example, there's a satisfactory conclusion, and Clay has asked Trixie to marry him, but she is going to think about it before giving her answer. And that's where the story ends. Why don't we get her answer?

A. I do like a story to have a generally satisfactory conclusion—I think that's an important part of storytelling. But I resist the urge to wrap everything up in a bow or have one of those "Where are they all now" epilogues. Life never answers every question, so neither do my books.

How much longer does Carrie live? What does Hannah do after college? Was Slade a truly good man or a manipulative con artist? Does Trixie marry Clay and live happily ever after?

Readers are quite capable of filling out the rest of the story in their own minds.

Q. Trixie is such a compelling character, and it feels like her life is just getting started. Is there potential for a sequel with Trixie? Or possibly a prequel about her life leading up to where this book starts?

A. Finally, an easy question. No. I don't do sequels, prequels, or series. When a book is finished, I have completed that character's story. Many writers do a phenomenal job with a series. I just can't. That character leaves me and moves on with her life and I have no idea what happens to her after that. And she doesn't tell me.

Book publishing and marketing experts will tell you that a series built on one character is the way to go as far as generating sales. Perhaps unfortunately, but that's not how my brain works with stories and characters. I write stand-alone novels.

So far, at least. Never say never.

Q. Your books have had a variety of settings, including Europe, Asia, Washington DC, New York City. But they're all centered in the southern

US, although different states. *Turning Trixie* is one of the few where the setting never really left the small town of Pineywoods. Talk about your settings, how you choose them, why the south in particular, and why Trixie's story never leaves east Texas, compared to your other novels where the protagonists often travel.

A. The easy answer is that the characters tell me their story, including where they're from and other places they have lived or visited. The deeper truth is probably that's how my life has been. I'm from small towns in the south, and we moved around a lot when I was a kid. We even ventured farther north for a couple of years in Illinois and Iowa, and then wound up in Arizona for a couple of years. As an adult, I've continued that pattern in my newspaper career. I lived in small towns in North Carolina, Texas, Missouri, and Wisconsin. I've also lived in DC and Tokyo. I traveled extensively through Europe and Asia for business and pleasure.

Sometimes my characters do the same. That small-town North Carolina girl goes to DC for college then to New York to appear on a TV show (*Hannah's Voice*). The good ol' boy from Texas winds up in Hollywood (*Slade*). Then there's the military brat who grew up all over the world, but her roots were a Cajun father and Japanese mother (*Carry Me Away*).

Q. One aspect of your writing that stands out, and has been commented on in reviews, is voice: the overall voice of the writing, but especially the characters' voices and dialogue. How do you develop all the various voices for characters and keep them so distinct yet realistic?

A. I listen. Let the character speak while I take dictation. I learn the story that way, as well as hear the character's voice in her own words.

I preach this to my editing clients. If you're writing down what you want the character to say, then handing the character the script and saying, "Here, read this," it never comes out as natural and realistic as when you just listen to the character speak.

Q. In contrast to your ability to create character voices, what aspect of fiction writing do you find most difficult?

A. I don't know if I find it most difficult or I just don't care for it, but I don't generally do detailed descriptions of settings, or even detailed descriptions of what characters look like. As a reader, I don't want to read paragraphs or pages of description. I want a sense of what it looks like, what it feels like, what it smells like even. But I want that blended into the story. I don't spend half a page describing how hot it is. Let the character wipe the sweat off his forehead. Don't give me two pages of how this particular species of pine tree came to be ubiquitous in east Texas, just show me some pine trees outside the house with a hawk sitting in the branches.

That's just a personal preference. I've read some amazing writers who can really draw you in with detailed, precise descriptions. But I'm always itching to get the story moving again, get some people on the page talking and going places and doing things that are important.

Sometimes, in the revision stage, I'll realize I need to add a bit more setting and description to ground the reader in the scene. I can see the scene so vividly in my head when I'm writing, I don't stop to show it to the reader, so I have to add it later. But just a few bits and pieces to ground the story in the real world.

Q. What's up next on the writing agenda for Robb Grindstaff?

A. There's always something. I'm working on the next novel now, but I'm still not completely sure where it's going. The working title is *For What It's Worth*, and it's the story of two powerful men, two teenage boys, and a missing girl — sometimes the past has a way of washing ashore at the most inconvenient times.

I just have to write for a while and then figure that out. I also want to write a few more short stories. I love those. Love reading them. Love writing them. As a writer, they are great to experiment with, try out different approaches, and maybe learn some techniques that can be applied to a novel.

I also do a lot of editing for other fiction writers — and memoir writers as well — and in 2023, I'll be teaching a couple of fiction writing courses. There's a yearlong writing course in Adelaide, Australia, that I'll be co-teaching with author Samantha Bond. I'll remote in by Zoom at some ungodly hour while Sam will be in the classroom with the students. And in June 2023, I'll be an instructor at the wonderful Novel-in-Progress Book Camp, in the Chicago area.

Other than that, I plan to do some fishing.

ACKNOWLEDGEMENTS

I absolutely must give a huge shout out to the international team at Evolved Publishing: Lane Diamond for taking a chance on an unknown writer ten years ago and sticking with me through some barren times, now publishing my fifth book; Kabir Shah and his continuing series of cover art that somehow captures the images in my brain; Jessica West for her editing expertise that pulls no punches, encourages, corrects, refines, and pushes me to dig a little deeper. She gets me.

A giant 'ta' to Samantha Bond, my partner-in-crime from down under, author, editor, and writing instructor, for her extraordinarily valuable insights as a guinea pig reader.

And all my love to Linda, my wife of nearly four decades, my biggest supporter and biggest critic (when needed) who puts up with me burying my head in the computer to spend more time with imaginary people than I do with her on writing days.

ABOUT THE AUTHOR

In addition to a career as a newspaper editor, publisher, and manager, Robb Grindstaff has written fiction most of his life. The newspaper biz has taken him and his family from Phoenix, Arizona, to small towns in North Carolina, Texas, and Wisconsin, from seven years in Washington, D.C., to five years in Asia. Born and raised a small-town kid, he's as comfortable in Tokyo or Tuna, Texas.

The variety of places he's lived and visited serve as settings for the characters who invade his head.

His novels are probably best classified as contemporary southern lit, and he's had more than a dozen short stories published in a wide array of genres. His articles on the craft of fiction writing have appeared in various writer magazines and websites, and one of his seminars was presented at the Sydney (Australia) Writers Festival. He also has taught writing courses for the Romance Writers of America, Romance Writers of Australia, and Savvy Authors.

Robb retired from the newspaper business in the summer of 2020 to write and edit fiction full time.

For more, please visit Robb online at **www.RobbGrindstaff.com**.

MORE FROM EVOLVED PUBLISHING

We offer great books across multiple genres, featuring high-quality editing (which we believe is second-to-none) and fantastic covers.

As a hybrid small press, your support as loyal readers is so important to us, and we have strived, with tireless dedication and sheer determination, to deliver on the promise of our motto:

QUALITY IS PRIORITY #1!

Please check out all of our great books, which you can find at this link:

www.EvolvedPub.com/Catalog/

Thank you!

CPSIA information can be obtained
at www.ICGtesting.com
Printed in the USA
BVHW060309070123
655722BV00005B/824